14 x 9/12 LT 7/12

WITHDRAWN

The Scarlet Contessa

The Scarlet Contessa

A NOVEL OF THE ITALIAN RENAISSANCE

JEANNE KALOGRIDIS

St. Martin's Press
New York

This is a work of fiction. All of the characters, organizations, and events portrayed in this novel are either products of the author's imagination or are used fictitiously.

THE SCARLET CONTESSA. Copyright © 2010 by Jeanne Kalogridis. All rights reserved. Printed in the United States of America. For information, address St. Martin's Press, 175 Fifth Avenue, New York, N.Y. 10010.

www.stmartins.com

Library of Congress Cataloging-in-Publication Data

Kalogridis, Jeanne.
    The scarlet contessa : a novel of the Italian Renaissance / Jeanne Kalogridis.—1st ed.
        p. cm.
    ISBN 978-0-312-36953-8
    1. Sforza, Caterina, 1463–1509—Fiction.   2. Nobility—Italy—Fiction.   3. Renaissance—Italy—
Fiction.   I. Title.
    PS3561.A41675S33 2010
    813'.54—dc22   2010013042

First Edition: July 2010

10 9 8 7 6 5 4 3 2 1

FOR HELEN,
FOR SAVING MY LIFE

ACKNOWLEDGMENTS

My deepest thanks to:

My best friend, Helen Knight, whose incredible generosity made this book possible;

My editor, Charles Spicer, whose professionalism, kindness, patience, and enthusiasm are unmatched;

His editorial assistant, Allison Caplin, who is likewise a sheer delight;

My super-agents, the amazing Russell Galen and the astounding Danny Baror;

My friend Sherry Gottlieb, who listens to me whine about my plot and always offers sage advice;

Mouse and Bill, whose hospitality brightens our days;

And most of all, to my partner of thirty-one years, George, who, during the writing of this book, did all of the cooking, cleaning, errand-running, and author-pampering—*cheerfully.* I love you something fierce, sweetheart.

THE TOWER

Ravaldino Fortress

December 10, 1499

PROLOGUE

The end of the world will arrive, say the mendicant preachers, on the first of January 1500; God can no longer bear the deeds of evil men and will strike them down. That most famous Cassandra, the monk Savonarola of Florence, says that God is especially outraged by the blatant sexual crimes of Pope Alexander VI, who brought his sixteen-year-old mistress and his illegitimate children to live with him in the Vatican.

On that terrible day, the prophets say, the earth will shake until it crumbles to dust, and we sinners will fall howling to our knees. For the wicked there will be no mercy. Those of us who have been faithless will be cast forever into the lake of fire. The world will perish in a cataclysm, and a new kingdom will take its place.

Christmas is a fortnight away, which means the coming wrath of God is barely three weeks away, according to the faithful. I wonder whether my lady Caterina and I will live long enough to see it.

For now, however, it is midnight, and beyond Ravaldino's fortress walls all is quiet. I lie upon the little cot in my lady's roomy closet—used now for storing ammunition and gunpowder instead of Caterina's headdresses and gowns, and thus stinking of war. I yearn for sleep, but it does not come easily these days.

Especially not tonight, with the noise emanating from the bed out in my lady's chamber. My arm has gone numb, and to wake it, I turn over on the narrow cot; it is lumpy and uncomfortable, and I am unused to sleeping on it. This leaves me facing the velvet curtain that covers the closet door.

Unfortunately, it does not cover it well enough. The swath of velvet is slightly too narrow, and through the cracks between it and the stone, I glimpse Caterina sitting up in the middle of her large bed, illuminated by the lamp on the night table. She is entirely naked, and the light infuses her white skin with a warm glow, as if she has been dipped in honey; her torso is long and lean, her waist, after many children, narrow. Her back is to me as she straddles her supine lover, and as she rides him vigorously, the handsome muscles of her shoulders, back, and arms ripple, and her thick dark blond braid, terminating at the base of her spine, swings like a pendulum across her back.

Her latest lover, Giovanni di Casale, lies passively beneath her, groaning with pleasure and exhaustion, his head thrown back against the pillow, his long, bony legs emerging from beneath my lady's firm buttocks. He is forty—only four years older than the insatiable Caterina—but he seems twenty decades older. He is red-haired, balding, with flabby skin the unhealthy white of a fish's belly; Caterina reaches out to brace herself against his chest for a moment, and his skin jiggles beneath her hands. He is my lady's secretary, not a soldier.

After a full day of leading military drills and testing the artillery, the Contessa Caterina Sforza, Lady of Forlì, is still full of lust and energy. She releases her hold on Giovanni's freckled chest and circles her hips atop his in a slow, grinding motion, as if to crush him. Inspired, Giovanni releases a gasp of mounting ecstasy.

The scene causes a faint, pleasurable stirring between my own legs, but anxiety steals my desire to seek release. Instead, I squeeze my eyes shut and turn my back to the curtain, wishing I had the energy to stick my fingers into my ears.

It is hard enough to sleep these days, even without such an interruption. A week ago, we left the comfort of Paradise, the name Caterina had given her magnificent apartments inside the fortress, with their breathtaking view of the nearby Apennine Mountains. A week before that, she secretly sent all her valuables—fine gowns, jewelry, furniture, carpets, as well as all her children, save one—to the safe haven of Florence. Now we are in the most secure tower in the fortress of Ravaldino, on the edge of the town Forlì, which Caterina rules. She is contessa, too, of Imola, a larger town half a day's ride away, which is now under attack by the Pope's army.

If Imola falls, odds are we shall fall, too.

There are few windows here in the main tower, no paintings or tapestries covering the drab walls, no carpets upon the rough stone floors, no furniture save for the bed, a single armoire, a night table, and a table for the washbasin, above which hangs the large, finely polished mirror Caterina insisted on bringing. The Lady of Forlì's cries of pleasure grow louder and more urgent, joining with those of Giovanni, finally fully inspired by her efforts.

Just as Giovanni lets go a howl of ecstatic release—and my lady laughs softly with delight at his abandon—a hammering comes at the thick wood and iron door. There is such urgency in the knock that I roll from my cot at once, slip the shawl folded near my pillow over my shoulders, and push the curtain to the closet aside. Politely, I avert my gaze as the lovers hastily uncouple, pull on their clothing, and move quickly to the door.

"Who calls?" I shout.

"Ridolfo Naldi, come from the fortress of Imola this night. I bear a message from my brother, Dionigi."

A thrill—hope and fear combined—passes through me. I peer through the peephole to confirm the identity of the messenger, and to ensure that he is alone. Satisfied, I nod over my shoulder at Caterina, who then curtly tells her lover with the brisk authority of a military commander: "Ser Giovanni. Fetch my son at once."

She nods at me to open the door.

I do. It swings outward; Giovanni exits and Ridolfo enters. The two men pass each other closely, emphasizing the difference in height and build. Giovanni is short and rather slender, though soft and unmuscled; Ridolfo is a full head taller and almost thrice as wide. His head is entirely bald, with folds of skin at the base of his burly skull; his neck is as broad as Caterina's thigh. Yet the huge hands that clutch his cap are trembling, and his round, thick features are slack with shock and fright. As Caterina gestures, rather impatiently, at him, he steps heavily inside; a pungent waft of aged sweat emanates from him as he passes. His blue uniform, clearly worn for days on end, is stained from the oil used to lubricate the cannons. As I close the door behind him, he does not merely genuflect, but sinks to his knees in front of the contessa.

I have met Ridolfo many times. Like his brother, Dionigi—castellan of the fortress at Imola—he is no coward, yet there is such panic in his eyes I expect him to start weeping at any instant. My lady and I know, of course, what he is about to say, but I will not allow myself to believe it until I hear the words.

"Your Illustrious Excellency," he says to Caterina. His voice, too high pitched for so great a body, wavers. "I bring news from my brother."

"So you've said," Caterina replies softly, and waits.

Ridolfo draws a shuddering breath and releases said news in a torrent. "The citizens, perhaps you know, all surrendered to the Duke of Valentino's army without a struggle. My brother, Dionigi, was able to hold the fortress for you . . . but Valentino's artillery breached the wall at last. Dionigi fought courageously and well, but without the support of the city, he could not hold them off forever." He bows his head and releases a small sob. "Dionigi showed such bravery. He is wounded, Your Illustriousness, in the head. Even after it was clear he would be defeated, and despite his pain, Dionigi would not surrender, would not leave his post, would not listen to the duke's threats and promises. He was so persistent in his loyalty to you, in his willingness to die for you, that Valentino was moved. He granted my brother a three-day truce, so that Dionigi might send me to you, to ask whether you wish to send reinforcements to try to hold the fortress."

As he speaks, a burning chill has forced its way upward from the base of my spine and spread outward, leaving me sickened.

The Lady of Forlì turns her face away from the kneeling giant; her lips twist with fury. *"Bastards,"* she mutters. "Dionigi would have prevailed if they hadn't spread their legs like whores for Valentino!"

She is speaking of her subjects in Imola, who so feared the duke's army that they surrendered to him before he ever entered the city.

"They have paid for it, Your Illustriousness," Ridolfo says. "Valentino's army has pillaged the city and raped every woman, even those in the convent. The duke himself took the prettiest women; it's said he sleeps with a new one every night."

At this, Caterina's anger hardens. She composes herself, squares her shoulders, smooths her brow, and assumes an air of dignity and confidence. Were it not for her disheveled hair and rumpled chemise, one might think she was holding court. But a long moment passes before she can gather herself to speak.

"Valentino knows that I can spare no troops," she says at last. "The fortress is lost, through no fault of Ser Dionigi's. He has behaved admirably. I must know, however, what the duke plans for him."

"He will allow Dionigi and his men to leave the fortress with a safe escort to Forlì," Ridolfo answers swiftly. "The duke is sincere, Your Illustriousness, else he would not have let me come. He says . . ." His voice begins to tremble again. "He says to tell you that he is coming next for you."

Caterina lifts a golden brow at the duke's threat, but otherwise refuses to respond to it. "Go back to Imola," she tells Ridolfo, "and relay our deep gratitude to Ser Dionigi. Tell him he has discharged his duty with honor, and that I am releasing him and his men from my service."

"Thank you, Your Illustriousness!" Ridolfo's broad face crumples with relief; he puts his massive hands to his eyes and weeps briefly, then looks up, cheeks and eyes shining. "May I . . . that is, my brother wished to know, with all respect . . . Does this mean you will now release his wife and children, that they might join him?"

Caterina lets go a short laugh; apparently she forgot that she had secured Dionigi's excessive loyalty by imprisoning his family. "Of course, of course!"

Just as Ridolfo thanks her profusely, the Lady of Forlì's lover and secretary, Giovanni, reappears with her eldest son, twenty-year-old Ottaviano. Caterina takes her secretary aside, all business, and whispers detailed instructions to him. When she is finished, Giovanni nods and helps the overwhelmed Ridolfo to his feet. The two disappear out the door, and Caterina turns her attention to her son while I try not to be noticed. Caterina is not shy about sending me away when she desires privacy; the fact that she has not dismissed me means that she wishes me to remain. And so I watch, at a respectful distance, the poignant exchange between mother and son.

Ottaviano is not an easy youth to love. He is as slothful and unmotivated as his mother is tireless and ambitious, as full of complaints as she is courage. Nor did he inherit Caterina's good looks, wit, or athletic talent. Though she has drilled him in the martial arts daily for months, his cheeks and body have not lost their childish plumpness; the swell of his belly is easily visible beneath his long wool nightshirt. His nose and lips are broad and thick, his face round, his general demeanor one of listlessness. He wears his dull brown hair in the manner of a page, chopped short so that it falls three fingers below his chin, with straight bangs ending just above his eyebrows. Even now, after the urgent summons to his mother's quarters in the middle of the night, he is still rubbing his eyes and scowling fretfully at being awakened. Though he is already twenty years old and will soon be the ruler of Imola and Forlì, he has little interest in the details of government and prefers to leave such matters in his mother's hands.

Caterina steps up to him and puts her arms upon his shoulders. He is less than half a head taller than she is, but much, much broader.

"My son," she says briskly, without drama. "The fortress at Imola has fallen. Ser Giovanni is fetching a scout; he will guide you to Florence. We cannot wait another minute. Your trunk and horse will be waiting at the western gate. Get ready at once and go to them."

"Imola has fallen?" Ottaviano's eyes widen; he seems honestly surprised, as if he had expected some other news to have caused Caterina to drag him from his bed at such an hour. "Mother, are you sure?" He glances to me as if seeking another opinion; I drop my gaze.

"Yes," my lady says firmly. "We've discussed this several times. Now we must act." She leans forward on tiptoe and kisses the center of his forehead. "Go. I will see you again soon—here, in this very fortress, when Valentino has been routed."

He hesitates. "But . . . are you sure you will be safe?"

Caterina laughs at the question and gives him a little shove. "Foolish boy! Hurry! Others will be waiting for you."

Ottaviano gives her a last woeful look; apparently this is the first time he has considered that he ought not leave his mother to fight the French and papal armies alone. But Caterina pushes him again, this time with a hint of irritation. He gives her a slow, solemn kiss on the lips, then turns and lumbers out of the chamber.

"I will summon you home as soon as it is safe," Caterina calls after him, her tone gay.

Once the door has closed behind him, her false cheer evaporates; she goes to the bed and sits down abruptly, heavily, on the edge. She presses her palms to her eyes, and as her lips suddenly contort, I go to stand beside her, and rest a hand gently upon her shoulder.

"I'm all right," she says from behind her hands, but I hear the tears in her voice. We remain as we are for a long moment, and then she lowers one hand and pats the mattress beside her. "Giovanni is not coming back tonight. Sleep here, beside me."

I do as I am told, and lie down beside her. For a long time, she does not extinguish the bedside lamp, but stares up at the ceiling, thinking. I close my eyes and do my best to feign sleep. After an hour, perhaps two, Caterina puts out the light. Some time later, I can tell from her breath that she will not fall asleep. Nor will I. We lie awake together until dawn, each of us lost in dread of what is to come.

News of Imola's fall spreads quickly throughout the town of Forlì; Valentino's massive army is only two days' march away. By the following evening, two town elders come to Ravaldino's fortress, where the Contessa of Forlì has taken refuge.

Unfortunately, I am not available to serve as my lady's ever-present talisman at the meeting. Caterina indulged in a hot bath half an hour before, and I am making use of the still-warm water when the elders arrive and request an audience with my lady. She gives me leave to remain behind, even though I suspect the citizens' appearance does not bode well. I therefore bathe as quickly as possible, and struggle to pull my chemise and gown over still-damp skin.

The encounter between Caterina and the elders lasts only minutes. By the time I hurry out of Caterina's new chamber and up the vertiginous steps to Paradise—the lavish apartment she had built for herself in more peaceful times and where she receives all her guests—the elders, Ser Ludovico and Ser Niccolò, are coming down the stairs and pass me. With them is one of the contessa's personal bodyguards, guiding them out of the maze that is Ravaldino Fortress.

They nod politely and cordially enough to me, though they seem preoccupied—who would not be, with Valentino's army on the way? I nod in response and make way for them to pass, deeply relieved that they seem calm. Obviously, there had been no argument with the contessa; perhaps they had come to express support for her.

Buoyed, I lift my skirts and hurry upstairs to find Caterina in the nearly bare reception chamber. She has left her chair, behind which a second impassive bodyguard stands, and is on her toes at the window, craning her neck to stare down at the stone courtyard Ser Niccolò and Ser Ludovico will cross on their way out of the fortress.

When I enter and pause to curtsy, she jerks her head over her shoulder to look back at me, and I know in an instant that all is lost.

"Bastard!" she swears. "Son of a filthy whore . . . !" Her lips are trembling, her teeth gritted, her blue eyes wide with rage. I do not move, but remain genuflected as she turns her face back to the window and continues her tirade.

"Luffo Numai!" she shouts. Numai is the richest man in Forlì; he has served on the city council for some years and considers himself the spokesman for the townspeople. "That's who it was—that's the traitor! He convinced them all that they had no chance with me, that Valentino's army would slaughter them, that they were safer surrendering to him." She lets go a wild laugh. "They'll learn soon enough what becomes of those who trust the Duke of Valentino!"

I lift my head. "The Forlivese?" I whisper.

"They will not fight in my defense," she says, still facing the window. The bitter words steam the glass, and she wipes them away angrily as she stares down at the courtyard below. "They are sending a messenger to Valentino to tell him so. And according to my apologetic guests, it was Luffo Numai who worked tirelessly to convince the citizens that surrender was their only hope for survival. Many of the people supported me, wanted to raise their swords for me, but Numai bullied them until they gave in." She lurches toward the window as her eye catches something below. "Hah! There they go!"

She turns toward me, skirts whirling, words tumbling out of her so rapidly I can scarcely follow them. "I was polite to Niccolò and Ludovico, of course. I was gracious; I told them that, given the fall of Imola, I could not expect the citizens of Forlì to defend me. But they would have, had it not been for Numai. How much money, do you think, Valentino promised him? And governorship, of course, since Valentino will not be able to look after the cities himself."

She moves swiftly to the chair and throws on her cloak, then strides out of the chamber, through the door, and down the same steps Niccolò and Ludovico had recently trodden; since she continues to address me, I follow, breathless from the effort to keep pace with her.

"Numai thinks he will steal my lands from me," she says darkly, "and from my sons, but he will pay. The bastard will pay! I will see to it personally."

I follow her down to the second level, where tunnels have been cut deep into the stone wall to accommodate artillery. Caterina leads me to the end of one of them and calls to a nearby soldier.

"Bring the gunners!" she shouts, and as the soldier runs off to obey, Caterina moves to the side of one of the long bronze cannons, which is tilted upward forty-five degrees.

My lady does not need to search for the long-handled ladle, or the great wooden box that houses the gunpowder; she knows where both are kept, and fills the ladle full of the sulfurous powder with practiced ease, then pushes it down the cannon's long barrel. At her bidding, I run and fetch a huge handful of hay to serve as wadding from a pile kept near the gunpowder box, and the long wooden rammer.

As I drop the hay into the muzzle and push it down with the rammer, Caterina goes to fetch the ball from a large pyramid-shaped stack. She staggers beneath the weight of the dressed stone sphere; she can carry it only crouched over, in both hands, with the ball at mid-thigh. But carry it she does, and as she steps toward the muzzle, I join her, and together we manage to lift the ball high enough to push it into the barrel.

By this time, six gunners have finally assembled, and they take over the rest of the duties.

"Aim it at Numai's palace," Caterina orders, knowing full well the likelihood of accurately striking such a distant target at dusk is poor. Even so, she watches avidly as one of the artillerymen uses a weighted plummet line to find the true perpendicular, then measures the angle with a quadrant and adjusts the muzzle accordingly. And when at last the metal cover is lifted at the cannon's base, and the botefeux holding the lighted match is applied to the touchhole, she claps her hands with dark glee.

"For you, Luffo Numai!" she cries, a split second before the officer in charge waves us back, then orders:

"Fire!"

I flinch and put my hands over my ears.

At once, I find myself living the fortune-telling card known as the Tower. The cannon roars, paining my ears, and the heavy stone of the fortress walls, of the solid floor beneath my feet, trembles. In my mind, I feel myself falling, falling amid shattered stone, to the ground, to certain doom, to the end of everything I know.

At Caterina's command, the cannon fires again, and again.

The Lady of Forlì and I have been through the experience of the Tower twice now, and survived. But this third time will surely be our last.

In the midst of the deafening song of the artillery, I see our end and our beginning. And my mind turns to the distant past. . . .

PART I

Milan

December 1476–April 1477

One

At dusk the screams came—outraged, feminine, shrill. We would never have marked them had it not been for the smoke and the singers' sudden silence. I heard them eight days before Christmas as I stood in the loggia, gasping in stinging cold air from the open window, brusquely unshuttered by a quick-thinking servant.

A moment earlier, I had been sitting in front of the snapping hearth in the duchess's quarters while one of her chambermaids roasted pignoli on a wood-handled iron peel—treats for the ducal heir, seven-year-old Gian Galeazzo Sforza, who stared blankly into the flames while his nurse brushed out the straw-colored curls covering his frail shoulders. Beside him sat his six-year-old brother, Ermes—thick-limbed and thick-waisted, slow to move or think—with a straight cap of dull red hair. To their left sat their mother, Duchess Bona, a sheer white veil wrapped about her coiled, muddy braids, her lips pursed as she squinted down at the needle and silk in her plump hands. She was twenty-seven and matronly; God had dealt her a stout frame, squat limbs, and a short, thick neck that dwarfed her broad face. Though her features were not unpleasant—her nose was short and round, her skin powder-soft and fine, her teeth small and fairly even—she had a low forehead with thick, overwhelming eyebrows. Her profile was flat, her eyes wide set, her small chin lost in folds of fat, most of it acquired after the birth of her first child; yet at the court of Duke Galeazzo, to my thinking, there was no lovelier soul.

To Bona's left sat the duke's two natural daughters, results of his dalliance with a courtier's wife. The elder, Caterina, was, at thirteen, an example of physical perfection, with a lithe body that promised full breasts, clear skin, and a straight, well-proportioned nose, though her lips were rather thin. Two attributes propelled her past mere attractiveness into true beauty: full, loose curls of a gold so pale and bright it glittered in the sun, and eyes of a blue so intense that many who met her for the first time let go an involuntary gasp. The effect was enhanced by the natural confidence of her gaze. That afternoon, however, her gaze was sullen, for she had no patience with the needle and she hated sitting still; she paused often in her embroidery to glare at the fire and emit sighs of vexation. Had it been summer, she would have ignored the duchess's insistence on a sewing lesson and joined her father on the hunt, or gone riding with her brothers, or chased them across the sprawling courtyard. No matter that such activities were exceedingly inappropriate for a young woman, already betrothed and certain to wed within three years. Caterina had no fear of the duchess's wrath, not just because Bona was disinclined to anger, but also because her father the duke favored her and rarely allowed her to be punished.

The same could not be said of her nine-year-old sister, Chiara, a rail-thin, timid mouse with bulging brown eyes and a narrow, sharp-featured face. For all the attention the duke showed Caterina, Chiara—a slow-witted, obedient girl—received only his unwarranted abuse; she rarely met another's gaze and kept close to Bona's side. For Bona's heart was so great that she treated all the duke's children equally; her own son, Gian Galeazzo, who would someday rule Milan and all her territories, was shown the same tender kindness as Caterina and Chiara, both living proof of her husband's philandering. She was also good to his two bastard sons, who were then almost men, off in Milan learning the military arts at their stepfather's home. Although she had encouraged all of us children to address her as our mother, Chiara alone called her *Mama.* Caterina called her *Madonna, my Lady*; I called her *Your Grace.*

Bona was kind even to me, a foundling of murky origin. She claimed publicly that I was the natural child of one of her disgraced cousins in Savoy, and therefore related to the king of France. I had only the vaguest memory of a beautiful raven-haired woman, her features blurred by time, who murmured endearments to me in French; surely this had been my mother. I had recollections, too, of kindly nuns who cared for me after the raven-haired woman had disappeared. But when I pressed Bona privately on the subject, she refused to give any details, hinting that I was better off not knowing. She adopted me as her daughter—if a lesser one, fated to spend my days as her most coddled lady-in-waiting. I was grateful, but ashamed of my origins. And being ashamed, I imagined the worst.

Almadea, she named me: soul of God. Over the years, I came to be called simply Dea, but Bona made sure I never lost sight of my soul. She was a pious woman, given to prayer and charity, eager to raise her children to serve God. Since Caterina took no interest in the invisible world, Gian Galeazzo was destined for a secular fate, and Chiara was slow, I alone was the diligent recipient of her ardent religious instruction.

The duke, who praised Caterina to the skies and cursed poor Chiara, had little to say to or of me. I was strictly Bona's project—although I, four years older than Caterina and often her chaperone, had many opportunities to be in the presence of His Grace, who doted on his blue-eyed, golden-haired daughter and paid her frequent visits. At those times, his eyes belonged to Caterina, and in those rare instances when his gaze strayed and caught mine, he quickly averted it.

On that eighth day before the Feast of the Nativity, the castle at Pavia—the duke's favorite country lodgings—was bustling. Every servant's expression was one of harried determination, every courtier's one of eager anticipation. In two days, the entire court of several hundred would make the daylong procession to the city, Milan, and the majestic Castle of Porta Giovia. There, on the day before Christmas, the duke would address the people, issue pardons, and distribute charity; when the sun set, he would ceremonially light the *ciocco*, the great Yule log, for his staff and servants in the great banquet hall. The fire would be faithfully tended throughout the night. The duke had never lost his childhood love of the holiday, so he also privately celebrated the *ciocco* ritual with his family each Christmas Eve, followed by a lavish banquet.

On that particular afternoon, in a festive gesture anticipating the annual pilgrimage, the duke sent a quartet of carolers to his wife's chambers. These were members of Duke Galeazzo's choir, the most magnificent in all Europe. The duke took only a vague interest in the arts, leaving the acquisition of books and paintings to his underlings, but music was his passion, and he took great care to seek out the most talented vocalists and composers in all of Europe.

Gian Galeazzo, Ermes, Duchess Bona, Caterina, Chiara, and I sat facing west before the fire, with the open doorway to our left, while the carolers—two men and two lads, the latter chosen by the duke for their pretty bodies as much as their talent—stood just left of the hearth, lifting their amazing voices in song. Behind us, two chambermaids were busy packing Bona's Christmas wardrobe into two large trunks. Sitting on the floor by his elder brother's feet, Ermes dozed while little Gian Galeazzo sat dutifully enduring his nurse's brush as he stared into the fire and listened; Duchess Bona hoped that the boys would catch their father's passion for music. She and Chiara were distracted by their embroidery, and Caterina by a wooden ball at her foot, a toy belonging to her younger half-brothers. She slyly nudged it with her toe until it rolled a short distance and gently bumped the nose of the dozing greyhound coiled at Bona's feet. The dog—three-legged and, like me, one of Bona's rescues—opened one eye and promptly returned to its nap.

The duchess's chamber was of comfortable size, with a large arched window, vaulted ceilings, and walls paneled in dark, ornately carved wood. Unlike the duke's, it consisted of a single room that featured a sitting area in front of the fireplace, a dressing area shielded from view by several garderobes, and a platform upon which rested a mahogany bed, its brocade curtains drawn. Near it were three cots, one of which I occupied on those nights my husband traveled. Bona's chamber resembled most of the other rooms in Castle Pavia, which consisted of a two-story stone square large enough to comfortably house five hundred souls. Each corner of the square was marked by a great tower, and these corner suites were reserved for the most important personages and functions. On the upper floor, the northeast tower housed the duke's suite of rooms, the northwest, his heir's; the southeast and southwest towers served as the chancery and the library, respectively. On the ground floor, the tower rooms held the reliquary and the prison. Except for the duke's, all rooms opened onto a long common hall, or loggia, overlooking the massive interior courtyard; the loggia on the first floor, which housed the servants, lesser visitors, butchery, prison, bath-house, laundry, and treasury, was open to the elements. For the comfort of the duke and his family, however, the upper loggia was bricked in, though there were windows to catch summer breezes, with shutters to close out winter winds.

As a girl, I used to race down the long, seemingly endless halls, barely avoiding collisions with the servants who filled them. One day I determined to count every room on both floors: There are eighty-three if you include the *saletti*, the little sitting rooms that protrude from the chapel, the chamber of rabbits, and the chamber of damsels and roses, the last two named for their murals. My favorite was the first-floor chamber of mirrors, with a floor of glittering mosaic and a ceiling of brightly colored glass.

Bona's fireplace rested in the center of the wall adjoining her son's apartment, and so we sat many steps away from either the window or the chamber door. I sat nearest the latter, which was open to allow the servants who were packing the duchess's Christmas luggage easy access.

I should have relaxed in the fire's warmth and simply listened to the singing. One lad's voice was so hauntingly beautiful that when he performed a solo, Bona stopped in her sewing and closed her eyes at its sweetness.

I closed my eyes, too, but opened them immediately at the sudden welling of tears and the unwanted tightness in my throat. For the third time in the last hour, I set my sewing down and—as discreetly as possible, moving behind the seated group—stepped rapidly away from the hearth into the cool shade at the arched window, and looked out.

To my left, the feeble sun was dying behind thick winter clouds that threatened snow; before me stood the formal garden, withered save for spots of evergreen. Straight ahead, to the north, the Lombard plain stretched out, much of it obscured by the bare, spidery-limbed trees in the nearby park where the duke hunted. A day's ride away, beyond the plain and my sight, stood the Alps; to the east, the kingdom of Savoy, where Bona had been born.

My Matteo would not be coming from the north, but court life required me to attend the duchess, and quash all yearning to run southward down the endless loggia to the library, where I could climb the steps to the southwest watchtower and stare out toward Rome.

Matteo da Prato served the duke as a scribe, occasional courier, and minor envoy. His mother had died giving life to him, and his father had died not long afterward; like me, he had been adopted by a wealthy family and educated. His talent for breaking ciphers and creating impenetrable code had earned him the attention of the duke's top secretary, Cicco Simonetta. I first set eyes on him seven years ago, when I was ten and he seventeen, new to Milan and freshly apprenticed to Cicco; I never dreamed then that we should ever marry.

I had never expected to marry at all.

Back at the hearth, Bona noted my dismay. When the singers caught their breath between arrangements, she called softly, "He will not come today, Dea. I've said a hundred times, there is nothing more certain than delays during winter travel. Don't fret; they've already found lodging and are sitting comfortably right now just as we are, in front of a fire." She paused. "Time to shutter the windows now, anyway. It's growing bitter."

She did not remark on the fact that it had been the coldest winter anyone at court could remember.

"Of course, Your Grace," I said. At my words, a gust of wind stirred the clouds; before my eyes they writhed and reformed into a haunting image: the shape of a man dangling in the darkening sky as if an invisible God held him by one ankle, his opposite leg bent at the knee to create an upside-down four.

The hanged man, Matteo had called him.

I pushed the heavy slatted panels into place and latched them, then hesitated an instant to flick away a tear. When I faced Bona again, it was with a false smile.

Reason, if not the clouds, said that I had no cause to worry. Matteo was a seasoned traveler, and the guests he was escorting from Rome to Milan were papal legates, too precious to risk by traveling in bad weather. Matteo was also armed against bandits, and the legates traveled with attendants and bodyguards. Yet my anxiety would not ease. I had awakened that morning in a peculiar panic from a dream of a double-edged sword pointed downward, dripping blood onto the frozen earth, while a voice whispered flatly in my ear, *Matteo is dead.*

Before morning mass, I had lit a second candle for Matteo, so that God would be doubly sure to hear my prayers. Bona noted it when she arrived in the chapel, and when I knelt beside her, she set a comforting hand upon my forearm.

"God hears," she said softly, "and I am praying, too."

Her kindness forced me to flick away tears, yet my worry did not lift; in my mind's eye, I saw Matteo suspended upside-down, pale and unconscious.

After mass, I was gratefully distracted by the task of supervising the chambermaids as they prepared the duchess's and children's households for the return to Milan.

At noon, I noted the gathering snow clouds but told myself stubbornly that Matteo, the smartest man I knew, would mark them, too, and hasten his progress; but as the sky darkened, so did my mood, and sunset brought a growing dread. By the time I shuttered Bona's window, I was again fighting back tears.

Yet I returned to my embroidery with a vengeance, and with each jab of the needle uttered a silent prayer: *God, protect my husband.* Surely God would hear. No one was more deserving of protection than Matteo; no prayers were worthier of being granted than Bona's.

My stitches were large and careless and later would have to be snipped and resewn—not today, though, for the light was failing and soon, when Bona gave the word, all needlework would be retired. The male quartet began again to sing, a lively folk tune that made Bona smile and Caterina keep time with her feet.

My eyes were on the pool of white silk in my hands; I did not see what caused the first loud clatter, but I looked up in time to see Francesca's iron peel drop with a resounding clang to the stone fireplace floor, scattering nuts in the flames. Francesca looked down at the carpet in horror, and threw up her hands; the act caused her shawl to slip from her shoulders. One edge spilled into the hearth and ignited, while she, unaware, stared down at a red-hot stone smoldering on the carpet at the very feet of the ducal heir.

Francesca let go a shriek, which was quickly seconded by Bona and the nurse, who dropped the brush at once and lifted her charge, Gian Galeazzo, straight up out of his chair, overturning it in the process. Ermes screamed for his mother. The quartet of singers—the coddled cream of Europe's musical talent, and loyal to the duke's family insofar as their generous salaries were paid—were quickly out the door.

While the area of the hearth filled with smoke and shouts, I rose, determined to stamp out the fire before it caught in earnest, and tried to move toward Francesca. But Caterina, already on her feet, blocked my way. Her blue eyes were wide and blank, her manner that of a mindless, terrified beast. As I pressed toward the fire and she away, she gave my shoulders such a mighty shove that I staggered backward and nearly lost my footing. She ran past me, the three-legged greyhound at her heels, out the door and into the loggia.

Behind her, Bona had gotten Chiara, stiff and weeping with fright, from her chair and was herding her, Gian Galeazzo, and Ermes toward the door. With her charges safe, she moved past me, allowing me to help Francesca stamp out the woolen shawl, now a heap on the carpet, its edges burning steadily, filling the room with the smell of burning hair.

One of the maids who had been packing the duchess's things ran forward and, with a poker, pushed the errant hearthstone—which had initiated the calamity by tumbling from the chimney and striking Francesca's peel—back into the fireplace. A second ran up and doused both the shawl and the smoldering carpet with water from the duchess's slop jar.

By this time, the nuts had begun to give off a scorched stink; the air grew noxious. Gasping, Francesca hurried to the window I had so recently shuttered and opened it, letting in the chimes from the nearby Certosa monastery and the freezing alpine air.

I joined the others outside in the loggia, where the window overlooking the interior courtyard had been thrown open. Gian Galeazzo's nurse was leading him, his brother, and the still-weeping Chiara next door, to the ducal heir's chamber in the northwest tower; the singers had all disappeared from sight. A few nervous servants had appeared in Gian Galeazzo's doorway in response to the outcry, but seeing the danger past, they were already receding back into the tower room.

Bona remained by the loggia window, waiting to make sure I was unscathed; she clucked maternally at the sight of my coughing and steered me directly to the opening. I bared my face to the painfully cold air and filled my lungs. When my coughing finally eased, I wiped my streaming eyes and drew back to examine the duchess.

The incident had left her unharmed, but some new disaster had claimed her attention: I followed her gaze east down the long loggia and saw Caterina standing at the far end of the great hall that separated the duchess's quarters from the duke's.

In the yellow light cast by a wall sconce, Caterina stood profoundly still with her back to us, her normally exuberant aspect hushed, her chin lifted and head canted to one side; I was reminded of a cat that, before pouncing on a bird, pauses to listen to its song. I paused, too: a woman was screaming in terror and outrage somewhere in the opposite wing of the palace.

The five doors that led into the great hall were uncharacteristically closed, and the servants inside oddly silent. The loggia, too, had grown abruptly deserted, save for an old servant who paused to light each wall sconce with the long taper in his hand; he made his way slowly toward us from the direction of the duke's apartments. Surely he had heard the lady's cries; perhaps he had even seen her, struggling in the grasp of Bruno, strongest of all the duke's bodyguards. Yet like all good servants of Galeazzo Sforza, Duke of Milan, he had learned to keep his eyes downcast, his pace steady, his expression blank as though he could not hear her ragged screams.

They emanated from the east, from the loggia in the men's wing, and they grew ever louder as they moved toward the northeast tower, and the duke's quarters.

Let me go, let me go!

For the love of God . . .

You there, help me! Someone, help!

I understood at once why everyone else had so efficiently departed the scene.

Caterina whirled to face us, her blue eyes avid, bright; she did not quite smirk.

"Madonna," she called, almost gaily, to Bona. "Shall we pray?"

Bona's dark, bovine eyes were wide with hurt. Yet she mastered her pain and, ignoring the servant and Caterina's insolent, knowing gaze, lifted her skirts. With calm, deliberate steps and all the grace her square, portly frame allowed, she moved down the loggia, past the closed doors of the great hall, to the open entrance of the family chapel.

Caterina and I entered the chapel with her. Just inside, to our right, stood the interior door that connected the chapel to the duke's dressing chamber. For safety and privacy, none of the duke's rooms opened directly onto the loggia. Instead, one had to enter the chapel and from there, gain entry to the duke's dressing chamber, which in turn led to the duke's bed-chamber, which in turn led to the duke's private dining hall in the north-east tower. The dining hall opened onto the northernmost room of the men's east wing, the chamber of rabbits. This sported a life-sized mural of the duke on horseback in the summer-green park, following greyhounds in pursuit of a warren of hares; the chamber opened directly onto the eastern loggia. In sum, there are only two ways to reach the duke's suite from the common hallway: either from the chapel off the north loggia, or from the chamber of rabbits off the east.

They planned, of course, to drag the girl in through the chamber of rab-bits, so that she could not be seen by anyone passing in or out of the duch-ess's chambers. If a stone had not chanced to tumble from the chimney in Bona's hearth, the duchess would have heard no one but the singers, and would have remained cheerfully unaware of the rape occurring under her husband's roof.

The chapel smelled of hot candle wax. It was paneled in ebony wood, like the duchess's chamber; the choir stalls were carved from the same. The room's sole spot of color could be found in the large stained-glass window, which depicted Milan's patron saint, Ambrose, white-bearded and stern in his golden bishop's mitre against a garden backdrop of emerald green. The sunlight had almost disappeared, leaving the window dark and the chapel shrouded in shadow, broken only by the glow from lamps flanking the entry and tapers burning on the altar, beneath the large wooden crucifix where a bronze Christ hung, his head bowed in death. The room was hearthless, dreary, and chill; Bona believed that God paid closer attention to the prayers of the suffering, which was why she often wore a hair shirt hidden beneath her fine silk chemise. No doubt she hoped God might post some of her ex-cessive contrition to her husband's account.

Beneath the altar, a dozen votive candles burned, two of them for my

Matteo's safety. By the time Bona knelt at the altar and I lifted one of the burning tapers to light two new votives—one for the duke's soul, one for his victim's—the shrieking had stopped. I replaced the taper on the altar, then returned and knelt on the cushion next to the duchess, who smelled of rosewater and smoke.

Bona's deep-set eyes were fast shut, her dimpled hands clasped, her lips moving silently. Her features were pinched but set; one who did not suspect her personal agony would think she was simply earnest at prayer.

Caterina did not kneel, but unabashedly pressed her ear against the door adjacent to the duke's dressing room; she did not test it, for she knew that it would be bolted from the other side. When Caterina was still quite young, but old enough to suspect what was happening, Bona had tried to send her to her quarters for the duration. The girl disobeyed and kept escaping to the men's wing in an effort to catch a glimpse of her father in flagrante. She was stronger, faster, and far cleverer than her nurses, with the result that Bona finally acknowledged the duke's trangressions and brought Caterina with her to the chapel, insisting that the girl should pray for her father. But Caterina refused to waste her time.

"If it is wrong of my father to do such a thing," she asked reasonably, "then why does no one stop him?"

Bona, devoted to God but no philosopher, had no answer. She soon despaired of trying to influence Caterina for the good, as the girl was obviously as stubborn as her father and most likely just as inclined to wickedness.

I, on the other hand, was desperately beholden to the duchess and eager to please her. My parents had no doubt been so horribly damned—my mother perhaps a shamed woman, my father perhaps too wicked to care for his own children—that Bona, unshakable in the face of evil, had never been able to bring herself to say much about them. I feared that whatever had driven them to unspeakable sin had infected me, and so I embraced the duchess's assiduous instruction concerning religion.

God is loving, Bona always said, *but also just. And though you might not see results at once, He surely hears the prayers of the meek. Pray for justice, Dea, and in good time it will come; and pray for yourself, that you might be wise enough to love sinners while abhorring their deeds.*

For Bona's sake, I believed it all, prayed often and sincerely, and waited on God to reward the faithful and punish the wicked. The duke was all-powerful, his bodyguards cunningly armed and ready to deal death to those who interfered with their master's pleasure; what else could I, a mere seventeen-year-old woman, do other than pray and offer Bona my comfort and companionship?

Yet when it came to sinners who relished cruelty, such as the duke and his coldhearted pet, Caterina, I could not match Bona's saintliness. My heart held hate, not love. And so, as I began to mouth silent prayers beside the duchess, I asked God not for patience or for charity, but for vengeance, of a swifter sort than He was accustomed to meting out.

In my mind's eye I pictured not the dying Christ or the Holy Mother, but the duke, who had invited the current silence by holding out his hand to the girl and speaking gently, quickly, as if soothing a frightened beast. He was telling her that all the stories about him were lies, that he was in fact a kindly man who wished her no harm.

And she—fifteen years old at most, lovely, unmarried, and a virgin from a decent family—was crazed with fear and desperate to believe him.

I yearned to be a man, one with a sword and the access to His Grace Duke Galeazzo. I pictured myself stealing up behind him as he murmured to the girl, and ending his crime with one short, swift, avenging thrust of my blade. Instead, I had only the opportunity to whisper one Our Father and two Ave Marias before Caterina, her expression one of fascination, hissed, "They are moving into his bedchamber now."

The screaming began again, this time wordless, outraged, animal. I clasped my hands until they ached and tried desperately to quash my imagination. From behind the altar wall came muffled thumping—bodies or limbs striking walls, perhaps—and the tinkling of glass. Beneath it all was the very faint, vicious sound of male laughter.

Holy Mother, take pity upon her. Lord, let the duke taste justice.

"Why do you not help her?" Caterina demanded. There was no concern or frustration in her tone, only a dogged insistence. "He is hurting her, after all. Surely God does not mean for you to stand idly by."

Without lifting her head, Bona replied, "We are only women, and far frailer than men. Should they not come to our aid, we can rely only on the goodness of God."

A corner of Caterina's lip twitched in disgust. "Only a coward waits on God."

Angered by the attack on Bona, I jerked my face toward Caterina's. "If that is so, Madonna, then why do *you* not stop your father? You're his favorite; persuade him. Save him from sin and protect the lady."

Without lifting her ear from the door, Caterina stuck out her tongue at me; still at prayer, Bona did not see.

"You all speak nonsense," Caterina said. "First you say that my father sins. Then you say that God chose my father to rule, so his will must be respected. Well, it's his will to lie with pretty young women. So where is the sin? And if it *is* sin, then why would God have such bad judgment as to anoint my father duke?"

Bona did not open her eyes, but behind her veil, a fat tear spilled from the corner of her eye and slid down her cheek. It was not her way to question God or her husband. "If you will not pray for your father," she said, her voice husky and uneven with sorrow, "then at least pray for the girl."

"The fact is," Caterina countered, "a duke can do whatever he pleases."

She began to say more, but her words were drowned out by a man's shouts coming from the direction of the chamber of rabbits: *"Duca! Duca! Your Grace!"* His rasping, nasal voice was soon joined by others, and grew muffled by the sounds of scuffling.

Intrigued, Caterina hurried into the hall to learn the source of the noise. Within a minute, she retreated back into the chapel in a fright, and dropped to her knees at the altar on the far side of Bona.

Boot heels rang against the loggia's stone floor; soon a trio of cloaked men armed with drawn short swords stood in the chapel archway. One of them, of powerful shoulders and good height, stepped inside. Upon seeing the interior door leading to the duke's suite, he rattled the handle, found it locked, then nodded to the other two, who began in turn to throw themselves at the door to break it down.

Ashamed, Bona turned her face from them.

Meanwhile, the first man—with straight dark brown hair, parted down the middle and falling a few fingers shy of his shoulders—bowed low to us, then straightened and said, "Good ladies. My deepest apologies for disturbing you at prayer and disrupting the peace in God's chamber, but one of your fair sex is in danger. I beg your forbearance while we work to bring this matter to a happy end."

His dialect was Tuscan, and his diction revealed an education reserved for the highest born, yet his voice was peculiarly nasal. He was in his twenties or thirties, but it was difficult to judge, for his face was remarkably strange. His jaw was very square, and his chin jutted far forward; he had a noticeable underbite and when he spoke, his lower lip stuck out while his upper disappeared. This would not have seemed so unfortunate had it not been combined with his huge nose, which was flat at the bridge where it met the inner corners of his eyebrows, then rose and swooped alarmingly off to one side; it had an unusually long, sloping tip. It made me think of a clay likeness that had waited too long for the kiln and begun to droop. He might have looked foolish or unforgivably ugly had it not been for the rare intelligence in his eyes and his unselfconscious, confident grace.

I stood, curtsied reluctantly, and said, with as much contained fury as I dared show a noble, "You have disturbed my mistress at prayer, my lord. And you have violated the sanctity of the chapel."

I looked pointedly at his two companions, gasping after their few failed attempts to break down the door. Like him, they were dressed in new winter cloaks trimmed with brown marten fur at the collars and sleeves.

"I am no lord," he replied, clearly troubled by the fact that the screams had turned ominously to muffled groans. "Only a commoner trying to help in an emergency. I beg your forgiveness in what surely must be a difficult time for you all. But can no one else in this palace hear that the lady needs help?"

Bona bowed her head low, still too mortified to speak; Caterina stayed on her knees but peered past Bona at the speaker, clearly eager to see where this unexpected development would lead. Before the man could say more, a low wail emanated from a distant room behind the door, followed by wracking sobs.

The self-professed commoner's strong, homely faced twisted with pity at the sound; pushing aside his fellows, he threw his shoulder against the door with all his force. The thick, solid wood did not so much as tremble at the blow. Rather than leave in frustration, the commoner knocked the wood with the hilt of his short sword.

"Your Grace! Good Your Grace!" he called, his tone playfully cajoling. "It is I, your secret guest, freshly arrived to enjoy your legendary hospitality. Let me repay it in small part now by offering the young lady an escort home." And when no reply came, he added cheerfully, "I am determined, Your Grace; I shall wait at this door, and my fellows at the other, until we have her."

With that, he turned to his men and gestured in the direction of the chamber of rabbits; they understood and left at once, while the so-called commoner remained, his ear to the door.

A long moment passed, during which Bona found her composure. She then crossed herself, rose, and turned to the man; at her side, Caterina rose as well, and watched with unselfconscious fascination.

"Your Magnificence," Bona said softly, slowly, as always in control, though I knew her heart was breaking. "My lord the duke informed me to prepare for a guest's arrival, but he did not tell me that it was you. I fear I cannot greet you properly at this time, given the unpleasant circumstance."

He squinted hard at her and took a slow step toward her, frowning, until his eyes suddenly widened and his jaw dropped.

"Your Grace!" he exclaimed softly, his voice hushed with embarrassment; his cheeks reddened. "Oh, my lady Duchess!" He bowed deeply from the shoulders, and remained in that position as he spoke. "I cannot— I would never have— Your Grace, I beg forgiveness for my cruel thoughtlessness! My judgment has failed me once again. Had I recognized you, I would have been far more discreet."

I applauded his desire to save the distressed lady, but could not forgive the humiliation he had just inflicted on Bona; my temper took abrupt control of my tongue. "How could you not recognize the duchess, good sir, when she stands directly before you? A poor excuse for such rudeness!"

Bona moved to me and caught my elbow. "Dea," she said, her voice very low. "His sight is poor. Now you, too, must apologize."

Behind us, Caterina giggled. Tongue-tied, I looked back at His Magnificence, and he looked back at me.

"Dea," he said, with faint surprise, and in his eyes curiosity dawned. He uttered my name as if it were a familiar one.

Before he could say more, we all turned at the sound of footsteps approaching the door leading to the duke's dressing chamber, and the squeal of the bolt being drawn. The door opened a crack; His Magnificence inclined his ear to it, and listened to whispered instructions from one of the duke's valets. He gave a sharp nod to show he had understood, and the door closed again.

His Magnificence turned to Bona and bowed to take his leave. "Your Grace, my apologies once more. When we meet tomorrow, I will greet you as you deserve and do my best to make full reparation."

"When we meet tomorrow, or any other day, dear Lorenzo," Bona said softly, "we shall not speak of this."

"Agreed," he answered, then nodded to Caterina and last of all, me. "Ladies," he said briskly, and was gone; I listened to his ringing steps as he made his way down the loggia toward the chamber of rabbits.

Like everyone else in Italy, I had heard tales about Lorenzo the Magnificent. At the tender age of twenty, he had become the de facto ruler of Florence upon his father's death. I had glimpsed him only once, in 1469, when I was nine and had been living in Bona's household only a year. Along with four other prominent rulers in Milan's great Duomo, Lorenzo de' Medici stood as godfather at Gian Galeazzo's christening. Unlike us lesser mortals, Lorenzo possessed such intelligence, confidence, and charm that he could speak bluntly to Duke Galeazzo without provoking his wrath, and the duke, who routinely abused his family, courtiers, servants, and peers, treated Lorenzo with respect.

Once Lorenzo had left the chapel, Bona turned to me, her eyes brimming with tears. "God surely answered our prayers, sending him to help the lady . . . and to teach me humility."

"Surely," I gently agreed, though I did not believe for an instant that Bona had any pride left after eight years of marriage to Galeazzo Sforza. But I was grateful for Lorenzo's attempt to intervene.

"Take Caterina with you," Bona ordered, "and make sure she gets to her quarters and stays there. You're free to do as you wish until I summon you again."

"I will deliver her to her nurse, then return, if you like," I said softly. I could see the duchess was in need of comfort. It is a hard thing to accept that one's husband is a monster, and harder still to endure that monstrousness in polite company.

Her gaze averted, Bona shook her head, and I suddenly understood: Lorenzo's appearance had so shamed my mistress that she was no longer able to control her tears. As I herded Caterina out, Bona knelt again at the altar railing, pausing before she returned to her prayers to call: "Please close the door behind you."

I did, leaving her to weep in private.

Caterina broke away from me the instant we were out in the loggia; she turned toward the men's wing and, cursing her full woman's skirts, lifted them high and half ran in the direction of the chamber of rabbits. I was taller, with a longer stride, and easily caught her by the elbow.

She tried to shake free, but I held fast, wheeled her about, and dragged her with me toward the women's wing.

"Bitch!" she snapped. "I'll tell my father!"

"That I am following the duchess's orders?" I paused. "What would your father say, were he to see you waiting in the chamber of rabbits?"

She said nothing, but accompanied me, sourly, back down the loggia toward Bona's chambers, where servants had managed to clear out the smoke and close the windows, though the smell of burnt wool and nuts lingered. Next to it was little Gian Galeazzo's and Ermes's quarters in the northeast corner, and just past them was the northernmost room in the ladies' wing, the pink chamber, so named because its walls were covered in rose moiré silk. It served as nursery to Bona's daughters, five-month-old Anna and four-year-old Bianca Maria, who had already been married off to her first cousin, Philibert, Duke of Savoy. Just past it was Caterina's room. I deposited her there and informed her nurse of Bona's order, knowing all the while that the duke's headstrong daughter would likely dash off the instant I had left.

I did not care. I proceeded southward down the endless ladies' loggia, with its life-sized murals of those in Bona's household, framed against a summer garden backdrop. Near the duchess's quarters, there was a painting of Bona, seated and gazing proudly down at the infant Gian Galeazzo in her arms. Her courtiers clustered around her: the duke's aunt, Elena del

Maino; Emilia Attendoli, who had served Duke Galeazzo's mother; and Emilia's daughter, Antonia. Farther down the hall, in the newest mural, Ermes handed his baby sister Bianca Maria an apple picked from a tree, while the image of ten-year-old Caterina made one of her beloved greyhounds sit for a morsel.

My likeness, like my heritage, was nowhere to be seen.

At last I arrived at the open door of the library, in the southwest corner tower. Here, the plain stone flooring became gray-veined white marble, and the ceiling rose three stories high. There were no murals here; the vast walls were covered in tall oak shelves. Upon the last rested stacks of parchments bound in brocade, damask, or velvet. Despite the duke's lack of interest in literature, his collection was priceless; he owned a copy of Virgil's *Aeneid*, annotated in Petrarch's very hand. For this reason, all works were attached to the shelves by silver chains.

Only three souls stood inside the vast chamber: the librarian and two young monks from the nearby monastery at Certosa. Unable to leave his domain unguarded, yet eager to retire now that the sun had set, the librarian scowled as I entered. I ignored him, knowing that I would be gone well before the monks, who stood with reverent awe in front of one of the manuscripts.

I passed them and headed for the library's interior staircase, thinking to climb all the way to the fourth-floor perch, where I could stare far to the southern horizon toward Rome, looking for signs of my husband.

As I moved to the landing, movement outside the window caught my eye. On the banks of the moat near the castle's main entry, two courtiers stood next to a servant who held the reins to two horses in one hand and a lamp in the other. In the faint arc of light, snowflakes sailed relentlessly downward.

I paused to stare at them. Though I could not make out their faces clearly, I recognized the build of one of them: Carlo Visconti, a black-haired courtier and member of Milan's Council of Justice, his bearing and gestures betraying violent emotion. Beside him was an older, white-haired man who might have been his father.

Approaching them from the direction of the castle was a third man carrying a swooning young woman. At the sight, the older man beat his chest, then threw open his arms; gently, the third man handed her to her father.

Visconti was not so conciliatory; he drew his sword and lunged at the man who delivered the girl. The third man reacted by taking a great step backward, then spreading his arms in a gesture of peace.

For the space of several seconds, neither party moved; I supposed that one of them was speaking. Abruptly, Visconti sheathed his sword and sagged with grief. The man he had threatened stepped forward to put a hand upon Visconti's shoulder, and in doing so, stepped into the lamplight.

I watched as Lorenzo the Magnificent kept his hand upon the courtier's shoulder, then put another on the father's, and spoke for a moment. Afterward, he dug into a pocket and discreetly handed Visconti a purse. The latter pocketed it without argument.

The snow grew heavier, prompting the father to mount one of the horses. He reached for his daughter, who was unsteady on her legs; it took both Visconti and Lorenzo to get her up into the saddle. Visconti and the servant then mounted the remaining horse; Visconti paused long enough to bow from the shoulders to Lorenzo, who returned the gesture before the trio galloped off across the drawbridge.

I remained at the window as Lorenzo turned, the wind whipping his dark hair across his face, and watched as he made his way grimly back to the castle. At its entrance he paused to glance pointedly up at the library window—at me, as if, impossibly given his poor eyesight, he saw me standing there.

Two

Snow fell that night. By morning, the clouds had gone, leaving behind a blue sky and an infinite white expanse that glittered beneath the sun. The weather was still bitter, but the wind had died; a good day for travel, Bona told me brightly, and promised that Matteo would be home within two days.

I smiled faintly at her cheer, though my anxiety had not eased; I woke with a gut so clenched I could not face breakfast. Instead I prayed earnestly beside Bona in the chapel: *Lord, guard Your servant Matteo da Prato and bring him safely home to me. Blessed Virgin, Mother of God, keep my husband from harm. Saint Christopher, patron of travelers, protect him . . .*

Afterward, I put on my heavy cloak and went downstairs to the passage that led to the garden, where the woodsmen had piled boughs of evergreen as high as my shoulders. I gathered several boughs into my arms, and made my way carefully over the slippery floor of the open loggia; on the opposite side, an old serving woman swept away the snow with a broom while her frailer husband followed, sprinkling ash from a pail onto the stone.

Matteo's chamber, situated on the first level, directly beneath the duke's bedroom, stood two doors from the garden passage. Only the highest of Galeazzo's officials were housed on the second floor along with the ducal family; Galeazzo's secretary and right-hand man, Cicco Simonetta, was privileged to live right next to the duke's suite, closer even than Bona. In recognition of Matteo's intelligence and loyalty, however, he had been rewarded with one of the better downstairs chambers.

I paused at the entrance to my husband's room, wrestling with my fragrant burden in order to get the key from my cloak pocket. Like his immediate superior, Cicco, Matteo always kept his chamber locked; the duke entrusted all his state secrets to Cicco, who in turn shared a few of them with my husband. In these perilous times, a prince was wise to encrypt any correspondence he did not want read by anyone other than the intended recipient; couriers could not always be trusted. The duke had promoted Cicco to a position of great power because of the latter's natural grasp of the art of encryption, and Cicco had promoted my husband because of Matteo's ability to create and memorize hard-to-break ciphers. Matteo could look at a letter in Latin or the vernacular and encrypt it in a matter of minutes, an unheard-of feat. After seven years of acquainting himself diligently with the duke's most confidential matters, Matteo was chosen to serve as a junior envoy to Rome. He had visited there once in the spring, before we were married, and was soon to return from his second visit. I asked him no questions, but I was proud: I had no doubt that he dealt with members of the Sacred College, perhaps even with the pope himself.

The melting snow had caused the wooden door to swell; even unlocked, it would not open until I gave it a hard kick. Once it was open, I set down a branch and wiped my feet upon it, then closed the door behind me and scattered the rest of the perfumed boughs onto the stone floor.

Matteo had been gone almost two months, but the room still smelled of him, of rosemary water and olive oil soap, of parchment and iron-gall ink, of the indescribable scent of male flesh. The room was chilly, the hearth long-unlit; I had told God that morning that I would set my oddly persistent fear for Matteo's safety aside and trust that my prayers on his behalf would be answered. As proof of my conviction, I would perform an act of faith and light the fire, so that the room would be cozy by the time my husband arrived.

Yesterday, I had loaded wood onto the grate, with strategically placed juniper bark as tinder; today, I took the tinderbox from the mantel and retrieved the flint and steel. It took several tries before a spark fell and caught; I sat on my heels and fanned it, thinking of my strange marriage.

Other women would think me exceedingly lucky. Though lacking noble blood and the convenience of well-placed family, Matteo had succeeded in using his wits to rise to an admirable station. And he was good-looking enough—taller than most of the other men, and long-limbed, if a bit too slender, with straight, thick auburn hair so dark it looked black after sunset. He kept it cut short and often hidden beneath a red felt cap, of the same close-fitting sort his master Cicco wore. His skin was naturally pale, though it had browned during his travels; his eyes were a clear, light hazel, thoughtful and calm. His lips were full and pretty, though the bow of his upper lip bore a scar from a childhood mishap. His words were spoken softly and always kind. Occasionally, when he was tired or forgot himself, his Tuscan accent became noticeable.

Over the seven years he had spent at Duke Galeazzo's court, Matteo was never far from me. On holidays, at picnics, at summer games in the courtyard, or at the hunt, Matteo always managed to seek out my company; he seemed to know a good deal about the particular circumstances of my life, and was always interested in how I was faring, especially in my studies. He wanted to know whether Bona was good to me, or Caterina rude, what my favorite subjects and hobbies were, what books I had read. I responded with questions of my own, and learned that he was from Florence—or rather, from the Ospedale degli Innocenti, the city's largest orphanage.

"I grew up there," he said, "but was rescued in my youth by a patron. I got my education from the monks at San Marco in Florence. When I was older, I went to the University of Pavia, where Cicco recruited me."

"So there is no one in Florence for you?" I asked. "No patron? No adopted family to return to?"

He almost answered, then stopped himself and gave a crescent moon smile. "None. But I have many dear friends there." He hesitated. "You would love it. There is no fear there, as there is here. . . ." He dropped his gaze suddenly, realizing that he had said a politically dangerous thing. "The people are happier and speak freely. The world's best artists live there because the nobles support them."

"Nothing could be more beautiful than Milan," I said firmly. I had never traveled and therefore feared it; Bona was my refuge.

"Once you see Florence, you'll change your mind," Matteo replied.

I did not think much about my friendship with Matteo, for his interest in me was kindly but not obsessive, though at times, I would look up from a conversation during a gathering for the ducal staff, and see Matteo looking at me; he always flushed and averted his eyes.

Perhaps, as I grew older, I was a bit attracted to him, but given Bona's stern religious instruction and my desire to cast off my parents' sin, I had no interest in marriage or the pleasures of the flesh. The world was a fearsome, wicked place, and I lucky to be alive and under Bona's pious wing; when I was twelve, I begged her to send me to a convent, but she would not. (I am grateful now she did not sent me to one, for I later learned that, when drunk, Galeazzo liked to pay nocturnal visits to the nunneries, in order to assert what he considered his ducal privilege upon the poor women there.) I vowed never to marry, but to remain celibate and serve none but God and Bona all my days. And so I paid no mind to Matteo's fraternal attentions.

The duke, however, paid no mind to my vow. When I turned sixteen, he pressed Bona to find a husband for me—no matter that I had no dowry, so that a decent match was impossible. After some months, when the duke realized that she was intentionally delaying the matter, he announced that I was to marry the master of Bona's stables, one Ridolfo, who had recently lost his wife. Ridolfo was gray-haired, potbellied, and profoundly uninterested in the arts. He understood only dogs and horses, and those none too well, for he had lost his front teeth to a stallion unappreciative of his constant lashes. His dogs despised him for similar cause; I had no doubt his late wife had been relieved to quit his company. Even before she died, Ridolfo always leered at me and the youngest women. Apparently the thought of tender virgin flesh made up for the lack of a dowry.

When I learned of the marriage, I wept and begged Bona to cancel the wedding or let me flee. She had enormous sympathy for my situation, but she could not disobey her husband. As my wedding day grew closer, I grew more frantic.

Then Matteo went to the duke and asked for my hand.

At the July wedding—a small affair in the ducal chapel, attended by Bona, her ladies, Cicco, and Matteo's fellow scribes—my groom was too stunned by his own decision to meet my gaze. After the ceremony, he kissed me not on the lips, as was proper for man and wife, but upon the brow. At the small banquet in the ground-floor servants' hall, his gaze was, for once, directed at everyone but me. He drank a bit more than his portion of wine that night, and I more than mine; clearly, the bride was not the only one to dread the wedding night.

We went to his chambers to find the bed strewn with rose petals; Bona's maid Francesca helped me quickly to undress down to my chemise, while Matteo hid behind the open doors of his wardrobe and fumbled with his own clothing. Once Francesca had left, I climbed into the bed, drew the covers up, and waited for my naked husband to appear.

Matteo emerged minus his doublet but still dressed in his short chemise and leggings. He pointed to a fur rug in front of the cold hearth. "I will sleep there tonight," he said, still without looking at me.

I stared at him in amazement. The thought of sexual congress had left me terrified, but the priest had pronounced us wed. We were, to my thinking, obliged to couple whether we wanted to or not. "Why do you not come to bed?"

"I . . ." His cheeks flamed. "Dea, I could not bear to see you forced into such a terrible marriage, to a cruel man far beneath your station. But I—"

"You do not love me," I finished calmly. How had I so misinterpreted all those longing glances over so many years? "You are doing this out of kindness, of course."

He drew a breath, squared his shoulders, and sat down beside me. Taking my hand, he finally looked into my eyes. "I love you more than anyone else in all the world, Dea," he said fiercely. "And I vow to protect you from harm and care for you tenderly. I am your truest friend, but I can never be more than that. Do you understand?"

"Yes," I said. "You don't fancy women, then."

He let go a short, unhappy laugh. "It's not that at all. It's . . . simply a very complicated situation. The time will come soon, though, when I can explain why things must be so. But for now, I ask you to trust me. And one more thing . . ."

I lifted an expectant brow.

"For your sake, and mine, we must pretend that we have consummated our marriage. It is the safest course. Could you do that, Dea, knowing that I love you and want only the best for you?"

His words and eyes radiated compassion; I imagined I heard honest anguish in his tone. Even so, my temper flared. He was lying about preferring women to men, I decided, because it was a mortal sin and one that, discovered, could lead to his disgrace and even death. Yet I was furious that he would not trust me with the truth. He had said we were true friends.

I dropped his hand, picked up the feather pillow beside me, and, with all my strength, struck him hard in the face with it. Then I flung myself down on the bed, turned my back to him, and lay there a few minutes before my indignation yielded to tears. Even now, I am not sure why I cried so abruptly and bitterly; I should have been relieved.

When he lay down beside me and put his arm around my shoulder, I did not pull away. We passed the whole night thus.

My pride was wounded, but I quickly recovered. After all, I now had something I had never known before: a family, even if it consisted only of Matteo. For the first time I truly belonged to someone else, and he belonged to me. And I did not, like all other women, crave children—in fact, I privately thought it cruel to bring a new soul into such a wicked world. I enjoyed Matteo's company, and resolved to live contentedly with him without relations.

Resolutions are such feeble things.

I had expected to love him as I might a friend, a brother. I had not expected that he would be ever thoughtful of me, that he would daily do me small kindnesses, bring me small gifts, take joy in my delight. I had not expected that I would lie in his bed pretending to sleep while he worked late at the small trestle desk in his chambers; I had not expected the way the lamplight would paint his skin golden, would cause shadows to nestle in the hollows of his cheeks and throat, would spark glints of copper in his hair.

During the days he worked upstairs in the men's wing with Cicco and the rest of the clerical staff while I spent the time with Bona. At night, he worked alone, in our chamber, on the most secret projects. I was proud that Cicco had entrusted the most delicate matters to him, even at the same time that I was annoyed that Cicco overworked him so. Matteo was discreet: he never discussed his work, nor left the papers out where I could see them. Sometimes he read; most of the time, he wrote and wrote. When he was finished, he gathered his papers together and quietly placed them in a compartment hidden in the wainscoting, which he locked; the key hung from a leather thong about his neck.

Once I passed by while he was working at his desk and failed to avert my gaze in time. I got a glimpse of cipher rendered in Matteo's even hand. It was a beautiful creation, a tapestry of numbers and Latin letters and mathematical symbols, elegantly woven upon the page without space or punctuation. I tried to forget what I had seen, but that was impossible—like Matteo, I was good at keeping secrets, too. Only Bona, who had taught me my letters, knew the truth: that once I saw something in writing, in my native tongue or French or Latin, I could not forget it. Bona was scandalized that God should have given a woman such a useless gift; at her urging, I kept my talent to myself.

I hid it from Matteo, too, for it comforted me to have him there as I fell asleep; I did not want him to worry I might be too curious.

Not long after we were married, I woke one night to find the lamplight blue and sputtering, and Matteo still in his chair. He had put away his work and was sitting up very straight, his arms by his sides. His eyes were closed, his face utterly relaxed; the corners of his lips were faintly turned up in the most beatific of smiles. Dreaming, I thought, and I stirred, thinking to rise and lead him to bed, but the instant I moved, his eyes opened slowly. He had been full awake.

"I thought you were asleep," I said, startled.

"I was just thinking," he said, as if that were explanation enough. His eyes were extraordinarily bright and loving. "If you don't mind, I would like to think for a bit longer."

"Suit yourself." I rolled back over, but I could not go back to sleep; I kept thinking of the look on his face.

In all dealings with me Matteo was patient, in all dealings kind. I saw his anger only once, one evening when his master Cicco kicked open our chamber door and hurled Matteo inside. As Matteo struck the floor full force, I yelped and ran to him. His upper lip was split and bleeding, his left eye swelling shut. I put my arms about his shoulders and pulled him up to sitting; trembling with rage, he pushed me away and tried to get to his feet, but Cicco moved quickly into the room and kicked him back down.

"Fool!" Cicco barked. He was forty years Matteo's senior and gray-haired, but stout and tall as an oak. "Are you thinking to get yourself killed? Stay here and soak your head in cold water until you can think clearly!"

With that, Cicco turned and left, slamming the door behind him.

I fussed over Matteo and cleaned the blood away. His front tooth had been chipped on the outside edge, his upper lip was split at the same spot as his childhood scar, and the tender skin around his eye was badly bruised. I asked a gentle question as to the cause of the fight, but Matteo was too troubled to speak for hours. I suspected that he had probably seen a woman being dragged through the loggia, and tried to intervene. After all those years of working for the duke, he should have known better.

We did not speak that night; I helped him undress and turned down the covers for him, but he would not go to bed. Nor did he bring out his papers to work; instead, he sat at his desk and stared straight ahead at the wainscoting.

It was well after midnight when I woke to see the lamp still burning, and Matteo still in his chair. His eyes—the one swollen and an alarming shade of purple now—were closed, and his expression was, if not blissful, then at least serene.

"What do you do in that chair?" I asked softly.

He drew in a long breath and released it with a faintly shuddering sigh. "I try," he said, "to see things as they really are."

There was something surprisingly optimistic in his tone. Barefoot, I went to him and blew out the lamp, then led him to bed. He slept with his arm around my shoulder. We did not speak of the fight with Cicco again, but I watched day after day as the swelling of his upper lip gradually retreated, leaving behind a thicker scar.

The months of our marriage passed quickly. July left, and August came; at every feast day, every wedding, Matteo and I sat together and danced, beaming as newlyweds ought. We blushed at jokes about the conjugal relations we were surely enjoying, and answered questions about the possible arrival of children with smiles and shrugs.

I began to fall in love. I had not meant to; I had not believed that any man could be as kind as Bona, or as gentle, or as able to put my needs before his. I blamed Matteo for my feelings. I would not have come to love him so much had he not gazed on me so often with such genuine affection, and I saw, from close daily observation, that he did not favor men over women.

What, then, kept him from my arms?

By late August, I began to experiment with small signs of affection. When the entire court celebrated the end of summer with an outdoor picnic, I held his hand after the dances had ended, and led him to a pond on the edges of the duke's hunting park. The moon was waxing fat and reflected in the dark, still water; I drew his attention upward, to the glittering diamond sky, and pointed at a cluster of stars.

And I shared with Matteo something I had never revealed to anyone. Somehow I knew that Matteo would understand.

"See those stars." I pointed up at the sky. "And the wisps of clouds beside them. Together, they make an upside-down numeral four."

Matteo noted them and looked sharply at me. "They do," he said.

"It's a man, do you see? He's upside down—and his one leg is bent and crossed over the straight one, to make the four."

"The hanged man," he whispered. I could not read his tone.

"Well, perhaps," I said, relaxing my focus and letting my imagination roam. "Perhaps, if one slipped a rope over his ankle and dangled him upside down, and he bent one knee . . . Matteo, that man is you."

I looked back at him to see his reaction. I expected him to smile and think it was a fanciful little joke. But he was studying me with the same intensity he turned on his ciphers.

"What does it mean?" he asked.

I looked back at the hanged man, and was filled with sudden dread. Some very bad things were going to happen, but they would bring about great good. Good that Matteo would heartily approve of.

"Changes are coming," I said truthfully. I could not bring myself to say that they would be unbearably hard.

It was a warm night, but the breeze stirred as I spoke. He shivered slightly, and composed himself.

"How often do you see these . . . signs, Dea?"

"They're everywhere," I answered, heartened by the fact that he did not scoff. "I just notice them at some times more than others. But they are always true." I hesitated. "Bona would say this was from the Devil."

"Bona would be wrong," he said, more quickly than I think he wanted to, for he stopped himself and remained silent for a moment. "Have you mentioned this to anyone else?"

"No one. I hoped you might understand."

"I do. And you should never, ever speak of this to Bona or anyone else." He paused. "It's not from the Devil. But some people think it is, and that makes it dangerous to discuss. People have been killed for less."

"I'll speak of it only to you."

"I would appreciate that—if you see something you think I should know about." His tone warmed. "You must be who you are, Dea, and must never stifle such a talent. But only you and I should know."

I smiled, pleased that my husband and I shared a secret.

He glanced back up at the sky. I took advantage of the moment to reach up and press my hand to his warm cheek. He smiled down at me, but upon seeing the look in my eye, drew away, and went back to the others.

I was, however, not easily discouraged. In those days my chaste pecks upon waking and retiring began to stray from his cheek toward his lips. I remarked on the fine appearance he made, on my great good luck of having him for a husband, on my constant gratitude for his kindness. When he worked too long past midnight, I would go to him and set my cheek upon his shoulder and plead sweetly for him to join me in bed. I yearned for yet feared his touch.

In every case, I was rebuffed kindly, subtly: Matteo avoided my kisses by turning his face gently away, and slipped his hand from my grip when I held on too long. My compliments brought small, tenuous smiles and averted gazes. In the first few days of November, as Matteo settled at his desk, while I, in my nightgown, stoked the fire, I asked over my shoulder:

"Would it be so horrible, then, if we were to truly live as man and wife?"

His long silence served as answer. I looked back at the flames, humiliated and struggling to hide my tears.

After a time, he said softly, "I love you, Dea. But never in that way." He paused. "I'll be leaving in a few days for Rome. Cicco has asked me to go on the duke's behalf. Perhaps when I return, I'll be able to explain things. Perhaps later we could go together to Florence, to meet some of my friends there."

"Florence!" I whispered harshly. "What has Florence to do with anything?"

His expression grew sorrowful; after a long moment, he said, "If you understood, you would not be angry. Please, Dea, trust me for a little while longer."

I answered nothing, but took a few more savage thrusts at the fire with the poker, then went to bed sulking. Eventually, I tired of my self-pity and fell asleep.

Some hours later I woke in the dead of night. The room was black; the single window was shuttered and Matteo had put out the lamp, but he did not lie beside me. Instead, he trod with bare feet slowly, lightly, over the carpet and the stone, gesturing with his arms in the darkness. As my eyes grew accustomed to the lack of light, I saw him pause in front of the south wall and make a complicated, sweeping gesture, and heard the faintest of murmurs—softer than a whisper, yet oddly authoritative—issue from his lips. After this, he made a quarter-turn to face west, and again gestured; by the time he faced the north wall, I surmised that he was drawing stars in the air, and connecting them with a circle.

The realization pricked the hairs on the back of my neck: Stars and circles belonged to the realm of magic, and Bona had drilled into me that such things were of the Devil. Yet only half of me took fright; the other half was keenly interested, and even comforted, for Matteo's circle enclosed the entire room, including the bed where I lay. Like him, I was sheltered from whatever evil lurked beyond the perimeter.

In the darkness, my husband summoned no demons, invoked no dead. Instead, he stood in the circle's center, at the foot of our bed, and spread his arms, his face turned toward the invisible sky. He was, I decided, praying.

The next morning I did not speak of it to him; nor did I mention it over the next few days, though he continued nightly to draw the stars. As he packed for his Roman journey, he grew increasingly pensive; I felt at times that he was on the verge of telling me a great secret, but something held him back.

Morning and evening, I prayed at Bona's side in the chapel: *Let Matteo's acts be good, not evil. Let him love me. Keep him safe.*

He departed for Rome on a chill November dawn. He would not let me go with him to the stables, even though it was early and Bona would not expect me for an hour. Instead, he turned, dressed in his heavy woolen cloak and cap, and stopped as I tried to follow him out the door of our chamber.

"Dea," he said. "Let me take my leave now, and quickly." To my surprise, he clasped both my hands very tightly, and studied my face as if he thought to find something unexpected there; his eyes were so bright, so filled with affection that I thought he was about to kiss me full on the lips.

"Quickly," I agreed. "I don't care for good-byes." I closed my eyes and leaned in, eager for the kiss.

It did not come. He let go of my hands abruptly, and when I opened my eyes, he was reaching for something around his neck. He pulled it over his head and handed it to me; I stared at it for an instant as it dangled from his long fingers.

A tiny black key, strung upon a leather thong. I stared at it in surprise.

"Use it," he said, "in case of emergency."

"For the compartment in the wall," I said, disbelieving, "where you keep your papers."

He nodded.

"Why do you not just give it to Cicco?"

"Because those papers are not for Cicco," he said, in a way that awakened gooseflesh on my arms. "Or for anyone else but you, and then only in an emergency."

"There will be no emergency," I warned him sternly as I took the key and hung it round my own neck. His statement provoked a thousand anxious questions: *If you haven't been working for Cicco, then who? Why? What sort of papers are these?* But I asked none of them; he was standing in his cloak in the doorway, ready to leave. "I'll return this to you when you come home." *At Christmas,* I almost added, and realized how very long he would be gone.

"Dea," he said softly, and tried to take my hands again; I threw my arms around him and hugged him. This time, my embrace was fully returned. "My Dea," he repeated, then drew back and gave me that pure, loving smile. "God keep you."

"And you," I said, struggling to keep my composure. "Oh, Matteo, be careful!" I wanted to say *Don't go to Rome!* I felt that if I dared let go, Matteo would slip from my grasp forever.

He leaned down and gave me a solemn, fraternal kiss upon the lips, then said, "You *will* see me again, Dea."

"Of course," I said, and he turned and was gone.

The whole time Matteo was away, I slept on the little cot near Bona's feet, where I had always slept in the years before my marriage. Without Matteo, his chamber seemed forlorn and empty; I could not sleep in his bed alone. I did not linger long; Bona would be waiting for me that morning, and there were countless preparations left before the annual Christmas trek to Milan.

Even so, I paused before leaving, and prodded the fire one last time, making sure that the smoke drew properly. As I stared down into the golden flames, I saw the chance design made by the smaller limbs I had heaped upon the logs: an upside-down four. The hanged man.

Three

Bona was surprisingly cheerful that morning. Normally, her husband's violent infidelities would have left her shaken and sorrowful for a few days, but the instant I arrived in her chamber, she informed me that Duke Galeazzo had yielded to her request that she be allowed to honor his "secret guest" with a luncheon. The duke was reluctant, but, apparently, Lorenzo was eager to make amends for "startling the ladies in the chapel."

It was to be an intimate event. Situated in a corner tower, Galeazzo's private dining chamber had an unusually high vaulted ceiling; the stone floors were covered in Persian carpets in shades of scarlet, pine, and gold to mute the echoing tread of servants and the clatter of goblets and plates. Two arched windows faced north and east; these were shuttered that morning to keep out prying eyes and the bitter cold, and the great hearth contained such a fierce crackling blaze that I began to sweat the instant I entered the room. A pair of large tapestries covered the walls on either side of the eastern window, and the bare walls had been painted with trellises of flowers. But what was most remarkable, to my mind, were the eight long oval mirrors—four hung on the wall behind the table, four on the wall in front—that allowed the duke to see his reflection's reflection, as well as those of everyone in front of or behind him. These, combined with his four tasters—who sampled everything before it appeared on Galeazzo's plate or in his cup—gave him some measure of comfort, for even he realized that he had earned many enemies.

Lorenzo was waiting when we women arrived, an hour before midday. He wore a great smile that emphasized his jutting lower jaw by revealing his bottom row of teeth, yet it somehow served to ease his ugliness. That morning, he was unaccompanied and dressed in a plain, long tunic of gray wool. He wore no jewelry, nor had his straight locks felt the kiss of a curling iron. Yet when Bona's arrival was announced, he bowed and kissed her extended hand with a seasoned courtier's finesse; though he presented himself as a commoner, his confidence and self-possession marked him as an equal. Caterina, too, was announced and received a similar reception. I entered silently, to no fanfare, and expected no greeting, but Lorenzo bowed deeply to me, and when I responded with a curtsy, said warmly, "Dea, isn't it? The wife of Matteo da Prato?"

"I am," I said, blushing. I was unaccustomed to being acknowledged by anyone save Bona.

"I am an acquaintance of your husband's," he said. "I have known him for many years. It was I, in fact, who recommended him to the duke for employment."

Tongue-tied in the face of his composure and charm, I had no response.

Duke Galeazzo was late, requiring Bona and Lorenzo to engage in small talk for half an hour. Galeazzo's secretary and right-hand man, the thick-necked, burly Cicco Simonetta, arrived first. With his peasant's hair—long on top, cropped sharply above his oddly small ears—and round, heavy face, Cicco could easily have been mistaken for an ignorant bumpkin were it not for his fine dress and the shrewdness in his eyes. The duke kept no secrets from Cicco, who greeted Lorenzo with no smile and much reticence.

After the silent appearance of three sullen, armed bodyguards, and the emergence of attendants and the ducal cupbearer from the kitchen, Galeazzo arrived—without the usual blare of trumpets, given that Lorenzo's arrival was to be known by as few residents of Castle Pavia as possible. The duke's pride, however, required that his entry be accompanied by the sung praises of one of the castrated tenors who had entertained us in Bona's chamber the day before.

A month shy of his thirty-third birthday, Galeazzo Maria was in his prime. Like all the Sforza, he was sturdy, muscular, and passionately devoted to sport. His tunic, of gray-green watered silk embroidered with bronze fleur-de-lis, with white ermine trim at the collar, was tailored to show off a powerful chest and shoulders. His cap of light reddish brown hair was cut in layers, long enough to cover his ears but too short to touch his collar; as was the fashion, carefully crimped curls framed his face. The latter was dominated by a strong nose, so badly broken in his youth that the bridge had a large bump. His green eyes were deep set, round, and ringed by shadows, his lips thin and permanently pursed in an arrogant sneer.

This was the man who had ordered one of his enemies to be nailed to his coffin before being buried alive; who had, instead of showing generosity to a starving peasant who dared catch a hare in the hunting park, killed him by forcing him to swallow the unskinned animal whole; and who had, in a spasm of jealousy, chopped off the hands of a courtier who had caressed one of Galeazzo's former lovers. The duke had been born not to heartless parents but to a brave warrior, Francesco Sforza, and a proud, strong-willed but charitable woman, Bianca Maria Visconti, daughter of the Duke of Milan. His parents were much loved, and as their eldest son grew to maturity, they were perplexed by his arrogance and cruelty. When his father died and Galeazzo claimed the duchy, he resisted his mother's advice; she died of a mysterious fever—or poison, some say, on the order of her own son.

As the singer's voice faded, Galeazzo glared at his wife and jerked his chin in my direction. "What is *she* doing here? I wanted as few people as possible to know of this!"

I stared intently at the carpet while Bona stammered.

Lorenzo interjected smoothly, "It is on my account, Your Grace; do you recall? I disturbed the three of them at prayer yesterday, and wished to make my apologies to each one today."

Galeazzo frowned; the weather had kept him from the hunt, which added to his usual irritability. I feared he would lose his temper at the subtle reference to yesterday's incident with the screaming young woman. The sight of Lorenzo, however, distracted him enough so that he gave a small, tight smile.

"Good Lorenzo! How do you fare?"

"Well, Your Grace," Lorenzo replied, "especially when I am surrounded by such lovely women." He gestured at us three.

Galeazzo's smile widened at the compliment. "She *is* beautiful, is she not?" he asked proudly, and went to take his daughter Caterina's hand. He kissed her on the lips, after which Caterina curtsied and shot the rest of us a gloating glance.

The duke moved to Lorenzo next. The two clasped hands and slapped each other upon the shoulder with more affection than I had ever seen the duke show his brothers. Milan and Florence were solid allies; Lorenzo's grandfather, Cosimo, had supported Galeazzo's father's claim to the duchy of Milan.

Questioning Lorenzo about his journey from more temperate Florence through the freezing weather, the duke passed by his wife with a careless nod, and took no further notice of me. As he moved toward the massive ebony table—carved, at the top of each leg, with the symbol of the Sforza, of a dragon-headed serpent swallowing a naked child—a servant scrambled to pull out the tallest chair for him. He settled against the red leather padding and snapped his fingers; instantly, his cupbearer leaned forward and set an amethyst-studded golden goblet into the duke's waiting hand. Galeazzo told each of us where to sit: Lorenzo on his right, the silent, stolid Cicco on his left. Bona sat directly across from her husband; Caterina sat to her left, facing Lorenzo, while I sat on Bona's right.

A pair of servants hurried to light the tapers in two heavy candelabra upon the table; Galeazzo turned to one of them. "Bring the wine now, and the food; besides, I'm hungry, and Lorenzo cannot tarry." He looked back at Bona. "Once we have eaten, you women must depart; we men have private business to discuss."

"Then with your leave, Your Grace," Lorenzo said, "I should like to present Her Grace the Lady Bona with a gift, for her hospitality, with hopes that it will ease some of the difficulties I have caused her."

If Galeazzo was angered or insulted by Lorenzo's second veiled reference to the violated woman, he did not show it. He nodded, faintly bored, and watched as Lorenzo reached into the pocket of his tunic and produced a box of red velvet studded with tiny diamonds.

"For you, Your Grace," he said to Bona, and smiling, rose slightly in order to hand it to her across the table. "I pray this humble gift pleases you."

Bona forgot her embarrassment and beamed. "Your Magnificence," she said, "dear Lorenzo, no guest of mine has ever been more welcome ... or more gracious." She took it from him and held the box so that the gold embroidery and the diamonds glittered in the candlelight. "How very handsome."

"Look inside, Your Grace," Lorenzo prompted.

Carefully, the duchess opened the lid. Inside, tied together with a silk ribbon, was a thick rectangular object, slightly longer and broader than Bona's hand; she lifted it out of the box, revealing a deck of cards made of thick parchment coated with white gesso and painted.

She did her best to mask her response, but I knew that she did not approve of playing cards. She forced a smile as she undid the ribbon. I stared with her at the backs, prettily illustrated with flowers and vases, and bordered by angels.

"They're lovely," she said to Lorenzo. "Thank you."

"Turn it over," Caterina said impatiently.

She did, and like Caterina, let go a slight gasp of amazement at the sight.

The front side of the card was covered in gold leaf, which had been painstakingly etched with numerous fine geometric designs; the texture made the bright gold flash with reflected light. Upon this dazzling backdrop was painted the image of a pauper, a young, wide-eyed man barefoot and dressed in tatters, with a walking stick resting against one shoulder. He stood on the very edge of a dark chasm; emerald and sapphire hills sprawled out behind him.

Bona began to set the cards out in front of her, one by one. "But these are beautiful," she breathed.

"I know of your love for illustrated manuscripts," Lorenzo explained. "I had hoped that these might please you. That one is the first in the deck; he is called the Fool."

Galeazzo let go a laugh. "I know of these!" he said. "These are triumph cards. Oh, I will dazzle my companions with these!" He lowered his voice and winked slyly at Lorenzo. "Yet another way for me to lose money at the gambling table!"

The duchess tensed; Lorenzo saw, and said diplomatically to Galeazzo, "It's true, my lord, that these are triumph cards. Yet this deck is special. Some would prefer to use it for more serious pursuits."

Galeazzo scowled in puzzlement. "Such as?"

"Seeing the future."

The duke lifted a brow and peered down at the cards with renewed interest. "Really?"

Beneath the table, Bona clenched one fist; only I could see, and only I knew that she wanted to cross herself out of fear. "These are devilish," she whispered, so faintly that I was surprised that Lorenzo heard.

"Far from it, Your Grace," he told her. "They reveal what God wishes us to see of the future, that he may deal more directly with our souls. Yet they could, I suppose, be misused by those with evil in their hearts."

He said more, but I did not hear it, for Bona had just turned over the twelfth card. I found myself staring down at the image of a man suspended upside down from a rope bound to his ankle. His hands were hid, helpless, behind his back, and his unbound leg was bent at the knee and crossed behind the other, to form an upside-down numeral four.

I was too riveted to stop myself from reaching for the card, from taking it and holding it before my eyes. At the time, I could not see the painting on the card of a man with golden curls; instead I saw Matteo, with his dark auburn hair falling straight beneath his head. On the card, the man's eyes were dark and open, but I saw only Matteo's eyes, shut, his features white and deathly still. Matteo, limp and dying...

It was the image I had read in the stars, in the fire. Despite the blazing hearth, I grew cold. Matteo was in danger of dying, and there was nothing I could do to stop it.

"*Dea,*" Bona said sharply in my ear, and snatched the card from my grasp. I looked up and realized that the others had been speaking for some time; I had been somewhere else entirely. In the interim, the soup had magically arrived; a plate sat steaming in front of me.

Lorenzo was studying me intently. "Madonna Dea," he asked softly, "what do you see?"

"My husband," I murmured, stricken.

He reached across the table and set a long, tapered finger down, pointing to the card. "This is called the Hanged Man. Yet you can see, he does not struggle." *Surrender to evil forces,* I imagined him saying, though he uttered not another word, *with the intent of sacrifice.*

"Does she see things in the cards?" the duke called gaily over Lorenzo. "Can she tell our future, then?" Ignoring Bona's tense expression, Galeazzo pointed at me. "Gather them up," he directed. "Mix them, and choose our futures." He chuckled. "No gambling, so long as the ladies are here."

Bona had stiffened in her chair, but she handed me the deck; Caterina's eyes were gleaming with curiosity and amusement at her and my discomfort. Galeazzo snapped his fingers again, and with a gesture, bade a servant clear away my plate.

The cards were overlarge, unwieldy, stiff from the gesso plaster. I had expected them to be cool to the touch, yet they were warm in my hands, as if they were living things. I stared down at the table's ebony surface, polished to a reflective sheen, and felt the present melt away.

I set them down and fanned them out facedown upon the ebony. They were too stiff to be shuffled, so I moved them about, again and again, until it was impossible to identify the cards that Bona had turned over earlier. When I was satisfied, I gathered them together and fanned them out again, and said to Galeazzo, "Your Grace, choose one card."

He shot an excited glance at Lorenzo and grinned, then indicated his choice by pointing. I took the card and pushed it slightly toward him but decided that it was not yet time to reveal it.

"Now His Magnificence," the duke said.

Lorenzo's smile was encouraging as he met my gaze. It was unsettling to encounter a stranger who was exposing my ability to recognize portents, yet I trusted him. He reached out and tapped the wood near his chosen card.

I pushed it from the deck toward him. Cicco, as always carefully appraising the others without revealing his own feelings, accepted a card without comment.

"Would it please Your Grace for the ladies each to have one, as well?" Lorenzo asked with consummate politeness.

Galeazzo gave a loud sniff of impatience, but nodded to me. I shifted in my chair toward Bona, but the duchess gently shook her head.

"The cards are exquisite," she said sweetly, "and I shall treasure them always, just as I shall treasure my friendship with the magnificent Lorenzo. But I am content to wait upon God to reveal the future in His own good time."

Galeazzo scowled at her and clicked his tongue. "Come now, don't spoil our fun!" His temper was rising, and he would have lashed out at his wife had Caterina not interrupted.

"One for me then! One for me!"

Lorenzo said cheerfully, "It seems, Your Grace, that the young lady does not wish to be kept waiting."

The duke sighed, yielding, and gestured for me to give his impatient daughter a card. I set it down and pushed it in Caterina's direction. Rather than wait for the others, she reached out and turned her card over immediately. As she stared down at it, her expression soured. "But it is only the Fool! I want another!"

Lorenzo looked to me before saying, very softly, "It can be a good card, Madonna Caterina. You might not want to dismiss it."

I studied it. The Fool's eyes were fearless and innocent, his posture unguarded. He was on the verge of a long and tumultuous experience, ignorant as a child of the perils awaiting him. He might well decide to turn and head for the serene mountains behind him, in which case, he could reach the highest pinnacle—or he could just as well take a single step forward and fall into the dark, yawning chasm.

"A long journey awaits you," I said. Caterina leaned past Bona, the better to see and hear me. Expression avid, the girl propped an elbow on the table and rested her chin upon her hand; the long golden curls framing her face spilled forward and caught the light. "The most important journey of your life," I continued. "Be cautious and reflective, lest you fall into danger."

She drew back, mollified. Aware that Lorenzo's eyes were on me, I did not wait for his prompting, but drew one last card, for myself, and set it aside.

Galeazzo was intrigued and once again smiling. "Let us go in ascending order now. *Her* card first"—he indicated me—"and then yours, Lorenzo, and Cicco's, and last of all, mine."

I turned over my card, and fell into the image, scarcely hearing Bona's soft, shocked inhalation.

I saw a woman dressed in flowing golden robes and cape and seated upon a throne. She wore a nun's white wimple, and upon her head, unmistakably, rested the triple crown of the papal tiara; in one hand, she held a holy book, in the other, a long staff atop which rested a large gold cross.

She was a female pope, a papess—a scandalous image, yet I was not in the least appalled. I trusted her, with the same unreasoning certainty I trusted Lorenzo. I stared at the landscape around her, seeking clues as to where I might find her; a green, carefully tended orchard lay in the distance behind her.

I must have stared for some time, but my reverie was interrupted by a sharp pain in my shin as Caterina kicked me beneath the table.

"She is . . ." I began, and searched desperately for a word that would not offend Bona; *papess* was out of the question, as was *priestess*. Finally I said, "The Abbess. She holds much wise spiritual advice."

Lorenzo's card was the male version of mine—a white-haired, bearded man wearing the gold papal crown, with a gold cross atop his staff. But the card had been accidentally turned upside down, and at the sight of it, I felt a thrill of fear.

Lorenzo's homely face grew solemn as he gazed upon it. "The pope, ill-dignified," he said.

I stared back at it, too, and saw a thousand fleeting things, too numerous to give voice to: an old, vengeful man weeping over a dead son, the swirl of frankincense, the glint of a blade, a spray of blood, an oddly familiar voice sighing, *Lorenzo* . . . My fear must have been visible, for when I looked up again, the women were wide-eyed and silent, and Galeazzo, though frowning, was chastened.

I struggled to put all that I had seen into words. "There is vengeance here," I said, "and sorrow, and great treachery. You must take care, or there will be blood."

Bona crossed herself; the duke and Lorenzo shared a troubled, knowing glance. "I know how to deal with the matter now," Lorenzo said, his tone firmly optimistic; I felt his words were not so much true as intended to comfort Duke Galeazzo. "I will take care. Thank you, Madonna Dea."

"All this seriousness!" Galeazzo scolded. "Here now, this was meant as lighthearted entertainment." He gazed sternly at me. "Read Cicco's card now, and see to it that it doesn't spoil our luncheon!" He nudged Lorenzo playfully as he addressed me. "Speak to us now of song and sport and love!"

I murmured an apology and turned over Cicco's card. Ten glittering golden coins rested against a white backdrop decorated with flowers; I sighed with relief. "You will come into a good sum of money," I told him.

Cicco gave the slightest of smiles and nodded; the duke grinned, pleased.

"That's because I pay him too well!" Galeazzo quipped. "Now, let's see if I am luckier than my secretary!"

I turned over the duke's card. Like Lorenzo's, it was upside down. Upon a throne, a crowned king sat in full gilded armor. In his left hand was a gilded shield, in his right, a long sword with a wicked sharp point. His hair appeared golden on the card, but my internal eye recognized a dark-haired man, a courtier wild with outrage, who had waved his sword at Lorenzo de' Medici.

I felt a welling of dark satisfaction. "Here is justice at last," I said.

The duke frowned. "Regarding which matter?"

I shook off the pull of the card and kept my wits. I wanted desperately to see what action this king of swords would take, and whether that action would succeed; I hoped that vengeance was coming at last to His Grace, but feared warning him. I did not want him to be able to protect himself.

And so I pretended to study the card further, then said, in as casual a tone as I could muster, "There is business that soon will be concluded, though not to His Grace's favor, unless he take exceptional care."

"Which business?" he persisted. The appearance of another negative symbol had awakened his ire; if I answered in a manner that displeased him, we would all pay.

I replied smoothly, "Political. I will speak no more of it, for I believe it concerns a secret matter. I have confidence that, should his Grace ponder the card, he will come to a clever solution to avoid the difficulty."

He nodded, feigning understanding, and studied the card thoughtfully until Caterina, her blue eyes narrowed with curiosity, said to me, "So it's true . . . your mother *was* a witch!"

I looked up sharply. Beside me, Bona turned to Caterina and hissed: "Mind your tongue!"

I had spent the past nine years of my life with Bona and had never heard her criticize Caterina, much less scold her in anger. Nor had the duke, who leaned across the table to give his wife a look that threatened imminent physical violence.

"Caterina jests," Galeazzo said witheringly. And to prove it, he laughed, but when by accident I caught his eye, I saw the fear in it.

An hour before dusk I made my way down to Matteo's chamber, ostensibly to rekindle the fire. In truth, I wanted to be alone so that I could cry. Since the appearance of the Hanged Man, I had been increasingly worried about Matteo. Bona had said that he would come today, but Bona was wrong; the triumph card had merely confirmed my feeling that something terrible had happened.

My mood had not been helped by Bona's reaction to the deck—or, more to the point, her reaction to *my* reaction. After bidding Lorenzo a warm farewell, the duchess had returned to her chambers in uncharacteristic silence, clutching the red velvet box containing the cards. Upon arriving in her quarters, Bona had given it to one of the chambermaids, with instructions to "hide it well, where I will not soon set eyes upon it again." Caterina, too, was unusually quiet, though her eyes were adance with amusement at the duchess's and my discomfort.

I confess, I paid close attention when the chambermaid moved toward a trunk set in a corner near the duchess's bed, opened it, and slipped the box beneath a fur throw.

While Bona retreated to her wardrobe to change into less restrictive attire, I moved to the front of the chamber to gaze anxiously out the window overlooking the duke's hunting park. Caterina followed, and when I was certain the duchess was thoroughly distracted, I asked the girl, "Madonna, why did you say that? About my mother being a witch?"

"You should have seen your eyes," Caterina hissed, widening her own until the whites showed ghoulishly. "There were times, I swear, when you had no idea where you were . . . you were carried off by visions!"

Impatient, I pressed: "What has this to do with my *mother*, Madonna? You speak as though you've heard rumors."

"I have," she said coyly.

"From whom?"

"From Nonna Beatrice," she replied. Nonna had been Bona's girlhood nurse and had accompanied the duchess from Savoy when the latter had married Galeazzo; Nonna had died the previous year. "She said your mother was a witch and saw the future."

I controlled the urge to shake the duke's favorite daughter by her shoulders. "What else did she say about her? What else?"

Caterina shrugged; her shell pink lips curved upward in delight at my agitation. "Just that."

Nothing I said could force her to say more. Shortly afterward the duchess joined us, with the curt remark: "No good ever came of fortune-telling."

With that, Bona dismissed the subject completely and ignored all of Caterina's attempts to revive it. I spent the rest of the day marking the movement of the sun and struggling to suppress my growing dread. When dusk came, Bona dismissed me. While she was undressing and the chambermaids distracted, I did an unthinkable, inexplicable thing: I went to the trunk, slipped my hand beneath the fur throw, and made off with the diamond-littered velvet box. I wrapped my shawl tightly around me, tucking the hand that held the box beneath it, around my waist, and headed down to the first-floor loggia, bound for Matteo's apartment.

Lorenzo was there, leaving one of the guest quarters with his two gentlemen; the three of them wore cloaks and caps and riding gloves, and carried saddlebags. My hand was on the door when Lorenzo caught sight of me and waved.

"Madonna," he called, and handed his saddlebag to one of the men, then gestured to both of them to go on to the stables ahead of him. It was an odd hour, I thought, to be setting out for distant Florence.

"A word with you," he said as he approached. But the loggia was crowded with servants headed wearily back to their quarters; a pair of Cicco's apprentice clerks brushed past us, laughing and joking. Lorenzo looked pointedly at the door handle to Matteo's room. "Might it be a private word, Madonna Dea?"

I dropped my gaze. He was a man in his late twenties—homely, to be sure, but with an accomplished swordsman's shoulders—and I a young woman. His request was faintly inappropriate, but his manner held no whiff of impropriety. He was also unquestionably my better, so I unlocked the door and gestured for His Magnificence to enter. As I did so, I could not help but reveal the velvet box in my hand; he marked it without comment, and I offered no explanation.

Inside, the fire was reduced to glowing embers, but the hearthstones still gave off a good deal of warmth. I stood near the door, the box still in my hand.

Lorenzo removed neither cloak nor glove; his expression was as darkly serious as I had ever seen it. "Forgive my brazen request, Madonna," he began. "I intend nothing improper. But I did not wish to be overheard." He paused. "As I said, I know your husband well. It was my understanding that he was to have arrived home yesterday."

"Yes," I said, embarrassed that my voice betrayed all my repressed tears. I expected him to reassure me then, to say something comforting, but Lorenzo was, apparently, no liar. Or perhaps, like me, he had recognized the danger in the Hanged Man.

"I am sorry for that," he said softly, "and for your worry. I had hoped for a word with him in private. But I can tarry no longer, as my wife and children will never forgive me if I'm not home by Christmas." He studied me for a long moment. "I can trust you to deliver a message for his ears alone, can't I, Madonna?"

"Of course," I answered, and he smiled faintly at my indignant tone.

"If Matteo returns before tomorrow evening, would you tell him that I have taken the route to the north, and will await him at the lodge? He knows which one."

I lifted my brows in surprise at the direction; Florence lay well to the south of Pavia and Milan. "I will be sure to tell him, Your Magnificence."

"Lorenzo," he admonished me cheerfully, then grew serious again; his gaze strayed to the velvet box in my hand. "God gave you a gift, Madonna Dea, one best practiced with discretion, and shown to few. I am glad to see your interest in it. It is not my place to give such a new acquaintance advice, but—"

"I should like to hear it," I interrupted bluntly.

"The duchess and others mean well, but . . . Do not let them keep you from it. Such a gift was meant to be used. Remember the parable of the servant and the talents."

"I will," I said.

"Good. Then God keep you, Madonna Dea, until we meet again."

"And you," I responded.

As I watched him slip out the door, I felt a sudden conviction that our next encounter would come too soon.

Four

I spent that evening staring at the gilded illustrations on the cards. At times, the images evoked something very like recognition in me, so much so that for long moments, I was able to forget my worry. When exhaustion overwhelmed me, I stacked the cards neatly and returned them to the box, which I hid in the trunk at the foot of the bed.

I slept poorly that night, pulled from sleep again and again by the clatter of frozen rain pelting Bona's window. By dawn, the storm had passed, leaving the glass coated with a wavy layer of ice; even though the window stayed closed and shuttered, the groaning of the trees was audible, and the occasional ear-splitting crack of a breaking limb made me start. By midday, all clouds had cleared, and the sun gained strength. The ice on Bona's window began to melt, revealing the hunting park beyond, glazed and glittering like a jewel.

On the sixth day before Christmas, all at Castle Pavia were filled with festive cheer as preparations for the procession to Milan intensified; even Bona had forgotten her distress over the incident with the young woman and my reaction to the triumph cards. The season inclined Bona to be even more generous than usual. She feted her servants and courtiers in the great dining room, setting out the Milanese sweet bread called *panneton*, cheese, and good wine. I had no taste for any of it. When the duchess kindly released me in the early afternoon to do as I wished, I went to light the fire in Matteo's quarters, then climbed the southwest tower steps and stood staring out toward Rome for hours.

They came at dusk, galloping across the Lombard plain: a solitary horse and rider, black against the graying sweep of snow and ice and sky. I let go a cry of infinite relief; my breath clouded the glass, and I wiped it away, compelled and squinting as I struggled to recognize the rider.

At last he reached the moat, reined in his horse, and shouted for the castellan to lower the drawbridge. Only then did I see the body slung over the saddle; I gasped and pressed my fingertips to the freezing glass.

Somehow I calmed myself, gathered my skirts, and hurried down the stairs. I ran outside, across the cold, endless courtyard to the main gate just as the horse's hooves struck a last, hollow thud against the wooden bridge and passed, ringing, onto the cobblestones inside the gate.

I ran to Matteo, his belly pressed against the saddle, his long legs hanging down one flank of the lathered steed, his head and torso down the other, his arms horribly limp and dangling. He would have slipped easily to the ground had the rider not held him firmly in place.

I cried out, thinking he was dead, but when the rider dismounted and helped him slide into my arms, he groaned.

I do not remember the rider carrying him to his bed or shouting for the doctor. Others ran to help, but I do not remember them at all. Of the breathless moments before the doctor came, I recall fragments: Matteo's hazel eyes, the whites now red, sparkling, utterly lost; Matteo's brow and cheeks, an ugly mottled violet; his skin slick and glistening; Matteo's limbs, spasming as cramps seized his gut. I held his head as he retched yellow-green vomit streaked with bright blood. I wiped his sunken face with a cold cloth that appeared magically in my hand and called his name, but he did not know me.

If I had to lose him, if he had to die, why did he not die as the Hanged Man, limp, peaceful, resigned? Why did he have to suffer horribly? *God is merciful*, Bona said, *and just*, but there was no mercy, no justice in Matteo's dying, only the most savage cruelty.

Plague, someone whispered, and crossed himself, but it was not plague.

Bona's physician appeared with leeches and a bitter draught, but Matteo vomited up what little he was able to swallow, and his limbs convulsed so violently at times that he crushed many of the leeches and the doctor removed the rest for fear of losing them.

Fever, the doctor said, but it was like no fever I had ever seen. Matteo's master Cicco came, his huge bulk huddled, his tiny eyes wide, his rounded features slack with fright; Matteo did not know him, either, and he did not stay long. Bona came and said that I must rest—a ridiculous suggestion, I thought, for I had no idea then that it was nearly dawn—and that she would sit with Matteo. I sent her away. I sent the doctor away. I sent the hovering rider away, until my husband and I were alone.

As the morning light filtered through the open shutters, Matteo's thrashing eased at last, and I closed them, hoping he might sleep. Amazingly, the hearth was still crackling; someone must have stoked it. As I turned to where my husband lay, his long, naked torso and limbs motionless against the dark soaked sheets, I heard a rasping croak.

"Lorenzo."

I moved swiftly to the chair by the bedside and put my cool hand to his cheek. His eyes were frighteningly dull; the purple flush had faded from his cheeks, now ashen.

"Lorenzo has gone back to Florence," I said. There was no point in mentioning Lorenzo's diversion to the north in hopes of a secret rendezvous. His Magnificence was already well on his way home. "You must not worry about him now."

His eyelids fluttered. "Dea," he gasped. His voice was so hoarse as to be unrecognizable; his throat must have been terribly sore.

I pressed my knuckles to my lips. "Oh, Matteo. Matteo, my poor darling . . ."

"I am dying," he whispered, and I felt as though I would melt—my blood, my bones, my flesh—and only the blinding pain in my throat and chest would remain.

"I won't let you," I sobbed, but he gestured desperately, impatiently with his right hand. He was so weak that I had to fall silent to hear him.

"My quill," he said.

I ran to his desk, retrieved the quill, and lifted the inkpot from its place, my hands shaking, clumsy. I fetched a piece of parchment along with his little lap desk, and propped him up against the pillows.

Once situated, he tried to dip the nib into the inkpot I held for him, but tremors plagued him; he dropped the quill. He squeezed his eyes shut and let go a moan of frustration, then gathered himself and looked back at me. His lips were dove gray and trembling.

"Swear," he whispered.

"Anything," I said. "Anything for you."

It pained him to speak; sweat dripped from his forehead as he formed the words. "On your life," he gasped. "Take me to San Marco. And my papers . . . Read them in secret. Tell Lorenzo: *Romulus and the Wolf mean to destroy you.*"

He fell abruptly silent.

"I swear," I said.

As I spoke, his body stiffened, and he let go a terrible strangled sound and lost control of his bowels. For several seconds, he lay thus—stiff and trembling—and then his arms and legs began to thrash. I cried his name and tried to hold him down, lest he harm himself, but I was not strong enough.

In the end, he fell still; his eyes closed, and his breathing grew harsh. Half an hour later, it stopped, and his eyes slowly opened; I looked in them and knew that he was dead.

I stripped the soiled sheets and set them outside, and used the basin of water someone had left behind to wash my husband. When he was clean, I dressed him in his finest tunic and leggings, then lay down beside him and held him until someone knocked upon the door.

I did not answer, but I had forgotten to throw the bolt and Bona entered. She tried to coax me away; I would not hear, would not leave Matteo. She left, and when she came again, she brought others, including Cicco, his foolish hair disheveled from sleep. The lumbering bear of a man, normally stoic, burst out weeping at the sight of Matteo, his star pupil. He tried gently to pull me from my husband, but again, I would not go; he had to recruit a second man. I clawed and kicked, to no avail; they caught my arms and tore me from my beloved.

I screamed, I thrashed; the sobbing Cicco held me lest I hurt myself. When I finally grew tired and had to sit, Bona convinced me to take a sip of strangely bitter wine. She had brought her priest, Father Piero, and after I had fallen into a strange state between sleep and waking, Father Piero told me, "You must accept this. We are human and frail, and do not understand as yet, but it is God's will."

"God is a murderer," I said listlessly, "and a liar. He bids us pray, yet will not hear us. He sets evil men over us, and takes no pity on their victims."

"*Dea,*" Bona chided, aghast. "God have mercy on you!" She crossed herself, covered her eyes with her hands, and wept.

I turned calmly to her. "When did He hear us? When did He ever hear us?"

She never answered. To my astonishment, a scarlet-robed cardinal entered and produced a vial of holy oil, dipped his finger into it, and touched my darling's eyes, ears, nose, lips hands, feet, and loins, praying: *Per istam sanctam unctionem et suam piissimam misericordiam, indulgeat tibi Dominus . . .*

Through this holy unction and His own most tender mercy may God forgive whatever sins you have committed . . .

Matteo needed no forgiveness, I decided. It was God who needed to apologize to my husband.

When Bona's draught had left me sufficiently compliant, Francesca and the chambermaids took me away to the duchess's room and dressed me in black skirts that were too long, and a veil that filmed the world darkly; I did not care. I did not want to see.

Miserable, pointless hours passed, after which I was taken to the ducal chapel to discover Matteo in front of the altar, lying in a wooden box, his arms crossed, a crucifix over his heart. The votive candles I had lit for his safety still burned upon the altar. I threw them across the room, ignoring the startled gasps of onlookers and the scalding wax that spilled down my arm.

I did not sleep at all that first night.

The next day, I sat beside Matteo in the chapel, Bona at my side, while most of the courtiers filed past his body. In the midst of familiar faces, one unknown appeared, with beard and hair and eyes black and shining as jet. I did not know him, yet felt I had laid eyes upon him before. He bore a saddlebag slung over his shoulder, and when he approached, he went down upon one knee and presented the saddlebag as if it were a gift.

I realized then that he was the rider, the man who had broken away from the caravan of papal legates my husband was leading from Rome to Milan, in order to bring Matteo swiftly home. He had remained in Matteo's room, awaiting the outcome, until I had thrown him out.

"This was your husband's, Madonna," he said. His voice was deep and soft, his gaze averted; if he felt any emotion, it was carefully contained. "He asked me to be certain you received it." He looked to be Matteo's age and would have been pretty enough to capture the duke's attention—Galeazzo occasionally indulged in affairs with his male staff—had it not been for his great sharp nose.

I thanked him. The bag was heavier than I expected, and when he handed it to me, it slipped from my grasp to the ground. I could not bring myself to look inside, not there, with others watching. The man bowed and retreated, and I thought no more about him.

Duke Galeazzo was last to appear. He stared with distaste at my husband's corpse and said flatly, "A pity. He was one of my most talented scribes. Poison, was it?"

At those last words, I gasped. The red-eyed Cicco was with the duke and drew him away with a word, but I rose, and called after him to explain himself. What poison? Had the doctor said this? Why had no one mentioned this to me?

I tried to push through the crowd and find the black-haired man who had given me Matteo's saddlebag. He had traveled with Matteo; surely he would know if my husband had been poisoned.

But the man was nowhere to be found, and Francesca and Bona pleaded with me to sit back down. His Grace was mistaken, they insisted. He was confusing Matteo with another man, another matter, but I did not believe them, and broke down sobbing.

After a time, there were priests and Roman legates, public prayers and psalms, but there was no burial. For the first time in anyone's memory, the ground was coated with a layer of solid ice; we could not lay him in the earth until it thawed.

Matteo's corpse was taken away—somewhere outside, I suspected, sheltered from animals but not the freezing cold; they were wise not to tell me where. Bona led me to a nauseating display of food in the common dining chamber near the chapel. I could not bear the sight of it, so her ladies returned me to Bona's chamber, where I drank more of the wine laced with the bitter tang of poppies. For hours I stared into the glittering fire.

Matteo had been murdered. Romulus and the Wolf had killed him in order to silence him, and they would kill Lorenzo next. And I was stripped of reason and will and could do nothing to stop it. Whom should I tell? Whom should I trust?

When night fell, Francesca helped me undress and put on my nightgown. She offered me more bitter wine, but I refused and was taken to my little cot. When Bona arrived, she paused before climbing into her own bed to pray; I lay listening to her whispers and began to tremble with silent rage. I wanted to strike her, to tear the rosary from her fingers, to scream that she had taught me only lies: God was neither loving nor just, and I hated Him.

I held my tongue and waited, anguished, until Bona fell asleep, until Francesca snored. By the light of the hearth, I rose and found my shawl and slippers, then slipped out into the loggia.

I pattered downstairs, gasping at the freezing air when I hit the open hallway. I staggered in the blackness, twice almost slipping on the ice, and was shivering uncontrollably by the time I got to Matteo's room. It was cold and dark and drafty; the fire had gone out and the flue was still open, but I did not bother to light it, as I did not care whether I caught cold or froze to death. I would have been pleased to die.

I am unsure why I went to my husband's chamber. I believe I meant to scream myself hoarse, though even with the windows shuttered, I would have been overheard. I only know that when I arrived and drew the bolt behind me, I spied Matteo's quill upon the carpet.

It must have been tangled in the bedding and fallen when I removed the sheets to clean him. I dropped to my knees before it and grief rushed out of me in a torrent. The sobs wracked me so that I sank down upon the carpet, the quill clutched to my chest.

I wept a good half an hour. When I was done, my eyes, nose, and mouth were streaming, the poor feather crushed. Gasping for breath, I pushed myself up to sitting, and felt something small and metal brush against my breastbone, beneath my nightgown.

Matteo's key.

Use it in case of emergency.

I drew my sleeve across my eyes and nose, and stared across the room at Matteo's writing desk and the secret panel next to it, hidden in the dark wooden wainscoting. Weak and trembling after the paroxysm of tears, I crawled on my hands and knees to Matteo's desk, and pulled myself up into his chair to light the lamp. The oil was low, and the flame feeble; I leaned down and had to run my fingertips over the wall to find the tiny black key-hole.

I slipped the leather thong over my hand, and put the little key into the lock.

The door to the compartment popped open with a faint click. Behind the wood panel, a large stone brick was missing from the wall; in the gap sat a thick stack of papers the size of a library manuscript. I drew them out carefully, set them upon my husband's desk, and pulled the lamp closer.

On the very top was a tiny black silk pouch, tied with a red ribbon, and beneath that, a letter on fresh paper, folded into thirds, sealed with wax, and addressed *For my Beloved.* At the sight, I braced myself for the emotional upheaval to come as I opened the little black pouch. I thought it contained jewelry—a keepsake, perhaps, by which I could remember him, but it contained only a coarse grayish-brown powder.

I turned to the letter, expecting to learn, at long last, why my husband had rejected my amorous advances.

I did not expect to be frightened.

It was not a heartfelt farewell letter but a diagram, in Matteo's hand, of a circle with the cardinal directions marked—oddly, with east at the top of the circle instead of north, and west at the bottom. At each direction, he had put a five-pointed star, with arrows carefully indicating how it should be drawn, and beneath each star, a word in what I suspected was Hebrew; underneath these were written phonetic translations in the vernacular, but no meaning was given.

Beneath this was a diagram of a second circle, again with the cardinal directions, this time accompanied by hexagrams and more barbarous words.

It was magic, the same magic I had seen him work at night when I pretended to be sleeping in our bed, and I remembered snatches of our conversation the night I had first told him that I saw portents in the clouds and sky and stars.

Bona would say this was from the Devil, I had said, and he had answered swiftly: *Bona would be wrong.*

Beneath both circles were sets of instructions in Milanese describing the rites that accompanied each. I could not focus my shattered mind long enough to make sense of them, nor could I keep the hairs on my arms and the back of my neck from lifting when I set down Matteo's diagram to examine the next page upon the stack.

It was a piece of yellowed vellum, brittle with age, many times folded and in danger of falling apart. Gingerly, I unfolded it upon the desk. The ink was rust brown, faded, the handwriting ancient, unfamiliar; Bona had permitted me no Greek, though I recognized it readily enough, and understood most of the Latin translation written in a later hand beneath it.

It was an invocation—of what, I could not fathom in my grief-addled state. I set it delicately aside; beneath it rested an unbound manuscript of text, consisting of several dozens of pages in Latin. The paper and the author's hand were modern; the title page read *De Mysteriis Aegyptiorium, Of the Egyptian Mysteries.*

Last in the stack of writing was a document written in Matteo's careful, even script. The letters of the Latin alphabet were written across the page, in order, and beneath each letter was written a different, random letter, number, or symbol. The letter *a* for example, was represented by the number 9, the letter *b* by an *x*, and *c* by an *l.* At the very top of the document was written *strike out every fourth.* It was, I realized, a key—one Matteo must have used when encrypting secret correspondence.

I propped an elbow on the desk and put my fingertips to my brow. "Why do you want me to have this?" I asked aloud.

The impulse to cast it all into the dying fire overtook me. Magic had been no more able to protect wicked men from killing Matteo than had God. But another thought damped my anger: the memory of the gilded triumph card displaying the Hanged Man. *Surrender to evil forces with the intent of sacrifice.*

I pressed the heels of my palms to my burning eyes and tried to make sense of it all. Matteo had clearly had a sense of his impending death before he left, else he would not have given me the key.

He had sacrificed himself to me in marriage out of innocent love. Had he again sacrificed himself to protect me? Had he left all this behind to warn me?

Had I not been furious with God, I would have burned it all. Instead I stared down at the meaningless tapestry of numerals and letters on the page and heard Lorenzo the Magnificent speaking.

It was I, in fact, who recommended Matteo to the duke for employment.

As if in answer, I heard Matteo in my memory.

I was rescued in my youth by a wealthy patron. . . .

Perhaps later we could go together to Florence.

Bury me in San Marco, the monastery in Florence that had educated him.

Read them in secret. And tell Lorenzo: Romulus and the Wolf mean to destroy you.

I sat very still, for perhaps an hour, then stoked the fire and stirred it until the flames leapt high and the room grew warm. I opened the shutters and discovered my husband's saddlebag, leaning against the wall beneath a window. I undid the straps and emptied it onto the bed. It held another quill, a vial of ink, a blotter, two pairs of leggings and two wool undershirts, a brass mug, comb, and a small book, bound in leather. Half its pages were covered in the same unfathomable cipher—numbers and letters mixed with an occasional star or other symbol—I had found on the papers hidden in the compartment. I examined the little book for some time, but could make no sense of it.

When the blackness outside eased to gray, I went back upstairs to the duchess's chamber, where Bona lay sleeping. I tiptoed up onto the platform, slid the bed curtains aside, and set a hand gently upon her shoulder. Even so, she wakened with a start.

"I must take Matteo to Florence," I said.

Five

The duke refused my request to take Matteo to Florence to be buried in the churchyard of San Marco. For one thing, Galeazzo said, the winter was far too treacherous for a woman to attempt five days' hard ride, even if it be southward—no matter that a day of feeble sun had melted most of the ice. For another, he insisted that every member of court attend the Christmas celebrations in Milan, whether they were in mourning or not.

Of the myriad princes in Italy, none celebrated Christmas with greater zeal than Duke Galeazzo. He required all courtiers, all ambassadors, all feudatories to come to Milan to celebrate the Nativity and renew their vows of fealty to him the day after, on the feast of Saint Stephen. Everyone, except the dying and the mortally ill, was required to attend, for the holiday marked the end and beginning of the year. The duke gave gifts to his underlings, alms to the poor, pardons to the convicted; during the week, he attended mass at different venues, the better to be seen by his loyal subjects. On the twenty-sixth, Saint Stephen's Day, he went to the church of Santo Stefano; on the twenty-seventh, Saint John the Evangelist's Day, he went to the church of San Giovanni, and so forth.

Bona had tears in her eyes when she told me of the duke's decision; the court was leaving the next morning for the Castle Porta Giovia in the center of Milan, and I, in my black veil, was required to go, too. I turned from her, speechless, but she put a hand upon my shoulder to draw me back.

"He is being embalmed," she said, and I realized she meant Matteo. "Come with me to Milan, please. And when we return to Pavia, the duke will be distracted, and I will see to it that you are able to take Matteo to Florence for burial."

The following morning found me riding silently on horseback alongside Francesca and the other chattering chambermaids next to the furnished, velvet-draped wagon that held Bona and the children. It was a sunny winter's day, harshly bright and blue, with a wind that stole all warmth. The roads were slush and mud; my cape grew quickly spattered. Matteo's saddlebag, packed with the little book in cipher and Bona's triumph cards, was strapped to my mount. From time to time, it brushed the back of my leg, bringing fresh grief.

Milan lies due north of Pavia, one day's easy ride away, on flat roads across the Po River basin. Given the size and lumbering pace of our caravan, however, we set out at dawn and did not reach our destination until well after dusk.

Nestled on a plain, the city stretches out to the horizon, where the distant, snowy flanks of the Alps graze the heavens. The light was failing by the time my horse's hooves struck cobblestone, but I could still see the four towers of the ducal castle, Porta Giovia, and the flickering yellow glow emanating from its windows. Across the broad avenue was the cathedral, the Duomo, its face covered with dark, skeletal scaffolding. Spires from other cathedrals—San Giovanni, Santo Stefano, Sant' Ambrogio—reared up from an endless span of red-tiled rooftops.

Normally I would have taken pleasure in the journey and the sights of the city, which we frequented only once or twice a year because the palace there was cramped compared to Pavia, and the city streets noisier and dirtier than the countryside. But that night I felt only bitterness; the festive spirits of those surrounding me were rude, the glory of Milan mocking. The ducal apartments were adorned with pomanders and evergreen, and fragrant with mulled wine; I found it all offensive.

In the little closet off Bona's room, I shared a bed with Francesca. Happily, she fell quickly asleep. I brought out the little book from Matteo's saddlebag and lit the lamp, and stared at page after page of my husband's mysterious cipher. After an hour, I realized that the headings for each separate entry must have been days or dates or times, and I distracted myself from miserable grief by trying possible substitutions for the different symbols.

I did not put out the light until Francesca stirred and complained drowsily a few hours before dawn. Even then, I did not sleep, but lay still, thinking of Matteo, the cipher, and the triumph cards.

Two days passed in a blur of audiences, masses, banquets, dances, and concerts, the last performed by Galeazzo's magnificent choir of thirty souls. Despite the weather, the streets of Milan were crowded with those who had come to watch the ceremony of the Yule log, and those who had come to proclaim their loyalty to Galeazzo for another year.

On Christmas Eve Day, the duke held a grand audience for petitioners; when sunset approached, we courtiers and servants stood in the first-floor great hall as His Grace lit the *ciocco*, the Yule log that was to be tended so that it burned for as long as possible. Once darkness had taken hold, Bona called for me to attend her in the ducal chambers. There, in the family's private dining chamber, I stood while Bona, her two daughters, two sons, and Caterina sat at the table watching the duke direct his brothers Ottaviano and Filippo. Together, Ottaviano—the youngest brother, slight and willowy, with a delicate, feminine face and long dark hair uncharacteristic of the Sforzas—and Filippo—second eldest, sturdy of body but feeble of intellect—carried a huge log of oak through the doorway and set it down atop a bough of juniper set in the hearth.

Despite the closed windows, the reedy wail of the traditional *zampogni*, the pipes played only at Christmas, filtered up from the duke's private courtyard below.

"Ugh!" Filippo exclaimed, once freed of his burden. "It's fatter than Cicco! This one will surely burn till New Year's."

"Back away, back away!" Galeazzo scolded excitedly, and took his place in front of the fireplace. His face was flushed, his words thick; he had already drunk a good deal of wine. A servant handed him a lit taper, and he held the flame to the juniper; it caught with a fragrant flare, and he laughed, pleased, as he handed the candle back.

With his right hand, he made the sign of the cross, and snapped his fingers at his cupbearer, who filled his goblet with fresh wine and gave it to him. Once the juniper had caught in earnest, the duke splashed a bit of wine on the log, as custom required, and took a long swallow from his cup. This he passed to Filippo, who handed it to Ottaviano, who respectfully delivered it to Bona; it made its way down the hierarchy to arrive last of all to me.

I emptied the cup, although there was less than a full sip left, thanks to Caterina swallowing far more than her share.

The duke then tossed a gold ducat onto the fire, and from a red velvet bag, handed one gold coin apiece to his brothers, children, and wife. My lowly status stifled his generosity, however, and he turned his back to me; Bona pressed her coin into my palm, so that I might enjoy an increase in wealth in the coming year.

Fortunately, the duke was not so stingy when it came to food and drink, and I was allowed to sit between his natural daughters, Chiara and Caterina. There was a surfeit of marvelous food, including a pigeon tart with prunes that normally would have tempted me, and ravioli stuffed with pig's liver and herbs, but I had no taste for it. I had not wanted to attend the family gathering, and had asked Bona to excuse me, but the duke had gotten wind of it and insisted that I come so that "things would be as they are every year." And to make sure of it, he had ordered that I dispense with mourning and dress in holiday attire; I had no choice but to obey, and so chose a gown of dark green velvet, but wore no gold and no smile.

Galeazzo and Filippo proceeded to get very drunk indeed, and by the time the feast was well under way, their conversation grew peppered with thinly veiled metaphors about the pleasures of defiling virgin flesh. At one point, the duke began to thrust a grilled sausage in and out of the stuffed capon on his plate, in a pointedly sexual manner, while Filippo howled with laughter. Caterina grinned, and Bona flushed and grew quiet. By the time supper was finished, Bona was eager to shoo the children out of the chamber and leave herself. I rose with her and accompanied her to the door; as she turned and bade her husband good night, he looked up from the table, his eyes heavy-lidded and glittering from drink, and said:

"Not her. You can go, but she must stay."

He had never made such a request, and both the duchess and I were troubled by it, until Galeazzo repeated, "She must stay. And you must have one of your ladies fetch the triumph cards Lorenzo gave you straightaway." When Bona hesitated to direct a fearful glance at me, he slammed his fist upon the table so hard that the empty platters rattled.

When silence followed, I said to her, "Your Grace, please forgive me, but the cards are in your quarters, inside the trunk at the foot of my cot."

Bona stared at me as if I were the Devil himself, come to steal her soul. Without a word, she curtsied to her husband and left, taking all the children with her; Caterina passed by last, pausing briefly to study me, her expression both curious and oddly worried. I stood awkwardly by the door for a quarter hour while the duke and his drunken brothers ignored me and the conversation grew ever more raucous. When Francesca finally arrived with the diamond-studded red velvet box, my anxiety increased.

"Sit," Galeazzo said, slurring, gesturing at the chair directly across from him. His brother Filippo made an exaggerated show of hurrying to pull the chair out for me, as if I were the duchess. He and the duke laughed, but I curtsied and sat with dignity, placing the box in front of me on the table and resting one hand atop it.

Only the girlish, delicate Ottaviano said hesitantly, "But you are in mourning, Dea. Was the loss recent?"

"My husband," I answered, and acknowledged his kindness with a nod. At that instant, a wave of grief mixed with rage overtook me, and I resolved that I would speak the truth to Galeazzo without fear. I would have been grateful to incur his wrath and die for it.

"Enough of that," the duke said, dismissing the gloomy subject with a curt gesture. "She's going to tell me my fortune for the coming year, boys." He leveled his dangerous gaze at me; for once, I returned it without disguising my hatred. "Except that this time"—his voice dropped to a malicious whisper—"my luck will be quite good, won't it, my dear?"

"Can we know our fortunes?" Filippo asked, with inebriated enthusiasm. His face was flushed, his lips crooked in an intoxicated grin. "My lord, may we know, too?"

Ottaviano seconded him so eagerly that the duke waved for silence.

"It all depends," he said, with a wink to his brothers, "on how cooperative the lady is. And such a lovely lady she has recently become."

Filippo laughed—half from nerves, half from delight—as the duke reached out and put a warm, sweating hand upon mine. Disgusted, I slipped mine out from under his and instinctively glanced behind me to confirm that Bona was indeed gone, as were all the servants save the duke's cupbearer and a pair of bodyguards who had appeared silently in front of the closed, and now bolted, doors.

I suppose I should not have been surprised, yet I had always believed that my relationship with Bona protected me, that the duke would no more lay a hand on me than he would his own daughters. For an instant, I considered screaming and pounding on the door, but I had heard too many times how little such behavior availed the other women who sought escape. I could rely only on my wits.

"Your Grace," I said, with feigned confidence, "I will read your cards. For the sake of accuracy, let us have silence. You must think only of the question you would ask and nothing else."

"I stated the question," the duke countered, with a hint of irritation, and slouched forward with both elbows on the table. He propped his chin upon both hands, as if his head had grown too heavy to hold up. "My future for the coming year."

"Then think on that, Your Grace," I said coolly, and took the cards from the velvet box. They were warm, as if they had been stored close to a hearth, and despite the fact that they were much larger than playing cards, they shuffled easily this time, as if tailored to my grasp. I mixed them for as long as I dared, praying silently all the while. I saw no point in calling upon God; I spoke to the only one I still trusted.

Matteo, help me. Help me to get out of here untouched and alive.

Filippo broke the silence with a drunken giggle; Ottaviano joined in, but the duke had grown serious and hissed at them to be quiet.

I, too, grew deeply still, and surrendered even my prayers in order to listen to the cards whispering in my hands. Instinct directed me to gather them up, stack them neatly, and push the pile to the center of the dining table, within Galeazzo's reach.

"Cut them, Your Grace," I directed. An odd calm descended upon me, turning my feigned confidence into something real, a strange and ancient authority.

Leaning heavily upon his left elbow, chin still propped upon a fist, Galeazzo reached out with his right hand. It was unsteady, and on his first attempt to cut the deck, he dropped the cards, overturning some, and swore.

"No matter, Your Grace," I said smoothly. "Gather them up, and cut again. It is all as fate wishes it to be."

By then, Galeazzo was scowling and visibly unnerved. Filippo's drunken grin had vanished; he and Ottaviano were paying careful attention to their brother's changing mood. Galeazzo pushed the cards back into a pile and cut them. I placed one stack atop the other, and took them back across the table.

I drew a card from the top of the deck, turned it over, and dropped into another world.

Before me, a glittering marble tower reared up against the bright blue sky, its pinnacle so high that wisps of clouds kissed it. At the top—so far up, they appeared as small as flies—two stonemasons wielded mortar and plane to build ever higher. This was the Tower of Babel, I realized, representing the hubris of man; and as I tilted my head far back to study its apex and the men working there, a roiling indigo cloud rushed from the horizon and enclosed the pinnacle and the men.

It was the wrath of God, this cloud, and it birthed a blue-tinged, blinding bolt of lightning; the crack and roar was so ominous, I shrieked and covered my ears. At the same instant, the Tower exploded, sending shards of shattered marble hurtling to earth. The masons' screams grew louder as they fell, headfirst, into oblivion. One of them, flailing a steel blade, I recognized as the King of Swords, he who metes out justice. I dropped to my knees and covered my head as he and a second man struck the earth beside me.

Just as swiftly, God's dark wrath disappeared, and the sky was again an unmarred blue—but the Tower was reduced to a shambles. Beside me lay the body of the second man. Impossibly, he was whole, and his eyes open in stark surprise, but he was no less dead and bloody, pierced through the heart by the King of Swords' weapon. His hair was a light chestnut, his lips thin, the bridge of his nose marked by a single large bump. He was Duke Galeazzo, and I knew that he had at last paid for his sins, and was glad.

"What does it mean?" Galeazzo demanded, and when I did not immediately reply, his tone changed from impatient to apprehensive. "What does it mean?"

Matteo, help me, I prayed again. I drew a deep breath and spoke the truth. My words were just loud enough to be heard over the crackling fire and the duke's quickened breath.

"That you will be attacked, my lord, by those against whom you have sinned. That unless you repent immediately and make reparation, you will not live to see the coming year."

His brothers looked on while Galeazzo let go a ragged gasp of amazement and clumsily pushed himself to his feet. Grimacing with fury, he let go a snarl and raised an arm to strike.

I glared back, defiant and ready to face my own unhappy fate. Matteo was dead, and I did not care to live. Yet it brought me wicked comfort to know that Duke Galeazzo would quake with fear until his own time came.

"You!" he roared, his voice shrill with outrage. "You rotting bitch, how dare you speak to us so! How *dare* you . . ."

He struck out. The stinging blow caught my upper lip, and almost tipped me backward in my chair. Stubbornly I held on and would not stir from my place, though my lip smarted enough to provoke tears. I refused to shed them, but looked boldly back at him.

"You," he hissed, his anger transforming in that exhaled word to curiosity. He stared at me, and his eyes narrowed in disbelieving recognition, then widened as his brows rushed together in fear. "Mother of God, it's her, she's a ghost! A ghost come back to haunt me! God help me . . . Save me, someone!"

He crossed himself and staggered backward, promptly falling over his own chair; Ottaviano and Filippo rushed to help him. As he struggled back to his feet, his brothers clutching his elbows, he bellowed, "Get her out of here! Get her *out!*"

I rose, and when the guards caught hold of my arms, I did not struggle, but let myself be pushed through the swiftly opened doors, and flung down upon the cold, hard marble in the loggia. Once there, I sat up and gingerly fingered my lip to find it greatly swollen. I touched my tongue to it, and tasted blood and morbid satisfaction.

Bona was sitting in front of her fireplace beside Caterina and Chiara when I returned from the duke's chambers. I knew she still felt betrayed over the cards, but at the sight of me, she let go a cry and rushed to embrace me. I put my hands upon her shoulders to comfort her, and when she realized I was otherwise untouched, she let go a sob of relief.

I admit, I was surprised to find Caterina there, wearing an unusually somber expression. Once she learned I was mostly undamaged, however, she grew at once insolent. While Francesca went downstairs to the larder to find a piece of fresh meat for a poultice, Bona made me sit in front of the fire and gently pressed her own kerchief to my lip to staunch the bleeding. She could not bring herself to ask how her husband had behaved, but Caterina, who had settled in the chair beside me, had no such reluctance.

"Did the king appear?" she asked.

Bona, Chiara, and I looked at her in puzzlement.

"The king," she prompted. "The one with the sword. You drew that card for my father before, when Lorenzo came to visit. Did it come again? Or does some new future await him?"

Bona's lip curled. "You ought not ask such impertinent questions," she said, with uncharacteristic asperity. "Let Dea rest. She's tired and has been through enough."

Caterina ignored her and turned her whole body toward me. "It must have not been a very good future, or he wouldn't have hit you."

Bona was right: I *was* tired—tired of secrets and lies. And Galeazzo's reaction had left me with an odd sense of power. No matter what punishment he was planning for me, I no longer cared. I had spoken the truth and it had squarely hit its mark; now I did not want to stop.

"The king was there," I said, my words muffled by Bona's kerchief and my huge upper lip. "But he appeared inside another card: the Tower."

Caterina leaned closer with avid curiosity. "And the Tower means?"

"The wrath of God will strike your father down," I said flatly, and tried not to care when Bona flinched.

Caterina caught her breath, her eyes oddly bright. "When?"

"I will not hear of this," Bona interjected. "Fortune-telling is pure wickedness, an abomination. . . . I wish to God that you had never seen those accursed cards! How could you have taken them from me?"

"Soon," I answered Caterina. To Bona I said, "Forgive me, Your Grace. Of late, my mind seems not to be my own."

Bona crossed herself. She was on the verge of weeping, I realized, and so I fell silent and answered no more of Caterina's questions.

The duchess never said anything more about the cards that I had taken without her permission, yet from that moment on, she developed a perceptible coolness toward me. I had stolen from her, and Bona would not forget it.

Six

On Christmas Day, three masses were said in the duke's chapel; custom demanded that Galeazzo and all of his courtiers attend. I missed the first, however, as I slept poorly, given my throbbing lip, and Bona told me to stay abed when the others rose.

I attended the other services and the great banquet, but wore my black veil to hide my swollen lip, and ate and drank little. When the dancing began, I retreated to Matteo's chamber and tried again to make sense of the cipher in the little leather-bound book from his saddlebag, without success. I also wondered what became of the triumph cards I had left with the duke and his brothers, but did not dare ask Bona.

The next day was the feast of Saint Stephen, the first martyr. As such, the duke was expected to attend mass at the church of Santo Stefano in the southeastern quarter, a short ride away. But normally temperate Milan was in the grip of the coldest weather most of its citizens had ever seen; an ice storm had glazed the city during the night, and been followed by a dusting of snow and a fierce wind that blew the clouds away, leaving trees, bushes, and roofs glittering in the early-morning sun.

The wind howled as I rose and dressed in my black mourning. A quick glance in the duchess's large hand mirror revealed that the swelling in my upper lip had gone down, though the skin was still purplish and bore a dark red scab where it had neatly split; I lowered my dark veil again. Bona kept her bed curtains pulled; she had been up retching during the night, and Francesca, I, and the chambermaids all agreed we would not wake her, but send a message to the duke that she was too ill to rise. Beyond the window, branches bowed low, snapping from the weight of the ice and groaning in the wake of the wind; I expected that most of the court, Galeazzo and his magnificent choir included, would refuse to go out in such weather, and instead celebrate the saint's day here at the castle.

I was wrong. An hour after we sent word to the duke that the duchess was indisposed, Caterina came running into Bona's chamber, her pale, pretty cheeks flushed and damp with tears. Her mother, Lucrezia Landriani, one of the duke's dearest, and most prolific, mistresses, lingered in the doorway, lest her presence offend the duchess.

"I won't go!" Caterina exclaimed, pouting, as she entered. She was dressed in a confection of white watered silk trimmed lightly in crimson velvet and studded with gold beads; her long yellow curls had been neatly contained in a hairnet littered with diamonds and tiny rubies. "Where is the lady duchess? I must speak to her!"

"Duchess Bona is ill, Madonna Caterina, and cannot be disturbed," I said in a hushed, warning tone.

Caterina recoiled slightly at the word *ill* and moved no farther; she gestured at me. "Help me, then! My father the duke is insisting that all of his"—she lowered her voice out of respect for Bona—"*ladies* and children accompany him to Santo Stefano!" His mistresses, she meant; perhaps it was Galeazzo's way of getting even with his wife for not accompanying him in the cold.

"In this weather?" Even I was surprised.

Caterina nodded; a cascade of diamonds and rubies sparkled at her ears. She was truly magnificent to behold that day, a porcelain beauty with gleaming golden hair, dressed in shimmering white, the dark red trim serving to accentuate her pale glory.

"He would have us *walk* halfway across the city in this wind," she said, and as if on cue, a gust rattled at the window. "Only the bishop and the ambassadors will be allowed to ride beside him on horseback. Please, Dea," she said, "can you not wake the lady duchess? She could send a note asking His Grace if my mother and I could ride beside him in the Lady Bona's stead. She could even say that I am weak from a recent illness. . . ."

Bona's flat, weary voice emanated from behind the tapestry bed curtains. "Have you been ill, Caterina?"

From the doorway, her mother, Lucrezia, called softly back, "Your Grace, she is being difficult because she is jealous—the duke called upon his sons to visit him this morning, but has ignored Caterina, who is eager to show him her lovely new dress. She thinks that if she rides beside him in a place of honor, he and everyone else in Milan will have a chance to admire her." She shot a sour look at her daughter. "You must not bother Her Grace. The duke has decided to go, and we must hurry. His priest and choir are already waiting at Santo Stefano; the others have all gathered in the courtyard."

"Dea," Bona called weakly, "will you go with her in my stead? And relay to the duke that I would humbly ask his favor for a horse for Caterina and her mother?"

"Of course, Your Grace," I answered, and in a lower voice said to Caterina, "but he will not give them if *I* ask."

"Why not?" she said, studying me carefully, and I remembered that I had, in fact, predicted Galeazzo's doom and walked out of his chamber alive and barely scathed.

I took a step closer to Caterina. "You must get your cloak and gloves, Madonna," I told her. "The duke will not suffer our being late."

Bona called again from behind the curtains. "Go," she said to me, "and pray for my husband. I have had a night of evil dreams."

We almost were late. I would have far preferred to remain inside the warm castle to tend the duchess that morning, but for Bona's sake, I borrowed Francesca's black woolen cloak and gloves and went down to the huge courtyard with Caterina and her mother. By the watchtowers, a crowd of perhaps fifty nobles—most of them women with their children, the duke's illegitimate get, and the rest of the duke's favorite male courtiers—had gathered, their splendid attire hidden beneath swaths of fur and thick wool. Nearby, a half dozen grooms held the reins to some thirty horses.

The mood of the waiting nobles was sour, their teeth chattering. Caterina and I joined them, and stamped our feet to keep warm until the grinning duke at last appeared in a crimson cloak lined with white ermine, his arms linked with a fellow hellion, Zaccaria Saggi, the Mantuan ambassador. The stooped, gold-mitered Bishop of Como and the duke's brothers, Filippo and Ottaviano, followed close behind, trailed by the Florentine ambassador and a dozen gentlemen of the chamber. The whole was flanked by a score of guards in full armor, long swords sheathed at their hips; among their ranks was a great tall Moor with yellow eyes and dark brown skin. In place of a helmet, he wore a large white turban; in place of a sword, a scimitar.

I moved toward the duke, paused a generous distance away, and bowed deeply as I relayed Bona's request.

He stiffened, unnerved by the sight of me, but cupped a hand to his ear to catch my words. A sudden bitter gust drove them away; impatient, he frowned and waved me off. Caterina thinned her lips and uttered an indignant curse beneath her breath as I returned to her side.

Galeazzo then briefly addressed the waiting crowd, speaking perhaps of the holiday and his gratitude for our loyalty, but his words, too, were swallowed by the wind. We shouted a perfunctory greeting, and watched as he climbed atop his black charger, caparisoned in white and crimson, the Sforza colors. Immediately, his inner circle and the guards mounted their steeds and closed ranks around him; we lesser beings were confined outside the protected inner circle.

Like the others, I drew the cowl close to my face and made my way over the slippery drawbridge and out into the street, across which stood the city cathedral, its unfinished walls covered with latticework scaffolding; the Alps loomed in the distance behind us. We kept pace with the horses for half an hour over icy cobblestones; on two occasions, Caterina slipped and her mother and I caught her before she fell to her knees. The wind drove my veil into my eyes, and would have blown it and my cowl off had I not clutched the edges of the latter. No one engaged in festive, lighthearted chatter; the howling wind drowned all other sounds, and forced us to walk with faces downcast against the stinging cold. Tradition demanded that the streets be filled with throngs cheering the duke, but on this feast day after Christmas only a few hardy souls huddled on the treacherous, snow-dusted ice and called out feebly when the duke and his entourage passed.

I was shivering uncontrollably by the time we arrived at the little plaza in front of the church of Santo Stefano, an ancient, unimpressive two-story edifice with a crumbling stone façade. The plaza was filled with merchants, peasants, and the starving poor; the church was so crowded inside that they had waited here in hopes of catching a glimpse of His Grace. The guards, their armor glinting with light reflected from the snow, dismounted and began to clear the plaza while several young grooms ran forward to take the horses.

Galeazzo dismounted and handed over his reins without looking at his groom; he squinted nervously at the plaza and, beyond it, at the door to the church. Like his daughter, he enjoyed public attention, but he also took enormous care to protect his person, and did not relax until the way was clear and the guards signaled him. The bishop, who was to celebrate the mass, moved ahead of him, and the ambassadors took their places at his left; his brothers moved to his right, so that the men stood five abreast, with the duke in the protected center. Behind them, in the favored retinue, walked Cicco's younger brother, the secretary Giovanni Simonetta, and a military adviser, Orfeo da Ricavo, followed by a row of *camerieri*, the nobles who attended the duke in his chamber and were considered his closest friends. The big Moor—a full head taller than any other man present, his hand on the hilt of his scimitar—led them into the church, while a pair of armored bodyguards flanked each row of the ducal procession.

Caterina pushed her way forward until we stood just behind the *camerieri*. When we finally made our way through the open door, she let go a sigh of relief at the rush of warmth emanating from the bodies of some three hundred faithful. At the front of the church, near the altar, scores of empty chairs awaited the duke and his party; most of the worshippers were obliged to stand and crane their necks as the duke passed by.

At the instant Galeazzo set foot inside, the choir, situated at the back of the sanctuary, burst into song, and a valet ran forward to relieve the duke and his companions of their cloaks. As the duke handed off his cloak, I saw he was dressed in a handsome doublet, the left half of which was gleaming watered white silk embroidered with tiny gold fleur-de-lis, the right of lush crimson velvet. His leggings were also of velvet—crimson for the left leg, white for the right.

I was not surprised to see that he sported his family's heraldic colors, but I was startled indeed to see that he wore no armor. It was the first time I ever saw Duke Galeazzo appear in public without a breastplate. Perhaps he shied from wearing metal so close to his skin in such cold weather, or perhaps it was an issue of vanity and the breastplate did not suit his fine new doublet; I will never know.

Beside me, Caterina let go a little gasp of pride, tinged with impatience, at her father's appearance. As we women handed off our cloaks, I saw why she was so eager for the duke to take note of her: her gown was made from the very same fabrics, with the same gold embroidery upon the white watered silk—a clever Christmas surprise for her father.

As the duke and his company followed the bishop down the center aisle, the rows of worshippers bowed, rippling like wheat in the wind. I kept an eye on Caterina; though she bore herself proudly, her gaze was riveted on her father and those surrounding him. She was seeking an opportunity, I knew, to get the duke's attention.

Midway to the altar, her opportunity came. Santo Stefano was very old, though not so old, it was claimed, as one great old stone abutting the sanctuary floor. Planted in the very center of the church, this large stone was unpolished and unremarkable, but it was nothing less than the Point of the Innocents, where, it was said, the blood of the innocent infants slain by King Herod had been spilled.

Galeazzo paused in mid-conversation and step to glance down at the stone and contemplate it in a show of false piety.

Seeing her opportunity, Caterina pushed forward, surging past the last row of the duke's chamber attendants and moving directly behind Cicco's brother Giovanni and the military adviser Ricavo. She was just one row from her father, and when her mother and I simultaneously hissed at her for such outrageous behavior, she glanced over her shoulder at us with a sly grin.

Her mother nudged me and gestured with her chin at her unruly daughter. I was of less importance than anyone else in the procession, so the task fell to me to retrieve her. I whispered apologies as I sidled between pairs of indignant *camerieri* and finally got directly behind Caterina.

As I touched her elbow, a cry went up—*Make room!*—and a middle-aged courtier stepped into the aisle just after the bishop passed. He was large and barrel-chested, with powerful shoulders, but one of his legs was withered; he moved haltingly, with a limp, and went down unsteadily on one knee right at the Point of the Innocents, blocking Duke Galeazzo's path.

His waving pale brown hair, brushed straight back and falling to his shoulders, was thinning at temples and crown; his anxious smile revealed overlarge yellow teeth. The soldiers nearby stiffened, and the big Moor stopped at once and drew his scimitar, but all relaxed upon recognizing Giovanni Lampugnani, a noble with a large estate just outside the city, and therefore bound to swear his fealty to the duke that very afternoon at Porta Giovia. I thought at first he wore the Sforza colors, white and crimson, but the red was far too bright. Lampugnani had long been a friend to Galeazzo, although rumor said the duke had lately taken notice of his comely young wife and vowed to bed her.

"A word, Your Grace," he said. His grinning lips trembled. It was not uncommon for a petitioner to stop the duke as he made his way to his seat near the altar, but Galeazzo's curled lip indicated it was unappreciated.

At the same time, Caterina reacted to my touch by surging forward to stand beside the military adviser, who walked immediately behind the duke. Ricavo, gray-haired but solid, glanced down at her with amused surprise.

Caterina reached out to tap her father's shoulder, and that was when another, younger man stepped out into the aisle to stand beside Lampugnani. His hair and beard were very dark, his long face handsome, his eyes hate-filled and haunted; he was Carlo Visconti, the man whose sister had been raped by Galeazzo. His hand was clutching the hilt of his long, sheathed blade. Like Lampugnani, he wore white and vibrant red.

He was the King of Swords.

I felt myself fall into another world, one where the wrath of God was gathering and roiling, a monstrous cloud about to birth a shattering bolt. With both arms, I pulled Caterina away from her father and held her fast.

"Not now, not now," Duke Galeazzo hissed at Lampugnani and waved him away just as dark-haired Visconti slipped beside the kneeling man.

Lampugnani began to rise awkwardly and fumbled with his sleeve. Still half crouched, he said distinctly, "Oh, yes, now. *Now.*"

With the swiftness of a viper, he struck. I did not see him draw the dagger, but I saw it come away bloodied, and heard the duke's horrified gasp. Beside him, the Mantuan ambassador made a feeble attempt to push the attacker away, but Lampugnani was on fire. He rose to his full impressive height, seized the duke's arm so that he could not run away, and thrust the dagger to the hilt into Galeazzo's chest. It came free with a sucking sound, and Lampugnani, his lips twisting with distaste and determination, plunged it into the duke again.

"I am dead!" Galeazzo exclaimed in surprise, and fell straight back against the chest of Orfeo da Ricavo, who tried vainly to support him.

Visconti was on the duke then, too, slashing with his long sword, and was joined by a younger third man. The Mantuan ambassador, Saggi, and Ricavo both began screaming for the guards.

The choir fell silent, its sweet strains replaced by a swell of frantic voices, the sounds of struggle. Bodies surged from the once-orderly rows; the church doors were flung open, and the crowd swelled toward them like a rising tide. The bodyguards were caught in the rush and fought their way back to their master, who had fallen upon the Point of the Innocents.

By then, even Saggi and Ricavo were struggling to flee; the duke's brothers Ottaviano and Filippo almost knocked me down as they pushed toward the door. I held fast to Caterina and pulled her away from the horror; she was limp and unresisting in my grasp.

The church emptied with astonishing speed. Outside in the plaza, courtiers and the duke's favorite chamber attendants called for their horses; those who had come on foot, including Caterina's mother, Lucrezia, were half running over treacherous ice back toward the castle. I paused in the doorway, the stunned Caterina still in my arms, and looked back into the sanctuary.

It was deserted save for the guards and the bloodied corpse of Giovanni Lampugnani, whose lameness no doubt hindered his escape. I watched as the tall, turbaned Moor, one hand pressed to his shoulder to staunch the weeping wound there, knelt over the motionless form of the Duke of

Milan. Galeazzo lay sprawled on his back, mouth agape, sightless eyes open, arms flung upward as if in defense. Blood spattered his clean-shaven face and soaked his doublet, now scarlet with no trace of white.

The tower of the duchy had crumbled.

Bona would have said that God had finally delivered His judgment, but that day, I knew she was wrong. God had had nothing to do with it; it had been the work of the King of Swords, who had avenged his sister. I looked upon the duke's pale corpse and felt exhilarating, if cold, satisfaction.

Justice: it was what I wanted for Matteo, and I would not rest until I found it.

Seven

Caterina and I returned to Porta Giovia to discover that, although the courtiers on horseback had arrived well ahead of us, none of them had had the courage to speak to Bona, who was still abed. Caterina, who was crying unrestrainedly, not so much from grief, I think, as terror, clung to me as I entered the duchess's chamber. I wound an arm about her shoulder as though I were her mother, who had so feared retribution from the duke's enemies that she had deserted her daughter and fled to her husband's house in the city. Together, Caterina and I went to Bona's bedside, where Francesca was just taking away a tray.

The curtains were open, and the lady duchess was sitting propped upon her pillows and wrapped in a heavy shawl, her disheveled dark blond hair plaited into a single thick braid. Her broad, ponderous face was drawn, her eyelids drooping with exhaustion, but she straightened at the sound of our footsteps and tried to arrange her features into a more pleasant expression. But at the sight of Caterina, who was pressing her tear-streaked face into my shoulder, Bona paled and grew very, very still.

My voice emerged, cracking and unsteady. "His Grace, the Duke of Milan is dead," I said. I expected her to shriek, to weep, to be inconsolable.

Bona's eyes widened, but the rest of her features did not move. A long silence passed between us, punctuated by Caterina's muffled sobs.

At last Bona's lips parted and formed a single word. "How?"

"At the swords of assassins," I answered. "Giovanni Lampugnani and Carlo Visconti. His Grace still lies on the Point of the Innocents."

"Visconti," she repeated tonelessly. "Is everyone else safe?"

I nodded. "I think so."

"Good." She looked at Caterina and sighed. "Poor child."

Francesca had set down the tray and was crying, but Bona threw back the covers and swung her thick legs over the side of the bed.

"Francesca," she said, a bit sharply. The chambermaid stopped her tears and looked up, anguished.

"Call Leonora, and help me get dressed," she said, and glanced up at me. "And Dea, go and tell Cicco the news if he hasn't already heard, then bring him to me."

After speaking with her husband's top aide, Bona ordered that Galeazzo's body be washed at Santo Stefano and dressed in a suit of gold brocade. By dusk, the duke's clean corpse was resting on a table in Santo Stefano's sacristy. There was no public viewing—or private, for that matter—as the duke had suffered fourteen disfiguring wounds. His mortal remains lay in the sacristy another full day, the twenty-seventh, the day His Grace was to have visited the church of San Giovanni to celebrate the feast of Saint John the Evangelist. All the while, Bona and Cicco worked together to prevent any chance of an uprising against the Sforza dynasty; soldiers were stationed at strategic points along Milan's empty streets.

Late that night, Bona sent a few trusted servants to Santo Stefano. Under cover of darkness, they stole into the church, removed the corpse, and took it across town to the cathedral known as the Duomo, across the broad street from Porta Giovia. There, they pried open the top of the casket holding the remains of the duke's father, Francesco Sforza, and laid Galeazzo on top of them.

Many a mass was said later for Galeazzo's soul, but there was to be no funeral, public or private, no tomb, no monument of stone, no plaque revealing where the duke lay. He had provoked such enmity during his thirty-two years that it was deemed safest to dispense with such things, lest those who despised him take revenge on his corpse.

Bona never came to bed that night, but remained conferring with Cicco and Galeazzo's other advisers. I undressed in the small closet off the duchess's chamber and, as I was pulling my nightdress over my head, Caterina's nurse entered and begged me to come attend her young charge.

I found Caterina huddled on her bed, arms wrapped around her knees, rocking. The slender, long lines of her girlish body showed beneath the fine wool nightgown; her long pale curls had been neatly plaited, though shorter tendrils framed her oval face. Her cheeks were flushed, the lids of her bloodshot eyes swollen. When I entered the room, she glanced up, oddly hopeful, and curtly motioned for her nurse to leave the room. I was surprised to see that the three cots where her attendants slept were empty, though the blankets were disheveled and the sheets still bore the impress of bodies. No doubt their mistress had thrown them from their beds without warning.

When we two were alone, she motioned for me to sit on the bed beside her—an unusual liberty for her to grant—and said, in a voice that was hoarse from weeping:

"You knew my father was going to die. You knew the very moment. How?"

"I don't know," I began, but she made an impatient gesture for silence.

"I will pay you." Her gaze was as naked and earnest as I had ever seen it. "Whatever you want, and I will say nothing to anyone about it. Only you *must* tell me the secrets of your magic."

I shook my head. "There is no secret, Madonna."

Her features contorted with anger. "Or I can have you tortured until you confess everything you know. I could turn you over to the Church as a witch."

I was too weary from grief to care, and it surely showed in my voice and expression. "Then turn me over to them, Madonna, and I will tell them what I am telling you: I know nothing about magic." It was true; I had not

yet studied Matteo's ritual. "I saw your father's death, but I don't understand *how* I knew."

She remained silent. I rose, intending to ask permission to leave, but she
motioned sternly for me to sit back down.

"Why did you save me?" Her voice was taut with emotion.

"Why would I not?" I countered.

She drew a long hitching breath and loosed a torrent of childish tears.
"Don't leave me," she sobbed, and threw her arms about my shoulders, pulling me to her. "Don't ever leave me, Dea!"

Her distress was so honest, so wrenching, that I returned the embrace.
"Hush, Madonna, hush," I murmured maternally. "I'll stay as long as you
like."

I soothed her for several minutes until she finally fell quiet, then let
loose a hiccup.

"I hated my father," she said suddenly, her chin resting upon my shoulder. "*Hated* him." I waited for her to speak of his heinous crimes, but instead, she added, "He never loved me—not at all. He loved my beauty. I
was only a bauble to him, like his jewels or his choir or his mistresses . . .
something he would parade in front of others to provoke their envy."

"That's not true," I said perfunctorily, but she drew back and looked
solemnly into my eyes.

"It *is* true, Dea. Men don't deserve to be loved."

"I knew one who did," I said with sudden vehemence.

Caterina did not let me leave her that night. She would not even let me
go to one of the cots, but insisted I lie beside her on her soft feather bed.
She was exhausted from weeping and quickly fell asleep; I lay listening to
her soft breath and thought about the duke, and Matteo, and the mysterious cards.

On the next day, the Feast of Saint John, news of the duke's assassins arrived in the afternoon and spread swiftly throughout the court. Shortly
after the murder, Lampugnani's body had been stolen from the Church of
Santo Stefano by a group of young toughs and dragged over the city's cobblestones. By the time the crowd was done, the corpse was mutilated beyond

recognition, and the citizens took gruesome glee in feeding the tattered remnants to pigs.

Visconti and the third conspirator, a youth named Olgiati, who had gone into hiding shortly after the murder, had been betrayed by relatives and captured; they were awaiting their fates in Porta Giovia's dungeon. Bona had coolly sentenced them to the wheel, where they would be ripped in two from neck to loins while still alive.

According to her chambermaids, the duchess had not shed a single tear since hearing of her husband's death. Newly widowed myself, I felt certain grief would soon overcome her, and wanted to be at her side when the storm finally broke. But one of Galeazzo's attendants informed me that the duchess would not need my services that day; I was at liberty, except for the fact that I needed to gather up my belongings, as the court was to return to Pavia the very next morning.

I headed for my little closet, thinking to make quick work of packing. I had not made it far, however, when Caterina, curiously unaccompanied, came running after me. She was breathless and pale in a high-necked black velvet gown; her hair had not yet been crimped, but hung uncombed and tousled about her shoulders, free of nets or veils. Apparently she had seen me pass by her chambers while her ladies were in the midst of grooming her. I stopped and turned to look askance at her, until I noticed the red velvet box in her hands.

"Where are you going?" she gasped.

There was no point in lying; Caterina would have her way regardless. "To my closet, Madonna," I admitted. I could scarcely lift my gaze from the box.

She looked about to reassure herself no one could hear us. A pair of launderesses were down at the far end of the loggia, laughing as they collected soiled linens from the rooms and paying us no heed.

"I will go with you," she said softly.

I bowed to indicate assent. Together we entered the little closet adjacent to Bona's chamber, and pulled the curtain so we would not be seen. I gestured for Caterina to sit upon the cot I shared with Francesca. She did so, and set the box down upon the mattress with a look of sly complicity.

With a small, triumphant smile, she said, "Ask me no questions; suffice it to say that Bona does not know I have the cards, and she need never know. You may keep them, on one condition."

"That I read them for you, whenever you wish," I said slowly. "Madonna, I cannot do that. Bona will discover the theft, and I will be blamed." I picked up the box and proffered it to her. "This was a priceless gift to her from Lorenzo de' Medici. It must be returned."

She rose quickly and stamped her foot, a childishly imperious gesture. "You *will* obey me!"

She would have added the phrase, *or I shall tell my father,* but clearly realized that she had lost a great deal of bargaining power. Instead she sputtered and cast about for some new threat to evoke my obedience.

Softly, I responded, "Bona of Savoy is my mistress. I am obliged to obey her."

"You took the cards from her once before!"

"Yes," I allowed, "but that was before I saw how it offended her. Surely you have seen it, too, Madonna; she no longer trusts me with her whole heart. And now she is regent of Milan, and obliged to mete out justice. Should she find me to be a thief—with me knowing full well she did not want me to touch the cards ever again—she would be forced to punish me."

Caterina sat back down and let go a grudging sigh. Without looking at me, she admitted, "That's true. But . . ." She leaned sideways and lifted the diamond-studded lid, exposing the cards inside. They were facedown, revealing the floral design on the back. I reached for them involuntarily, and Caterina caught my wrist.

"Read them for me," she said. "Tell me my future."

The fire flared suddenly as it found a bit of pitch; Caterina and I both started. She laughed nervously, and let go of my wrist.

I took hold of the cards. "Only this once, Madonna," I warned. My lip still felt the sting of the duke's blow. "And if you wish me to be honest with you, you must swear that if the future is not to your liking, you will not turn your anger on me. Otherwise, I will confess everything to Bona."

Caterina nodded eagerly in agreement. I did not trust her, but I also could not resist the cards.

Just as I had for the duke, I mixed the cards thoroughly, instructed

Caterina to cut them, then gathered them up and set three cards facedown in front of her.

"The past," I said, turning over the first card. Four golden goblets were painted against a white background decorated with green leaves and tiny flowers; a banner reading *a bon droyt, rightfully,* was unfurled across the center of the card. It was a motto often used by the Sforza, indicating that God had made them earthly princes because they were deserving of it.

Words came unbidden to my lips. "The Four of Cups. Luxury. A coddled childhood, and much wealth." I paused; the shining, gilded cups held something as dark and bitter as the draught Bona had forced me to drink when Matteo had died. "Yet this is not a good thing, but a tarnished past to be overcome. This is a dream from which you must wake."

I turned over the second card. There again was the image of a barefoot young man in rags, with a walking stick resting upon his shoulder.

"The present," I said. "Once more, the Fool. The beginning of a long journey, one that will leave she who takes it much changed. The fool loses his naïveté in the end."

Caterina leaned an elbow upon the desk and frowned down at the image. "Of course, we're returning to Pavia, but there will be no more journeys after that."

"Perhaps not immediately," I countered, "but soon." I turned over the third card, and announced, "The future."

I had barely set it down again when Caterina reared up, almost knocking the cards from the bed.

"No!" she whispered harshly. "It's a trick, all of it! You're doing this to frighten me!"

She began to weep as I stared down at the image of the Tower, torn asunder by a lightning bolt. Abruptly, I saw myself standing inside a wall made of thick stone; not only Caterina but I, too, dwelled inside the very Tower that would someday be blasted to its foundations. I heard a sudden deafening boom, like thunder, and put my hand against the wall to steady myself. It trembled violently, but did not fall.

A second boom, and the wall quaked harder, but it did not crumble. Not yet.

But in time it would be lost, just as the duchy of Milan had been torn from Galeazzo's iron grip.

My attention returned suddenly to Caterina; I cast about for whatever truth might calm her. I, too, was shaken. I had not wanted to scare her.

"This does not mean death," I said honestly. "Not for you. You will not die as your father did, Madonna. But..." I gazed at the image, and fancied the ground shook beneath my feet. "This is an upheaval, an end to old ways. This is destruction."

"I don't want it!" Tears streaked Caterina's cheeks as she wrung her hands. "I don't want any trouble! *A bon droyt! A bon droyt!* Why does God give us noble blood? Why does He give us power, but refuse to protect us? It isn't right!"

"Perhaps not," I answered soothingly. "But the Tower stands a long way from you, and you have a long journey ahead. Perhaps along the way you will find the means to avert whatever disaster this represents." I paused. "But there is one thing you must know."

She looked over at me, stricken.

"These are castle walls. Your castle, Madonna. You will rule someday."

She wiped her streaming eyes and nose upon her black sleeve and settled back onto the cot, faintly mollified.

"You must never leave me," she said. "Never."

Though I was sorely tempted to keep the triumph cards, I convinced Caterina to return them to the duchess's trunk. Early the next morning, on the twenty-eighth of December, the court returned to bucolic Pavia. Bona traveled in a private carriage, accompanied only by Galeazzo's right-hand man, Cicco, and the military adviser, Orfeo da Ricavo, in whose arms the duke had taken his last breath. I would have made my way on horseback, but Caterina insisted that I sit in the wagon beside her on the long ride home, along with Bona's children and their nurses. Caterina had frantically demanded that I sleep in her chamber every night, and Bona kindly allowed it, even though I far preferred the duchess's calm company to that of the duke's selfish daughter. The weather had finally warmed, and a slow drizzle of rain accompanied us as the wagon's wooden wheels slung mud on the soggy journey home.

Once back in Pavia, eight-year-old Gian Galeazzo and his younger brother, Ermes, moved into their father's luxurious bedchamber, while their mother, Bona, declared herself regent and formally assumed power until Gian Galeazzo reached his majority. She spent her first day back privately consulting Cicco in the duke's gloriously appointed study.

She summoned me briefly to the study, where she sat at Galeazzo's huge ebony desk. The new regent of Milan looked haggard and distracted by numerous worries; at the same time, there was unmistakable relief, even lightness, in her gaze and bearing.

As Cicco looked on, Bona handed me a letter. I glanced down at it. It was dated the twenty-fourth of December, and it bore the signature of the abbott of the monastery of San Marco in Florence.

"You will be allowed to bury your husband at San Marco," Bona said gently. "I have made arrangements for your travel. When you arrive in Florence, you will stay at the convent of Le Murate."

I put my hand to my mouth in an effort to stifle a sob, but failed altogether. Bona rose from Galeazzo's desk and wrapped her arms around me as I wept.

Late that afternoon, I resorted to subterfuge by asking Francesca to pack my things and leave them in Matteo's room. After nightfall, when Caterina was fast asleep, I went to my husband's chamber and retrieved his secret papers and the little black pouch containing the mysterious brown powder, and slipped them into the trunk Francesca had filled with my things.

At Caterina's insistence, I lay beside her in her feather bed, and woke well before dawn. Happily, Galeazzo's daughter did not stir, but lay so silent I could not hear her breath. I slipped from the bed, dressed quickly, and hurried down to Matteo's chamber. Just before sunrise, a pair of grooms came to take my trunk, and the three of us headed for the stables. The cold, light mist settled upon my cheeks and eyelashes.

My covered wagon was waiting. The driver, who before age had taken its toll had been master of Bona's stables, was a tall, skeletal man with sunken cheeks and a cottony white beard. Beside him sat his aged wife, a tiny, equally frail-looking creature with one blind, clouded eye. To my amazement, the driver leapt from his seat and helped the young grooms push my trunk into the back of the wagon with ease. He then caught my elbow and, with an arm thinner than my own, pulled me up into the wagon with impressive strength.

I would have sat beside the pair, but the driver, Gennaro, gestured emphatically for me to sit in the back, and held open the canvas flap for me; he pointed in the direction of the sun, which had just begun to infuse the thick, gathering clouds with a pinkish red glow. The mist would soon turn to cold rain.

I yielded, and crouched low as I moved inside the wagon, half of which was covered with cushions, pillows, and fur throws. The other half bore my trunk, and a coffin fashioned from fresh-hewn, fragrant pine.

I fell to my knees upon the cushions and threw my arms about the coffin as if it were Matteo himself; I put my cheek against the smooth, sanded wood and wept. I had known, of course, that my husband would accompany us, but I had not realized he would travel at my side.

Perhaps later we could go together to Florence.

In the distance, thundered rumbled, and the mist turned abruptly to steady rain. The driver called to the horses; the wagon shuddered and began to sway. I held fast to the coffin, and did not look up until I heard a girl shriek and the horses neigh. I poked my head out through the half-open flap and saw Caterina.

She was barefoot, clad only in her woolen nightgown, her long braid bouncing as she rushed toward the wagon. I watched, stricken, as she waved her arms, her face contorted with grief, and shrieked my name.

"Dea! Dea!"

Her desperation and fear were unfeigned, her voice so heartrendingly shrill that I squeezed my eyes shut.

I retreated back into the wagon and clutched the coffin, sobbing, until distance and pelting rain swallowed the sound of her cries.

Eight

We traveled southeast across the plain, along the banks of the Po, and crossed the rushing waters at San Pietro, before the river grew wildly serpentine. From dawn to dusk I rode inside the covered wagon next to the pine coffin, my palm pressed to the wood as if it were Matteo's hand. From time to time, the rain grew deafening as it pelted the canvas, but it stopped altogether as we passed Piacenza's city walls in the late afternoon; I opened the back flap and glimpsed the region known as the Emilia, its hillsides terraced with vineyards. We did not pause there, but continued half an hour after the sun had set, coming to rest finally at an inn. By then, I was chilled to the bone; the wagon's interior had been so cold I could see my breath.

There was but one room to be found, so I took the straw mattress while the driver and his wife—who, I learned, was totally deaf—lay snoring upon pillows on the floor. While they slept like the dead, I left the candle burning and delved into my trunk to take out Matteo's papers. I meant to slip them into my cloak, intending to read them the next day, but was so restless that I began to read *On the Egyptian Mysteries*, attributed to Iamblichus.

I did not read for long. It had been four years since I had applied myself to Latin, and my understanding was at times wanting, but what I understood frightened me. Iamblichus spoke of pagan gods, demons, astrology—

and a personal demon whose name could be known by studying one's natal stars. Worse, it spoke of telling the future: *Ecstasy or alienation of mind is the basis of divination, also the mania which accompanies disease.*

Troubled, I soon left off reading. Even so, I slipped the papers into my cloak; if Matteo had thought this subject worthy, I was obliged to understand why.

The next day we passed Parma, and more carefully terraced rows of grapevines, bare and gnarled in winter. I had no opportunity to read more; the elderly wife had begun to cough, and I made her lie in the wagon beside Matteo while I sat beside the old driver and stared at the nearby Apennine Mountains, forested with bare-limbed chestnut, beech, and oak.

That night we stopped some hours past Modena. This time, the accommodations were better, and I had my own room. I stayed up quite late rereading Iamblichus; at the manuscript's end was a letter in the vernacular, written in the same modern hand that had provided the translation of the ancient Greek ritual, yet not part of it.

To my beloved, it said,

This is in reference to the ritual I sent for your edification, in hopes it—and this translation of Iamblichus of Syria, a follower of our dear Plato—will set you well upon the path to union with the Divine.

The ritual predates both men by centuries, but was assuredly used by them and their students. Its purpose: to invoke the personal daemon, as the Greeks called him; we know him better as the Holy Guardian Angel, that divine inner genius which guides our soul surely to union with its Creator. For God cannot be grasped through the mind, or through contemplation alone, but through the heart, which is exalted in ritual. As a pagan, Iamblichus was not blessed with the knowledge of our Savior, and so much of his writing reflects this ignorance, but much of it is of great use to us today. I am of the belief that God granted His grace even to the heathens, in order that those ignorant of Christ yet men of good will could come to know Him through the dedicated practice of the rite of the Bornless One.

How shall we know, you ask, whether the ritual has been successful? Heed Iamblichus, who says, "The arrival of the archangels is preceded by the appearance of light."

Of the angel, I must say little, for each man has his own, and each soul must travel its own path to divine union; one man's salvation cannot be another's. It is therefore imperative that once you have attained conversation with the angel, you speak of it to no one, lest you fall into the error of believing that you alone have a special connection to the Divine, or that the lessons meant for you alone should be inflicted upon others.

As for the precious contents of the little bag: Immediately before commencing the ritual, take half a small spoonful, no more; use wine to cut the bitterness. See that it never falls into the hands of the profane, or is used wastefully. This, too, must be accomplished in strict privacy, and never be mentioned to outsiders.

May this rite, which was handed down to us by the ancients, guide you to a greater knowledge of the One Who created us all.

In eternal friendship,
Your servant,
Marsilio

On the third day, the wife was so ill that she lay coughing all day inside the wagon; I sat beside the driver again as we skirted the mountains. The weather was dry, sunny, and mild, and remained that way on the fourth day. We stopped at other inns, but I read no more; the letter by the mysterious Marsilio had assuaged some of my fears, but raised other uncomfortable questions. I remained puzzled, confused, thoroughly intrigued.

Late on the morning of the fifth day, we passed over a series of gentle hills; at the apex of the last one, I spied Florence, nestled in the basin below, and let go a gasp of appreciation. Beneath a dazzling blue sky, the city looked golden, its southern flank bisected by the winding silver Arno. As we descended, the separate rooftops grew distinct, and the driver, who knew the city well, began to point out landmarks. The greatest of them, dominating the skyline, was the vast orange-red dome of the great cathedral, Santa Maria del Fiore, Our Lady of the Lilies, matched in height only by its slender campanile; farther south lay the tower of the Palazzo della Signoria, the Palace of Lords, seat of the city's government.

Most of the buildings were made of stone—some of the costly pietra serena, a dove gray rock that turned shimmering white in the strong sun, others of a pale brown or gold. Some were of stucco, but almost all had the same orange-red brick roof and were built in the classical style, which lent a pleasant uniformity. Perhaps it was the light or the clement weather or the languid hills that embraced the outskirts, but I judged Florence to be the prettiest city I had ever seen. Next to it, Milan seemed drab and cold and dirty.

We passed through the northern gate onto the broad, cobblestoned Via Larga, swarming with pedestrians, wagons, carriages, horses, and street merchants; the sun hung at mid-heaven, and all over the city, church bells were chiming to mark Sext, the sixth hour after sunrise. From the upper-floor windows of all the buildings, fluttering banners hung. Most bore the city standard, a bright red fleur-de-lis against a white background, or the Medici crest, a gold shield adorned with six balls, five of them red and the topmost blue, with tiny gold stylized lilies.

I was so exhilarated that I wanted to keep riding, but we arrived at San Marco all too quickly, and the wagon wheels slowed to a stop at last. I was disappointed; I had wanted a cathedral with a great dome and tall spires for Matteo, but instead saw a spare single-nave church with a bland stone fa-çade, and tucked next to it, a square, plain, two-story cloister. I climbed down from the wagon, my legs wobbly from disuse, and waited with the horses while the driver entered the monastery.

He returned with a lay brother, Domenico, a cheerful young man with red curls who wore a white tunic and scapular beneath a black cape that fell below his ankles. Domenico led me just inside the cloister, to a public area known as the chapter house. He explained in a whisper that San Marco's church and convent had been some two hundred years old when Lorenzo de' Medici's grandfather, Cosimo, paid for their renovation thirty years earlier; the crumbling wood and mortar were replaced by the more durable and handsome pietra serena and cream stucco.

I sat, only half listening as Domenico spoke in hushed tones. He told me that the abbot was expecting me, and that the next afternoon at None, the ninth hour after dawn, a service for Matteo would be held in the sanctuary, followed by burial in the churchyard. I left, relieved that I had survived the discussion without tears, and returned to the waiting driver, his wife, and the now-empty wagon.

We continued south down the wide Via Larga and the driver continued his narration. He pointed out the home of Lorenzo the Magnificent, an unremarkable, square, three-story fortress of stone, with the Medici banner hanging from every window.

The driver pointed straight ahead. "And that way lies the church of San Lorenzo, where Lorenzo's father and grandfather are buried."

We rolled past similar palazzos and gardens, then artists' workshops, goldsmiths, and jewelers. Not long after, we approached the massive cathedral of Florence, also called the Duomo because of its magically unsupported dome, the largest in all the world. Across from it stood the pale stone octagon of the Baptistry of Saint John, its gilded bronze doors dazzling in the sun.

We turned east to drive alongside the long stone spine of the cathedral, and followed the road as it curved due south again. Eventually, we came to a grim, four-story fortress with a crenellated tower, which housed the city magistrate; there we veered sharply left onto the Via Ghibellina. A few minutes later, the driver pulled the horses over to the curb.

"The convent of Le Murate," he announced, and hopped down from his seat to help me down.

I descended to find a long expanse of stone wall broken by a tall, narrow wooden gate. Two rusting iron grates, one at the level of my eyes, the other of my ankles, were set into the door; the uppermost grate was covered on the inside by a black cloth. While the driver waved down a street lad to help him fetch my trunk, I clanged the brass knocker and called out softly; as I did, I caught a sudden whiff of vinegar and felt inexplicably nauseated.

Within a few minutes, the gate opened far enough to allow the driver to shove my trunk inside the door, though he was not allowed entry himself. He promised to come for me the next afternoon, and as I passed through the convent walls I saw the vinegar—used to prevent plague—in a bucket that held alms thrown through the grate by passersby.

Le Murate was old but in good repair and very clean; the furnishings were spare but elegant and comfortable, even by the court of Milan's standards. The abbess, who had received Bona's letter, welcomed me personally and gratefully accepted the duchess's generous donation, which I pressed into her palm. Even so, the place evoked a strange anxiety in me.

I went at once to the cell assigned me, closed my door, and studied the star rituals written in Matteo's hand. "For banishing," he had written beneath the first, "start here." I was not certain I wanted to know what needed banishing, but the alternative was to sit and think deeply on the funeral that was to come. I chose instead to practice drawing the five-pointed stars in the air with my index finger, the way I had seen Matteo do it in the darkness. I began, also, to memorize the strange words that went with the banishing. I did not emerge from my cell until supper; afterward I walked the grounds alone, and came upon the carefully tended gardens. In the center of them stood an unusual tree: a cedar, as tall as four men standing upon each other's shoulders, its branches broad and sweeping.

The sight jolted me, as if I had seen Matteo himself standing there. I hurried to the tree and reached past the bristling blue-green needles to press my hand to the bark; it was ridged and rough, as I knew it would be, though I had supposedly never seen such a tree before. I leaned against it and drew in its pungent fragrance; tears came to my eyes as I heard a woman's voice whisper in my memory.

A cedar of Lebanon.

My mother's voice. The convent's outer walls loomed close and began to spin; I closed my eyes, panicked. The Duomo's red cupola, the cobblestoned streets, the whitewashed convent walls, even the grates on the door and the smell of vinegar . . . hadn't I recognized them all?

I do not know this place, I told myself firmly, and hurried back to my cell through halls grown terrifyingly familiar.

That night, I silently performed Matteo's banishing ritual, and did not emerge from my cell until the next day at half past two, when it was time to leave for my husband's funeral.

The driver delivered me to the main entrance of the church of San Marco, where the redheaded Brother Domenico waited for me. He led me into a modest chapel, where a small candelabrum burned in front of a magnificent altarpiece painted with a scene of the Last Judgment. Nearby, a balding priest was lighting coals for the censer, muttering prayers as he did so. Two monks in white tunics and black capes stood together just left of the altar, and lowered their gazes as I entered.

As the church was the recipient of the Medicis' charity, there were wooden chairs for the worshippers. In the last row sat a tall, spare woman dressed in a rich but modest gown of dark gray velvet; her face and bowed head were veiled in black silk gauze. She did not look up as I passed, but kept her head inclined toward the rosary in her prayer-steepled hands.

Domenico deposited me in my seat, in the first row directly before the altar, and departed without a word to the woman. The priest sprinkled frankincense upon the now-hot coals, and put the lid on the censer; smoke streamed out through the holes. Swinging the censer from a chain, he made his way down the aisle, chanting. I turned as the door to the chapel opened and Domenico and five other men carried Matteo's casket as far as the threshold. There they waited while the priest censed the casket, then took a brass asperger from the font by the door and sprinkled Matteo with holy water.

As he did, the two monks by the altar began to sing a hollow, aching melody.

De profundis clamavi ad te, Domine . . .

Out of the depths have I cried unto Thee, O Lord . . .

The priest then led the slow procession into the chapel. I turned away, struggling to contain my tears, and did not look at the coffin again until the priest took his place at the altar, and the pallbearers gently set the casket down a few steps from him.

For the first time, I noticed the pallbearers. One was Brother Domenico and two others his fellow monks. But three of the men were wealthy gentlemen, given their exceedingly fine but unostentatious clothes. The first was small and delicate-looking, with graying red-gold hair; the second was Matteo's age, young, handsome, dark-haired and muscular. And the third was Lorenzo de' Medici.

At the sight of Lorenzo, my tenuous grip on my emotions failed. Tears spilled from me, hot and fierce. I remembered Matteo's suffering on that last horrible night; I thought of how Lorenzo must have waited for him and finally realized that something had gone horribly wrong.

I heard Matteo's ragged whisper: *Tell Lorenzo . . .*

I remember little else of the ceremony—only the sacred Host dry upon my tongue, and the priest circling the coffin twice with more incense, more holy water. Only when it was over, and the pallbearers returned to take the coffin, did I realize that they had been sitting behind me the entire time.

The priest caught my arm and led me after the coffin; as I left the chapel, the tall veiled woman rose and stood respectfully.

We went to a deep hole flanked by a large mound of reddish dirt in the churchyard; the gravediggers were waiting for us, leaning on their shovels. The coffin was set upon ropes, which the diggers used to lower it into the ground. Matteo was laid to rest so that his head lay due east of his feet, since Christ would appear in the eastern sky when He returned to raise the dead.

Lorenzo and the younger man flanked the veiled woman, their arms wound about hers in support; the delicate middle-aged man stood on Lorenzo's other side and dabbed at his red-rimmed eyes. They remained a short distance from me, as if unwilling to intrude on my grief.

I listened, dazed, as the priest spoke of Saint Martha and her profession of faith that her brother would indeed rise from the dead.

At last, the priest made the sign of the cross over the grave, and chanted: *Requiem aeternam dona ei, Domine, et lux perpetua luceat ei . . .*

It was over. At the priest's prompting, I clutched a fistful of cold, wet soil and sprinkled it onto Matteo's coffin. The other four mourners watched me, hesitant. I turned to them, gesturing at the mound of earth.

"Please," I said.

The woman was first to add her handful of dirt; the men followed. Once I had handed a coin to the priest for his services, and a purse for the monastery from Bona to Brother Domenico, the gravediggers took to their work with haste. I turned to the others.

"Ser Lorenzo," I asked, "may I have a private word with you?"

He nodded, and moved to my side; the others retreated a few steps, while Lorenzo led me over to a bare-limbed tree, swollen with pink-red bud in response to the unusually mild weather. I tried not to flinch each time a clod of earth struck Matteo's coffin.

"I was so sorry to hear of Matteo's death," Lorenzo said. For once, his glorious confidence and equanimity were gone, his strong shoulders slumped by sorrow. "We learned of it from the abbot less than a week ago." A rock struck the pine coffin resoundingly; he looked over his shoulders toward the gravediggers and turned back to me. "When did it happen? Was he ill?"

"The night after you left Milan," I answered. "Ser Lorenzo, he was poisoned." I struggled to keep my voice steady, but it broke on the last word.

He drew in a deep breath and turned his face away, though not before I glimpsed his guilt and pain. For a long moment, he stood speechless, staring at distant church spires; when he was able to look back at me, he whispered, "I am so sorry."

"As he was dying, he gave me a message for your ears alone," I told him. "He said, 'Tell Lorenzo: The Wolf and Romulus mean to destroy you.' I would have given you this sooner, but I did not trust putting it on paper. Matteo asked me to bring him here, to San Marco, and I tried to come immediately, but the duke would not give me leave."

He gazed past me at the far distance and clenched his jaw, the lower jutting a finger's breadth beyond the upper; a muscle in his cheek twitched. "I had expected as much," he said softly. "And I apologize, Madonna, for involving you in such sordid matters."

"But who is the Wolf? And who Romulus?" I tried, and failed, to hide the hatred, the bitterness, in my tone.

He heard it and though his expression never flickered, something in him recoiled from it. "You must trust me, Madonna, that Matteo did not die in vain. Those who are guilty will be brought to justice in due time. But I would be remiss in my responsibility to Matteo if I told you. It would place you in great danger and would only increase your suffering."

"Then he *was* murdered!" I let go a bitter, gulping sob. "And you know who has killed him—and will not tell me!"

He gave me a moment to collect myself, and asked, very quietly: "Madonna, did you trust Matteo?"

"Of course!" I snapped.

"Of all the people in the world, he sent you to me. He sent you here, to San Marco. Did he tell you that we Medici are the benefactors of this church and monastery? My grandfather Cosimo rebuilt it from a crumbling pile of bricks. He spent much time here in his last years, meditating in one of the cells. Nothing happens at San Marco without our notice.

"Matteo sent you here because he trusted me most of all. Will you not trust me, too, Madonna Dea? We Medici were the closest thing Matteo had to family ... and I tell you that in the strictest confidence, just as Matteo entrusted his warning for me with you."

By then, my tears were no longer so angry; when Lorenzo stretched out his hand, I took it.

"Come," he soothed. "Come and meet our family, and our dearest friend, who loved Matteo greatly."

He led me over to the group of mourners: the dark-veiled woman, the handsome young man, and the small, frail-looking older gentleman with silvering red hair.

"This is Madonna Dea, Matteo's wife," Lorenzo told them. He emphasized the last word, pausing as he did so to shoot the other two men a peculiar warning glance. As they nodded a solemn greeting, the woman faced me and lifted her veil.

She was silver-haired and elegant of bearing, with very large, heavy-lidded eyes and a sharp chin; she might have been lovely had it not been for her astonishing nose, which veered forth from a flattened bridge to curve alarmingly to one side. Like the cedar in the convent garden, her face was hauntingly familiar.

"My dear," she said kindly; like Lorenzo's, her voice was reedy and nasal, yet her tone was so well modulated and gracious that the sound was not as grating as it might have been. "I am Lucrezia Tornabuoni, mother to Lorenzo and Giuliano de' Medici." She gestured at her sons as she spoke, then at the small middle-aged man. "And this is our dear friend, Marsilio."

"Marsilio Ficino," the man said; his voice was hoarse from weeping. "I knew Matteo for some years, and kept up a correspondence with him. Did he ever speak of me?"

I thought of the translation of Iamblichus, and the letter written at the end of the manuscript. "I know the name," I answered, "but nothing more."

Madonna Lucrezia stepped forward and took my hand. Hers were cold and bony, but her eyes and voice drew me like a hearth in winter. "We have known Matteo since he was a boy. We made a little feast, for us alone, in Matteo's honor; would you do us the kindness of joining us?"

My driver followed their carriage to the rusticated stone palazzo on the Via Larga. Giuliano—the younger brother, with his mother's lean, handsome face and large eyes, though, fortunately, not her nose—helped me from the wagon while Lorenzo tended to his mother. There was a sweet timidity in

Giuliano that his older brother lacked; Giuliano averted his eyes and said nothing while we waited for Lorenzo and Lucrezia to join us.

Lucrezia led the way through the ground-floor loggia, where a pair of bankers sat at a long table, writing up loan agreements for eager clients. We exited onto a large colonnaded courtyard; in its center was a burbling fountain at the feet of a life-sized bronze Judith, grasping Holofernes by his hair as she grimly prepared to hack off his head with a sword. Nearby, a bronze, naked David smirked as he rested one foot atop Goliath's severed head.

We made our way inside and up to the second floor, crossing over shining, inlaid marble floors and passing displays of crumbling marble busts, ancient armor and tasseled, jewel-encrusted scimitars, thread-of-gold tapestries, and painting after painting after painting in gilded frames. We arrived finally at an intimate dining room, where I was encouraged to sit close to the fire, and servants—not courtiers in finery, but common folk, plainly dressed—brought wine and bread and pasta in broth for the first course. It was nothing like the court of Milan; for one thing, the diners were cordial and entirely relaxed with one another; for another, they addressed those waiting on us as though they were part of the family, and inquired after their well-being and loved ones. The servants, too, were relaxed, and though courteous, did not bother with bows and curtsies.

"I am so glad that you have come, Madonna," Lucrezia said, smiling faintly across the table at me. Lorenzo sat beside her; Giuliano and Marsilio, on either side of me. "Lorenzo says that he made your acquaintance in Pavia." She paused to stare down at her steaming bowl; her gaze turned inward for an instant as she contemplated her words. "We were heartbroken when we heard of Matteo's passing," she added finally. "Tell me, did he ever speak of us to you?"

"No," I answered awkwardly. "Well, that is, I knew that he was friends with Ser Lorenzo."

"My late husband, Piero, saw to Matteo's education," Lucrezia responded. "Marsilio here was his teacher." She took up her spoon, the signal for the rest of us to begin eating.

Marsilio let go a sad, small sigh; his pale eyes were bright with affection. He was more emotional than the others, quicker to gesture, to smile, to weep, with a dreamy distraction in his gaze that marked artists and scholars.

"A gentler, kinder lad never lived," Marsilio said. "Nor a quicker one. He took to Greek and Latin as if he had been born knowing them; of course, he already had his French." He colored suddenly, as though realizing he had said too much.

I ventured the truth. "I have read the manuscript you gave Matteo, the one by Iamblichus. When my husband was dying, he told me where to find his hidden papers. I found Iamblichus, and three rituals—"

"We will speak of that, and many other things," Lucrezia said swiftly, pointedly, "after we have dined. There is much to discuss in private. But for now, let us speak of Matteo's youth."

And she proceeded to tell me how one day an eleven-year-old boy came to scrub the floor of old Cosimo de' Medici's cell at San Marco. Cosimo had left him to his work, and returned to find the boy absorbed in reading a manuscript in Latin: one of Plato's works, recently translated for Cosimo by his grandsons' tutor, Marsilio Ficino. The boy apologized profusely for abandoning his scrubbing and for touching the manuscript. But when Cosimo asked him a few questions about what he had read, the boy responded with such intelligence that Cosimo was deeply impressed. He went to the abbot, and learned the boy was orphaned; his mother had died the year before, and he claimed to know nothing of his father.

"And so," Lucrezia said, "with Cosimo's blessing, my husband, Piero, took charge of the boy's education. Though he lived at San Marco with the monks, we often brought him here to play with the boys and take lessons from Marsilio. On holidays, we brought him here so that he could celebrate them with a family. And when he grew older, Piero sent him to the University of Pavia.

"Lorenzo here often visited Duke Galeazzo—God rest his soul—in order to maintain good relations with Milan. While he was there on business on his father's behalf, he learned that the duke's secretary was looking for a good apprentice. And so we recommended Matteo to him."

Next to me, Giuliano half turned, smiling. His eyes held an exuberance that his brother's lacked; his full lips were framed by fetching dimples. "He used to go with us to the Epiphany celebrations. He was my age, and he and Lorenzo and I would walk together behind the horses."

"Not too closely, and even then with great care where we stepped,"

Lorenzo observed drily, and Giuliano responded with a short laugh before continuing.

"Epiphany is tomorrow," Giuliano said. "There will be a street procession from the House of Lords all the way to San Marco; Lorenzo will be on horseback dressed as Balthazar, one of the three Wise Men. Two other notable men have been selected to play magi, and I will be riding in Lorenzo's entourage. It's quite a beautiful old pageant. We were hoping that you might take part in it this year, and join us afterward for the feast."

He spoke with such warmth, such poignance, that I was moved, yet grief left me unwilling to countenance anything so festive. My eyes burned, and as they filled, Giuliano saw and took my hand in brotherly fashion.

"Oh, dear Madonna Dea," he said, genuinely stricken. "I did not mean to make you cry." He cast about for something to cheer me, and said, "Perhaps I should now tell you how Matteo used to carry a slingshot, and one year struck the rump of one of the Wise Men's mounts with a stone. The poor horse reared and sent the crowd scattering; it was a miracle the rider held on."

I managed a small smile, which satisfied him. Meanwhile, his mother said, "Don't press her, Giuliano. Madonna Dea is in mourning and may well wish to forgo the procession."

"Please," I said to them both, overwhelmed by the affection with which they spoke of Matteo and showed toward me. "Please call me Dea."

"Dea, then," Lorenzo said with authority, as if establishing it for all. "Matteo has entrusted you with a great deal, Dea. He wrote to us of you." He gave his mother a knowing look; Lucrezia responded with a nod, then spoke to the servants.

"Matilda, Agnes," she said, "and Donato, would you excuse us? We will summon you when we are ready for the next course."

The servants quietly took their leave. Once the great door was shut, and we four were alone, Lorenzo said softly, "Epiphany is very important to us Medici. Seven generations ago"—his voice took on a storyteller's rhythm, as though he uttered a speech often rehearsed—"my family was entrusted with a great deal of oral wisdom—knowledge that was at once both a great privilege and a great burden—by a wise man of Egypt who called himself Baldazar. It was nothing less than the spiritual tradition of the ancients, and was later confirmed in writing by several sacred texts which my grand-father Cosimo was blessed to discover."

"A spiritual tradition?" I half whispered.

"A means," Marsilio interjected, in his breathy tenor, "by which the soul might unite itself with God."

"We are the bearers of holy gifts," Lorenzo said softly. "Each man, each woman. Like the magi of old, we follow the star, knowing it will guide us to even greater treasure. Those of us who have been granted the knowledge and conversation of the angel have a duty to use our gifts to shine the light of the sacred star on others, not just for the good of Florence, but for the good of Italy, for the good of the world. This is why we Medici collect all the sacred things, all the ancient things; it is our duty, so that the old wisdom is not forgotten. It is why we have painted the Procession of the Magi on our cha-pel walls, why our family celebrates Epiphany as our special day."

"The angel," I murmured, and when Lorenzo looked askance at me, I added, "the Holy Guardian Angel, the one Marsilio mentioned in his letter . . ."

"The same," he answered shortly. "We vow to obey that divine inner ge-nius, even unto death. But it is something to be experienced, not discussed."

"Matteo must have known the angel," I said, struggling to understand.

"And he sent you to us, with his dying breath," Lucrezia said. "Clearly, he wanted you to know this, else he would not have allowed you access to his papers." She paused. "There is much we have to discuss, Dea, and more we will explain. In the meantime, it would be best for us to finish our lun-cheon." She nodded to Giuliano, who reached behind him to pull a tasseled cord hanging from the ceiling.

In less than a minute, the servants reappeared, bearing more food. We finished eating while the others told me humorous stories about Matteo's youth. I treasured each one, yet none of them explained the secret that troubled me most of all: why my husband would not take me to his bed.

After the meal, Lucrezia wished to speak to me alone; we left the men downstairs and went up to her chambers on the third level. Although the rest of the rooms were filled with exquisite paintings, relics, busts, and jewels on display, Lucrezia's suite was austerely elegant, without a single painting on the wall save one of an angel announcing the coming of the Christ child to a young, golden-haired Mary. It was also entirely empty; the Medici matron had apparently informed her staff of her desire for privacy.

Lucrezia settled in the antechamber, in a padded chair in front of a writing desk by the flickering hearth. A second chair had been set beside hers, and she patted it in invitation. I sat, struggling to digest what I had already learned.

Clearly, Matteo, Lorenzo, Marsilio, and probably Giuliano had all performed the rituals I had discovered in my husband's secret cabinet, and had evoked the angel.

It was also becoming clear to me that my husband—a close intimate of the Medici, gone to serve at Galeazzo's court—had also served as Lorenzo's spy. Why else had Lorenzo, a secret visitor to Milan before Christmas, been eagerly awaiting a message from Matteo? A message that had been utterly cryptic: *Romulus and the Wolf mean to destroy you.*

"This has not been an easy day for you," she remarked, drawing me from my thoughts. "Too sad, and filled with too many shocks." She opened the little desk drawer and pulled out a small rectangular bundle wrapped in black silk. "I'm afraid it isn't over yet."

She set the bundle upon the dark glossy wood and untied the silk, then spread it out over the desktop, revealing the hidden contents.

It was a deck of triumph cards—not so large as those Lorenzo had given Bona, nor as fine, though the backs of the cards bore a similar design, of vases, twining leaves, and flowers. But the thin film of gesso plaster on which the illustrations had been painted was cracked and chipped in places from heavy use.

I gasped and picked them up without asking permission, turned them over, and fanned them in my hands. Here were images I had known since childhood: the terrifying Tower, with its lightning bolt and shattered stone; the barefoot pauper called the Fool; the Wheel of Fortune; and, of course, the Papess, in her golden tiara and white veil.

The Papess. I looked up at Lucrezia, and recognized her at once.

"Do you remember these cards?" she asked softly.

"I do . . ." I spread them out upon the table; the chalices, the swords, the coins, the batons: I knew them all, yet did not remember how. I fingered the cards wistfully, tenderly. There, the Hanged Man, my poor sacrificed Matteo. There, the flighty, vengeful Knave of Swords, the courageous Queen of Batons. I caressed them as I would family.

"These were your mother's," Lucrezia said.

I glanced up, dumbstruck. My hand, which had been hovering over the Queen of Batons, picked her up and clutched her tightly.

"Before she died, she came here to Florence," Lucrezia continued. "To the convent of Le Murate. The Medici men support San Marco, and go there to meditate and pray; we Medici women do the same for Le Murate. The abbot, the abbess, are our dear friends. Nothing happens at either cloister that we do not soon learn about."

I closed my eyes briefly and thought of the great cedar in the convent garden; I understood now why its fragrance had provoked my tears.

"Do you remember anything about your mother?" she asked gently.

I shook my head.

"Matteo indicated to us that you did not." She drew a long breath. "I know only that her name was Elisabeth, that she was French, that her husband had cast her from his house when you were very small. She fled to Milan first, and there she suffered the misfortune of reading Duke Galeazzo's future." She paused; her voice dropped to a low murmur. "Your mother was a very beautiful woman."

My hand, which still gripped the Queen of Batons, began to tremble. "You needn't say more; I know what the duke did to beautiful women."

She bowed her head. "Elisabeth foretold a bad end for the duke, and warned him to change his ways, or he would die at the hands of his enemies. Such talk enraged Galeazzo, who beat her almost to death, then raped her."

The light dimmed suddenly, as if someone had blown out a taper; the walls in the spacious antechamber grew abruptly close. I closed my eyes and saw the duke staring down at the Tower card: *Mother of God, it's she! A ghost come back to haunt me!*

Lucrezia's gaze was focused on the distant past. "After the duke was finished with her, her young son struck Galeazzo with a candlestick and they managed to escape. Galeazzo's secretary, Cicco Simonetta, is a decent man who abhorred his master's cruelty. While the duke was incapacitated, Cicco saw her and her children to the stables, gave her a horse and provisions and instructed her to head to Florence, where she would be safe.

"She rode with her children here, and sought refuge at Le Murate. The attack left her pregnant; even though the nuns took good care of her, she lost the baby. Afterward . . . she was never the same. She lost her reason, and desired only revenge against the duke." Lucrezia sighed. "As a mother, I understand. There were rumors that Galeazzo had vowed revenge against her little boy. And so one day she left her children behind to return to Milan. She had acquired a dagger, and managed to get near enough to him to graze him with it, but she was quickly surrounded by guards." She dropped her gaze. "She was hung in the public square outside the cathedral in Milan."

"Children," I said. "So I was not the only one. Are the others still alive?"

She shook her head sadly. "There was only one other, a boy. He was older than you, perhaps ten, when it happened; you were only three. You must have seen it all. When his mother was attacked, the boy threw himself on the duke and pummeled him; the duke struck him so hard that he was slammed back against the wall.

"Elisabeth fled Milan in part because she was terrified for her son's sake; striking the duke's royal person is a crime punishable by death. So when she came to Le Murate, she asked that the boy be moved to San Marco, and his name changed."

"What was his name?" I pressed.

"Guillaume. And yours was Desiree."

The names were meaningless to me. I drew a deep breath and asked a question whose answer I feared. "What happened to him?"

Lucrezia faced me squarely. Her eyes were very large and sorrowful. "He died. But not before he grew into a man. We educated him and sent him to the university at Pavia. Because of his great heart and talent, Marsilio initiated him into the secrets of the Magi. But once he learned that he had a sister at the court of Milan, he insisted on finding employment there, so that he could watch over her himself. He could not tell her the truth, lest the duke get wind of it and punish him and his sister. But he intended to bring her to Florence eventually, and to reveal all. Of course, he had pressing business to finish for Lorenzo before he could leave the duke's employ."

I heard my husband whisper: *Perhaps we could go together to Florence, to meet some of my friends there.*

The Queen of Batons slipped from my fingers; I pressed my palms hard against my eyes. "Matteo," I whispered, and drew a ragged, hitching breath, then released it as a wail. "Oh, Matteo, my dear brother . . ."

Nine

All my doubts concerning Matteo's affection for me fell away. I had never realized just how deep and constant his love for me had been.

"Why did no one tell me he was my brother?" I moaned, bitter at the realization that I had lost my only surviving family member. "Why?"

Lucrezia wrapped her arms about me tightly until I grew calm enough to listen again.

After my mother had left me in the nuns' care to meet her fate in Milan, I became withdrawn and mute and forgot everything about my former existence, including my family. For almost five years I lived at Le Murate as an orphan until I came to Lucrezia's attention; the abbess had kept her promise to my mother to reveal my identity to no one, for my own safety. But two years later, the abbess and many of the sisters died during an outbreak of plague in the convent; only one surviving sister remembered my story and relayed it to Lucrezia some time after. She in turn compared notes with her husband, Piero, and realized that she had finally located Matteo's lost sister.

But by then, Bianca Maria, the duke's mother, had learned from Cicco that the boy and girl of the hanged mother were in Florence. Eager to make amends for her son's wickedness, Bianca Maria secretly searched for them, hoping to adopt them. She could not locate Matteo at all, and by the time she located me at Le Murate, she was dying, so she confided in the duke's good-hearted new wife, Bona of Savoy, who was also determined to right Galeazzo's wrongs.

In the middle of the night, Bona's agents stole into the convent and took me away, back to Milan, where I became the "natural daughter" of one of Bona's "disgraced but noble" cousins.

Lucrezia was terrified that the duke had taken revenge on me; it took her months to discover what had actually happened. By then, she deemed it safest to let me remain under Bona's gentle care. But Matteo was inconsolable at the thought of his sister living under the same roof as their mother's murderer. As soon as he was grown, he went to Milan to look after me . . . and, in time, to bring me back to Florence.

"The nun who took care of your mother at Le Murate kept the cards because Elisabeth asked that they be given to you, when you were old enough," Lucrezia told me, after I had calmed. A note of regret crept into her tone. "I wish I had had the chance to meet her, because such a talent must not be misused. I would have offered her the secrets of the Magi . . . and the knowledge of the angel, so that she could have offered her ability up to God. Instead, her anger destroyed her."

She paused and leveled her serene, knowing gaze at me. "You have your mother's gift, Dea. Lorenzo saw it, and Matteo told us as much."

"How do I know it doesn't come from the Devil?" I demanded, suddenly fearful. "The manuscript spoke of demons, not angels, and of pagan gods. And the rituals Matteo left behind . . . they use stars and circles and barbarous names."

"The names of God," Lucrezia corrected. "And the Greek word *daemon* usually refers to a divine genius, not an evil spirit." She gestured at the cards. "Dea, do you truly believe these are evil?"

"Bona says they are," I said, and stopped myself. What did *I* believe? "They represent . . . people, sometimes. And forces, like fire, or the wind." I pondered it a moment. "I suppose the wind is neither good nor evil."

"It can destroy and shatter," Lucrezia agreed, "or power a great ship.

Forces simply *are*, Dea. Their worth depends upon the purpose for which they are used." She gathered up the cards in her long, bony hands and held them out to me. "These are yours now. So are the rituals and the manuscript that Matteo left for you."

I hesitated. "The ritual is for summoning the angel?"

Lucrezia nodded.

"And if I summon it, then what?"

She smiled faintly. "That is between you and the angel. It will show you the purpose of the life God has given you, and give you special help so that you might fulfill it."

I took the cards. They were warm from Lucrezia's touch, and worn from my mother's hands.

I had many more questions for Lucrezia, some of which she answered that day. For example, the brown powder in the little pouch—"which must never be discussed, as the profane cannot understand it," she said—was to be taken in a bit of wine just before the ritual was begun, and all three rituals were to be performed in a certain order.

The revelations of the day strained my nerves and emotions and left me exhausted. Lucrezia insisted that I stay the night at the Palazzo Medici, and sent word of the fact to my driver, asking that my things be brought to me. I stayed alone in the modest bedroom that had belonged to Lucrezia's now-married eldest daughter, Nannina, which overlooked the courtyard.

I did not have the will to come down to supper, or to join the carnival celebrations beginning outside in the street; instead, I lay on Nannina's straw and feather bed and stared up at the stucco ceiling, overwhelmed by sadness, regret, love, and bittersweet gratitude.

I was filled with other, darker emotions, too: hatred, and the craving for swift and bloody justice. I was pleased that Duke Galeazzo had died violently, as my mother and I had predicted; her death had already been avenged. But Matteo's had not.

I decided that I already knew my life's purpose: that of taking revenge on my brother's murderers—on the Wolf and Romulus, whether Lorenzo was willing to reveal their identities or not. And so I resolved to use the powder, the rituals, and the angel for a cause I believed to be just.

A maid brought me a warm supper that evening. The singing and shouting out in the broad Via Larga kept me awake until very late, as did the happy voices of visitors inside the palazzo.

I woke the next morning to a muted cascade of church bells from San Marco, not far down the broad cobblestoned street, and San Lorenzo just to the east, and from the magnificent Duomo farther south. I opened my eyes knowing that I would tell Bona I had discovered Matteo's surviving family—it was not entirely a lie—and wanted nothing more than to return to Florence, and to them. I knew that if I made my plea passionately, she would grant it. After all, Lorenzo was my one connection to the Wolf and Romulus; he had the answers I sought.

I declined that morning to join the parade through the city streets. Instead, I attended mass with Lucrezia in the Medici family chapel, whose walls were adorned with a fresco of the procession of the Magi, rendered in vivid scarlets, greens, and sapphires, all gilded and gleaming with candle-light. Afterward she and I went up to a second-floor window and waited for the pageant to pass by in the street below.

Clad in black and white, the trumpeters marched at the head of the parade, blaring notice of their arrival. Behind them strode the standard-bearers, dressed in brilliant stripes of saffron, red, and blue and carrying the red and white flags that bore the fleur-de-lis of Florence. Next came costumed pedestrians, some of who threw brightly colored streamers of cloth into the cheering crowd.

And then came Lorenzo, first of the Magi, upon a white horse grandly caparisoned in gold and red; the rider was similarly dressed in gold brocade and a red velvet cape, with a tasseled Moorish turban upon his head. Lorenzo's smile was broader, more carefree, than I'd ever seen it; in a grand, giddy gesture, he threw coins into the crowd. Beside him, dressed in a red felt cap and the plain tunic of a servant, was his younger brother, Giuliano.

I stared down at them, at the fluttering gold and blue pennants, and could think only of how Matteo must have looked riding there.

I attended the banquet that afternoon. The sweetly beaming Marsilio attended, along with a number of young men whose names sounded vaguely familiar, among them Leonardo da Vinci and Alessandro Botticelli. Lucrezia sat at my side and smoothly answered questions on my behalf, deftly disarming any that were too prying, too painful.

Afterward the men adjourned to a meeting hall on the ground floor; Lucrezia took my elbow and steered me away, whispering, "It is a meeting of the Society of the Magi, for those who are initiated. Don't worry, Lorenzo will merely repeat what he told you before. I'm afraid we women are not allowed to attend, as most of the men are too foolish to realize that we are just as capable of spiritual attainment as they are." She chuckled softly. "May God grant them all wisdom."

By then, I had resolved to leave for Milan as soon as possible, and informed her. She was sad that I would be leaving so soon, but I told her of my intent to return to Florence very quickly, and to remain here forever.

I asked her then whether she would read my triumph cards for me; she hesitated, and shook her head. "That is not my gift, but yours."

"And what is your gift?" I asked.

She gave a secretive little smile. "Similar to yours. But I use no cards. I simply see."

Quietly, so that servants passing in the hall might not hear, I murmured, "And what do you see for me, Madonna Lucrezia?"

The smile faded; her gaze grew somber. "A longer and more unusual journey than you expect, dear Dea."

She would not elaborate. I sat with her an hour that evening, asking questions about Matteo—what he had been like as a boy, what he had said about me. She showed me the most recent letter he had written to her in his lovely cipher; Marsilio had kindly written the decrypted message above it, in his distinctive hand.

My brother described me as intelligent, beautiful, generous, and thoughtful. He spoke of how the deception of marrying me broke his heart, though it was necessary to protect me from physical abuse; he spoke of his worry that I would never trust him again once I learned the truth. I could not listen to his words without weeping.

When all the servants were out of earshot, I whispered to Lucrezia, "When should I perform them? The rituals to summon the angel?"

She raised her thin dark brows in mild surprise. "That is not for me to answer, child. You will know when it is time."

Worn from emotion, I again retired early to Nannina's bedchamber, and when the maid left me for the night, I took out my mother's triumph cards. Sitting upon the bed, I mumbled a prayer to the angel—whatever, whoever it might be—then set out three cards facedown, just as I had for Caterina.

Past, present, future.

I turned over the first card. Upon a white background, four gold-tipped swords pointed at the ground; a second set of four downward-pointing swords crossed them, forming a diamond-shaped lattice at the card's center. I sensed steel clashing against steel: there was dissension here, interference of an internal sort, deception and confusion; and when I saw a ninth sword, its hilt upon the ground, its tip pointing straight up through the center of the crossed blades, I felt as though it pierced me to my core.

The Nine of Swords represented the past, one that held pain to the point of madness. As I stared at the swords, I fancied blood dripping like tears from the tip of each blade, and felt a strong sense that while this had been my past, it might also be my present and future unless this pain was resolved.

"The present," I said aloud, and turned over the Fool.

At the sight of it, I felt an unreasoning dismay. *This is wrong,* I thought involuntarily; this was someone else's destiny, not mine. But then I cast about for ways that it might have a desired meaning; and, as minds often do, mine misled me, with the comforting notion that *This is merely the trip back to Pavia, then to Florence again. Not such a long journey after all.* It was coincidence, and nothing more, that I had drawn the same card I had given Caterina.

At least, I convinced myself of it, until I turned over the third card representing the future, and saw the Tower.

Caterina's terrified words echoed in my mind. *It's a trick, all of it! You're doing this to frighten me!*

The stucco and tapestry of Nannina's bedroom walls changed suddenly to the thick stone of a castle keep. Thunder roared in my ears so violently that I reached out to press a hand to the stone, and felt it shudder violently.

Panicked, I tried desperately to remember what I had told Caterina.

This does not mean death. But this is an upheaval, an end to old ways. This is destruction. . . .

You have a long journey ahead of you. A journey, I knew, of years. *Perhaps along the way, you will find a way to avert whatever disaster this card represents.*

"I do not want this," I hissed. I wanted nothing to do with spoiled, selfish Caterina and her undoubtedly well-deserved fate.

I put the cards away and did my best not to think of them again that night. The destiny they revealed seemed senseless, the angel a vague and distant philosophical concept.

Nonetheless, I spent the hours before sleep studying the three rituals. Even after I blew out the lamp, I lay on the bed, arm raised, and, just as I had seen Matteo do, traced stars in the dark.

In the early morning, my driver and wagon were waiting for me out in the Via Larga. I took my leave of Lucrezia with a familial embrace and kiss; I did not have the opportunity to say good-bye to Lorenzo or his brother, who were both still sleeping after the previous day's revelries. Hidden in my cloak pocket were the rituals, the powder, and my mother's triumph cards.

The first two days of travel were uneventful. The weather remained unusually warm, and the driver's wife's health was much improved; she sat on the seat beside her husband while I sat inside, the canvas flap closed, and set to memorizing the barbarous calls that were to accompany the drawing of the stars and circle.

By the evening of the third day, a cold breeze stirred and sent dark clouds scurrying across the sky. The air smelled of rain, and the driver stopped at the inn a few hours' south of Modena, where we had stayed before. I dined on cabbage, bread, and wild boar, then bought a half flagon of wine and carried it to my private room. Although it had no hearth, the innkeeper's wife brought me heated bricks for the bed.

I bolted the door, shuttered the windows, undressed to my wool chemise, and drank most of the wine; the prospect of asking Bona to release me from her service made me anxious. In time, I fell into an uneasy sleep.

Some hours later, a boom jolted me full awake. I sat, heart pounding, and listened to thunder roll off the nearby mountains. I felt an odd anticipation, as if an event of enormous import were about to pass.

A profound determination seized me: it was the time to summon the angel.

The thought left me exhilarated and terrified; my hands shook as I laid the rituals out upon the bed and found the little pouch containing the powder. As Lucrezia had instructed, I put some of the powder into the wine—only a pinch at first, then another, then a third, and finally, a larger amount, for I suddenly could not remember how much I was to use.

The draught was noxious. I downed half of it before deciding that I had probably added too much powder, and set to performing the rituals at once. The whole business took half an hour. At the end, I stood in the center of my invisible circle, waiting for the angel to appear.

Nothing happened. I felt a sudden hot flush, followed by nausea, and staggered to the bed, realizing that my limbs were difficult to move. I lay down beneath a crushing heaviness and closed my eyes; even so, I felt the walls slowly revolving around me.

After a period of misery, the nausea grew urgent; I leaned over the edge of the bed and emptied my stomach onto the worn stone floor. Relief came immediately; with the dizziness gone, I fell back into a delightful languor.

The low, many-times-patched ceiling no longer spun. Instead, it began to shimmer, as if each tiny, golden atom were dancing and twinkling like stars. I watched, delighted, as they began to form shapes: wreaths inside infinite wreaths of bas relief flowers and vines, as if the creamy stucco were blooming tondi sculpted by artists, as if I lay staring up at the inner dome of a great cathedral and not the tired ceiling of an aging inn. The wreaths swelled like clouds, like rising dough, then sank again, only to repeat the process.

Abruptly, the walls fell away: I lay alone on the bed in the center of the inky storm. Overhead, rain fell in sheets, though magically none of it struck me; it pulsed with distant lightning while the racing clouds parted fleetingly to reveal glimpses of a filmy, luminous moon. Images born from the storm coalesced, only to be dissolved again by the wind: the Tower, whole and as yet unshattered; the Fool, one foot lifted in mid-step toward the chasm; the Nine of Swords, every blade dripping blood. Each time lightning kissed the dark, distant Apennines, coins, chalices, swords, and batons glittered in the sky.

The absurdity of the present moment struck me: of my lying there in the storm, of Matteo poisoned and dead, of my mother's cards, still hidden in the cloak upon the chair, of Duke Galeazzo crying *I am dead!* It was so hideous that I wept, so meaningless that I laughed. So much struggling, so much pain, and all of it for nothing.

At the clutch of grief, I told myself not to weep; Matteo was at peace, with God, his suffering ended. Or was it? If God did not hear my prayers, if God had let Matteo die, then how did I know He would take him to Heaven?

Worse, if the angel had let Matteo die, then how could I trust it?

"Matteo," I groaned aloud, clutching my head, then laughed to remember that he had been my own brother all along, and I too much of a fool to see it.

The nocturnal scene above me shuddered. I sat up to find that the bare wall had been replaced by smoke; fingers of white mist were streaming up from the threshold where the wall had once met the floor. They rose, swirling against the backdrop of dark sky to form a column slightly broader and taller than I. Faster, faster the mist swirled, until it grew entirely opaque; just as swiftly it stilled, and began to part.

In its place stood the living night: the outline of a grown man, its form blacker than the sky surrounding us, and darkly glittering, like coal. Its features, hair, and dress were obscured by impenetrable shadow, yet I knew it faced me. For long seconds, we remained motionless, watching each other.

"Who are you?" I breathed at last, and remembered enough of Matteo's instructions to demand: "By what name shall I call you?"

The sentient darkness took a step toward me; as it did, the sky behind it transformed into a yellowed stucco wall with scarred wainscoting. In a wholly human gesture, it lowered itself onto its haunches and leaned, glistening onyx, against the wall.

I stared, transfixed, terrified, exhilarated.

Dea. The words formed themselves distinctly inside my skull, but they were not my thoughts. *You will know that only after you vow to obey me unto death. Only then will I be able to share with you my secrets.*

Thinking myself clever, I countered, "How can I do that, when I cannot even see who or what you are?"

You know me. You've always known me. If you cannot see me, it is because I reflect the darkness in your own soul.

"What darkness?" I had spent my entire life trying to be good, to please God and Bona and everyone but myself. It was not my fault that God had failed me.

It gnaws at you. If you do not expel it, it will ultimately devour you.

"What darkness?" I insisted.

The key to it has already come to you in the cards. The key to your past. It must be expunged if you are to move into the present, into the future . . . toward your destiny, as one of the magi.

"But I have done nothing wrong! I am an innocent victim trying to discover who . . ." My words grew thick. "Who killed my brother. Please, help me."

The angel was suddenly upon his feet; the swirling darkness that was his form dulled as its glittering motion slowed.

The key to your own darkness has already come to you in the cards. When you have mastered it and taken the vow, you will see me. I am but a mirror of your soul.

"Can you not help me now?"

The help you need is not the help you seek. Vow to obey me unto death, and I will reveal all.

I hesitated. Even though my darling Matteo had trusted the angel enough to have left me instructions for contacting it, it had not protected him from a terrible death. And I had no intention of giving up my quest to find his killer.

"I will obey," I replied cautiously, adding silently *insofar as I am able.* I bowed my head. "Please, come to me, and reveal your name. Reveal how and why my brother died, and I shall trouble you no more."

My feeble attempt at deception failed.

I am already here. But your darkness shackles my tongue and hides my true form. If you would be a true magus, and know all things, seek me honestly.

A cold gust howled through the room, lifting my hair and chilling me to the core. I lifted an arm to shield my eyes, and watched as the black form began again to swirl and glitter like coal dust. Invisible drops of freezing rain stung my face, my shoulders.

"Tell me what I must do!" I cried, but my words were swallowed by the gale.

The angel's form grew thinner, sheerer, until I could see the wall behind it; the words that had sounded so clearly in my head now faded to something less than a whisper.

The key has already come to you in the cards. . . . The key to your past is also the key to your future. . . .

The wind roared in my ears; thunder rolled off the mountains. I shut my eyes against the stinging rain, covered my ears with my hands, and howled.

By morning the storm had passed, and I had mostly returned to my senses, save for a lingering appreciation of color and form. I remembered the encounter with the angel vividly, and over the next two days of travel, sat inside the wagon meditating on my mother's triumph cards—specifically, those of the Fool, the Tower and, especially, the Nine of Swords.

The key to your past . . .

I set the three cards beside me on the cushion, faceup, then fanned the others in my hands and stared at them: trumps, batons, swords, chalices, coins. Words came to mind, words that seemed to spring from an external source.

Batons represent will; swords, thoughts; chalices, feelings; coins, material goods. Trumps represent experiences that all of us must pass through, in this life or another. . . .

I stared back down at the Nine of Swords, and heard: *Cruelty, and self-cruelty. Pain to the point of madness.* I closed my eyes, and saw blood dripping from the blades of the eight lowered swords—and from the one sword pointed heavenward.

If there had been cruelty in my past, I told myself, it had never been self-directed. The duke had killed my mother, and a different monster my brother. Any wound I suffered was their fault, not mine.

Thus deluded, I rolled through the Emilia into Lombardy, and back to the Castle Pavia.

We arrived home in the late afternoon of a fine, sunny winter's day. I went from the stables to Matteo's room. I intended to sleep there from now on, with Bona's permission. I needed privacy to decipher Matteo's letters, to work with the cards, and to communicate further with the angel.

I bathed and dressed and went to seek the duchess. I waded through a crowd of courtiers and petitioners waiting in the hall to find Bona in Duke Galeazzo's gilded, mirrored office, looking dwarfed by his enormous carved desk. Bona was quite short, and the effect would have been enhanced had she not replaced his thronelike seat with her own smaller, feminine chair. She was dressed with more care than she had ever been; her black mourning gown had a bodice quilted with thread of gold and studded with seed pearls. Rubies sparkled at her ears and throat, and her veil was held in place with a headband of gold filigree inlaid with tiny diamonds.

Cicco Simonetta, tall and thick as an oak at sixty years, stood beside her as she squinted down at a letter on the desk. Across from her stood a nervous young lad in noble dress.

I pressed to the front of the crowd and bowed low. "With your permission, Your Grace," I called, ignoring the guards flanking the doorway, each of whom directed a scowl at me for calling to the duchess out of turn.

Bona looked up. She seemed weary, and her brow was lined; her pale, small eyes were limned by purple shadows. But at the sight of me, she broke into a bright smile and waved for me to approach.

"Dea! Dea, my darling, my prayers have been answered! God has brought you safely home to me! How do you fare?" She did not rise from her seat—though before the duke died, she would have rushed to embrace me—but instead held out her jeweled hands and inclined her cheek toward me. "Come, come!"

Dutifully, I kissed the proffered cheek and took her hand; it was cold, even though the room was stiflingly warm from the blaze in the fireplace.

She maintained a slight air of formality—great responsibility had changed her—and beyond that, an odd emotional distance.

"You look well," she said, smiling.

"And you look grand, Your Grace."

"How was your journey?"

"Uneventful," I said.

She let go of my hand to cross herself. "Thank God!" She paused. "I am afraid I have little time now for conversation, but perhaps after supper, we shall speak again. As you can see, I have more petitioners than I have minutes in a day. However . . . if there is anything you have need of today, on your return, ask it now, and I will grant it."

I had not meant to speak of my plans so soon or so publicly, but I could see how enormously busy she was; it might be impossible to get her attention for some time in the future. "Your Grace," I said, "I do have a petition of my own."

Bona smiled, waiting.

"I discovered that Matteo had family in Florence. It is my hope that I might return to live there, to be near them. However, I can remain here for as long as Your Grace wishes, of course . . ."

Bona listened, her expression mildly pleasant; if she was offended that I wished to spurn her generosity, she showed no sign. "You had best take this up with Madonna Caterina," she said.

I looked up. "Caterina?"

Bona let go a sigh. "She is your mistress now. She was so distraught when you left that she came to me weeping and begged me to place you in her service. Her father's death has not been easy for her, and she said your company would give her great comfort. What else could I do?" She rubbed her eyes, then gazed back down at the letter upon her desk; her tone grew distracted. "I will abide by whatever she says."

With those words, I was dismissed from Her Grace's care and presence.

Ten

Caterina was at the hunt, taking advantage of the warmer weather. I went to the stables and watched the riders return, their forms dark against the coral glow at the horizon. Caterina rode at the head astride a chestnut mare, her stockinged calves bared, one hand on the reins, the other dangling a dead hare by the scruff of the neck to tease the pair of eager hounds in the basket fastened to her saddle. Her hair had been woven into a single plait, to keep it out of her eyes, but her headdress had come off during the hard ride, leaving a disheveled gold halo about her head. Her face was flushed from exercise and sun; the young master of the hunt rode beside her, and laughed with her at the hounds' desperation.

There was something newly womanish in her appearance and manner; she had passed her fourteenth birthday in my absence and, I suspected, a feminine milestone. Over the past year, her cheeks had thinned, losing their girlish plumpness; her breasts had grown full, her waist narrow. Now, for the first time, I watched her flirt with a man. She made a saucy comment to the master, and tossed her head, laughing, as she gazed sideways at him.

I watched unobserved until Caterina finally glanced in my direction. She urged her tired mare into a trot, deserting the others, and came to a halt a few arms' lengths away. She ignored the help proffered by a stablehand, gathered up her skirts and neatly swung down from her mount, then tossed the reins to the groom.

She strode up to me, and, to my utter astonishment, embraced me so urgently that it pushed the breath from me; her heart was hammering beneath her bodice.

Just as suddenly, she pushed me away, and struck me so hard across the cheek that it sent me staggering; I bit my tongue, and spat blood upon the damp earth.

When I looked up, her blue eyes were narrowed and gleaming with tears.

"You will never leave me again!" Her voice was hoarse, her tone bitter. "Never again, do you hear?!"

Imperious, furious, she turned and left me standing there, with my hand to my jaw.

I did not dare broach the subject of Florence with Caterina for some weeks. By then I had learned that Bona, worried about uprisings and eager to gain the protection of the pope's army, had agreed with Pope Sixtus IV that the best strategy would be to marry Caterina off quickly to her betrothed: Girolamo Riario, the pope's nephew (such was the euphemism for Sixtus's son) and captain general of the Papal Army.

In February, Pope Sixtus sent Cardinal Mellini to Milan to arrange a proxy wedding. When spring arrived, Caterina was to travel to Rome to meet her new husband and take up permanent residence with him there.

And I was to go with her, as her first lady-in-waiting.

It was an honor, Bona chided me, when I finally went to her, weeping, begging to be permitted to go to Florence, or at the very least, to remain with Her Grace—anything but be forced to go to Rome with the duke's spoiled daughter.

My efforts were in vain. Bona took offense that I was not honored and pleased by my new role, and reminded me that Caterina's husband, Girolamo, was the second most powerful man in Rome after the pope, and that my new role as her chief lady-in-waiting afforded me much greater status. I was an ingrate, Bona said; it was the harshest word she had ever spoken to me.

Caterina reminded me at least daily, sometimes hourly, that I was to remain by her side, and to keep the triumph cards nearby so that she could consult them whenever she wished. I never slept again in Matteo's chamber, but in Caterina's bed. She was slow to forget her bitterness over my departure, with the result that I found myself in the odd position of being both favored—with sumptuous clothes, jewelry and perfumes, and the choicest food—and constantly chastised for all manner of imaginary misdeeds.

After one such scolding—when I was slapped at the dining table by Caterina, who claimed that the goblet she knocked over herself was somehow my fault—I reached my limit and strode away from the table, brazenly refusing to ask my lady's permission. I knew I would be punished, but did not care. I half ran to Matteo's chamber, and bolted the door behind me.

"Tell me," I whispered passionately to the angel. "Must I go to Rome? Can I not go to Florence?" I bowed my head, awaiting an answer. But in my heart, my head, there came only silence.

At last I lifted my face as, for the first time, reason dawned. Matteo had died returning from Rome. He had been traveling with papal legates, had he not? And the mysterious rider who had delivered him had also spoken with a Roman accent.

His murderer was in Rome. Fate—and perhaps the angel—had not failed me after all.

"Very well," I whispered. "I will go to Rome. I will obey you. Now reveal yourself to me."

A long silence followed; the angel was not fooled. But I was resigned to my fate. I slowly returned, back through the courtyard and up the stairs to face my punishment.

A fortnight later, Caterina and a small entourage traveled to the castle of Porta Giovia in Milan, still draped in black in honor of the late duke. We went to meet Cardinal Mellini, who had arrived earlier from Rome. There, in a solemn, hushed ceremony, Caterina was wed by proxy to her betrothed, Girolamo Riario, who was far too preoccupied to attend the ceremony. Because of the official state of mourning, no celebrations followed.

Now a contessa, Caterina was eager to leave the memory of her father's assassination behind in order to head to Rome. But Girolamo was adamant; a spell of abnormally hot weather had brought an outbreak of deadly fever to the Holy City. Worse, there had been unrest among feuding noble families, which had led to battles just outside the city walls. The situation had grown so grave that Girolamo had narrowly escaped assassination. *I cannot in good conscience expose my young bride to such dangers,* he wrote.

Caterina and patience, however, remained strangers. At least once a day, she disturbed the overburdened Bona to make her case for an immediate departure for Rome. Worn down, Bona at last wrote Girolamo asking for permission to send him his eager bride. It was all the duchess-regent could do to make Caterina wait long enough to receive a reply.

Girolamo was a determined man: *Under no circumstances can I permit her to come to Rome at this dangerous time,* he wrote. *But if she will not be placated, let her start her journey southward and go to Imola. I will notify the townspeople that she is coming, and make certain that she is feted and well cared for. But she must stay there until I send for her.*

Imola—a little town in the Romagna, south of Milan and north of Rome—had long been owned by the Sforza; upon Caterina's engagement, it had been promised as her dowry to Girolamo, who eagerly accepted the terms. Born of peasant stock, Girolamo had been a customs clerk in a fishing village until his "uncle's" elevation thrust him into a more glorious role, and Imola gave him the opportunity to finally acquire the title of count. All of Imola would turn out to properly welcome Caterina, their contessa, and would see that she was well cared for until her husband summoned her to Rome.

Caterina accepted the invitation with great excitement, and was elated when Girolamo insisted on sending an escort of more than a hundred men, including the bishop of Cesena and the governor of Imola, as well as trumpeters, guards, and assorted dignitaries from Caterina's new kingdom. On a bright morning in late April, I took my place beside her in a luxuriously appointed carriage, and left the life I had known at the court of Milan behind forever.

PART II

Rome

April 1477–October 1484

Eleven

We made our way southwest over the ancient Via Emilia, worn by the tread of Roman legions. It was the very path Matteo had taken on his last journey, and I thought often of him as our great caravan wended its way from town to town, from Piacenza to Reggio nell'Emilia, and beyond. The road was level and boringly straight; we passed dozens of travelers who paused to gape at our magnificent cavalcade with its fluttering flags and banners: the crimson and white Sforza arms of a basilisk swallowing a naked child, the golden oak against sky blue of the della Rovere and Riario, and the golden tiara and keys of Pope Sixtus himself. At every city, our messengers rode ahead to announce the imminent arrival of Her Illustrious Highness, Caterina Sforza, and all the local dignitaries rode out to greet her, to the blaring of trumpets and cheering of hastily assembled crowds.

She dined and slept in the palaces of the ruling families, who publicly praised her grace, beauty, and manner and sent additional escorts with her to add to the carnival atmosphere. With each day, her bearing grew prouder, her behavior toward underlings ruder; by the time we reached Bologna to be welcomed by the family Bentivoglio, she had adopted her father's arrogance. During the day, she treated me with such contempt that I came to despise her for it; only at night, when I lay beside her in a strange bed, did she sound like the frightened child who had wept when I abandoned her.

After eleven days of torturously slow progress, we rolled into the lush, fertile region dotted with orchards, vineyards, and wheat fields known as the Romagna.

By Milanese standards, the Romagna was provincial and fiercely independent; the region was broken into several small fiefdoms. The Malatesta family held the town and outlying areas of Rimini, and the Ordelaffi clan the town of Forlì; various other families claimed other towns, and skirmishes between rivals were common. They agreed on only one thing: their shared disdain for the pope, who yearned to unite them, preferably under his rule.

An hour before sunset, our carriage rolled over a slight promontory. When we reached the crest, Imola lay before us, a trifling town with its eastern flank nestled against the languidly snaking Santerno River.

At the sight of it, Caterina let go a small gasp of delight and beamed.

I followed her gaze, perplexed; had I been in her place, I would have been painfully disappointed. Compared to Milan or even bucolic Pavia, Imola was one of the more provincial hamlets we had passed. West of it stood a great square fortress, its towers bleached to bone by the sun, its base ringed in dark green mold from the moat. Beyond it lay the redbrick city walls; inside them was a sparse collection of buildings set upon a few dusty roads. I counted five churches and as many convents, a small government hall, a marketplace, and a half dozen dwellings suitable for nobility. The rest of Imola was given over to pasture, crops, or hovels for the poor, most of the latter huddled on the riverbank.

"All mine," Caterina whispered to herself, her eyes wide with awe and desire. She was staring at the garlands of flowers set upon either side of the road leading to the gate, its doors thrown open beneath a huge crimson and white Sforza banner, with smaller banners of the Riario and Sixtus flanking it. A crowd had gathered to welcome the new mistress; church bells rang in a sonorous cascade.

We were covered with dust from travel, and the contessa bedraggled from the heat. Caterina ordered the caravan to stop at a nearby castle outside town. There she bathed, and I directed the chambermaids as they dressed her—first in a gleaming white chemise of the finest spun silk, then a kirtle of white satin to which was sewn gold braid. The sleeves were tight and slashed, and the silvery-white chemise was pulled through the slashes and puffed. Over all this went an overdress, open at the sides and cut deep at the neckline, of pure, glittering gold brocade textured to create a pattern of stylized pomegranates. I tucked Caterina's long braids into her favorite gold and diamond snood, and drew forth tendrils round her face; a poker, swiftly heated in the kitchen hearth, coaxed them into tight ringlets. Upon her head went a veil so gossamer as to be invisible; around her neck, a heavy gold necklace studded with large diamonds; and around her shoulders—at her insistence, despite the heat—went a cloak of rich sable velvet, lined in gold satin. Imola was in the grip of unusually warm weather for the first of May; sweat was trickling from Caterina's forehead by the time we set off again, but she scowled at my suggestion that she looked just as splendid without the cloak.

My lady set off upon a horse, caparisoned in crimson and white; I rode close behind, with her two maids. Preceded by the trumpeters and Girolamo's escort, heralded by church bells, Caterina rode through the gate onto streets covered with garlands of spring flowers and lined by townsfolk, who cheered her beauty.

Our procession stopped at a pavilion draped with banners, where Girolamo's sister, Violantina, wife of the governor, stood waiting alongside the dignitaries of the town. When Caterina dismounted, several lads came to blows over the honor of claiming her horse, which delighted her further.

By the time she had been properly welcomed, with speeches, the keys to the city, poems, and the songs of a children's choir, her features were incandescent with joy; I had never seen her behave with such charm, such poise, such confident authority. Violantina then led us to the Palazzo Riario, a stern square building covered in the ubiquitous terra-cotta. Caterina's chamber walls and ceiling had been covered in white silk and gold brocade, but the view from the windows was still that of a small, dreary town, whose most notable landmarks were the house in which we resided and the grim, weathered fortress on its outskirts.

The first few days saw Caterina too busy to take much note of her surroundings; she was escorted to feasts, entertained by jesters, musicians, plays, and spectacles. Peasants surrounded the Riario palace and presented gifts of local delicacies, wines, and preserves.

Her husband, Girolamo, had promised earlier to meet her at Imola, but after four days, she began to chafe. Her instructions were to wait for him until he gave word that danger from assassins and plague had eased. After twelve days, a letter came from Girolamo, but she would not open it. Instead, she set out the following morning for faraway Rome.

We continued on the Via Emilia to Cesena, then due south. With each passing day, the weather grew warmer; by the time we passed Perugia, midway to our destination, we women stripped down to our chemises in the carriage, and hung out the windows, hoping to catch a stray breeze.

After more than a fortnight of dull, miserable travel, our messengers went ahead of us into the Holy City, while we stopped a few hours shy of it, at Castelnuovo, owned by the powerful Colonna family. Caterina was again feted and overfed, and put in luxurious quarters.

The next day she was anxious, and snapped irritably at me and at the maids as they outfitted her again in the grand gown she had worn on her triumphant entry into Imola. Our host, Stefano Colonna, honored her that afternoon with a banquet; by the time our unwieldy caravan again headed south, three hours before dusk, all of us were sated and drowsy. The Roman sky was cloudless, the sun merciless, the heat so sweltering that Caterina abandoned all notions of wearing the velvet cloak.

Along with Caterina, I craned my neck out of the carriage at the driver's shout: Rome lay shimmering in the near distance. They say the Holy City rests upon seven hills, but age has worn them to gentle swells, enclosed by the crumbling, overgrown remains of the Aurelian Wall. Bona had been to Rome, and while I was still a girl, she had had me schooled carefully in its culture, geography, and history. She had always spoken of it with such reverence that I had expected to see a crowded but shining heavenly paradise—and indeed, there were hundreds of palaces, cathedral domes, and churches of shimmering white marble, dazzling in the afternoon light. To my disappointment, however, there were far more squalid, crumbling structures, small forests, overgrown meadows, abandoned vineyards and orchards, and ancient ruins playing host to grazing flocks of sheep and goats, all within the city walls. The gleaming new Jerusalem was far too small to fill them; in ancient days, it had held close to a million souls. Now it was home to barely forty thousand.

Nestled against Rome's western flank, a brown river flowed north to south; on its eastern bank, which contained little more than rolling countryside, sat an isolated, aging complex of massive rectangular buildings. These were Saint Peter's Basilica and the Vatican, whose name meant vacant, uninhabitable. The land on which these were built had acquired its name in the first few decades after Christ's death, when Caligula's mother, Agrippina, had ordered the marshy, spring-laden hill to be drained so that she could plant her gardens there. Later, her son began construction of a circus nearby, which was finished by the tyrant Nero.

Nero entertained the pagan masses by martyring hundreds of Christians on the spot. Many were crucified, others covered in tallow and burned alive; still others, forced to wear the bloody pelts of beasts, were torn to pieces by wild dogs. They died as the mad emperor himself took part in wild chariot races around them.

The bones of these martyrs were too many to be recovered and properly buried, so a church was erected upon them to consecrate the remains, including those of Saint Peter, who had been crucified upside down in the very center of the circus. *A blessing,* the priest who tutored me had said, *for he died looking up toward heaven.*

We traveled another half hour before those riding ahead of us issued a series of shouts; our carriage rolled to a stop. As the driver helped the Countess of Imola from the carriage, I followed, and glimpsed for the first time her husband.

He had dismounted a black charger, and carelessly tossed the reins aside without waiting to see whether the groom caught them. His entourage was no match for his wife's; he had brought with him a dozen men, including the Bishop of Parma, a pair of red-caped cardinals, and a man dressed in bright blue silk who turned out to be the Milanese ambassador to Rome.

Girolamo Riario, the unacknowledged son of Pope Sixtus IV, wore a tunic of dark brown velvet embroidered with silver thread and trimmed with white ermine, despite the heat. His attendants wore the same brown velvet, sans embellishment, and they watched his every move with the same anxious attention I had seen Duke Galeazzo's underlings pay him.

Girolamo gazed frowning upon his young wife. A gigantic, solid man, long of torso and limb, he stood three-quarters of a head taller than his tallest companion. His low forehead was hidden beneath light brown bangs, his dark eyes were wide set, his nose short and straight. His lips were red and small and round as cherries. His hair, cut like a page's, fell just to his shoulders, framing a long, horselike face with a massive jaw that overwhelmed his face, though he could not be called ugly. It was not until he walked toward us that I saw he had a sparse mustache and goatee, both better suited to a raw youth than a man of thirty-four years.

When he stepped up to Caterina, he smiled, revealing crowded, over-large teeth, but his eyes held no joy, only guardedness. He took in the golden glory of his bride—precisely twenty years his junior—with only the briefest flicker of carnal admiration. He was ill at ease; he glanced anxiously about until a sextet of armed guards encircled him, and the chief of them gave a short nod that it was safe to proceed.

"Madonna Caterina," he said stiffly, in a husky bass, and gave a perfunctory bow. "Beloved consort, Countess of Imola, I'm glad to meet you. How lovely you look." His unimpressive little speech was halting and clearly rehearsed; he spoke with such a pronounced Ligurian accent—nasalizing half his words and swallowing most of his *r*'s—that we all had to listen keenly to make out what he said. All the ermine and silver embroidery in the world could not hide the fact that he still sounded like a backward commoner from a tiny fishing village.

When Caterina, flushed from heat and nerves, proffered her hand, he took it clumsily and led her to the Milanese ambassador and the bishop, whose florid praise for her beauty made her husband's words seem all the more lackluster. After the two dignitaries fawned over her a moment more, Girolamo grew impatient and led her over to a copse of tall, ancient oaks, accompanied by the guards.

I watched from a short distance, discreetly trying to swat away mosquitoes as the two of them spoke. Girolamo presented a necklace of very large pearls to his wife, and Caterina responded with gratitude; he tried, awkwardly, to fasten it about her neck, but grew frustrated and left the task to a guard. Through it all, he kept glancing about, utterly distracted and wearing a faint, sullen scowl; at the end, when Caterina ventured a few questions, he cut her short with a wave of his giant hand. And then he raised his voice so that Caterina's maids and I, and all his male companions, could hear.

"I wasn't happy," he said, in his peasant's accent, "when I heard you were coming. I wasn't joking when I said there was plague, and there are men plotting to kill me—and now I'm forced to expose myself in a public procession through the streets! I sent a letter to Imola explaining these things to you. Didn't you get it?"

For the first time, he fastened a distinctly menacing gaze on his bride, and became very, very still. He drew up to his full height to emphasize the point that the crown of Caterina's head did not come so high as his shoulder; although his hands remained at his side, they coiled into fists.

Caterina, too, grew still. She dropped her gaze, now flinty, and tucked her chin in a manner that usually preceded an outburst of temper. She held this pose for only a few seconds and looked up at her consort with a smile only slightly less disingenuous than his had been.

"I did not," she replied with cloying sweetness, in a breathless, feminine voice I would never have expected from her lips. "I would never want to endanger you or disobey you. Forgive me: I was so eager to see you in the flesh that I could wait no longer. And now, having met you, my happiness is complete."

The last sentences were uttered with gushing obsequiousness; Caterina was mocking him openly. Girolamo, however, did not yet know Caterina well enough to know it. He digested her words and nodded to indicate her reply was acceptable.

"Let's go then," he said flatly, "and make quick work of this. I have pressing business." He turned his back on his noble-born wife without the simple courtesy of leave-taking, and waved to his men as he headed back to the horses.

Caterina did not move. Instead, she stood staring in the direction of the vacant spot where Girolamo had stood, her craven smile rapidly fading, her eyes narrowing with suppressed rage. While the others were mounting their horses and hurrying back to carriages and wagons, I touched her elbow.

"Your Illustrious Highness," I said. "We must go, too."

Her back was to all the others; only I could see her face, hear her voice.

"Ignorant fucking fisherman," she muttered softly, then fixed the artificial smile upon her lips and turned back to her waiting entourage.

Caterina rode on horseback the rest of the way while the maids and I rode in her carriage; as we drew closer to the city, we were obliged to stop every quarter mile for Caterina to dismount so that she could be greeted by scarlet-clad cardinals and prominent Romans. By nightfall, we arrived at the palace of the Cardinal of Urbino on the northern outskirts of the city. Despite the grandeur of the dwelling—newly renovated, with a marble façade, columns, friezes, and pediments—the street leading to it was in disrepair. Weeds sprouted between the bricks, and our coachman had to shoo away grazing goats; hares scattered in front of the horses' hooves and quickly took refuge in a field across from the palace.

Exhausted, Caterina slept soundly despite the unrelenting heat; she did not stir even when wolves howled beneath our bedchamber window.

I woke at daybreak to the sounds of retching, and rolled from the bed to discover my naked mistress huddled over the basin, emptying her stomach. I found a cloth, wet it with water from the pitcher by the basin, and gently lifted her damp hair to press the cool cloth against the back of her neck.

When she had finished, she straightened and looked up at me. Her face was ghastly pale, her eyes and nose streaming.

"Was it the food?" I asked. We had both dined on a surfeit of rich dishes and a good deal of wine.

She shook her head. Her entire body was trembling and her brow slicked with sweat from the oppressive heat. "He is a horrid man," she whispered. "A boor and a bully. I want to go home."

I freshened the cloth with more water and cleaned her face. I considered telling her that her bridegroom had simply been nervous and in ill sorts, that he was surely a nicer fellow than he had seemed, but that would have been a lie. Instead I said, "I am with you, Madonna. He would have to kill me first before I let him hurt you."

Perhaps I said the wrong thing; her eyes filled with sudden tears. But she

144

swallowed them deliberately, and said, in a stronger voice, "I'm not sick. It's just this damnable heat."

I judged the first statement to be true, the second a lie, but did not contradict her. Instead I rinsed the cloth, wrung it out, and pressed it to her warm brow.

"Ride with me," she said. "I want you by my side today."

She would not listen to my protests, but made me put aside my widow's unadorned black, and gave me a gown of cobalt silk embroidered with silvery white leaves; it was only slightly too short, and a bit too full in the bodice.

Despite the heat and the sun, already relentless at that early hour, she dressed in her full wedding regalia: a kirtle of black damask imprinted with a pattern of roses, and quilted with gold thread in a diamond pattern; her black bodice and sleeves were similarly quilted and studded with gold beads. Over this went an overdress of crimson satin and a heavy black damask cloak embroidered with the Sforza crest. Large rubies hung from her ears and around her neck on gold chains thicker than my thumb, along with the long strand of pearls from Girolamo.

It was Pentecost, and all of Rome was in a festive mood. Girolamo arrived wearing a faint, forced smile, a sullen gaze, and a shimmering silk tunic of Riario sky blue, embroidered with the golden oak. He and his male entourage led the way on horseback, followed by Caterina on a white mare. I rode just behind my mistress, ahead of representatives of the most powerful Roman families—the Gonzaga, the Orsini, the Colonna—and her large Milanese contingent. We made our way through the heart of the city, along the broad Via Recta, roughly paralleling the course of the River Tiber and recently repaved with brick and widened by Sixtus. Rome hosts hundreds of churches, more than I had ever seen, and every bell was ringing; their chimes, along with the cheers from the crowd that lined the street, deafened me.

Caterina's nerves were forgotten. Once in public, she was again the poised, confident contessa, wife of the second most important man in Rome; she turned her head from side to side as she waved to the masses, allowing me a glimpse of her joyous, beaming face.

We wended our way past countless churches, most of them in serious disrepair, with broken spires, missing bricks, broken windows, and stone steps so badly worn by the centuries as to be unnavigable. There were shops—some new, some old, most selling religious items to pilgrims, who were obliged to traverse the Via Recta on their way to holy sites—and parks, some desolate and overgrown, and the occasional cluster of filthy shacks. There were also massive palaces belonging to the wealthy families and to the equally wealthy cardinals; I imagined that the ancient Roman temples, when new, had appeared much as these square white travertine structures, their entrances flanked by marble columns topped with ornate pediments, the whole embellished wherever possible with the forms of gods and cherubs.

Our cavalcade turned west and crossed the bridge leading to the imposing papal fortress that once housed the emperor Hadrian's bones. This was the Castel Sant'Angelo, a squat, stark cylinder, many stories high, of brick so bleached and weathered its original color was uncertain. Some nine hundred years earlier, it was said, when the city was in the throes of a deadly plague, the Archangel Michael appeared atop the fortress and sheathed his sword; with this act, the pestilence retreated and Rome was saved. As we passed over the River Tiber—murky brown, littered with floating garbage and reeking of raw sewage—bile rose in my throat, and I covered my nose with my hand.

From there, our way led straight to Saint Peter's Square, where papal guards held back the cheering throngs. At the steps leading up to the gatehouse in front of the basilica, we dismounted. I stayed close behind Caterina as she, Girolamo, and a Milanese orator were met by a middle-aged cardinal, whose height and long limbs marked him as one of the groom's many cousins. This was Giuliano della Rovere, who otherwise resembled Girolamo not at all: Giuliano's features were even, his jaw square, his cheeks sculpted, his nose straight, his chin delicate, with an attractive cleft. He was, in a word, pretty, and his gestures and movements graceful and refined. The rest of the nuptial entourage followed us through the arched gateways and across the atrium known as the Garden of Paradise to the church proper.

As I write this some thirty years later, the old basilica is no more, having been replaced by something new and shining and obscenely grand; I am grateful to have had the opportunity to set foot in it before its destruction. For the original Saint Peter's—worn and stained, patched and crumbling as it was—dazzled not the eye but the soul. Its most impressive trait was not its architecture; the sanctuary was laid out in the simple shape of a Latin cross, with a broad central nave supported on either side by interior columns and flanked by two smaller aisles on the right and left, the whole covered by a leaky gabled roof. Nor was its adornment impressive; the great dark wooden doors were plain and deeply scarred, the marble floors worn and patternless, the small windows set high, admitting only narrow shafts of sunlight. Set upon a high platform of dark gray marble, beneath a plain, scarred wooden crucifix and a frieze supported by four spiral columns, was the altar, covered with gold brocade. Above the frieze, in a small half-cupola built into the wall, was the basilica's most notable work of art: a mural of Christ attended by Saint Peter and Constantine, its builder.

None of these things awed me as much as its overwhelming vastness and its age. Its length and breadth allowed the gathering of several hundred souls in the central nave alone, and its height was more than three full stories. The windows were so high they blocked all view, forcing one's attention away from external matters onto the spiritual. The instant I stepped inside, I felt a thrill, knowing that beneath my feet lay the bones of the first martyrs and all the popes, including Peter himself. Here trod Nero and Constantine and all the powerful men of Rome, past and present. And though the air was close and warm, filmed with the smoke of incense and redolent of human sweat, I breathed it in, and felt sanctified.

We made our way down the right aisle, passing the marble columns and the hushed congregation of hundreds, rich and poor alike. Upon the tall dais containing the altar, Pope Sixtus IV sat on an overlarge throne, surrounded by a scarlet flock of some two dozen cardinals.

Bona had raised me to revere the Holy Father, and despite my anger at God over Matteo's death, I was still awed by the realization that I stood on the very ground hallowed by the bones of Saint Peter, staring at his successor.

The former Francesco della Rovere was grotesquely obese, a mountain of jiggling flesh covered by white linen robes and a chasuble of bright gold brocade edged with panels of crimson velvet; his cloak was of white satin embroidered with red and gold thread. On his crown sat a mitre of white silk trimmed with gold braid and studded with rubies, amethysts, topaz, and emeralds. A large pectoral cross of gold inlaid with diamonds rested upon his wheezing chest.

His square head was massive, his body even more so; even seated, he was clearly as tall and long-limbed as his gargantuan "nephew," Girolamo, though his large bones were covered by mounds of fat. He was clean-shaven and nearly bald, with a bloated, jowly face that dripped sweat despite the efforts of two attendants who stood on either side of his throne waving two great ceremonial fans. His nose was straight and long, with a hooked tip, and wide, flaring nostrils; the whole looked as though it had been squashed deep into full, puffy cheeks. His long chin and jaw were lost in folds of fat, and he seemed to have no lips at all. The whites of his eyes were yellowed beneath heavy lids and fine, sharply arched brows; the jaded intelligence in those eyes was unsettling.

Della Rovere was a brilliant man, born to an impoverished peasant family in the Ligurian village of Savona. Young Francesco realized early that the church was his one way out of a miserable existence as a fisherman and joined the Franciscan Order. He rose quickly to the highest ranks, eventually becoming its general. He claimed surprise when Pope Paul II gave him his cardinal's hat, and was outraged when, after Paul died and della Rovere was promptly elected pope, charges of bribery were leveled at him.

We paused before the altar, where two braziers and a censer hung. I took my place beside the orator from Milan, the ambassadors, and the rest of the wedding party while Cardinal della Rovere, Girolamo, and Caterina ascended the gray marble steps to the altar, genuflecting there, then crossing to the right hand, where the pope and his cardinals sat. At the top of the stairs, Cardinal della Rovere turned to take her elbow, and led her to the pope on his throne. She knelt with swanlike grace, her shoulders square, her neck held high to emphasize its sweep, and kissed first the pope's slipper, then his ring.

Sixtus's bored, pompous expression transformed into a brilliant grin, revealing at last his lips—small and round, like his son's—and gray, toothless gums. He squeezed Caterina's hand affectionately, and patted the chairs on either side of him. Girolamo sat on his right, Caterina on his left, and for the next three hours, we suffered through an interminable mass, during which Sixtus, from time to time, favored Caterina with smiles, and the Spanish ambassador, obliged to stand with the wedding party the entire time, fainted dead away and was carried off.

When mass was over, every soul in the expectant crowd remained to see what followed. Cardinal della Rovere rose and directed Caterina to kneel again before His Holiness. She kissed the pope's red velvet slipper a second time, and remained kneeling while the orator from Milan stepped from beside me and, after clearing his throat nervously, produced a piece of paper from his cloak and read a summary, in Latin, of Caterina's marvelous virtues. This went on to nauseating excess, until Sixtus, smiling and with the kindliest of manners, cut him short with a wave and praised him for a job well done. He then motioned for Girolamo to stand up and take his place beside his bride.

Girolamo took Caterina's hand while Sixtus recited the marriage ceremony; his voice was forceful, deep, resonant, his enunciation as lacking as his teeth. His consonants were indistinct, his sibilants as slurred as a drunkard's. Even so, his delivery was compelling, for as a young man, he had devoted himself not only to the diligent study of theology and philosophy, but also to the art of diction and oration, with the result that the only remnant of his peasant origins was a slight nasality to his speech.

At the pope's direction, Girolamo, ashen from nerves and unsmiling, slipped a plain gold band onto Caterina's finger, then bent low to kiss her quickly.

At this, Sixtus clapped his hands in boyish delight, his lips curving upward in a black cavernous grin, the corners disappearing beneath the ponderous folds of his cheeks. "Come, my darling, come!" He held out his giant, pudgy hand to Caterina.

She took it and began to kneel again, but he stopped her and signaled to Girolamo, who stepped behind his wife to unclasp the pearls around her neck. Sixtus snapped his fingers at Cardinal della Rovere, sitting nearby; the cardinal rose with alacrity and handed a small velvet box to His Holiness.

Sixtus opened the box and held up the necklace to the dim light, so that those near the front of the congregation could see it: four heavy chains of gold, each thick as two plump papal fingers, hung from a single clasp; a large emerald was set in the center of the first, with six smaller emeralds on either side. The second chain was similarly adorned with rubies, the third with diamonds, and the fourth with sapphires. Such a piece could easily have purchased a cardinal's large palazzo in the city. A collective sigh of appreciation echoed through the sanctuary.

"This," the pope announced, with hissed and slurred sibilants and explosive *p*'s, "befits you better than plain pearls. Girolamo could not be a luckier man. I had heard you were a beauty, my darling, but such a simple word cannot properly describe you. You are more dazzling than any of these jewels."

"I lack the proper words to thank you, Your Holiness," Caterina said in her still-girlish voice. "Your generosity is beyond measure, and more than I deserve." With that, she knelt.

As she did, Sixtus drew her toward him, pulling her head and shoulders toward his lap and obliging her to stretch out her lovely neck. The position was awkward and vaguely unsavory, yet she held perfectly still as His Holiness managed, with thick, clumsy fingers, to fasten the necklace. Then he bade Caterina rise, and along with Girolamo, she turned and faced the sighing congregation to show off the jewels.

Sixtus lifted an upraised palm at the cardinals seated nearby on the dais; they immediately rose, and Cardinal della Rovere introduced Caterina to each one. Besides the pope's relatives, there were an Orsini, a Colonna, three Frenchmen, a pair of Spaniards, and a Greek.

But the one I remembered best was the first, who held the envied seat closest to the pope: a tall Catalan, with a faint accent and the deep black hair and olive complexion of his people. After studying law, he had served many years as vice-chancellor of the Curia. Though he had passed his fortieth year, he was still tall and straight, with a powerful chest and square shoulders and an aura of virile masculinity. From the moment Caterina ascended the platform, he rarely took his gaze from her. His oval face was marked by a broad, prominent nose, full lips, and a high forehead; his brown eyes, set beneath striking black brows and high, angular cheekbones, revealed a sensitive, lively spirit and shrewd intelligence. When the young Countess of Imola looked up at him, he met her gaze with a brazenly flirtatious smile before he murmured a blessing. Even after Cardinal Giuliano delle Rovere had led her on to the next introduction, the Spaniard continued watching her with intense desire, coupled with growing determination. I remember thinking, with faint outrage, *He means to have her.*

Borgia was his name. Cardinal Rodrigo Borgia.

Twelve

The postnuptial festivities continued at the Orsini Palazzo across the Tiber from Saint Peter's. Though exhausted and flushed from the heat—even the grand halls, liberally sprinkled with costly perfumes and garlanded with roses, could not hide the smell of sweat—Caterina kept her diplomatic smile firmly in place as she suffered through a twenty-two-course banquet that continued late into the evening.

After the last toast was made to the health and fertility of the happy couple, Girolamo Riario collected the bridal entourage and drove us a short distance north to the Palazzo Riario. Near the front entry stood a large fountain featuring the god Neptune, encircled by lit torches so that the flowing water sparkled golden as our carriages passed. We passed several windows, all of them glowing yellow in honor of the bride, and rolled to a stop in front of an intimidatingly huge brass door.

Caterina's suite of rooms was grander and more lavishly furnished than any she had ever enjoyed in her father's court. I oversaw the undressing of my lady, and the brushing out of her pale gold hair all the way to her narrow waist. I myself drew the white satin sheets up over her exposed breasts before leaving her to her fate. Caterina's eyes were wide, her tone clipped, yet she made a brave effort to joke; I regretted knowing little about the marriage act, as I wanted to comfort her, but found myself without words. A Ligurian house servant led me to adjacent quarters—larger, more luxurious than those I was accustomed to, with a curtained bed all my own, and two generous cots for the chambermaids Caterina had brought from Milan. I opened all the windows to catch the humid breeze, then fell naked onto the soft feather mattress.

I was wakened little more than an hour later by the bell suspended from my ceiling; my mistress was summoning aid. The memory that this was her wedding night brought me to my feet, where I pulled on a nightgown.

In the contessa's new quarters, the table lamp was still burning. The bed drapes were open; Caterina sat propped against the pillows, one arm across her breasts to hold the sheet against them. The pooling white satin bore the imprint of more than one body, the extra pillow an imprint of a large head; all the coverlets had been kicked aside onto the floor. Caterina's long hair was tangled, disheveled, and her eyes narrowed in an effort to hide the misery in them.

"Wine," she said brusquely.

A carafe and upturned goblets sat on a low table several steps away, near the long arching window, unshuttered to admit the stink of the nearby Tiber; beyond lay the Holy City, dark and brooding save for a few faintly flickering palace windows. I filled a cup halfway from the carafe and looked about for the pitcher. Married or not, Caterina was only fourteen, and still took her wine mixed with water.

She caught my eye and shook her head. "Just wine," she said.

I filled the goblet to the brim and handed it to her. She was full awake and could easily have fetched her own drink; I lingered, waiting for her to initiate a conversation.

She took a large gulp; her eyes watered and she coughed a bit, but she immediately forced down another swallow, then another.

"The poets are all liars." She spoke offhandedly, with a forced dark humor, but her lip trembled faintly.

I suppressed a yawn as I asked, "How so, Madonna?"

"He is oafish," she said sourly, "and his breath stinks. He has hair all over his back and chest and stomach, like an ape." She stared at me. "Are all men so hairy?"

She moved her legs aside; I noted the subtle request, and sat down upon the cool sheets. My experience in the subject was limited to the fact that I had twice seen Matteo without his shirt. "I cannot speak for all men," I said. "But I know one who did not have so much, just a small bit at his chest. I believe it varies."

"It's disgusting," she said. She took more wine, then fell silent a long moment. When she summoned her courage, she added, "Is it supposed to hurt?"

The question took me aback; Caterina had no clue that Matteo and I had not lived as man and wife, and I meant to keep her ignorant of the fact.

"Only the first time," I said; of that, I was fairly certain, and the rest was embellishment for my lady's sake. "After that, it grows . . . pleasurable. With practice."

"I hope so," she said, "but the brute spent little time at it. He was here and gone in five minutes." She let go a single wracking sob and reached for me.

I performed the duty for which I had been summoned: I wrapped my arms about her, lifted her heavy hair off her damp neck and stroked it, murmuring words of comfort.

When she finally composed herself, she said darkly, "I will do what I must. But he has nothing but contempt for me, and I only hatred for him. I will bear him children—for my purposes, not his."

The following day Caterina's moodiness was replaced by incandescent joy as she presided over a tournament in her honor. Like her father, she adored the pomp and ceremony that went with noble status. So long as she was not forced to endure Girolamo's company by herself, she was infectiously cheerful, and with good reason. While her husband might have been stingy with his affections, he was generous when it came to matters of money. Caterina's every request was indulged. Even though she had received a new trousseau of the most fashionable clothing, Girolamo allowed her to have several new gowns of her own design made, and new jewelry. He also left the running of the house entirely to her, so that she might make whatever changes she wished to the staff or the furnishings. Her first decision was that I should sleep in her bed when her husband was not present.

Over the next weeks, she had ample opportunity to enjoy herself, as she and her husband had been invited to the palaces of every noble family and several cardinals. On most occasions, I accompanied her, introduced as her "cousin," and came to see that there was little difference between the face Girolamo presented to the world and the one his wife and her entourage saw. He took advantage of his position by being surly and remarkably crude to all, telling the most raucous jokes in mixed company. He smiled and laughed in earnest only when he was being led off to a game of dice or cards. At such times, he would disappear for hours, and Caterina and I would return home without him. To her relief, he came only rarely to her bedroom.

Only once during those days did I glimpse Girolamo's human face, when the young couple's connubial bliss was interrupted for a visit to the eight-hundred-year-old basilica of Santi Apostoli, a short walk from our palazzo. We were joined there by His Holiness and several of his cardinals, including Rodrigo Borgia, the Catalan with the sensuous, leering gaze.

His manner markedly somber, Sixtus wore a simple red skullcap and red silk chasuble over his white linen robes. We waited patiently as he made his way up the steps to the basilica's entrance; it took two cardinals, each gripping the old man's arm, to hoist his corpulent form up the stairs and into the church. By the time Sixtus tottered up to the sanctuary's threshold, sweat streamed from the edges of his skullcap down his brow and ashen cheeks. Girolamo went at once to his father's side and, in an uncharacteristic display, embraced him with grim, urgent affection.

The two walked arm in arm—Sixtus huffing and teetering as his son did his best to shoulder the bulk of his father's weight—to a side chapel, where a temporary throne had been placed for His Holiness. This rested directly in front of a shining marble funerary monument, the floor beneath it still bearing dust from the artist's chisel.

Four times my height, and half as wide, the monument had a massive rectangular base as high as my shoulder, upon which was inscribed the name of the deceased: the noble young cardinal Pietro Riario, Archbishop of Florence and "nephew" to Sixtus, had perished at the age of twenty-nine.

Above this was carved a bier, its base supported by the busts of three winged seraphs. Upon the bier lay the three-dimensional, life-sized figure of a young man with even, rounded features, more attractive than Girolamo's, though I saw the similarity in the nose and eyes. His form was draped in priestly robes and his head bore a plain mitre; his face wore an expression of placid repose. Behind him was a marble wall featuring a bas relief of a seated Virgin with the Christ child on her lap; on her left was an adoring, kneeling Girolamo, and on her right, a kneeling and notably thinner and younger Sixtus, the former accompanied by Saint Paul and the latter, Peter.

Girolamo had had an older brother, Pietro, the recipient of Sixtus's special favor. At a young age, Pietro had been singled out by Sixtus for an education from the Franciscans, followed by time at universities. Sixtus lavished appointments—bishoprics, benefices, and ultimately a cardinalship—upon the lad, who, unlike his dull younger brother, had inherited his father's shrewdness and wits. Pietro had also inherited a fondness for food and drink and women, which some said led to his early, unexpected demise: he had been discovered dead in his bed by a servant trying to rouse him. Others, including one of Caterina's chambermaids, Teodora, said that he had been poisoned because his unchecked power had provoked a great deal of jealousy among the other cardinals.

The tragedy had occurred three and a half years earlier; only now had the grand monument to him finally been unveiled. At the sight of it, Sixtus pulled away from his surviving son's grasp, and staggered up to the towering sculpture. He put his hand upon the marble and let go a low wail before sinking to his knees.

Girolamo hurried to him. Giant though he was, he lacked the strength to pull the massive pontiff to his feet; he signaled for help, and a trio of cardinals and the patriarch Stefano Colonna managed to get him to the papal throne, where he sat, gasping for breath and weeping.

Girolamo remained at the monument only briefly. All eyes save mine were focused on the grief-stricken Sixtus, but I saw something unsettling in Girolamo's profile, in the way he, too, pressed his palm to the marble. When at last he took his hand away and turned to join his father, his eyes made me think of how my own must have looked in the hours after I learned my Matteo had died of poison: narrowed with love and grief, and the bitterest rage.

The days and nights passed quickly, and the miserable heat, along with the deadly fevers it brought, finally abated somewhat, though it was still much hotter than Milan had ever been.

I despised Rome. Outside of the grander, newer churches and palaces, and the few main thoroughfares recently repaved by Sixtus, the streets were narrow, uneven, and heaped with horse manure and stinking sewage. Sometimes the breeze from the nearby Tiber was so foul that we closed the windows despite the heat. The homes of the wealthy were new and beautiful, but they were few compared to the hovels of the poor, who fed themselves by hunting down the small game that roamed the less trafficked streets, or by trapping the fish that swam in the river's filthy waters. Some areas were so unsafe, we dared not go there even by carriage, and at night, even the wealthiest areas were so dangerous that few ventured out without an escort of armed guards. We had lived at the Palazzo Riario for nearly a week before I discovered, aghast, that the windows on the uppermost floor and friezes on the flat, square roof hid crossbowmen and artillery, and that by sunset, soldiers patrolled the entire perimeter of the dwelling.

I assumed at first that this was due to the fact that Girolamo, as captain of the papal army and recent recipient of death threats, was being overly cautious. Such was not so, for as Caterina responded to social invitations, we saw that every palace was similarly guarded. Rome then was a far more dangerous place even than it is now. Wolves, wild dogs, and bands of armed thieves roamed the dark streets, and the Orsini and Colonna families, while maintaining polite relations during the day, carried on a continuing bloody vendetta each night. Each morning brought with it fresh corpses huddled on doorsteps or alleyways, or sprawled in public streets, or bloated and floating in the Tiber.

The world inside the walls of the Palazzo Riario could not have been more different. Caterina and I were accustomed to life with Bona, who, for a duke's wife, eschewed finery and overt luxury. Although the hundred-year-old castle at Pavia was marvelously appointed, it seemed aged, spare, and cramped when compared to the glory of the Palazzo Riario, with its vast rooms filled with ornate furniture, statues, paintings, and frescos, and its walls, floors, ceilings, spiral staircases, and columns made of glittering marble. The size of its courtyard and gardens was that of Milan's and Pavia's combined.

Such luxury came with a price, however. Just as the court at Pavia had trembled in fear of Duke Galeazzo's wrath, so did those at the Palazzo Riario tremble when Girolamo was in an ill mood. Unfortunately, it was a rare day that found Girolamo in good cheer; the entire household rejoiced when its lord traveled, often to oversee troops fighting to extend Riario control of the Romagna.

Luckily, Girolamo wanted little to do with his wife. They spent no time together privately, and did not dine together. Girolamo never invited Caterina to his chambers, nor came to Caterina's wing of the palace except to demand his conjugal privilege, usually late at night, when he was incoherently drunk.

On those nights, I felt sorry for my lady, thinking that she would never find happiness in love. Until, that is, we attended a party hosted by Cardinal Rodrigo Borgia.

One evening in early June, Caterina and I rode with Girolamo in a carriage flanked by eight mounted guards, though the Palazzo Borgia was less than a twenty-minute walk away. At first, I didn't understand why Girolamo rode with us—a carriage with his male attendants followed ours, indicating that Girolamo intended to return later than we ladies—until he began to speak.

That night, Caterina was a vision in a gown of shimmering silver silk, with pale blue velvet sleeves, and a rolled silver headdress from which hung a diaphanous veil; Teodora had spent an hour with a hot poker creating the long, loose curls artfully framing the contessa's face. At fourteen, Caterina was growing quickly into a stunningly beautiful young woman, and only the crudest, most self-absorbed of men could have looked on her that evening and not drawn in his breath, then released it with a torrent of compliments.

Girolamo climbed into the carriage, gave her a glance, and launched into a lecture.

"Look out for Cardinal Borgia," he told his wife, though his obvious cheer at the prospect of revelry undercut the direness of his warning. "Don't let him get you alone; he can't keep his paws off women. If he touches you, push him away and come tell me. I'll give him an earful."

His peasant's accent was thicker than usual; his breath reeked of wine and for once he was inclined to talk. Borgia, he said, was the worst sort of scoundrel, who openly kept a mistress and had a young son, whom he had convinced Sixtus to legitimize (a fact that obviously infuriated Girolamo). Borgia was also a political opportunist who, when his uncle became Pope Calixtus III, was made cardinal while only in his twenties. Extraordinarily ambitious, he sought the most lucrative position in Rome: that of vice-chancellor of the Curia, which oversaw the administration of the entire papal government . . . and thus had the most opportunity to collect bribes.

However, the position called for a doctorate in canon law, which Borgia lacked. Years of study were required, but Borgia attained his degree after less than a year. This attracted a good deal of enmity from the other cardinals. Yet Borgia proved himself to be not only competent, but also so talented at his role that all complaints ceased and were replaced by admiration. With the full approval of his colleagues and later popes, he had continued at the job for twenty years, growing wealthier than them all.

This latter fact soon became apparent. As we approached the street leading to Borgia's home, we were stopped by a line of armed soldiers, who, upon recognizing Girolamo, saluted and waved us through. The large public square in front of the Palazzo Borgia had been cleared of all but partygoers and was encircled by a hundred massive, flickering tapers on brass candlesticks as tall as my shoulder and garlanded with red roses and wreaths of blooming jasmine. The cobblestones had been swept and sprinkled with perfume and dried rose petals to mask the river's smell, and as guests milled about the square, musicians with flutes and tambourines played a distinctly Spanish tune while a tenor wailed a passionate love song in Catalan.

Our carriage rolled to a stop near a statue of a larger-than-life bronze bull, its horned head rearing upward in a display of ferocity, its hooves lifted in mid-trot. Beside it stood a large fountain, surrounded by lanterns on poles, the better to display the bull and the splashing water. I tilted my head back to get a good view of the palazzo itself. Clearly it belonged to the richest man in Rome, for it was five stories tall and boasted thirty massive windows across its breadth. From the top floor, a huge banner of the Borgia bull—purplish red, the color of ripening mulberries, set against a field of pure gold—had been unfurled across the width of twelve windows, and fell to the second floor, grazing the triangular marble pediment above the main entrance. Lanterns hung from the windows to illuminate the banner and to distract viewers from the castellated roof, where the mouths of cannon and artillery guns peeked out from between the battlements.

As Girolamo stepped from the carriage, and the coachman helped Caterina out, a pair of trumpeters blared notice of our arrival. Borgia, who had been talking nearby with a group of fellow cardinals, hurried over to greet us.

He wore a gown of white silk, neatly tailored to show off a narrow waist and broad shoulders, with a short scarlet cape lined with cloth of gold. The hair beneath his red skullcap was thick and black, without a hint of silver, and the eyes beneath his severe brows were filled with such celebratory giddiness that I thought at first he was drunk. But his tone was brisk, his words unslurred. Borgia was moderate in his approach to wine and food; he preferred other forms of excess.

He greeted Girolamo so perfunctorily as to be rude, but the captain of the papal army seemed relieved that all attention was immediately diverted to his young wife. When Caterina took a step toward Borgia and extended her hand, the cardinal gasped as if he had just seen a vision of the Virgin.

"Your Illustrious Highness," he said loudly, in order to be heard over the music and the crowd, "you are assuredly the most beautiful creature here! How the silver suits you; it makes your blue eyes gleam like the stars!" He bent low and kissed her hand, lingering over it a long moment to breathe in her perfume—attar of roses—until Girolamo fidgeted.

At that point, Borgia gave Caterina's hand a squeeze before letting it go, then turned grinning to her husband. "Again you prove yourself the better man, my lord Girolamo, to have succeeded in winning the loveliest woman in Italy as your wife! You honor us all by bringing her here. And," he added as an afterthought, "by your presence, of course." He winked at Caterina. "All this is in your honor, my dear"—he gestured sweepingly at the celebration around us—"to celebrate your marriage to our beloved captain."

He then turned to me, and took my hand. His own was hot and slightly damp, and it held mine with an unsettling strength. He bent down and pressed his lips tenderly against my skin, then raised his head and looked on me as if I were the only woman in all the world, and he the only man.

"Madonna Dea," he said. "A suitable name for a goddess. What a perfect companion you make for our beloved countess here: the two most beautiful women in Rome, one golden, one dark and mysterious like our Spanish women!" He chuckled. "And they, of course, have the hottest blood. . . ."

I began to pull my hand away, but he gripped it fast, trapping it for an instant before finally releasing it with a wolfish grin.

By this time, a maid dressed in a mulberry red gown with a gold apron appeared with a tray of wine-filled goblets. Borgia urged us all to take a goblet, then murmured into the maid's ear. She departed with a careful curtsy and disappeared into the milling crowd, where tens of servants in mulberry and gold livery delivered wine and samplings of food to cardinals and nobles.

In the interim, we were led to the group Borgia had recently abandoned, and presented to each person there: to Cardinal Giuliano della Rovere, of the handsome face and delicate hands; his sixteen-year-old cousin, Raffaele Riario, a girlish lad; and Bishop Girolamo Basso della Rovere, a heavyset man who much resembled a younger Sixtus. Girolamo greeted them all with casual familiarity, if not affection, and after briefly praising Caterina's loveliness, they returned to their previous topic of conversation: the hopes of Girolamo Basso and of Raffaele that Sixtus would give them cardinals' hats before the year's end. Borgia proclaimed his enthusiasm and support for both candidates, while the handsome, effeminate Giuliano della Rovere, already a cardinal, looked on Borgia with thinly veiled disgust.

In the middle of a flowery explanation as to why Raffaele's exceptional piety and brilliance had earned him the red hat despite his youth, Borgia stopped suddenly and pointed directly overhead.

"Look!" he crowed.

His exclamation was punctuated by a series of muted booms. We tilted our heads back and looked up at the cascade of fireworks lighting the night sky. A starburst of white gave birth to a bloom of spiraling crimson stars, which spun across the sky, then faded, only to be replaced by more bursts of white.

Borgia was standing beside Caterina, and nudged her gently. "In honor of the Sforza," he said, smiling slyly.

Another series of fireworks were born in the sky, expanding ever outward. These were of brilliant blue, followed by gold: the della Rovere/Riario colors, and all the men around us clapped, save Girolamo, who nodded in acknowledgment. Caterina kept her gaze fastened on the sky, her expression rapt, her lips parted as the light played upon her golden hair and silver dress. Borgia watched her from beneath lowered lids, pleased by her reaction.

When it was done, Borgia signaled the trumpeters, who played a short refrain. This was the cue for the servants in the street to usher the guests inside, beneath the great banner of the red bull. As we moved slowly toward the entrance, accompanied by the della Rovere clan and our host, a little boy—no more than three years old, with black hair and great dark eyes—pushed his way through the crowd and ran, on sturdy little legs, into Borgia's arms.

"Papa! Papa!" he cried, stretching out his arms, and set himself on a collision course with Borgia's knees.

Count Girolamo and Cardinal Giuliano della Rovere glanced down at the boy with irritation; a child was clearly out of place at such an event. But Borgia laughed, and in the instant before the boy crashed into his knees, reached down and swooped him up into his arms, with a playful bounce that made the child giggle.

"Cesare!" he exclaimed, with pure delight. "How did you find me, my boy? Where is your mother?"

"Over there." Cesare gestured carelessly behind him, without looking. "She says if I am good, I can stay a little while."

Borgia jiggled the boy in his arms and smiled dotingly at him. "And so you shall—if you are good." He looked up at the rest of us. The men were clearly familiar with the boy; Giuliano della Rovere smiled at him and pinched his cheek. "Your Illustrious Highness," Borgia said to Caterina, "this is my son and legitimate heir, Cesare Borgia. Cesare, this is Her Illustrious Highness, the Countess Caterina Sforza, consort of Captain Girolamo Riario."

He gently set Cesare down upon his feet. Scarcely past his toddling years, the boy executed a low bow with such a serious expression that Borgia, Cardinal Giuliano, and I could not suppress our chuckles.

Caterina directed her most charming smile at the boy and made an exaggerated curtsy. "Cesare Borgia," she said liltingly. "You are very wise for your age. And you have the name of a king."

"And I shall be a king!" he announced, wielding an imaginary sword and pretending to run Girolamo through. To my surprise, Girolamo let out a yelp and, clutching his gut, staggered as though wounded, which delighted the boy no end.

We adults laughed again. "But there are no kings in Italy," I ventured good-naturedly—though, in fact, I was shocked by the fact that Borgia, long a cardinal, had a young son, "save for the King of Naples."

Borgia lifted him off his feet again. "You shall be a cardinal, like your father," he reproved him fondly, tapping the tip of the boy's nose playfully with a finger. "And perhaps one day, by the grace of God, a pope."

"Papa, wouldn't you rather be the father of a king? Or an emperor?" Cesare persisted stubbornly, which prompted more laughter. Something he saw made him fall suddenly silent, and cling more tightly to his father; we all turned, following his gaze, as two women approached.

The first was older, her loveliness long faded, her hair a dark ash blond streaked with silver. She was thin and short, with a sharp chin and large, faintly bulging eyes; her dress was of heavy black velvet and gold damask, despite the heat, yet she seemed unwilted. Her stern, humorless gaze was fixed on Cesare, but at the sight of Girolamo and Caterina, she paused and curtsied low, her face downcast. She remained in that position until Borgia said to them:

"My cousin, Adriana Mila, from Valencia. She is the widow of Ludovico Orsini, and helps to care for the children." He nodded at the second woman and said, "And this is their mother, Vannozza Catanei."

Caterina and I smiled and murmured greetings when Borgia introduced us in turn, though my lady's eyes widened a bit and remained so throughout the encounter. I could only hope I did not seem so dazed.

Vannozza—a solid woman, half a head shorter than Borgia, with a waist twice as thick—was dressed as grandly as any other woman in attendance, in a gown of gray-blue silk and a necklace heavy with sapphires and diamonds. Yet the effect was undercut by her décolletage—her bodice had been tightly laced, pushing her huge breasts up so comically high that she could rest her chin upon them. Her hair, which I suspected naturally matched her black eyebrows, was the flagrant orange of a dried apricot. She had recently put on weight; her flesh bulged out through the slashes in her sleeves along with her gossamer chemise, and the seams of the bodice just above her waist were straining. Her face was pleasingly oval, and her features were regular enough to be deemed handsome, if not beautiful. She could not have been more than twenty, and her flawless skin was as pale as the glittering marble on Borgia's walls, her eyes dark and lined with kohl. There was a vacancy in them, and a cold insolence.

She did not curtsy; the naked six-month-old infant on her hip precluded anything more than a polite nod. She studied us women carefully, solemnly, and when she shifted the plump babe to her other hip to keep it from pulling on her jeweled necklace, I saw the gold wedding band upon her finger. It had been put there not by Borgia, but by another man.

Borgia told her our names. I thought again of Bona, and what she would say if she knew I had just been introduced to a cardinal's courtesan and his son.

"Your Illustrious Highness," she said to Caterina, in a soft, low voice meant to please the male ear, but that was difficult to hear over the noise of the crowd. She nodded at me. "Madonna Dea."

"And this," Borgia said, brimming with paternal pride, as he took the infant from Vannozza's arms, "is our darling little Juan, the future captain of the papal army!" At Girolamo's sudden scowl, he added: "May he learn much from your magnificent example, Your Illustriousness!" He ignored the towel Vannozza had tucked under Juan's bare bottom, and held the giggling infant up to his lips to pepper him with loud, exaggerated kisses.

Vannozza watched without a breath of maternal emotion; instead, she glanced down at her elder son, who was jealously watching the exchange. A crease appeared between her black brows. "Cesare, are you disturbing your father?"

Cesare began to whine, but Borgia shook his head to silence him and placate Vannozza, and answered easily, "He has been behaving himself quite nicely." Nonetheless, he handed both children off to Madonna Adriana and Vannozza, who disappeared.

I was no stranger to luxury, having lived in the Castle Pavia and the Palazzo Riario, but I had never before seen such large rooms, so much fine marble and brightly colored Spanish tile, or so much gold (in the form of vases, spoons, pitchers, statuettes, inkpots, lamps, plates, plaques, and candelabra) so prominently displayed. Nor had I ever seen so many tapestries, most of them glittering with thread of gold, nor so many daybeds with covered canopies, all of them wide enough for two souls, in velvets and tasseled satins and one of vivid red silk. We were led past portraits of Borgia's illustrious ancestors in heavy gold frames—born in Spain, he was related to Alfonso the Great of Aragon, the first king of Naples—and into a banquet hall, where we were plied with Spanish wines and sherries, and treated to a number of exotic dishes, including a roast peacock with its plucked tail feathers artfully replaced in a dramatic display.

Borgia took care to sit next to Caterina during the feast; I was separated from my mistress by the French ambassador—a charming, sophisticated man—and his aide—a striking, athletic youth with tight blond curls—and could not hear everything Borgia said to her. But the gist was clearly flirtatious; Caterina laughed and tossed her head, enjoying the attention, while the Spanish cardinal leered shamelessly and made a point of constantly refilling her goblet himself. At one point he said something so outrageous that she let go a loud laugh that was also a startled gasp, and stifled it by clamping her hand over her mouth, too late.

I worried whether I should intervene. But a single dark look from Girolamo, several seats away from his bride, made her lower her hand and affect an air of dignity; Borgia noted it, too, and their conversation immediately grew more sedate.

After the feast, we were led to another hall, this one cleared of furniture. Musicians with flutes and tambourines reappeared, and Borgia led his cousin Adriana in a stately pavane, followed by Caterina and Girolamo, who were being honored that night. For Matteo's sake, I refused all invitations to dance.

Afterward the players struck up rousing galliards and hopping saltarel-
los. Girolamo was clumsy on his feet, and disappeared back into the crowd
after the first dance; Caterina, an excellent dancer, found her match in Rodrigo
Borgia. She partnered several times with him, and also with Monsieur Gerard, as he called himself, the young Frenchman with the tight milky blond
curls.

While I chatted with the French ambassador's wife—a haughty young
duchess with striking green eyes that perfectly matched her emerald satin
gown—I spied a young woman entering the hall. She did her best not to
draw attention to herself, sidling along the edges of the chamber, amid the
mulberry-and-yellow-clad servants, but her appearance was striking: she was
dressed like the Turkish women, swaddled from head to toe in a purple
cloak, with a purple veil held in place by a silver band just above her eyebrows. A matching veil covered her nose and mouth, leaving only her kohl-
lined eyes visible.

The duchess smiled slyly at her, and nodded as she passed by some distance away; the girl gave a quick nod, but did not slow, lest too many others
notice her. She moved directly to Caterina's husband, Girolamo, who was
off in a private corner having a very tense conversation with his young cousin,
the would-be cardinal Raffaele.

The mysterious woman walked up to Girolamo, bowed deeply to him,
and took his hand. She stood facing the corner so that, when she opened
her cloak, others could not see what lay beneath save for Girolamo and Raffaele, who gaped like the naïve boy he was.

The woman closed her cloak and led the now-smiling Girolamo from the
hall. The prurience in the duchess's tight-lipped little smile kept me from
asking her what had just happened; I could well imagine what plans the
Turkish woman, obviously hired by Borgia, had for the captain of the pope's
army. But before I could broach a new subject of conversation, a second
woman in a saffron-colored robe and veil appeared and led the Spanish ambassador away. When a third one appeared in bright blue-green and led the
French ambassador away, only steps from his duchess-wife's nose, the duchess clicked her tongue in feigned disapproval, but her cheer never faded.

I watched a dozen men leave the hall in the company of veiled women.
By this time, Borgia, red-faced and sweating, had retreated from the dance

floor. He was just lifting a goblet to his lips when Vannozza appeared; she caught his elbow and whispered into his ear. Whatever she said pleased him, and he kissed her full on the mouth before she quickly left the room.

My expression must have darkened when he did so—I could not help thinking of those of deep, sincere faith, like Bona, who would have been scandalized by such behavior—because my French companion said easily, "You must forgive Rodrigo. He is not one of those men who can easily hide his passion for life, for women, for love. He would far have preferred the life of a soldier to that of a cardinal, but the decision was made for him when he was born." She eyed me carefully. "Perhaps God made a mistake in designing him so. Or perhaps the fault lies in the Church, for making such demands upon its clergy."

I blushed and changed the subject.

Some time after, Cardinal Borgia made his way toward the exit, pausing, as he passed by us, to wink at the duchess, who tossed her head and laughed aloud.

I did my best to put the Spanish cardinal's behavior out of my mind, until a veiled girl in yellow appeared and led the French duchess away. I was curious, and followed them at a discreet distance; as I stepped over the threshold into the hall to see them disappear down the corridor, a hand touched my forearm.

I started, and turned to see a veiled woman with smiling eyes standing before me.

"Madonna Dea," she said distinctly, in an accent more Roman than Turkish, "will you come with me?"

Taken aback, I demanded: "Where to?"

The crinkles in the corners of her eyes deepened. "To the garden of delights," she replied. "My master wishes to honor his special guests."

I hesitated, then decided to take her offer at face value. Borgia was certainly a grand entertainer, and he had planned the event to honor Caterina and Girolamo's marriage. It would be reasonable to have designed special entertainment for the more notable guests, instead of the entire three hundred now packed into the ballroom.

My guide navigated the corridor surely; we passed through another empty reception hall, then under graceful Moorish archways supported by slender, delicate columns. These led outside to a square courtyard of formal design, with a pair of carefully clipped orange trees flanking a fountain; a single lamp suspended from a pole beside the fountain provided the only illumination. We crossed to the far end, where a narrow corridor lay hidden between the outer and garden walls. My guide led me down the dark, moldy-smelling corridor, which, after some two dozen or so paces, terminated in a tall wooden gate.

My guide lifted the brass ring and struck it four times, slowly and delib-erately. The gate swung open to reveal Adriana Mila waiting on the other side, her thin, sallow face looking slightly ghoulish in the yellow glow of a lantern by the door.

In its light, I could see the vague outlines of a large square garden, en-closed by tall walls topped with delicate stone lattices in an arabesque de-sign. In the garden's center was a long, narrow reflecting pool, around whose perimeter were set small candle lamps covered with bags of paper cut out in Moorish designs. At the far end of the pool sat a stone fountain, its base supported by ten small stone lions; the gurgling water splashed with such intensity that it created a cool mist. Slabs of marble flanked the longer sides of the pool to create a small patio, and surrounding these were low box-wood hedges, then a carpet of grass.

Ten paces or so from the reflecting pool were canopied daybeds—three on one side of the pool, three on the other, separated from each other by several paces and a pair of broad potted palms that gave each a measure of privacy.

The single wall lamp and the few votives that flickered on tables beside the beds were insufficient to dispel the darkness and slight haze, which added to the sense of seclusion. I could make out the shapes of bodies stand-ing beside some of the daybeds, and hear the murmur of feminine voices, accompanied by the burbling of the fountains. From somewhere in the blackness came the low reedy warble of an exotic instrument playing a sen-suous, plaintive Arabian tune.

As we entered, my guide shed her cloak to reveal her costume: a tight, sleeveless bodice of tinkling coins that covered only her breasts, leaving her arms and waist bare, and pantaloons that were sheer from the top of her thigh to her ankle, completely revealing her legs. She pulled off her veil and shook her hair free; it fell unfettered to her waist, and she caught my hand again and led me deeper into the garden.

As we passed the first of the daybeds, the flickering votives on the adjacent table revealed a gowned woman reclining upon the bed, but my guide would not permit me to linger. She took me to the next daybed; it was covered in cool satin and stuffed with the softest down. It took some urging before I relented and settled back against the fat pillows. When I realized something was moving behind me in the darkness, I started, but it was only another girl in Turkish guise, waving a large fan to keep me cool.

When I nervously sat back again, my smiling guide went to the little table beside my bed, poured from a large golden pitcher into a silver goblet, and handed the latter to me.

"Drink, Madonna," she said sweetly.

I drank. Surprisingly, the wine was chilled, a welcome condition given the heat. It was also delicious, being mixed with a sweet cordial that tasted of blackberries and some mysterious herb that gave a bitter finish. I took a second sip and set it down, but my Turkish girl said, "Drink, Madonna, you must be very thirsty from dancing."

My guide pressed sweetmeats on me before I could protest, handing me a golden plate that held fried pastries dipped in honey and salted almonds.

Three small votive candles burned on my bedside table; above them hung a brazier, from whose sizzling coals wafted sweet, spicy-smelling coils of smoke. There was also a golden bowl filled with liquid, atop which floated rose petals and white jasmine blossoms. The girl picked up a folded cloth, dipped it in the water, and ran it over my forehead. Like my wine, this had also been chilled, and I shuddered at its delicious touch; even though I had done nothing more strenuous than converse, the reception hall had been filled with overheated bodies, and it was a great relief to enjoy the cool drink, cloth, and the breeze from the fan. I submitted as the girl tenderly wiped my brow, cheeks, and neck, then urged me to dip my hands in the golden bowl; she took them in her own and washed them with great care, then dried them in a fresh towel.

When she was done, she took the bowl and moved to my feet as a third girl appeared out of the darkness and began to remove my slippers. This caused me to sit up and launch a fresh protest.

"Hush, Madonna," she said with a supremely knowing smile. "The night is long; there is time to refresh yourself. His Holiness does not wish for his guests to become overtired too quickly. This is all for your delight."

As uncomfortable as I was with such familiar behavior from strangers, I was impressed by Borgia's hospitality. The girls knelt down, took my slippers, and began to wash my feet in the cool water. Despite myself, I surrendered with a sigh and settled against the comfortable pillows to sip my wine. Once my feet were washed and patted dry, the girls began to massage them with fragrant oil.

After several minutes of this, the girls drew nearer and began to massage my hands. The girl who had led me to the bed smiled down at me, her face captured in the flickering light of the votives; I smiled back and noted that her eyes were pale and her black pupils as tiny as mustard seeds, her lids half lowered in a dreamy expression.

I felt a sudden giddiness and a surge of relaxation and weariness and pleasure so great that I let go a soft moan without realizing it; my guide's smile widened to show small white teeth. This was truly a garden of delight, I decided, with its sensual music, the sweet wine, the breeze from the fan, the mist from the fountain, and the light of the little lamps shining upon the dappled waters.

I heard the French duchess's throaty laughter from the daybed next to mine, hidden at the moment by the thick, low palms between us. I sat up and leaned forward to peer past the fronds, and saw a pair of Turkish girls moving away from the bed where the dark form of the duchess lay giggling softly.

My third girl set a courteous, tentative hand upon my shoulder. "May I loosen your bodice, Madonna, so that you might breathe more easily? It must be so very tight."

Perhaps it was not a proper suggestion, but the girl's attitude was so consummately respectful and polite that I nodded drowsily. As the girls efficiently loosened the laces, I let go a great sigh, and watched the snaking film of the sweet incense rise and dance on the fan's breeze.

As I did so, I saw a blur pass by, and glanced up to catch the light glinting off the bright silver of Caterina's gown. I pressed my palms against the soft bed, thinking to push myself up, to dismiss the girls and sit with her in order to make sure nothing improper took place. Married or no, she was still only fourteen, and my charge; Bona would never forgive me if I allowed Caterina to indulge in scandalous behavior.

Yet I was more strongly disposed to remain motionless and silent, lest I break the spell of pleasurable languor that had overtaken me. Surely, I reasoned, Caterina would be treated to the same delightful hospitality I had been shown—and, after all, there was not a single man present. I remained settled against the pillows and sipped my wine.

After a time, my breathing slowed and my body sagged heavily against the satin-covered down. I closed my eyes and felt the strange, keening music pulse throughout my body. For a time, I forgot myself entirely, and fell into a light doze where there was nothing but the music, the perfumes, the breeze, and waves of pleasure each time I drew or released a breath.

When at last I opened my eyes, my attendants had all disappeared, leaving me to gaze out at the pool and the gurgling fountain, the drops of water now glittering diamonds. The thought that I should rise and look for Caterina occurred to me again, but my repose seemed too precious to disturb.

Sudden loud laughter broke through the soothing warble of the exotic reed; it was so clearly ribald in nature that I sat up, and was surprised that the act left me nauseated and dizzy. Disoriented, I half crawled to the foot of my bed, set my pillow there, and rested my head upon it; thus situated, and looking to the right, past the palm fronds, I could see where the French duchess lay.

The faint light from the votives on her table left her face hidden in shadow, but revealed her exposed white breasts. A dark form sat on the edge of her bed, facing her; it leaned forward and down into the light, and I recognized Vannozza Cattanei just before she kissed the duchess's mouth. As she did, her hands caught the duchess's breasts.

Any shock I felt was muted, distant. I watched as Vannozza, her lips still locked with the duchess's, reached down and skillfully gathered up the woman's skirts, then plunged a firm hand between her legs. The Frenchwoman pulled free of the kiss to let go a gasp; encouraged, Vannozza slid her face downward, over the woman's neck and collarbone, down to her breast, and took the nipple. There she suckled while the woman shuddered and buried her fingers in Vannozza's orange hair.

I should have risen; I should have run and found Caterina. Yet it was easier at that moment to watch, breathless, as Vannozza suckled the Frenchwoman, and moved her hand between her legs rapidly back and forth.

This continued until Vannozza spread the duchess's bared legs into a wide vee, so that her feet hung over the edges of the daybed. A shadow fell over her, and Rodrigo Borgia's face caught the light as he lowered himself onto the bed. His cloak was gone, and his skullcap, revealing a fringe of black hair around his shaved crown, pale as bone. Vannozza retreated as Borgia buried his face in the dark hair between the Frenchwoman's legs.

I closed my eyes so I would see no more. "Caterina," I said softly; I had meant to cry out. For several minutes, I struggled against the crushing inertia, finally managing to push myself to sitting; the effort brought nausea, and I was obliged to hold very still until it eased. Meanwhile, the moans from the daybed near mine turned to gasps and finally, a single drawn-out, strangled roar of pleasure.

When I looked up, Vannozza Cattanei stood smiling over me.

"Madonna," she said sweetly, "are you feeling unwell? Here . . ." She dipped a cloth into the golden bowl on the table, wrung it out, and pressed it to my brow. The coolness brought some relief, but I pulled away from her.

"I must leave," I murmured. "Where is Caterina?"

She laughed slowly, languidly. "You must relax, Madonna, and rest. Sleep. I will help you . . ." She put her plump hands upon my shoulders, intending to push me back against the pillows, but I resisted.

"No," I said.

She disappeared. I gathered my strength to rise, but before I could do so, a shadow fell across my bed. Rodrigo Borgia, his rumpled collar pulled open and down, sat on one hip beside me. He wore a sensual smile; his lips and chin glistened with saliva. He was altogether sober, unaffected by wine or the mysterious potion.

"Madonna," he said, "were you dreaming? Hush, now. If Vannozza cannot help you, perhaps I can. . . ."

He reached for me.

I pushed myself to my feet. I was unsteady and lost my balance, falling against him. Instantly, he wrapped a strong arm about my waist, pressed his hand like a starfish to my left breast, and covered my mouth with his. He stank of the Frenchwoman.

I shook off my stupor and kicked upward with my knee. The blow failed to connect with his most vulnerable spot, but when he recoiled to protect himself, I pulled away and struck him across the face with all my strength.

My feeble effort hurt him little; he laughed as he rubbed his jaw, but he also set me free at once. I took a tottering step away from him.

"Poor Dea," he said coyly, still grinning. "Am I so very terrifying?"

"You are a monster," I gasped, "and Vannozza a whore." Even as I reacted with revulsion, it seemed far away, as if I were watching something that had happened to someone else a long time ago.

He laughed. "And *you*, my darling, have lived a very sheltered life. All this has been done with no thought other than to make you happy. If it does not, if you are frightened, you are free to go. Only remember that if your outlook should change, we are always here for you."

"If you touch my mistress, I will kill you," I said.

He lifted his chin; a sudden dangerous intensity shone in his eyes. "Is that not for Her Illustrious Highness to decide?" he asked softly.

I began to walk past him. He caught my wrist with painful force, and, while I struggled to free myself, he very deliberately turned my hand palm downward and kissed it. Then, as he had before, he held it fast for an instant—just to show that he could—before letting it go with a scornful laugh.

I staggered about, calling Caterina's name and trying to find the daybed on which she lay. Dizzied, disoriented, I found the wooden gate only because Adriana Mila led me to it, opened it, and pushed me out to the other side.

The gate slammed fast shut. I started to hammer frantically on the wood—I dared not abandon my mistress—but was soon distracted by the sound of mewling nearby. It grew so insistent that I forgot Caterina and moved slowly toward the sound. Though my eyes were accustomed to dim light, the corridor was completely dark.

Despite my care and pace, my foot came down on something fleshy and yielding; the creature yelped. I heard the sounds of scrambling, and my other foot went out from under me as it met something cushion-soft and slippery. I fell hard onto my rump, and let go a cry as a creature the size of a hound flung itself onto my lap.

"Mama?" it asked timidly, and fell silent. I could hear it breathing rapidly as it nestled against me; I reached out and set my hand upon its head, and felt silky hair.

"Who is it?" I asked.

"Cesare." His voice was very small and very sad. "Madonna Dea, have you seen my mama? Aunt Adriana said to go to sleep, but it's dark here and I'm scared. . . ."

I felt a distant sorrow for him and anger at his parents, who were so lost in their own pleasure that they had no time for a lonely, frightened boy—one so alert and precocious that he remembered my name and recognized my voice in the dark.

"Oh, Cesare," I said. "I'm here. You don't need to be afraid." On impulse, I kissed the top of his head.

Immediately, the face of a man flashed before me: olive-complected, with the same dominant black brows and magnetic gaze as his father, and a dark mustache and goatee that made his features appear more handsome than they actually were. In his black eyes I saw ambition verging on madness, grief giving way to rage, and a predatory thirst that nothing could slake.

The earth beneath me shuddered. I glanced up and found myself again in the Tower—one of timber and stone, one whose very walls were rattling as if in the grip of an earthquake. Cannon boomed, punctuated by the *rat-a-tat* of heavy artillery; overhead, the trembling ceiling loosed a stream of grit.

Somewhere nearby, Caterina was calling for the men to fire on the enemy.

It was not just the Tower meant for Caterina; it was the Tower meant for us both.

"Cesare," I gasped, and pushed him from my lap onto the cool, dank stone.

Thirteen

Little Cesare began to cry again at my apparent rejection of him; the instant I came to myself, I scooped him up in my arms, ignoring my dizziness and the vision of the Tower, which lurked on the periphery of my dulled awareness. I found my way out of the corridor and back across the courtyard, where I peered into windows in an effort to find my way back into the palace proper. Once there, I flagged down a serving woman and handed the boy off to her, explaining that he should be taken to his bed and watched after.

Struggling to emerge from my disoriented sloth, I wandered far too long down a maze of corridors and became lost in the massive palace. Finally I came upon a closed door; the light limning its edges and the raucous laughter emanating from inside drew me. I opened the door a crack and peered inside.

In addition to many daybeds, where partially unclad men were being tended to by Turkish courtesans, there was a great long table in the room's center covered with red felt. Upon it lay a naked woman, her eyes lined with kohl, her long hair loose and streaming past her exposed breasts. At the table's edge, looking down at her and grinning, were Girolamo Riario and the French ambassador. Girolamo had a pair of dice in his hand, which he rattled vigorously in his fist, blew on for luck, and cast onto the woman's body.

The half dozen men watching held their collective breath as the dice came to rest. One landed on the woman's belly, in the slight recess at her navel, while the other struck the crook of her elbow, then tumbled down onto that part of the table covered by her hair.

Girolamo squinted down at the dice, then struck his forehead with the heel of his palm and let go an oath; the French ambassador, however, smiled and clapped his hands.

"She is mine!" he crowed, and as he took her hand and helped her from the table, to much cheering, another woman finished undressing and took her place.

I closed the door silently. After half an hour of wandering, I finally found my way back to the courtyard. I was beginning to recover by then, and more determined than ever to demand that my mistress be released, though I feared that I would be too late to protect her honor.

As I made my way across the courtyard, Caterina came walking toward me from the direction of the garden of paradise. She was frowning slightly, with her eyelids half lowered, as if she were dazed. I ran and caught her arms just as we reached the lamp beside the fountain; like the Turkish girl's, her pupils had shrunk, and her gaze was glassy.

"Madonna Caterina!" I exclaimed. "Did Borgia touch you?"

"No," she answered calmly.

I took stock of her: Her bodice was only partially unlaced, and her hair still neatly arranged; I let go a sigh, and busied myself with refastening her bodice. "Thank God!" I said. "Did he try to force himself on you?"

Her lips curved upward in a dreamy smile. "Oh," she said, "he *tried . . .*" She held up her right hand with a swift motion, and I flinched: her coiled fingers gripped a stiletto Girolamo had given her.

I gasped. "Did you cut him?"

She shook her head. "But he will think twice about inviting me to his garden again." And she let go an explosive laugh that sounded very much like herself.

Though still mildly affected by Borgia's potion, Caterina insisted on returning to the reception hall, where only two-thirds of the revelers remained. In particular, she wished to dance with the dashing young Gerard de Montagne, the curly-haired aide to the French ambassador. I sat watching as Caterina and de Montagne enjoyed themselves. At one point, I dozed off, and a maid woke me and helped me to a couch in the adjoining room.

I was taken aback to find the French duchess lying nearby, upon a daybed. I thought she was asleep, but after the maid left, the duchess lifted her head and let go a languid, throaty laugh.

"Foolish woman," she said, "to make an enemy of Rodrigo Borgia... and so soon after your arrival in Rome."

"What can he do?" I countered, indignant. "Tell Count Riario that I rebuffed his advances?"

Her head fell back against the pillow; she stared up at the ceiling and laughed again. "Oh, far worse than that."

"What will he do?" I demanded, but by then, she had already closed her eyes, a small but ecstatic smile upon her lips, and fallen into a reverie.

I, too, fell into a dream.

I woke, startled, when someone roughly shook my shoulder. Count Girolamo towered over me, scowling. His eyes were bloodshot and he smelled of wine and the fragrant oil the Turkish girls had used to anoint my hands and feet.

"Where is Caterina?" he demanded. "Shame on you, sleeping, when you're supposed to be keeping an eye on her! Go, find her at once!"

I rose in haste, and hurried for the door as Girolamo called out to me.

"Have the carriage brought round; you two are going home! I can't bother watching after a mere girl, especially if her chaperone can't stay awake!"

In the reception hall, few were left dancing. Many guests had gone home, or retired to the gambling room or pleasure garden. Although there were several groups engaged in earnest, drunken conversation, only two pairs of dancers were still on their feet. Caterina was not among them.

I made a swift tour of neighboring rooms, which housed daybeds and sofas, some occupied, though not by Caterina. I panicked and headed out the door for the courtyard, worried that Borgia had somehow managed to get her back into the garden.

Once in the courtyard, hemmed by its graceful Moorish colonnades, I did not need to look far. I crossed the lawn as far as the gurgling fountain and the hanging lamp when I detected movement in the periphery of my vision, and turned.

In the long shadow cast by one of the orange trees, a pair of lovers engaged in a passionate embrace. I would have given them their privacy had I not recognized the female half from her height and shape. I moved toward them, stamping my feet as noisily as possible.

"Madonna!" I whispered harshly.

The man started and impulsively pushed the woman away from him, stepping as he did so into the light cast by the lamp. Gerard de Montagne's blond curls were no longer so tight; his lover had run her fingers through them with such passion that a wild halo of frizz surrounded his pretty face. He was drunk, but murmured the politest of apologies and bowed, hoping that excessive courtesy might somehow deflect my wrath.

Caterina, however, lifted her chin regally. "Do not use so harsh a tone with us, Dea," she warned.

We locked gazes. Hers was implacable and utterly unapologetic. I let go a silent sigh, suspecting that my duties now included deceiving Girolamo.

"Forgive me, Your Illustrious Highness," I said, my tone barely civil. "But your husband asked me to find you. He is concerned by your disappearance, and wants us to return home at once."

Caterina and Gerard turned to each other, crushed, and engaged in a farewell kiss while I turned my disapproving visage away and waited.

When at last the two lovers parted, and Caterina walked back with me inside the palazzo, I lectured her about her lord's anger and the dangers to which she was exposing herself.

In mid-lecture, she silenced me with a withering look. "I am not some silly girl that you or Girolamo or anyone else can order about. I am a Sforza, and had I been born a man, I would have been the best of all my father's sons. I am more fit to rule than any of them. And like my father, I will not be told whom I can love, or when, or where. If you disagree, I can send you back to Bona tomorrow."

Perhaps I should have insisted on returning home to Milan; at least then Bona might have given me leave to go to Florence. But even so early in our Roman adventure, I already knew that fate had irrevocably bound me to Caterina.

. . .

Caterina rose late the next morning, though earlier than her husband arrived home. She took her breakfast out on the balcony because the sun was mild and the breeze pleasant; when she finished, she summoned me. The dancing and the wine had tired her; she sat back in a cushioned chair with her legs propped upon an ottoman. Though she was inclined to be surly in such situations, she forced a wan smile as I appeared. No doubt she wanted a favor from me, one that I would be reluctant to grant.

I delayed her request by speaking first. "Madonna," I said, my tone polite but concerned, "I should warn you that you must take a great deal of care around Rodrigo Borgia. I learned last night that he is a very dangerous man, and does not forget insults easily. I am concerned that he—"

"Oh, don't worry about that," she interrupted. "I spoke with Vannozza about it. I told her that I reacted too harshly by drawing the stiletto. I told her that the wine had gone to my head, and that I was worried I had insulted my host. And she told me that, had I been a man, I might well be dead by now. But that Rodrigo is too chivalrous to harm a woman. At least, not physically."

"I hope she's right," I countered darkly.

She changed the subject swiftly. "Your Matteo was a scribe. A very talented one, according to Cicco. Did he ever speak to you about ciphers?"

Despite her casual tone, I was unnerved. Had she learned of Matteo's magical papers, of his spying for Lorenzo? Had I been careless?

"No," I said, and averted my gaze.

"You know nothing of ciphers, then?"

I shook my head.

"Then you shall just have to learn about them," she said. "You're quick enough. I want to send a letter to Gerard—"

I delved into my memory, and realized that she was talking about the French aide, Monsieur de la Montagne.

"—and I want you to put it into cipher for me. Then ensure that Gerard receives it. Don't use any of Girolamo's messengers. I trust no one but you to do this for me. Quickly, find a quill and some paper."

I hesitated. "Madonna, I do not even know—" *Where to find a quill in this house,* I would have finished, but Caterina silenced me with a curt gesture.

"I don't care *how* you do it. Just find them, and come back to me. But get them yourself, so no one else knows."

I used common sense and went to Caterina's office, only two rooms away. Inexplicably, there was no quill in the inkwell, or ink, or paper of any sort. I made my way downstairs, to the middle floor, the whole of which was taken up by Count Girolamo's clerks and advisers. Most of the chambers were empty; perhaps the count's men were all still sleeping after the late night at the Palazzo Borgia. I found a door that opened onto what appeared to be shelves of clerical supplies; relieved, I entered and silently closed the door behind me.

The shelves held parchment and stoppered vials of ink; I helped myself to some and looked about for a quill and penknife. When I turned to look at a different shelf behind me, I saw light emanating from the far corner, where a narrow door had been flung open. I wandered back and found a tiny room equipped with a writing desk and a three-legged stool. Beside the slanted writing surface, a quill rested in an inkpot; as I debated whether to steal it from its owner, my gaze fell upon the half-written letter resting there. Or rather, two letters: one in Roman, in abbreviated note form, and one half-written, in an incomprehensible, artful mix of letters, numbers, and symbols.

Cipher.

I got only the briefest impression of either letter, for I had just glanced down when a male voice interrupted me.

"What are you doing? Get away from there!"

A gentleman Matteo's age stood in the little doorway. He was only slightly taller than I, of wiry build. He was also clearly the wielder of the quill; his fingers were stained with dark iron-gall ink, as was the lap of his pale blue tunic, still damp from a recent, unsuccessful attempt to remove a spill.

Though he spoke in a hushed tone, he startled me badly. It was not simply the fact that I had been caught looking where I should not have been; his features were familiar in a dark, unsettling way. He had a trimmed blue-black beard and hair, dark gray eyes, and a face that might have been handsome had it not been for his sharp, prominent nose. He stared at me with an expression of indignant outrage.

"Sir, forgive me," I said, lowering my gaze. "I simply seek a quill. I confess, I was eyeing yours, but I see you have need of it."

He studied me closely, as if he, too, found me familiar. Finally he demanded, his tone still barely above a whisper, "How long have you been here?"

"Less than an instant," I said cheerfully.

He stepped past me to open his desk drawer, and handed me a fresh quill.

"Here, then," he said. "Now go, and don't come back."

I did so, and he closed the door behind me; the bolt slid shut on the other side.

I returned to Caterina and sat beside her on the balcony, writing while she dictated the contents of the letter. It revealed her desire to meet "privately" with Monsieur de Montagne "as I want to see you again, to continue the discussion that began yesterday evening." She faltered a good deal before finally waving her hand in disgust at her inability to summon a flowery turn of phrase.

"Do you wish to speak of your feelings for him?" I asked, wondering what Bona would think of me for assisting Caterina in this illicit endeavor.

Honestly perplexed, she lifted a golden brow; the fine white skin above it furrowed. "Feelings?"

I lowered my voice. "Do you love him, Madonna? Does he have your heart? Do you think of nothing else but him?"

"Love," she said sourly and gave a short, sharp laugh. "Don't tell me you believe in the nonsense peddled by troubadors, Dea!"

I flushed. "Many do. He will want to know your feelings, Madonna."

She sighed and leaned back in her chair, setting her palm against her forehead and closing her eyes, as if the very idea wearied her. "He is very handsome," she said. "I desire him."

"And . . . you have some affection for him, surely?"

She opened her eyes halfway, annoyed by the very suggestion, and began to massage the point between her eyebrows. "I hardly know him," she muttered. "But I will not live my life without learning the joys of the flesh, and Girolamo cannot be bothered to teach me. I have heard that the French are very talented lovers."

My eyes must have widened at her cold, calculating heart; she let go a little grunt and waved her hand in frustration.

181

"I don't care about such things! Just tell him whatever sounds best, whatever will make him want me," she said irritably. "Pretend for once that you are not shy, and are writing a love letter to your husband. And don't forget to put it in cipher. I have enough of a headache now without Girolamo or anyone else finding out about this."

And with that, sitting in the sunlight listening to the songs of birds and drone of bees in the garden, I remembered where I had first seen Girolamo's secret scribe: riding across the Lombard Plain, with Matteo's limp body slung over his saddle.

Fourteen

That day, while Caterina lingered on the balcony nursing her headache, I went to the walk-in closet where Caterina's vast assortment of gowns, head-dresses, and trunks of jewelry were kept. The closet also held the single trunk I had brought from Pavia. I dug beneath the carefully folded sleeves, bodices, and overskirts, drew out the papers Matteo had left behind, and riffled through them for the encryption key. The rest I returned to their hiding place beneath my clothes.

I took the document, paper, and quill with me to Caterina's office and locked the door. It took me far longer to write a convincing love letter than to encrypt it; using Matteo's cipher as a guide, I created my own by making a few changes.

It was an easy business, really—or perhaps, like my brother, I was talented at espionage. Once I created my new key, I translated my original love letter to Monsieur de Montagne into cipher, and wrote out a second copy of the key. I folded both the second key and the encrypted love letter into thirds and sealed them with wax. I fed the original love letter to the candle flame, letting the curling, blackening remnants drop into the empty hearth.

I returned to the closet and hid my encryption key in my trunk, then went to the stables. A lone groom was mucking out one of the stalls, a young boy with a silky shock of carrot-colored hair and a face so smudged with grime that the whites of his blue eyes stood out alarmingly. I offered him two denarii to deliver a message "from the master to the French ambassador, but it must be done discreetly, for it contains a secret." I told him that he should take the letter to the aide, Gerard de Montagne, personally, and explain that he should show it to no one, but wait for a second letter to arrive. And if the first were delivered safely, I would give the boy two more silver coins, and a second letter the next day to take to Monsieur de Montagne.

Intrigued by the thought of danger, he agreed eagerly. "I'll be free at noon, to go to mass," he said, "but the stablemaster need not know I've gone elsewhere. No one shall know, I swear it."

I gave him the encryption key with a reminder that we would meet again the following day at the same hour and place. I dared not send the key and letter together, lest they be intercepted.

I went back to Caterina's chamber to report my accomplishment only to discover that she had returned to bed and was dozing. I went out onto the balcony to sit in the shade of the awning, and thought about Matteo's death, and the rider who had brought him home.

I knew nothing about the late Duke Galeazzo's reasons for sending Matteo to Rome. Clearly, he had been on a sensitive mission, one that involved Lorenzo de' Medici; why else would Lorenzo have come secretly to visit the duke? Why else would Lorenzo have hoped to speak to Matteo in private immediately upon his return? Before his imminent death required his swift return home, Matteo had been escorting papal legates back from Rome to meet with the duke. Try as I might, I could remember nothing of the cardinals who had come to see Galeazzo; the days immediately following Matteo's death were a blur. I remembered only the black-haired rider.

A rider who served Count Girolamo as a scribe, one who sat alone in a tiny room hidden from view, encrypting secret messages. One who had traveled to Pavia alongside Matteo and the papal legates sent from His Holiness and Girolamo.

On his journey, had he discovered that my brother had been the Medici's spy?

A wave of grief and rage swept over me; I steepled my hands and pressed the tips of my fingers to my lips, but I could no longer pray. Instead I spoke to the angel.

"Come to me," I whispered. "Show me the truth. If he killed Matteo, give me proof."

As if in reply, the angel's words surfaced in my memory, blotting out all other thoughts.

I am already here. But your darkness shackles my tongue. . . .

Vow to obey me unto death, and I will reveal all.

I closed my eyes and saw the Nine of Swords: four swords crossed over four others, with a ninth sword thrust, tip pointing heavenward, through the center of the others . . . and all of them weeping blood.

"I will obey," I whispered, "if you will only show me who killed my brother. . . ."

In my heart, in my mind, only silence answered. Silence, and gnawing, bitter pain.

I slept poorly that night, and in the hour before dawn, surrendered to wakefulness and slipped on an overdress to cover my thin linen chemise. As it was still dark, I took a lamp and stole down the stairs to the second floor, and the east wing, Girolamo's province. I was surprised to find the sconces there already lit, though the corridor was silent.

I headed to the far end of the hall and the little room where I had found paper and ink. It was a purely irrational act; the door was no doubt locked, and I had no plan, only an urgent need to discover whatever I could about the scribe.

The sconce mounted on the wall near the supply chamber door was lit, and the door stood ajar. Holding my breath, I stepped up toward the threshold and peered inside.

In a neat row against the eastern wall stood tall wooden shelves, upon which were stacked various items: reams of paper, scrolls of clean parchment, ink vials, inkwells, blotters, ledgers, boxes, awls, magnifying lenses, rules, penknives, pumice stones, ribbons, portable writing desks, wool dusters, and a fresh new pile of untrimmed quills.

At the far end of the room, near the closed door to the scribe's tiny chamber, a woman with a black scarf wrapped about her head was stooped over, reaching for one of the portable writing desks on the lowest shelf; beside her was a broom and dustbin. Her cheeks were weathered and sunken, her eyes almost hidden by heavy folds; she was broad of shoulder and hip, and dressed in a black, uncorseted peasant's kirtle and white apron, and a leather thong round her neck, from which hung half a dozen or so keys. These clanked together as she sank, groaning, to her knees, then lifted the corner of one of the slanted lap desks with a gnarled hand; with the other, she reached beneath the desk and brought forth yet another key.

She set down the desk and, with one hand pressed hard against the adjacent wall for support, rose with a groan. I watched as she unlocked the door to the scribe's office with the key, and took her dustbin and broom into the scribe's office.

When she was done sweeping, she locked the door and replaced the key beneath the lap desk; I darted into the nearest open doorway on the opposite side of the corridor and remained pressed against the wall as she moved out into the hall—not without first locking the door to the supply chamber as well, then rising onto her toes to set this second key flat against the arm of the nearby wall sconce.

She moved on to the adjacent chamber, a library. I scurried across the corridor, took the key hidden on the wall sconce, unlocked the door to the supply chamber, and slipped inside.

I closed the door behind me, and set my lamp down upon the shelf as I retrieved the second key hidden beneath the little writing desk.

Within seconds, I stood inside the scribe's tiny quarters, lamp in hand. There was no sign of any letters, in cipher or regular text. I tried the desk drawers, but both were locked. Stymied, I lifted my lamp high and turned in a slow circle about the room, looking for a likely hiding place for another key.

Just before I gave up, I noticed that the right rear leg of the desk was darker than the rest. I crouched down beneath the desk and turned the lamp on it. In the gloom, it had seemed merely dirty; now I saw the imprint of hundreds of inky fingerprints at the base, where the foot of the leg rested against the unfinished stone floor.

Girolamo's scribe was not only slovenly, but also careless.

I set my lamp far to one side and with both hands, lifted the right desk leg a finger's breadth off the ground. There, gratifyingly, lay the key.

The leftmost top drawer held two documents: the abbreviated letter and half-page of cipher I had seen the day before. Our scribe had made little progress.

There, in the little closet of an office, I sat upon the scribe's stool and, with the lamp perched beside me on the desk, read the abbreviated letter. It had apparently been dictated, as the scribe had written in haste.

> *YGrace, mst highly est. Montefeltro etc.*
>
> *We r now fully committed to removing 1st citizen fm pwr, yr assistance crucial to our success, need u to gathr min 600 trps outside Flor's walls, our agents will tk care of both bros, when they r dd, Cow will ring as signal, then yr troops storm walls, go to P. d. Signoria, join Pazzi in denounce Lor. & fam. Must destroy opposition. HH promises u not only handsm purse we discussd, bt also favrs & land. Reply swiftly to signal yr agreemt—plan will be enacted shrtly. Will give u notice of day, hr.*
>
> *W grtest esteem, etc.,*

I let go a gasp that would have been audible to anyone passing by in the hall, and clamped my hand over my mouth. I knew where *Flor* was and who *both bros* were, for I had stayed at their palazzo after Matteo's funeral. I knew the *1st citizen, Lor.* I even knew that the *Cow* was the low, "mooing" bell that summoned all citizens of Florence to the city square, the Piazza della Signoria. And I understood all too well what *dd* meant.

Girolamo Riario and *HH,* His Holiness, were plotting to kill Lorenzo de' Medici and his brother.

I do not remember replacing the letter or locking the doors and returning the three keys to their places, though I surely did. I only vaguely remember returning to Caterina's chamber and dressing silently as she snored, then taking the encrypted letter for Caterina's admirer, Gerard de Montagne, to the stalls. I paid the little red-haired groom his two silver coins, and hinted that, once his mission was accomplished, he might get a third.

All of this I did in the cold grip of fear. Girolamo was a murderer, and

Lorenzo de' Medici and his younger brother, Giuliano, were in terrible danger. It was my duty to warn them quickly.

Caterina was still sleeping when I returned to her chamber. I fetched a copy of the cipher I had created for her correspondence with de Montagne and went down the hall to her study and bolted the door. Making good use of the quill, ink, and paper I had recently obtained from the supply room, I made a second copy of the cipher and wrote a very brief letter.

Ser Lorenzo,

It is I, Dea, Matteo's sister. I now reside in Girolamo Riario's household and I have learned that he and the Pope are plotting to murder you and Giuliano. Beware: Girolamo has asked the Duke of Montefeltro to wait outside Florence's walls with an army of 600 men, and intends to give him a signal to storm the city once you and your brother have been eliminated. Take great care; Girolamo plans to strike soon.

I encrypted the letter carefully. When I was done, I fed the letter in plain text to the lamp's flame; it caught and quickly blackened and curled. I let it finish burning in the cold hearth while I folded the cipher key and the encrypted letter, and sealed them both before placing them snugly in the pocket hidden in the folds of my skirt.

I returned to my lady's bedchamber to fetch another silver coin for my little messenger; unfortunately, Caterina had awakened by then, and was in a surly mood upon hearing that her would-be lover would probably not reply to her that day, as he would not receive the encrypted letter until after midday.

I was desperate to take Lorenzo's letters to my little groom that morning, so that they would be delivered that day to the Florentine ambassador; instead, I spent the morning tending to Caterina's whims.

The two letters hidden in my skirt pocket weighed heavily on me; unfortunately, Caterina was demanding, and engaged me in a dozen other tasks. At several points, Caterina interrupted me to complain:

"What is *wrong* with you, Dea? Your mind is elsewhere today!"

For her own safety, I could not confide in her, so I murmured vague excuses and apologies. Time passed swiftly and I was startled when I heard a sudden cascade of midday church bells. I made up a hasty lie, telling Caterina that I had forgotten to pay my messenger, and had to do so immediately. I then ran as fast as my skirts would allow to the stables, to no avail. My little groom had already left on his mission.

Crushed, I headed back to the contessa.

Late in the afternoon, I finally escaped Caterina and went down to sit in the large kitchen garden off the servants' ground-floor dining hall in the far western wing. When the cook finally emerged to ring the supper bell, the outdoor workers—gardeners, stonemasons, artisans, and the stableworkers, who crossed over the gravel courtyard separating the stables from the estate proper—made their way wearily toward the hall.

I spotted my little messenger; as he neared, I called softly. Clearly, his mission had been successful, for he grinned broadly at me, revealing a newly missing front tooth.

"Madonna!" he exclaimed happily.

I shushed him and led him away from the gathering diners, back toward the gardens behind the palazzo's central wing. We stopped in an alcove beside a softly burbling fountain, the whole sheltered from view by an ancient rose thicket, loaded with fragrant blooms.

"Your letters are delivered, Madonna," the boy whispered, beaming. "The French aide, the one whose name sounds like a mountain, he came himself for the second one, and tipped me!"

"You've done an excellent job," I answered softly. "But now I have a far more important, and even more secret, task for you."

He squared his thin shoulders proudly. "I can do it!"

"Is there a chance that you could go into the city tonight?"

"Tonight?" He grimaced, and I felt a strong pang of guilt.

"It's all right," I said abruptly, deciding that I would have to figure out a way to go myself. "It's wrong of me to ask you to do something so dangerous."

"It's safer for a boy to go out than a woman," he said wisely. "Besides, Madonna, I just thought of a way to do it. Where is it that you want me to go?"

"To the house of the Florentine ambassador," I said. When Caterina had first arrived in Rome, her regular secretary had been overwhelmed by the amount of correspondence required to thank the hundreds who had given wedding gifts. I had helped, and learned where most of the ambassadors lived; I gave the boy the address.

He nodded and thought for a moment. As he did, I brought the two sealed documents from my pocket, and showed them to him. I was extremely reluctant to send both at the same time, for if they were intercepted together, Girolamo would discover that he had a spy for the Medici in his household, but I was too frightened for Lorenzo and Giuliano's sakes to wait the extra day.

"No one but the ambassador himself must see these," I said sternly. "What is your name, child?"

"Angelo, Madonna."

I fought not to smile. "Angelo, our lives depend on keeping these secret from everyone except the ambassador. If anyone else in this household learns about these, you will at the very least be severely punished. And I will die."

His pale eyes widened. "Why, Madonna? Are they going to harm anyone?"

I shook my head. "No. They're going to save someone's life. That's why they need to be delivered as soon as possible. I would do it, but my mistress does not like for me to be far from her for very long."

Squaring his shoulders bravely, he nodded. "It is for good, then. I will do it. You are a nice lady, and I want no harm to come to you."

"Thank you, Angelo. You are a good, brave boy. When the letters are safely delivered, I will give you a gold ecu. In the meantime . . ." I took a silver coin from my pocket and handed it to him along with the letters. "Take this for your pains."

He took the coin and letters eagerly, and hid them inside his grimy tunic. I made him repeat the phrase, several times: "Deliver these to Lorenzo de' Medici, each by separate courier. It is a matter of life and death."

When he had memorized it to my satisfaction, I dismissed him and watched him run back to the stables instead of the dining room, and whispered a prayer on his behalf to the angel.

The light was failing quickly by the time I headed back along the garden path and across courtyards to Caterina's wing of the palace. I was lost in a reverie where fear warred with relief now that I had taken action on

Lorenzo's behalf. What would I do if the boy failed in his mission? I was so caught up in my anxious thoughts that I didn't look carefully where I was going, and when I made my way up the back stairs leading up to Caterina's apartments—it was dim because the sconces had not yet been lit—I ran into someone coming down.

"Sir, forgive me," I said, flinching. I lifted my head up to see the scribe, and recoiled as though I had just stepped on a viper.

He had not been moving but had been waiting, motionless, in the dimness.

He was dressed magnificently, in a tunic of dark silver brocade, with sleeves of lilac silk laced with silver braid; his black hair and beard were freshly trimmed and the feathered end of a quill protruded from behind his right ear. The whites of his deep gray eyes were bloodshot; he was exhausted but, like me, animated by unsettled nerves.

"Madonna Dea," he said, his tone soft but utterly serious.

"I do not know your name, sir," I said.

"Luca," he answered, with a cursory bow. "Luca da Siena." His words were polite, but his tone was darkly urgent and none too friendly. "Forgive me for not remembering you earlier, Madonna; your face seemed especially familiar to me, but I assumed that I had seen you only in Her Illustriousness's household. I do not know whether you remember me."

"Oh, yes," I said, my heart pounding violently; my tone was no friendlier than his, but I knew that I dared not behave in a suspicious manner.

I had been so concerned with the Medici brothers' safety that my mind had not yet focused on the implications of Girolamo's secret correspondence. Up to that moment, I had only been suspicious of the scribe Luca. But now I remembered my prayer.

Come to me, I had begged the angel. *If he killed Matteo, give me proof.*

And then I had discovered Girolamo's clandestine letter stating his intent to murder Lorenzo.

My thoughts returned to the previous Christmas season, and Lorenzo's secret visit to Milan. According to Caterina, he had come to speak to Duke Galeazzo Sforza about Imola, the town that now belonged to Girolamo Riario, the papal captain.

But at the time, Lorenzo was strongly opposed to allowing Pope Sixtus control of Imola. It was too close to Tuscany, and Girolamo's possession of it would set a dangerous precedent. The pope already controlled the Papal States; to give him more power would seriously destabilize Italy and lead to more war.

Up to that point, Imola had been under Milan's control, but Pope Sixtus had pressured his soon-to-be in-law, Duke Galeazzo, to give Imola to Caterina, and thus Girolamo and Sixtus, as a wedding present. Lorenzo, however, had swayed Duke Galeazzo to his point of view, and ultimately, Galeazzo refused the pope's request.

A fortnight later, Galeazzo lay murdered in the cathedral of Santo Stefano, and my Matteo was dead.

These thoughts raced through my mind as Luca leaned forward to say, in a barely audible voice, "You were in my office again, even though I warned you once. That was unwise and very dangerous."

"I was not in your office," I whispered.

"But you were," he whispered back. "In fact, you were in my desk."

"Sir, I was not!"

"Lying does not become you, Madonna," he admonished, "though I must give you credit for being so observant. There is the matter of the key to my desk. If it is not replaced a certain way under the leg, the desk wobbles."

"That is of no concern to me, sir."

"You're quite right about that." He took a step closer to me, and caught my wrist, pulling me close to him so that he could whisper directly into my ear. "The two documents were not replaced in the drawer correctly, either. You read the letter, didn't you?"

I wrested my hand away from him. "I don't know what you're talking about!"

"Then why were you speaking to that boy in the garden? Why did you give him two letters? And why do you look so terrified?"

I pushed him away; he lost his balance but caught himself from falling. I cursed my heavy skirts as I gathered them up in an attempt to run, but he reached down and caught my elbow, this time holding me fast and pulling me round to face him. We stood nose to nose, close enough to kiss; his breath was warm on my face, his eyes narrowed with piercing urgency.

"I would hate to see what happened to your husband happen to you," he whispered. "And if you do not stop the course you are on, Madonna, it will."

At that point, Teodora appeared on the landing above us. "There you are!" she said. "Her Illustriousness has been looking for you."

As soon as Teodora gazed down at us, Luca released his grip on my arm. I gathered my skirts at once, and without giving the scribe a backward glance, hurried up the stairs on trembling legs.

Fifteen

I slept poorly that night as my mind examined all the possible responses to the threat issued by the scribe Luca. He could have already told Count Girolamo of my meddling, in which case I was doomed and my safest course was to rise from my bed in the dark, take one of the horses, and embark on the long trip to Florence.

But if Luca had informed the count of my transgression, why then had the scribe come to me in secret, to warn me? Count Girolamo was known for his lack of restraint and finesse; if he knew, I would already be dead, or lying on one of the racks in Castel Sant'Angelo's dungeon.

By the hour before sunrise, I still had no clear plan for escaping or protecting myself. I had determined only one thing: that I could no longer be patient and wait to discover the truth about my brother's death.

In the darkness I rose, dressed myself and, careful not to wake my lady, leaned over her to find the handle of the sheathed dagger tucked just beneath the mattress, in the upper corner where her head normally rested against the pillow. Fortunately, she had rolled into the center of the bed and lay sprawled on her stomach. I teased the dagger out silently, situated it in my skirt pocket so that I could quickly retrieve it, and slipped out the door.

Most of the servants had not yet risen and the halls were empty, the sconces unlit; I took advantage of the dimness to move unobserved from the contessa's east wing all the way to the count's wing in the west. The servants' dining room was in the bottom corner of the west wing. I hovered a fair distance from it, waiting in the gray morning mist until the strong Roman sun began to rise and the kitchen maid began to ring the large brass dinner bell.

I peered anxiously at each form making its way through the changing light across the gravel courtyard. The men were grim and shuffling, faces cast downward; the boys ran, giggling and playful, into the dining room. My little messenger was one of the last to arrive; he was limping slowly, and as he neared, I saw that his eye was bruised and swollen.

When he caught sight of me, he stiffened with fear and glanced over his shoulder, as if thinking to bolt back to the stables. I caught his arm before he could run away and drew him around the corner of the palace, where a tall juniper bush blocked us from the view of those still headed for breakfast.

"Angelo, what's happened? Are you all right?"

He turned his narrow face away from me and tried to stifle a sob; a huge tear slid down his thin cheek. "I don't think I should speak to you again, Madonna."

A wave of guilt overtook me.

"Oh, Angelo, did they hurt you? I am so sorry! Just tell me what happened to the letters and I won't bother you ever again."

"The stablemaster," he said, and began to weep in earnest. "He caught me trying to take one of the horses yesterday evening. I explained that I was doing it at the request of one of the contessa's ladies, but he did not care. He beat me." He drew in a stuttering breath, and wiped his streaming eyes and nose upon his sleeve.

"I am so sorry," I repeated. "I was wrong to involve you in this. You are a good boy, Angelo, and the stablemaster was wrong to hit you. Give me the letters back; I'll find another way. Please keep the coin."

His words spilled out so rapidly and so distorted by a fresh storm of emotion that I had to strain to understand them.

"I can't. I don't have them."

Sickened, I caught his thin arm. "What do you mean?"

"The stablemaster took them. Even the coin." He shook his head. "He said he was going to give them back to the count so that they could be delivered by someone more responsible. But I am never to take a horse without his permission again. I'm sorry, Madonna. I hope they don't punish you, too."

"It's all right," I said, numbed. "You're a good boy, and I'm sorry I caused you this grief. Thank you for your help."

Reason and self-interest said that I should flee at once, yet as I slowly made my way back into the palace, I thought not of the murderous count or his sinister scribe, or of the torture that likely awaited me. Instead, I thought again of Matteo, his dark auburn hair soaked with sweat, the whites of his eyes flushed with blood. With that image came his last request: *Tell Lorenzo: Romulus and the Wolf mean to destroy you.*

It seemed ridiculously clear; the symbol of Rome was a she-wolf, and Romulus the child who had suckled at her teat. Who could these be but Pope Sixtus and his murderous son, Girolamo?

I recalled how, in Milan, the courtier Carlo Visconti had sagged with anguish upon recovering his violated young sister from Duke Galeazzo's clutches. I recalled the look of bright hatred, of infinite satisfaction, in his eyes at the instant he ran the duke through with his sword.

For months now I had lived unawares in the household of my beloved's murderers. If I sought revenge on them, it was unlikely that I would survive long enough to warn Lorenzo that the danger to him had increased manyfold. But if I could not, then I would see to it that the architect of the assassination plot and his henchman were destroyed.

It was a brilliantly foolish plan, encouraged by the fact that I had brought Caterina's dagger. I would confront the scribe in his office, learn whether he had told Girolamo of my letter to Lorenzo, force him to confess his role in the murder, dispatch him, and then hurry the short distance to Girolamo's chamber. I would tell them that I had a private message from my mistress, meant only for her husband's ears.

So absorbed was I in these dark thoughts that I found myself in the corridor outside the supply chamber without remembering how I had gotten there. The old servant woman had already lit the wall sconce by the door and replaced the key; as I took it and opened the chamber door, I realized the scribe would have changed the locks. To my surprise, the iron key to the inner office was hidden where it was before and the door opened easily with a single turn of the key.

To my relief and disappointment, the scribe had not yet arrived, though the lamp was burning. Impulsively, I reached beneath the desk leg, and discovered the key in the same spot. I unlocked the top drawer of the desk and opened it, marveling at the scribe's carelessness.

The drawer was empty, save for two items: My encrypted letter to Lorenzo de' Medici and the cipher key, both with the wax seals broken.

I grew light-headed as I took the letters. I stuffed them into my pocket and—at the sound of the opposite door opening, the one that led back to Count Girolamo's chamber—pulled out the dagger.

It was the scribe, Luca, holding a plate of cheese and grapes in one hand, and smelling of soap. His jet hair was damp and neatly combed, and he wore a fine indigo tunic trimmed with black and gold braid, as if he were headed to a reception or a holiday mass. He had been waiting for me, cheese in hand, and when he kicked open the door with a flourish, thinking to surprise me, he apparently did not consider how the plate of food detracted from the air of danger he meant to exude.

His other hand held a knife.

He moved quickly to set down the plate on his desk, all the while holding the knife on me, and noticing only at the last minute that I, too, held a weapon. He recoiled, especially since he very nearly leaned unawares into the blade.

I waved the dagger at him as he drew back and pointed his own at me.

"You killed Matteo," I hissed. "Admit it!"

His black brows lifted in surprise. "You are a troubled young woman," he said. "Either you are a complete fool, which I doubt, or you wish to die and will not do it by your own hand."

"Matteo da Prato," I repeated. "You killed him on Count Girolamo's order. Last Christmas, when you came to Milan. Confess and accept your fate!"

He narrowed his eyes first at me, then at the point of my steel dagger. "You could not be more wrong."

In the next instant, he lunged at me.

I forced myself not to recoil, but stepped forward on one foot, as I had seen men do so many times, and struck out with Caterina's blade. He was too practiced, too nimble, and I swiped at nothing but air. Before I could draw back and go at him again, he grabbed my right wrist and twisted it; Caterina's dagger clattered to the stone floor. Holding his own knife on me, he reached out with his foot and kicked my blade into the far corner.

Panting, I contemplated the sharp, shining tip pointed at me and for the moment, stood still. The drawer to the desk was still open; he saw that it was empty, and gestured at me with the knife.

"The letter, please." His tone was flat and weary. "And the encryption key. Don't argue with me; I know you have them."

I took them slowly from my pocket, thinking to drop them on the floor just in front of me. He read my intent, and gestured with his weapon at the oil lamp on the desk.

"Don't you dare," he hissed. "Lift the glass."

I moved slowly to the lamp and lifted the glass cover, exposing the flame.

"Go ahead," he said. "Burn the letters." He took a step forward and pushed his food-laden plate so that it was flush with the base of the lamp. "You can catch the ashes with this. Spare the cheese, if you would."

I held the incriminating letter to Lorenzo to the flame first. As it caught, Luca said softly, "I knew Matteo, if only for a little while, and in that short time, we became friends. But we knew of each other for years."

"You lie," I answered, glancing up from the blackening paper in my hand.

"I traveled with him from Rome, as one of Girolamo's envoys along with the papal legates," he said. "If I killed him, why would I have then deserted my post to get him to help as soon as possible? Why would I have made sure to keep his saddlebag out of unfriendly hands in order to bring it to you, just as he asked me to?"

I shook my head; the thought was too painful to consider. "You have no proof."

"Fool!" he snapped. "Don't you see that I'm risking my life to protect you?" He lowered his knife and sat down upon his stool as I stood alongside him, and rubbed his forehead as though it pained him.

By that time, the first letter, the only evidence of my disloyalty to Girolamo, was reduced to a pile of blackened ash resting between a chunk of strong-smelling cheese and a cluster of grapes.

I began to feed the extra unnecessary copy of my encryption key to the lamp; as I did, he rubbed his brow again.

"Forgive my temper," he said. "But you have no idea of the danger you have put us both in. If I give you proof that Matteo and I were friends and swear to you that Ser Lorenzo has already been warned—time and again, yet he chooses to ignore the danger—will you stop your reckless behavior? Will you promise to stay far from my desk and quit endangering your life and those of others?"

Intrigued but unconvinced, I stared down at him. "Give me proof."

He hesitated. "Matteo was an orphan. Like you," he said, and when I reacted strongly to his words, he added, "Like me. All of us owe our current circumstances to the same generous benefactor. And if you reveal that last fact to anyone, I am dead. Now, perhaps, you can understand why you must not come here again, for my sake, and why you need not be concerned for Lorenzo."

I closed my gaping mouth to stare at the wavering flame, dark and smoking where the paper met it, and wondered where else he could have learned this information.

His thought must have followed mine, for he said, "I don't understand why you would suspect me. I returned Matteo's saddlebag with his journal intact. Surely the truth is written there."

I turned sharply toward him. "I have no way to translate it; I could not find the key. Were you able to read it? Do you know where the key is?"

He shook his head. "No. I assumed that you had it."

"If you didn't kill him," I asked, less than kindly, "then who did?"

He studied me; his eyes were guarded but held compassion. "Madonna, I don't know."

"You had best give me more proof," I said.

The papers were now nothing but a pile of whitening ash on a plate. Luca returned his knife to its sheath, and walked over to the far corner to pick Caterina's dagger up from the floor.

"More proof," he said, as he approached me, the knife in his hand.

"Madonna Dea, Matteo would be sad to see you so tormented by the desire for revenge. Besides, how can you be so sure he died of poison and not a strange fever?"

I lifted my chin and said coldly, "He told me to warn Lorenzo of Romulus and the Wolf."

He did not pretend that he did not understand the names. "There is no question that Girolamo and Sixtus are devoted to destroying Lorenzo," Luca said. "But they had no cause to kill Matteo. I will say this: he would not have hated his murderer, as you do. He may have suffered physically at the last, but he did not torture himself mentally, as you are doing now.

"And now, even after I brought Matteo home in an effort to save him, gave you his saddlebag, and have let you destroy the very documents that damned you—not to mention the fact that I am risking my hide by letting you inside this chamber—you want more proof. So I will tell you this, Madonna: that you saw the Hanged Man in the stars. And that your brother was very happy before his death. Why trouble me with these questions? Why do you not consult the one who would gladly guide you?"

He turned the dagger carefully in his hand so that he held it by the sharp tip, and presented the handle to me.

I took it, resheathed it, and placed it back in my pocket. *Your brother was very happy before his death.* Brother, not husband—a secret I shared only with Matteo and the Medici. I covered my eyes with my hands and began to cry.

"Ah, no," I heard him say. "Anything but tears. Hush, this is too dangerous! Please be quiet! Go back to your mistress! And never speak of this to anyone!"

I felt myself being pushed toward the door, then over the threshold; the door closed behind me, and the bolt behind it slid shut with a click. After a moment I gathered myself, and made my way slowly back to Caterina's wing.

I was still stunned by my encounter with Luca a few hours later, when a messenger on horseback arrived "with a social invitation from a friend, for Her Illustrious Highness's eyes only." I took the letter from a house servant, who explained that the messenger was outside, awaiting an immediate reply. I handed it to Caterina, who was sitting in her study dictating her regular correspondence to her social secretary. She cracked the seal on the letter, opened it no more than a finger's breadth, then swiftly closed it again, her eyes wide with anticipation, her lips firmly pressed together to prevent a smile. She waved her secretary and cupbearer outside, but gestured for me to remain; when the door had closed over them, she opened the letter to reveal it was written in cipher—my cipher, rendered in a French hand.

"It's from Gerard!" she hissed, and motioned for me to fetch my cipher key.

I did and returned to sit at my lady's desk to write out the translation for her. When it was done, I handed it to her.

She snatched it, and read it aloud to herself in a barely audible voice. She was slow when it came to letters, and stumbled a few times, but the rising excitement in her tone indicated that she did not miss the gist.

My darling,

I, too, yearn to see you alone, in private, to speak of all that is in my heart. Like you, I have never been so stricken by love. So preoccupied am I by the memory of you—of your extravagant beauty, your sweet charms, your generous soul—that I cannot eat, sleep, or focus my mind on my duties. Your eyes are like sapphires, your skin as delicate and sweet as cream, your hair like spun gold. When may I see you? Give me a time, a place, and I shall come to you! No duty can keep me from your side.

Your adoring servant,

G.

Caterina laughed at some of the lines. "Eyes like sapphires!" she said scornfully. "Hair like spun gold! How trite! A good thing he has chosen politics and not poetry as his profession."

Yet she giggled with excitement and instructed me to schedule a rendezvous between them that very evening, knowing that Count Girolamo had invited a number of men to his private quarters for political discussions that would likely last well into the night.

"You want him to come *here*, to the palazzo," I breathed, "while your own husband is entertaining guests? I can think of nothing more foolish!"

She grinned, in far too expansive a mood to be irritated by my scolding. "It makes it all the more exciting, doesn't it?"

"It does *not*," I replied sourly. "Bona instructed me to look after you. You are not even fifteen years old, and your judgment concerning romantic entanglements is—"

"None of your concern," Caterina finished icily.

"If your husband discovers you, Your Illustrious Highness," I said, my tone formal, "he will at best beat you. He might well kill you, and no one in Rome would dare stop him, or avenge you."

Her full lips twisted into a pout. In a cross, childish tone, she demanded, "The messenger is waiting. Do as I say!"

I sighed, and wrote a reply.

Beloved,

Come to my palazzo tonight, when the church bells proclaim the hour of Compline. Go to the servants' entrance behind the east wing; I will arrange for the gate to be unlocked and unguarded. To your left, leading to the back of the estate, is a path lined by cobblestones. Follow where it leads, and when you find a fountain in the shape of a nymph beside a large olive tree, wait there, and I will find you.

You have my heart. I yearn to give you more.

C.

Before I sent the letter, I persuaded Caterina to consult her secretary about the count's plans for the evening: Girolamo was meeting with "important personages who preferred to remain anonymous," but the secretary confessed that one of them was the Archbishop of Pisa, Francesco Salviati. This troubled me, for I knew that the Medici had opposed Salviati's appointment; Pisa was Florentine territory, and a Medici had always served as archbishop until Sixtus appointed Salviati, a distant relative, knowing it would infuriate Lorenzo.

But what troubled me most was the fact that Cardinals Borgia and della Rovere were coming later in the afternoon to the palazzo, and might well dine with Girolamo and his guests, after which all would meet with His Holiness at the Vatican.

Caterina, however, had made up her mind to find pleasure with Gerard, and could not be dissuaded. For the rest of the day, we were all preoccupied with embellishing my lady's beauty: her body was bathed and plucked, her hair washed and rinsed with an expensive concoction of cinnabar, sulfur, and saffron, to coax out the gold; her teeth were polished with ground marble, and her blue eyes washed with rosewater.

Despite the chaos, I found the time to think about the scribe and all that he had said.

You saw the Hanged Man in the stars. Your brother was happy before his death.

Why do you not consult the one who would happily guide you?

He had been speaking of the angel, of that I had no doubt. And he had recognized Matteo as a fellow Magus. Luca, too, was a spy for the Medici, and the more I considered how much he had risked in order to protect me—and how much he still risked, by trusting me to remain silent—the guiltier I felt about suspecting him.

But the phrase "Romulus and the Wolf" still troubled me. Clearly it referred to Girolamo and Sixtus, and my Matteo had died trying to warn Lorenzo of their plan. Why would some other hand have taken his life?

During Caterina's bath, the midmorning bells of Terce rang; as she sat out on her balcony, drying her combed-out hair in the midday sun and soaking her hands in milk, church bells throughout the city marked the hour of Sext. By the time they announced None in the midafternoon, her gleaming curls were dry, and by the time the sun had set at Vespers, her hair was done up in a fat braid wound just above the base of her skull; long golden ringlets had been artfully arranged to frame her face.

Caterina's other attendants had retired by the time the bells marked Compline, and I had dressed her myself in silvery blue silk—at her request, a simple gown with no overdress or stomacher, and no sleeves save those of the white lawn chemise she wore underneath; the fewer impediments to passion, the better.

I felt a good deal of guilt as we hurried down the stairs, I holding an oil lamp, the wick adjusted so that the flame provided just enough illumination to guide us to our destination. I held the lamp low and close, so that it would be almost impossible to see from Count Girolamo's balcony on the opposite end of the palazzo. The windows in the count's wing still glowed yellow, and torches still lit the path back to the stables—he and his guests had not yet left for the Vatican.

With a silent apology to Bona, I led the way as Caterina and I hurried toward the back of the gardens. As we passed the servant's side gate, Caterina began to whisper excitedly upon catching sight of the beautiful Arabian horse tethered nearby: clearly, her beloved had already arrived. We made our way over smooth flagstones, past long, waist-high hedges of boxwood, rosemary, lavender, and rose, the whole punctuated by marble Roman gods, stone benches, and citrus, fig, and olive trees.

At last we reached the clearing where an alabaster nymph knelt to empty her pitcher into a scallop-shaped fountain. Water rushed forth from the pitcher into the fountain with enough force to create a pleasantly cooling mist, one that glittered faintly in the muted glow cast by Gerard de Montagne's lantern, covered by an oilcloth.

A few strides from the fountain stood a long stone bench in the shade of a large, gnarled olive tree, heavy with unripe fruit. The Frenchman stepped forward and went down on one knee, doffing his plumed cap with a flourish. He bowed his head, revealing tight, blond-white curls, and kept his face cast downward as he spoke.

"Madonna Caterina," he said softly, with only a trace of a Gallic accent, "I am unworthy even to look upon you; I cannot believe that I have won the affection of one so charming, so young and so beautiful, and so far above my lowly station. Say the word, and I shall be your servant, to do as only you command."

Delighted by the display of humility, Caterina grinned as she stepped up to the kneeling man, took his hat, and tossed it aside carelessly. Then she bent down and took his hands, and made him rise to his feet. Although Gerard's shoulders and chest were rather narrow, his dark leggings revealed shapely, muscular legs.

"Is that so?" Caterina responded coyly. "Then take off your tunic, Gerard, so that I can see what a real man looks like, and take me in your arms."

At that point, I turned away, blushing. Lamp in hand, I moved half a dozen steps away, to give them the stone bench and some privacy. I would have moved farther away—despite the gurgling fountain, I could still hear more than I wished to—but that would have made me more easily visible from the contessa's wing of the palazzo. For a few minutes, I paced uneasily and stared at the flagstone beneath my slippers, trying to ignore the sounds of limbs intertwining and lips and tongues kissing.

"So perfect," Gerard murmured behind me. "Like pearls! Let me kiss them. . . ."

Silk rustled; there came the sound of suckling. I closed my eyes and forced myself to think about the scribe, Luca, and how I could apologize to him without further endangering him. When I had exhausted that train of thought, I tried to ignore the sighs floating on the humid Roman air.

How strong you are, Gerard. . . .

I have waited so long for this, sweet Caterina. . . .

Pull it down. Let me see you.

The lovers fell ominously silent. Long moments passed; I set the lamp down and shifted my weight from one hip to the other.

Abruptly, the silence was broken by Caterina's sharp gasp, followed by a long, low moan of delight. I wanted nothing more than to cover my ears with my hands.

And I might well have, had I not also heard rustling, not of silk or flesh against flesh, but of a body brushing gently against leaves. This was accompanied by carefully muted footfall, coming not from the direction of the lovers but the palazzo.

I turned toward the fountain. "Madonna!" I hissed. "Cover yourself, someone is coming!"

My gaze was averted, but not enough to spare me the sight of Caterina lying faceup, her breasts lifted out of her bodice, her pale hips exposed, her white legs and fine silk skirts draped over the side of the stone bench. Her jaw was slack, her lips parted, and her chin lifted heavenward in ecstatic abandon; her arms were tightly wound around her partner's bare shoulders. Atop her lay the shirtless Frenchman, his dark leggings pulled down low enough to reveal the slope of his buttocks.

I cannot say whether Caterina heard me, but de Montagne did, and immediately uncoupled and pulled up his leggings. I turned back in the direction the sounds had come from, and when I lifted my lamp again, I glimpsed the dark form of a man running away through the garden, toward the west. Just as swiftly, he passed out of view, hidden by foliage.

I told Caterina that we had been discovered, that someone was running directly back to report to Count Girolamo what he had seen.

"Did you see who it was?" She did not rise or cover herself. Her tone was languid, and her pitch a full octave lower than normal.

"No, but it was a man."

"Perhaps it was just a servant, trying to slip into the city unseen," Gerard proffered. He and Caterina shared a look; it was clear that neither of them intended to be interrupted, regardless of the consequences.

In the end my objections were steadfastly ignored; both Caterina and her lover insisted that if I had not been able to see the man clearly, then he surely had not been able to see me, and certainly not the two of them behind me.

Once again, I set my lamp down on the ground, and some minutes later, when Caterina could not completely stifle her first howl of pleasure, I pressed my hands hard against my ears.

Much later that night, when Gerard had gone and I lay beside my sated mistress in her bed, I thought again of the dark figure fleeing through the garden, and wondered how long Caterina and I had before retribution came.

It was indeed forthcoming, though not in the manner I expected.

Sixteen

Caterina slept quite late, and woke in a languid but decidedly jovial mood. While the laundress gathered up the contessa's linens to be aired and a chambermaid polished the marble floor in her bedchamber, Caterina took a late breakfast out on her balcony beneath awnings that shielded her from the already withering rays of the summer Roman sun. In a few hours, the heat on the balcony would be intolerable, but for the moment, Caterina desired privacy—and my company.

I took my place beside her at the table, facing west to look past the count's wing, gardens, and stables toward the Tiber and the round fortress of the Castel Sant'Angelo. My lady faced her gardens, casting dreamy glances in the direction of the spot where she and Gerard de Montagne had consummated their tryst. She was still incandescent from the night before. She wore a small conspiratorial smile as her cupbearer filled her glass and a second chambermaid set plates before us holding blue-veined cheese, bread, and figs. When we were alone, she said in a soft voice, so those still inside her chamber could not hear:

"I cannot thank you enough. I was beginning to think that only men experienced sexual gratification, and I was growing quite frustrated and desperate. I am, after all, my father's daughter." She leaned toward me and, to my surprise, caught my hand; her tone grew uncommonly earnest. "Dea, why have you never spoken to me of this? Of this incredible capacity for pleasure that we women are born with?"

Tongue-tied, I dropped my gaze to the plate in front of me. I must have blushed scarlet, for when I dared glance up, Caterina was grinning wryly.

"Don't tell me that Bona managed to turn you into such a prude," she said. And when I still could not bring myself to respond, she added, "Did no one instruct you about the marriage bed?" Her eyes widened with mild horror. "Dea, don't tell me that Matteo didn't know how to satisfy a woman!"

I lifted my face and looked steadily at the horizon, unable to meet Caterina's curious gaze. "We were both virgins," I responded truthfully. "Please, Madonna, I am not comfortable discussing such things."

"Well, everyone should be," she countered. "Physical love is only the most important thing in life! If it isn't, then why did God create Eve?"

"Because Adam was lonely," I ventured shyly.

Caterina dropped my hand. "Bah! Then why not create a second man, if all Adam needed was a companion?"

I had no answer for that, and so I stared disconsolately down at the blue-veined slab of cheese in front of me, and lifted my knife to cut off a chunk.

"Poor Dea," Caterina murmured. "You really don't know what I'm speaking about, do you?" As she spoke, she shifted in her chair toward me; we sat so close together that our knees were touching.

She caught hold of my new amethyst gown beneath the table, and slowly pushed back the silk and petticoat beneath, until her warm palm rested against the outside of my thigh, just above the knee.

"The secret," Caterina breathed, her eyes wide and bright, her gaze focused intently on mine as she half rose from her chair to slide her hand up my thigh, "lies *here*. . . ."

Her hand found its way to the top of my upper leg, and rounded the soft, inner curve of my thigh; in an instant, her fingers found the delta of hair between my legs, and began to probe there.

"Madonna," I gasped, mortified, and got to my feet.

Caterina laughed at me. "You are a beautiful woman, Dea—too beautiful to fear the best things in life. Why do you not take a lover?"

Before I could answer, a door banged open inside the countess's bed-chamber. The laundress and chambermaids emitted soft bleats of fear as a man's voice demanded: "Where is she? Where is the conniving little bitch?"

Caterina and I shared a fleeting look of terror. My lady smoothed her skirts, composed herself, and with an air of consummate dignity, rose and moved toward the open French doors leading to her chamber.

She never passed through them. Count Girolamo stood in the doorway, stooping so that his enormous head did not graze the lintel. His huge hands were clenched into fists, his teeth bared.

"Whore!" he snarled.

Caterina acknowledged his entrance with a curtsy and approached him fearlessly—an impressive act, given that Girolamo was fully twice her size. Her posture was straight, her chin lifted in regal defiance.

"My lord," she countered, her lips pursed to show the perfectly appropriate degree of righteous indignance. "Why do you address me so discourteously? What possible cause have I given, for you to—"

Girolamo took a step forward and struck her full force with the back of his hand. Caterina stumbled backward two paces and fell, tangled in her skirts. I rushed to her side.

"Harlot!" he screamed, spraying spittle upon his fallen wife. "I marry a virgin of respectable lineage to bear my children, but it turns out that she is an irresponsible wanton!"

Caterina struggled to her feet with my help; Girolamo moved closer, forcing her to step backward until she stood pressed against the balcony's waist-high stone railing. Her lower lip was bleeding freely, and the crest of one cheekbone was red and swelling.

Girolamo neared, half crouching to bring his face level with hers. For an instant, I thought he would strike again, but Caterina's reaction gave him pause. She calmly wiped her bleeding mouth upon her sleeve.

"Of what crime am I accused, husband?" Her voice was strong, unyielding.

"Do you deny it?" Girolamo thundered.

With equal fervor, Caterina responded, "Deny *what?*"

Girolamo seized her shoulders and, pressing her back against the balcony ledge, shook her; she was obliged to cling to him, lest she fall into the garden three floors below.

"You were flirting!" he shouted. "At Borgia's party, with one of the Frenchmen. I have the word of an eyewitness! You *kissed* him!"

In the midst of terror, I felt the urge to laugh. Girolamo had no idea of the extent of his wife's infidelity. Whoever had seen us in the garden the previous night had kept our secret.

The instant Girolamo ceased shaking her, Caterina replied triumphantly, "*Who* accuses me? Let me question him, and I will expose this vile, disgusting lie!"

Her confidence was so genuine that Girolamo let go his grip.

"It was a reputable man," he said, still smoldering. "One that I trust."

Caterina glared at him. "One that you trust more than your wife? And might this 'reputable man' have any hidden motive for stirring up discord in your household? Are you so sure that this person has no cause to act maliciously toward you?"

At this, a glimmer of doubt crossed Girolamo's features; he stepped back. Unafraid, Caterina moved forward to close the gap between them.

"This is a dangerous city," Caterina said firmly, "and you have more than enough reason to distrust all those who set foot in your home. But I swear, my lord, that my one aim in life is to help you and the House of Riario ascend to the greatest possible heights of power and glory. My fate is tied to yours."

Her expression transformed into one of reluctance and modesty; she suddenly blushed, as if she were the demurest of maids. "It is true, a Frenchman took unpardonable liberties with me and tried to kiss me. I was too ashamed to mention it to you and wanted no trouble, so I dealt with him myself. I see now that my behavior was wrong, and I therefore accept your husbandly correction.

"I do not know what your eyewitness saw, but I can tell you that once the Frenchman's intentions became clear, I slapped him and commanded him never to take such liberties again. I promise you, he will never make the same mistake. Nor will I ever put myself into a situation where a man can take similar advantage of me."

The count's fury had eased, but his expression remained sullen and mistrustful. He turned to me, studying my expression carefully. "Does she speak the truth?"

I thanked Heaven that my inferior status allowed me to avoid meeting his gaze. "She does, Your Illustriousness."

Girolamo narrowed his eyes at me. "See that she does not stray again from your sight."

With that, he pivoted on his heel and departed.

I turned at once to my wayward mistress. Caterina's expression was one of triumph soured by fury; her lip was still bleeding and she held the lower edge of her sleeve to it to staunch the flow. I reached out gently to lower her arm, so that I could examine the wound, but she waved me away and said, her voice muffled by the swelling and the fabric, "Get them out."

I obeyed and shooed the still-gaping laundress and chambermaids out the chamber door while Caterina came inside. She sat in front of the hearth while I brought the basin and dabbed at her purpling upper lip with a cloth. I was weak with relief; clearly, had Girolamo known that his wife was an adulteress, he would have thrown her over the balcony and dashed her brains out on the flagstones below.

"Thank God," I murmured, as I dabbed at Caterina's wound with a none-too-steady hand. "Thank God . . ."

Caterina let go a vehement sigh. "Fetch my mirror."

I hurried over to the dressing table where the hand mirror rested. When I brought it to her, she scowled at the polished steel surface.

"Fucking bastard! Look at my lip! And my cheek is swelling, too." She lowered the mirror and looked grimly at me. "How long before the bruises are gone?"

"A week, at the earliest."

"I cannot wait a week! I must see *him* again—if not today, then certainly tomorrow!"

I gasped in disbelief at the realization that she was speaking of Gerard de Montagne. "Madonna, you are mad!"

She grinned. "Perhaps I am, but if you had ever experienced what I did last night, you would understand my desire to see Gerard again. From now on, however, I will exercise more caution." She lifted the mirror and frowned again at her reflection. "Now, bring me some salve and cold water. We must get this swelling down!"

At Caterina's insistence, I penned another letter to Monsieur Gerard.

> *My darling,*
>
> *My husband is suspicious; we were spied upon at the Palazzo Borgia, and news of our embrace traveled back to him. I am still concerned that whoever spied upon us in my garden may still tell what he knows. My husband is not a tolerant man, and has already indulged his temper upon me; I fear what retribution he might take should he know the full truth.*
>
> *Even so, I cannot bear to wait until I see you again; you transported me to heights of ecstasy I have never before known. Tell me when and where I can meet you next, safely and discreetly—and quickly, my love, for each moment apart from you is pure torment.*
>
> *Your secret beloved*

This time, I bribed one of the French artists working on a mural in the chapel. He had no loyalty to Girolamo, and no one would find it odd for him to visit the French embassy. Monsieur Gerard was so eager to receive the message that he made the artist wait while he encrypted a reply on the spot.

Bellisima, Gerard wrote, *O most beautiful one, my heart breaks to tell you that I cannot see you today or tomorrow. But early this Friday morning, your husband is leaving on political business for Faenza and Forlì—did he not tell you? The trip itself will find him on the road twenty days.*

He then gave directions to a palazzo owned by someone who would gladly permit its use and was "a champion of love, utterly discreet about such matters."

Meet me there at midday on Friday, after you are certain the count has departed, he wrote. *Let us waste no time!*

For the next three weeks, every weekday at noon, Caterina and I rode into the city in a carriage driven by her favorite groom—a shy, taciturn young lad who blushed wildly every time his mistress appeared. So smitten was he that he would accept no bribe for keeping his lady's secret, "for it is," he said, "my honor to serve her."

I wanted desperately to remain behind. I thoroughly disapproved of my mistress's scandalous behavior, but it would set household tongues wagging if I did not accompany her as a chaperone.

"Besides," Caterina told me, "I would not feel safe without you."

We traversed the city in an unmarked carriage, ostensibly to indulge Caterina's desire to adorn herself and her surroundings. We visited goldsmiths, jewelers, silk merchants, artists' workshops, each time making some purchase to prove that the contessa had, in fact, gone where she claimed to be going.

But always, before the church bells rang at midday, Caterina and I climbed back into the carriage and lowered the black gauze curtains as our driver urged the horses to the northeastern edge of the city proper. We made our way to the neighborhood surrounding the Piazza di Spagna, the Spanish Plaza, to a narrow road that terminated in a cul-de-sac, where a few small palaces stood, each walled and gated for protection's sake.

The property was obviously owned by someone very wealthy, for a gatekeeper was always on duty and the driveway was covered with new flagstone. The original structure had been razed and replaced by the ubiquitous three-story rectangular palace of classical Roman design in polished stone. The interior, although sparsely furnished, featured the finest marble floors and walls covered by breathtaking tapestries.

We were welcomed inside by a jaded-looking, middle-aged noblewoman whose palpable boredom did not waver when she first looked on the dazzling Caterina, dressed in gleaming white and gold.

"Good day, Your Illustrious Highness," she said, with a faint foreign accent as she curtsied to Caterina. She led us upstairs to a bedchamber that was far more sumptuously appointed than the rest of the house.

Standing beside the bed awaiting his beloved was Gerard de Montagne, dressed in only his short white chemise and blue leggings.

"My God," he said, as Caterina entered, "I had forgotten how lovely you are! But what is this?" He rushed to take Caterina's hands in his and stared at her bruised lip and cheek. "My darling! Oh, my sweet, what sort of ogre could dare despoil such a beautiful face? I should kill him!" This last phrase was said with altogether unconvincing bravado.

Caterina waved his words away, and simpered. "Small cost for such enormous pleasure."

The conversation that followed was painfully vapid. I directed my face toward the carpet and studied the exotic Moorish pattern there until the two lovers began to grope each other, at which point I murmured a request to be dismissed.

To my surprise, the middle-aged servant was waiting for me just outside the door. "Come," she said pleasantly. "There is cool watered wine and refreshments waiting for you."

She led me across the corridor, to a sitting room where an open window overlooked a view of a landscaped garden. She gestured. "Sit. Don't worry, you'll be able to hear your lady when she calls."

I settled into a red satin chair next to a table that held a carafe of watered wine, an empty goblet, and a tray of pastries and figs; the instant I did, a lad hurried into the room, picked up a large feather fan, and began to wave it solemnly. I felt quite guilty—it did not seem right that I should enjoy being party to such a wicked venture—but the day was hot and the fan directed the breeze to me so nicely that I did not tell the boy to leave. Familiarity with crime, however, soon eases guilt, and by the fifth day, I had not only become comfortable at the little palazzo in the Spanish neighborhood, but had also come to enjoy the excellent wine served there, as well as the little dishes doña Maria, the greeter, brought me.

Caterina's proclivity for the sexual act shocked me; her temper was beastly on Sundays, the one day she did not visit the little palazzo, and remarkably agreeable the rest of the week. And her visits with Gerard, during the month Girolamo was gone, grew progressively longer.

On the seventh visit to the palazzo, Caterina spent an additional hour in the bedchamber with Gerard beyond our allotted time. I was in the sitting room, reading one of the books I had discovered upon a shelf—and thinking of Luca, who had accompanied the count to Faenza—when I heard doña Maria greet someone entering through the front door downstairs.

A man answered her, and a brief exchange followed. I could make out the voices but not the gist. His arrival alarmed me, especially when I heard heavy footfalls on the stairs. The open door to the sitting room was only a few paces from the landing, so I signaled for my little fan-wielder to stop and retreat to a corner while I hid behind the half-ajar door.

I peered through the crack and watched as Rodrigo Borgia, in his scarlet robes and skullcap, ascended the stairs and made his way down the hall. Directly across from my hiding place, only a few paces from me, he paused at the closed door to Gerard and Caterina's chamber, and inclined his ear toward the lovers' muffled groans of pleasure.

I feared he would open the door to their borrowed bedchamber; instead, he grinned and nodded in approval, and continued down the corridor. When I heard a door farther down the hallway open and close, I peered out cautiously; the way was clear.

I hurried across the corridor to the lovers' chamber and rapped softly on the wooden door. No reply came, so I cracked open the door and stepped quickly inside, my gaze averted—but not enough to escape a glimpse of a naked Caterina kneeling on all fours on the edge of the bed, her shins hanging free, and an equally unclad Gerard standing on the floor just behind her, fully erect and parting her flesh in anticipation of entry.

"Forgive me, Madonna, forgive me, Monsieur," I hissed. "Rodrigo Borgia has come. He is in a room down the hall. We must leave at once before he discovers you."

Gerard backed away and covered himself with his chemise. "Good God!" he exclaimed, then caught himself and lowered his voice to a whisper. "I should have taken note of the hour." He turned his bare back to me and balanced on one foot as he pushed the other into his gathered leggings.

Displeased, the contessa whispered to him, "What is Borgia doing here?"

"He owns this house. I received permission to use it at midday, when it is always vacant, from a dear friend of his. He has many friends who use this place when they desire privacy." Gerard pulled on his chemise, tunic, and boots with practiced speed as he spoke. "I of course told no one the name of the lady I was bringing here."

Once he had finished dressing, he moved swiftly to take Caterina's hand and kiss it. "Forgive me, my darling, but I must go; it is better that I not be seen with you. I suggest you leave at once, and quietly."

Caterina opened her mouth to reply, but Gerard dropped her hand and darted out of the chamber and down the stairs.

I gathered up all of Caterina's clothing and stuffed her into it.

The corridor was clear. I signaled to her, and preceded her out into the hall. She had just made it into the doorway when one of her slippers came loose; she paused to press one hand against the jamb and adjust the slipper with the other.

I was already on the landing, and glanced back at her just as she stepped into the hallway. At the same instant, several rooms behind her, a door opened, and Cardinal Borgia emerged in a long undershirt and mulberry and yellow leggings.

"But what fair lady is this?" he called after her. "As your host, I must welcome you!"

Caterina froze. We stared at each other for an instant, uncertain whether to bolt or stand fast. My lady's expression transformed from one of anxiety to one of dignified repose. She turned to face Borgia, and bowed shallowly from her shoulders.

"Your Holiness," she said sweetly.

Borgia's lips parted in amazement; the gesture transformed into a great wolfish grin. "Why, Your Illustrious Highness! What a delightful surprise to see you again!"

"And you," Caterina answered. "But I am late and must go."

She took a step toward the staircase, but Borgia caught her arm.

"Ah, my lovely Madonna Caterina," he said, still showing his teeth. "Do not leave just yet. Your husband is away; who will notice if you are late returning home?"

Caterina remained calm. "I have obligations. Unhand me, please."

Borgia's grip tightened. "Women are never so beautiful as they are after satisfying lovemaking," he murmured. "And Caterina, you are the most beautiful of all. I did not take offense at your earlier rejection, nor press my cause because you are so young—and, I thought, sheltered and inexperienced, but I see now that is not the case. I will give you the world, my darling, if only you would grant me some small favors. . . ."

He stroked her cheek; she turned it brusquely away, and he laughed softly.

"Am I wrong in believing you are much like me?" he asked. "Practical and aware that life is too short to deny oneself pleasure? More awaits you, Madonna. Come to my chamber"—he gestured behind him at the open door to his room—"and see what a far more experienced man can do for you. Your Frenchman is a callow youth, so eager in satisfying his own desires that he does not know how to lead a woman to the brink of ecstasy and keep her there for hours. Besides, someone else is coming to join me, one who would dearly appreciate your company. I can promise you an afternoon you will never forget."

Caterina lifted her free arm and slapped him full across the face.

A murderous blaze flared in his eyes, then dimmed. "Boldness becomes you," he said approvingly. "Without it, you would be just another pretty trinket, but I am that rare beast who admires strength in a woman."

To prove it, he pressed her to him for a lingering kiss intended to impress her with his finesse. Caterina pounded his chest with her fists, and kicked his legs, but he was the stronger. When he was satisfied, he pulled back, amused, and held her at arm's length to study her reaction.

Caterina's features were contorted by hate as she spat into the cardinal's eyes. Borgia wiped them on his sleeve as Caterina said, her voice trembling with rage, "You are old and disgusting and stink of garlic. Let me go."

Borgia's smile was gone now as he caught both her arms. "I may be older, Caterina, but I am far wealthier than even your Girolamo, and twice as powerful. He is too foolish and hotheaded to live very long. I can give you more than he could ever hope to."

"I could never love you," Caterina sneered.

"That's altogether beside the point, my dear." A threatening note crept into Borgia's tone. "I would think that you would be more concerned about the fact that I might reveal your affair to your husband." He glanced pointedly at her swollen lip. "I have come to know Girolamo rather well; it seems you have noticed, too, that his impetuous temper often leads him to violence. I would hate to see what he might do should he learn his young wife has been unfaithful."

Seething, Caterina pulled away with a jerk; this time, Borgia let her go.

"And I will tell my husband that *you* made this tryst possible—and that you have tried repeatedly to seduce me!"

He laughed scathingly. "Girolamo strikes first and asks questions later. I doubt your pretty mouth would be able to form the words after the initial blow. I doubt, in fact, that you would live long enough to tell him anything about me. Or that your Frenchman would survive such a revelation."

"You are quite right," Caterina replied hotly. "Therefore, *I* will go first to my husband and tearfully confess to him that *you* are my lover, and that you first took me by force in your pleasure garden, using your drugged wine. I don't doubt that Girolamo has heard of it. I will go to him begging for his protection and forgiveness, saying that I never wanted to become involved in the first place, and am overwhelmed by shame—and that I expect the worst sort of retaliation from you, a man who thinks nothing of corrupting beautiful young women. I may be forced to endure a beating, but I will not lose my property or my position, as you well may.

"Perhaps, before my husband returns home, I might make my confession to Pope Sixtus, who is especially fond of me and weakens at the sight of a woman's tears. Good day, Your Holiness." Caterina gathered her skirts, turned her back to him, and nodded for me to head down the stairs.

In the instant before I turned, I caught a glimpse of the cardinal's expression as he watched Caterina leave. His simmering anger had vanished; in its place was a look of fascination, determination, and total infatuation.

As we hurried down, he called after us, his tone oddly lighthearted.

"You can always change your mind. I understand that your husband will not be returning from Faenza for some weeks."

By the time we reached the entryway, doña Maria was just opening the front door. As I dashed over the threshold, I nearly collided with a pretty, green-eyed brunette—the French ambassador's wife—who was trying to enter. She stepped back to let us pass, and at the sight of the somewhat disheveled Caterina, let go a short laugh of astonishment.

"Your Illustriousness!" she exclaimed, with a sly, evilly delighted grin.

"Your Grace," I muttered beneath my breath.

Caterina swept past her without a word. Together we made haste to the carriage.

Seventeen

Caterina refused to stop seeing her French lover; on four occasions, she returned to Borgia's secret palazzo—always at the stroke of midday, when it was the Spanish cardinal's custom to give Pope Sixtus a daily report on Church affairs while the two dined together. She never again made the mistake of staying at the palazzo more than an hour. On other occasions, she rode with Gerard to empty meadows or forests on the edge of the city. I would leave her and her lover in the carriage, and, with the blushing driver, walk far enough away that we could not hear the pair's impassioned cries as the carriage rocked.

In the meantime, Caterina informed her lover of Borgia's unwanted attentions, but Gerard reacted with insufficient outrage, instead warning her to take care "not to insult the cardinal unnecessarily, for it is not good to be his enemy." Although Gerard's cowardice disgusted her, she did not let her opinion of his character intrude upon her enjoyment of his physical attributes.

I scolded Caterina constantly; she was playing with not just her reputation, but with her life. I gathered my courage and told her that once Girolamo returned home, I would no longer go with her to meet Gerard.

For that, she slapped me, but I held my ground. It was during this time that a letter arrived addressed to the contessa and bearing Borgia's seal. Caterina read it aloud to me with a good deal of triumph and sarcasm:

Your Most Illustrious Highness,

I perceive in you great bravery, intelligence, and determination. To me, such qualities are as appealing as physical beauty, which of course you also possess to an infinite degree.

Forgive me; I was wrong to treat you so rudely. You are clearly worthy of respect. Although you are still very young, I realize now that, were you a man, you would be as great and formidable a ruler as your father, the Duke of Milan.

Alas, Nature has made you a woman—a tragedy for you, but good fortune for men such as me, who perceive that females of strong character and wit are to be valued and encouraged to utilize their talents. What a shame that I am wed to Mother Church, and you to another—for were we to join forces, all of Italy would be ours for the taking.

Consider that, and put aside your pretty Frenchman; he is a witless boy, and will amount to nothing. I, however, promise you unimaginable wealth and power. I stand ever ready to become

Your servant,

Rodrigo Llançol y Borgia

When she had finished reading, Caterina laughed until her face was flushed. I, however, remained solemn as I contemplated what the cardinal had written.

"Unbelievable," I said at last. "He has trusted you with an unencrypted letter, signed by his own hand. You could easily shame him with this."

Caterina gave an indignant little snort. "Only if I wanted to implicate myself. See how he says here, 'Put aside your pretty Frenchman.' I can hardly show this to Girolamo."

I nodded. "But he is apologizing. I saw the look on his face as we were leaving. Madonna, he is in love with you."

She made a noise of pure disgust. "That is *his* misfortune. I would rather join a nunnery than make love to him. He is old and oily."

"He's only ten years older than Girolamo," I countered. "Although I agree, the thought is disgusting. Still . . . be careful not to insult him, Madonna. He is too wily and knows too much."

The Spanish cardinal was indeed wily. The very next day, a messenger wearing the Borgia livery arrived. He knelt as he presented Her Illustriousness with a long rectangular box, which contained six long strands of perfect pearls.

Please accept this gift of friendship, Borgia had written, *although it cannot do justice to your fair skin. Forgive my impertinence, and think of me kindly.*

Caterina gave a small, self-satisfied smile at the sight of the jewels, then dictated a reply to the messenger. "Thank His Holiness for the gift," she said. "But I must send it back. Tell him that my husband gave me a trunkful of pearls for a wedding gift. I have no need of more."

The following day, another gift arrived from the same messenger: a pair of solid gold candlesticks, with a note in the cardinal's hand comparing them to Caterina's shining hair. The contessa rejected them as well.

On the third day, Borgia sent a large mirror in an ornate silver frame. At that point, Caterina sat and dictated a letter to me.

You were right, she said, *that I am as brave as any man. And I must tell you to quit wasting your time, as I care nothing for trinkets or flattery. Far from it. My greatest wish in this life is to become a soldier. Like my father, I have a head for military strategy, and the fearlessness to implement it. In truth, I would make a far better captain of the papal army than my husband. Politics, power, war—these are things that pique my interest, not gowns or jewels.*

"There," she said triumphantly as the deflated messenger departed to return yet another gift to his lovelorn master. "That should give him pause."

On the fourth day—and the fifth, sixth, and seventh—no message from Borgia was forthcoming. I believed that he had finally been discouraged or was plotting revenge.

Then, on the eighth day, when the contessa and I returned home from another midday rendezvous with Gerard, the messenger in Borgia livery was waiting for us. This time, when Caterina swept imperiously into her reception chamber, the messenger was down on one knee, his head bowed, his arms outstretched as if pleading.

Across his open palms lay an unsheathed halberd.

"Your Illustrious Highness," the messenger said timidly, not daring to lift his head. "His Holiness wishes to convey that this is made of Toledo steel. The hilt is pure gold. He says, 'To the fearless wife of the captain of the papal army: may all her enemies be defeated.'"

It was a lovely shining creation, polished to a dazzling gleam. The blade was slender but deadly; the golden hilt was cruciform, and the pommel an open sphere of ornate gold filigree.

Caterina took it reverently from the messenger's hands and hoisted it easily, despite its heft; it was shorter than a man's sword, as though it had been made expressly for her. She lunged and slashed the air with it, then, grinning, pointed it at me.

Her gaze was still on me as she spoke to the messenger. "Is there a sheath for it?"

"Yes, Your Illustriousness." Still kneeling, he gestured at the finely tooled leather sheath on the floor in front of him, threaded onto a thick belt sized for a woman's hips.

"Excellent," Caterina said, slowly tilting the blade from side to side to watch the light glint off the steel. "Tell your master that I accept this gift in the spirit of friendship, and thank him for it."

The servant bowed his head, rose, and backed out of the room.

When he was gone, I scowled in disapproval. "Do not think for a moment, Madonna, that he has only friendship in mind. I don't trust him."

Caterina lunged forward, striking at an imaginary foe with remarkable grace. "Nor do I," she said, and swung the blade backhandedly. "Do you think I can't protect myself from the likes of him? You underestimate me, Dea."

She pivoted on her heel, skirts swirling, to attack the opposite direction with vigor.

"I hope you are right," I said. But the truth was that I knew that, as clever as my lady was, she was no match for Rodrigo Borgia.

Nonetheless, Caterina recruited one of Girolamo's drill instructors to sharpen her skill with the sword, and practiced diligently with the weapon every day.

Eventually, Count Girolamo returned home from his journey and for two nights demanded the nuptial company of his reluctant wife.

The third day after his return was the pope's birthday. Custom demanded that His Holiness appear outside Saint Peter's to address the crowd gathered in the square; however, Sixtus's health allowed him only to wave at the cheering throngs for a few moments before being carried on a litter back to his apartments. Caterina, Girolamo, and Cardinal della Rovere joined him on the dais, and della Rovere spoke after His Holiness had departed; unfortunately, those gathered were too impatient to listen to anyone other than the pope himself, and della Rovere's words were drowned out by the sound of his audience departing.

I stood just in front of the platform, straining out of courtesy to listen to the cardinal's exaggerated praise of his kinsman, when my eye caught movement in the periphery of my vision. I inclined my head toward it, and saw the dark-haired scribe, Luca, with a politely attentive expression frozen on his face.

I almost turned away quickly; I was still embarrassed over my distrustful behavior toward Ser Luca, and expected that he was still angry with me. Yet when my unwilling gaze accidentally caught his, he smiled brilliantly at me before turning his attention again to the unfortunate speaker.

I smiled back, with great relief.

That day, Girolamo and the contessa held a feast for dozens of cardinals and other notables at the palazzo, as Sixtus was feeling unwell and did not wish to entertain at the Vatican. It was by far the most lavish banquet ever prepared at the Palazzo Riario; two enormous tables were brought in to seat a hundred diners. Among them were Cardinal Borgia and Cardinal Giuliano della Rovere, who, though he still despised his cousin Girolamo, came for Caterina's sake. I stood behind Caterina, supervising her cupbearer and making sure that della Rovere received the special attention due a guest of honor.

Despite the mounting heat, the banquet dragged on for hours, until everyone was sweating and exhausted, including Caterina, who grew suddenly pale before the final course was brought, even though one of the little slave boys was fanning her furiously. By the time I was at her side, she had pushed herself from the table and, without a single word, hurried out of the stuffy chamber.

By the time she made her way down the corridor to the stairs leading up to her apartments—with me following a step behind—she was overcome. Pressing one hand to her stomach and the other against the wall, she hunched over and retched up the contents of the feast, which splattered against the white marble landing.

I caught her elbow and helped ease her down onto the first stairs, where she caught the cool stone railing and pressed her forehead to it, her eyes closed.

"Madonna, tell me how you feel." I pressed my hand to her damp forehead. It was warm from the heat, but not feverish.

She groaned without opening her eyes. "Don't make me talk," she murmured. "Let me just sit. . . ."

The effort of speaking proved too much, and another wave of nausea overtook her. This time, she vomited mostly foamy yellow bile before resting her head again. We sat there until Caterina grew steady enough to go up to her bedchamber. I sent one of the maids down to the banquet hall to apologize to the guests, while another brought a pitcher of cold water and a soft cloth, which I dampened and pressed to my lady's forehead.

An hour later, Caterina was still weak but much improved, and insisted I return to the banquet chamber to make sure Cardinal della Rovere was properly looked after. I did so, only to discover that he and almost all the other guests had left immediately after the final course. Only a few lingered, making conversation with their sated, drowsy host. As was common in summer, plague and a deadly fever were making their way through the poorer quarters of the city, and those remaining in Rome panicked easily when reminded of the fact.

I curtsied to Count Girolamo and announced that his wife was recovering quickly, that she had only been stricken by the heat because of her heavy gown. He accepted this with distracted relief.

I returned to my mistress, who was sitting up in her bed and hungry; I sat with her while she ate her fill of plain broth and bread. Soon afterward she fell soundly asleep. I would have remained with her, but by then one of the servants, a kindly old nurse, promised to watch over Caterina, and urged me to join the rest of the house staff in the banquet chamber; now that the guests had gone, the dining chamber was open to the household staff so that we could consume the remainders of the feast.

By the time I arrived in the chamber again, the room was crowded and a queue had formed of polite but insistent staff members and servants, all waiting to get their share of the spoils, which were being doled out by the cooks. I was obliged to wait my turn. Others, who had already sat down at the cleared banquet tables, were eating their fill; still others had finished, and were dancing to the tune played by lutists and pipers.

I intended to get my plate and cup and return to the contessa's apartments to dine in private, but as I stood in line, watching the dancers, someone stepped in front of me to block my view.

The scribe Luca held a kitchen tray in his hands, bearing two heaped plates, two finger towels, two goblets, and a carafe of wine. He wore his dark silver brocade tunic with the lavender silk sleeves; an ink smudge adorned the very tip of his prominent nose, a fact of which he was charmingly unaware. The summer humidity had coaxed a few half-formed ringlets from his blue-black waves, and left the plume of the quill tucked behind his right ear bedraggled. His neatly trimmed beard was speckled with what appeared to be breadcrumbs.

I stared up, startled, at the dark gray eyes so close to the level of my own; they revealed no intimacy, no recognition, merely the polite detachment of a friendly stranger.

"Madonna," he said loudly, in order to be heard over the music, conversation, and clatter of plates. "I have taken enough food for two, in case I discovered a friend with whom I wished to sup. Would you do me the honor?"

"Of course, sir." My swift, affirmative reply astonished me. "Lead the way."

He took me to a corner of the banquet table farthest from the musicians and the dancing, and chose a spot a few chairs distant on either side from the other chattering diners.

"I am so glad," I said more softly as I sat and he set my cup and plate before me, "that you are not still angry at me. I want to apologize for my stupidity, my thoughtlessness."

His gray gaze, still congenial but somewhat distant, was as blank as stone. "I don't know what you're referring to, Madonna. To my knowledge, we have not met before today."

Confused, I opened my mouth and closed it again as the corners of his mouth finally curved upward and a glimmer of amusement passed over his features. I realized that, outside of the scribe's hidden office, without any incriminating documents to bind us together, no one would be suspicious were we to "meet" for the first time under Count Girolamo's roof and become friends.

"Of course," I said, and did a half curtsy in my chair. "I am Dea, chief lady-in-waiting to Her Illustriousness."

He finished emptying the contents of the tray onto the table, and turned to bow to me. "And I am Luca, one of His Illustriousness's clerks."

"How do you do, Ser Luca?"

"How do you do, Madonna Dea?"

"Please, just Dea." I patted the chair beside me, and he sat.

"If you will call me just Luca."

"Luca," I said, savoring the name until an ominous thought struck me. "And have you a wife and children, Luca?"

"No," he answered wrily. "The count keeps me too busy. I expect our energetic young contessa keeps you rather busy as well."

I smiled, enjoying the pretense, and grateful that he did not inquire directly after my husband. "That would be an understatement. And are you from Rome?"

"Of that I am uncertain," he replied. "I was orphaned."

"Such a coincidence! I am, too."

Our gazes met as we laughed, knowing we shared a secret no one else in the room would ever guess. We made amiable if meaningless conversation as we ate; I yearned to speak frankly to him, to ask him more about his friendship with Matteo, but one of Girolamo's bookkeepers sat down beside us to eat his dinner.

After we finished eating, I deemed it too hot and stuffy to join the few sweating dancers. We took our wine out onto the deserted balcony, lit by a single torch, to enjoy the view of the night-shrouded gardens behind the palazzo. As I placed a hand upon the stone railing and peered down into the darkness, wondering awkwardly what I would say next, Luca began speaking.

"I first met Matteo six years ago, when Sixtus was elected," he said softly, his unfocused gaze directed outward, like mine. "I started working for His Holiness when he was still a cardinal. Later, when he was made pope and brought his nephews to Rome, I was assigned to Girolamo.

"But before I came to live in Rome, there was an enormous celebration when Sixtus was elected. Rulers from all over the world—including the contessa's father, the Duke of Milan, and Lorenzo de' Medici—came to pay their respects to the new pope. The staff was fed separately from the nobles, and I shared lunch with Matteo, among others, more than once. Neither of us dared speak to or of Lorenzo, of course, but I caught a look Matteo shared with His Magnificence, and realized they knew each other well. And so I set out to befriend Matteo."

His voice grew even softer. "We never spoke about the Society"—he gave me a sidewise glance, to gauge my reaction—"or the secrets our masters entrusted to us. But we spoke about what it was like to grow up orphaned and receive the help of a wealthy benefactor. We talked about the homes that we knew, and our friends, and Matteo spoke a great deal—not about his wife, but his sister."

Despite the heat, I balanced my goblet upon the railing and rubbed my upper arms, as if chilled.

Luca set down his own goblet—rather precariously, I thought, but I was far too captivated by his words to interrupt him as he continued. "Matteo described her remarkable goodness, intelligence, and beauty . . . and whispered of her uncanny talent for interpreting signs and portents.

"Of course, one can forgive a brother for exaggerating his sister's attributes, as I assumed he did. But Madonna"—he turned his face toward mine—"now that I have had the incredible good fortune of meeting you in the flesh, I must say that his descriptions do not do you justice."

I lifted my gaze from the dark gardens to look at him in surprise. Caught in the dim, flickering light from the torch, his expression was as intent and earnest as any I had ever seen. Here, I decided, was a man as good, as dedicated, and as brave as Matteo; my brother would never have revealed the fact that I was not his wife to any but the most trustworthy soul. I had not seen it before because Luca was amazingly skilled at keeping his emotions from registering on his face.

Now he did not hide them, and as I looked into his eyes and saw the timid but insistent affection there, I drew in a breath. When I released it, the world had shifted from a place of grief and evil to a haven of hope and grace.

I could have remained all night on the balcony speaking to Luca; I told him of my amazement over discovering that Matteo and I were related, of my grief over his death, of my hope to someday decipher the little diary, still in my possession. I mentioned my desire to live in Florence and my great disappointment at being ordered to go to Rome with Caterina. I said little of my meeting with the Medici, for I did not truly know the angel, and considered myself a fraud—a fact I did not want Luca to know, lest he realize that Matteo's sister was not as perfect as he presumed.

After speaking his heart, Luca grew charmingly flustered, and at one point, gestured sweepingly as he spoke. His hand struck his brass goblet, still balanced uncertainly on the stone railing, and sent it clattering down to the courtyard below—not without first splattering both of us. My neck and décolletage were soaked, and I laughed gently as I took his proffered kerchief to dab at myself, a feat that could not be performed with any discretion, as the wine had quickly trickled down between my breasts.

We parted with me grinning and thoroughly won, and Luca roundly embarrassed. I could not, after all, remain all night. There was Caterina to worry about, and I had spent two hours instead of the quarter hour I'd planned at the banquet spoils.

To my relief, the contessa was still sleeping soundly when I arrived, and did not stir as I undressed and took my place beside her in the bed. For hours, I lay happily awake, recalling again and again Luca's words about my brother failing to describe my virtues adequately.

Morning, however, brought renewed worry. I woke to the sound of Her Illustriousness heaving. She stood beside the bed in her nightgown, and as I leapt up and hurried round to her, she clutched the thick bedpost, slid slowly down onto her haunches, and closed her eyes. She was frighteningly pale.

"Let me die," she murmured crossly as I hovered, pelting her with inane questions. "Just go away. . . ."

I did, but brought back towels and the basin. I cleaned up the small mess and was dabbing her white brow with cool water when she slowly opened her eyes again.

"Bread," she said with abrupt certainty. "Bring me some plain bread, and some salt. I'm so queasy I could die, but if I had something in my stomach, I know I'd feel better."

I looked down at her with dread and tentative joy.

"Madonna," I asked, "when did your monthly bleed last come?"

Caterina was pregnant, of course, and unlike me, completely unconcerned about the child's paternity.

"Girolamo's a halfwit," she said. "He'll never notice if the child doesn't look like him."

"Your husband did enough damage to you when he only suspected you had kissed Gerard de Montagne," I countered. "What will he do when you present him with a baby whose curls are tighter and paler than your own?"

Her expression soured, but she had no answer. I took advantage of her queasiness and sudden disinterest in romance to press home the fact that she should break off the affair immediately and tell him he was no longer welcome in the Palazzo Riario. If Girolamo were not reminded regularly of the Frenchman, he would be less likely to think of him when he gazed on the face of his newborn child.

To my delight, Caterina chose to take my advice. She had finally had her fill of the amorous Gerard, and after the baby, there would be other men to conquer. But she had no desire for an unpleasant emotional confrontation. Rather than meet with him, she decided to visit the French ambassador at the embassy to deliver a gift: a barrel of the wine he had complimented when last dining at the Palazzo Riario. While Caterina was speaking to the ambassador, I was to find the unfortunate Gerard and deliver the last encrypted message he would ever receive from the contessa.

"I don't care what you tell him," Caterina said, when I asked her to dictate the contents of her final letter to Gerard. "Say that I don't love him anymore, or that I'm afraid of getting caught."

I sat down and wrote the kindest farewell letter possible. So far as Gerard would ever know, Caterina's heart was sorely broken. She was ending the relationship for the noblest of reasons: the child in her womb, which she prayed was her lover's, as she would treasure it all the more. The child whom she was, sadly, forced to protect from Girolamo's wrath, lest he strike her again out of jealousy, possibly ending the pregnancy.

Two days later, I rode with Caterina to the offices of the French ambassador. Caterina had eaten an egg and quite a bit of bread that morning in hopes of settling her capricious stomach, and by late morning, she decided she was steady enough to risk the carriage. We made it to the ambassador's palace without incident only to learn that Monsieur de Montagne had not yet reported for work that morning, and was most likely still at his residence.

Caterina duly delivered the wine to the ambassador. Afterward she directed the driver to take us directly to Monsieur de Montagne's dwelling. The minute we arrived at the modest building that housed Gerard's ground-floor apartments, Caterina pushed me out of the carriage.

I knocked on de Montagne's door. It seemed cruel to dispense of him in such a cold manner. As I tried to think of what I should or should not say, the door was flung open. A willowy, dark-haired youth stood just inside the threshold. He wore a noble's finely tailored clothes, and his expression was one of pure panic; his eyes were red and puffy from weeping.

"Where is the doctor?" he demanded, in a thick French accent. He gestured at the carriage where Caterina waited behind black gauze curtains. "Is he there? Tell him to come inside at once! My master can pay!"

"I'm sorry," I said, thoroughly flustered. "I've come from the contessa, Caterina Sforza. I have a letter to deliver to your master."

"Ah, is the contessa here?" The lad peered past me at the carriage. "Her presence would comfort him."

Before I could reply, the youth wrung his hands and burst into tears. In a lowered voice, he admitted, "Madonna, I am afraid he will die before the doctor comes! I'm no sickmaid. . . . I don't even know what's wrong with him!"

A groan of misery came from the sitting room behind him.

I glanced over my shoulder at the carriage, where Caterina waited. I had not intended to do anything more than hand the letter over, but the young man's panic was impossible to ignore. "Your master is very ill?"

The youth's face contorted again. "Please, Madonna, help him!"

I sighed and stepped over the threshold, knowing that, back in the carriage, Caterina was cursing my inability to follow her instructions exactly.

The youth led me back into the sitting room. Light streamed in through the open, unshuttered windows and fell directly on Gerard, who lay limp and half-conscious on the couch. His grayish skin glistened with sharp-smelling sweat; I moved beside the couch, and stared down at his sunken face. He stared back through half-closed, glittering eyes and did not know me.

I whirled on the youth, who was again wringing his hands. "Close those shutters!" I ordered. "And bring a basin, a pitcher of cool water, and some towels."

I set Caterina's letter on a table and crouched down beside the ill man. "Monsieur, can you hear me?"

He tried to answer, but the effort nauseated him; too weak to sit, even to speak, he turned his head to one side and vomited down the side of the brocade couch. The former contents of his stomach were bilious yellow-green, streaked with bright blood. Without thinking, I pulled a kerchief from my pocket and wiped it up.

But the sight of it—and the painfully familiar convulsing of his limbs that followed—reduced me to the same level of panic as the servant, who reappeared a moment later with the pitcher, basin, and towels.

"What's wrong, Madonna?" he asked, after seeing my expression. "Is it the plague?"

I shook my head, for a long moment unable to speak.

"Poison," I said at last.

Eighteen

How does one describe being pulled back into the unwanted past? As I crouched beside the dying Monsieur de Montagne, I saw only my beloved Matteo, the whites of his hazel eyes bloodied, his cheeks a mottled red violet. Even when de Montagne looked up at me to whisper, *Caterina*, it was not his voice I heard but my dead brother's. The grief that overtook me was as shattering as that I had felt the morning Matteo died.

I would have stayed to hold Gerard's hand until the last breath came, but the doctor finally arrived and ordered me to leave. Stunned, I made my way back to the carriage, where a very irritated Caterina was waiting.

"I almost sent the coachman after you!" she scolded as I climbed in beside her. She would have launched into a tirade, but the sight of my face silenced her.

The carriage lurched as the driver goaded the horses.

Caterina spoke again, this time in a low, if anxious, tone. "What is it, Dea? What has happened?"

I stared out through the curtains at the streets of Rome, sheerly veiled in black, and struggled to contain tears that should have been shed months ago.

"He is dying," I said finally. "He asked for you."

"Dying!" Caterina recoiled from me. "Of what? Fever? Don't tell me he has plague!"

I shook my head. "He was poisoned, Madonna."

She drew in a sharp breath and lifted her fingers to her mouth in a gesture that revealed not sorrow, but fear. She did not tell the driver to reverse his course and return to the Frenchman's house; instead, she leaned out the window, the gauze curtain hiding her from the scrutiny of passersby, and shouted for him to hurry home.

Then she turned to me, and in the same fierce, heartless tone, demanded: "How do you know this? How can you be so sure?"

"Because Matteo died of poison," I replied in angry disgust, flicking away unwanted tears. "Because I know the symptoms."

This revelation shocked her. We rode the rest of the way in silence, Caterina frowning down at her hands in her lap, her mind working at lightning speed, I staring out at Rome, darkly veiled.

We heard nothing more about Gerard de Montagne. Two days later, Count Girolamo decided that he wished to dine with his wife in private, something he had rarely done since the marriage. When Caterina received his invitation, her bravado momentarily deserted her, and she begged me to serve as her cupbearer. That way, I would only be a step or two away from her throughout the meal, and although I was not strong enough to save her from Girolamo's blows, she felt that my presence would bring her luck.

Dinner was a tense affair, held in the private dining chamber just off Girolamo's study. Caterina and I arrived first, and the contessa took her chair while I positioned myself two steps behind her. She would not take the water mixed with wine that Girolamo's cupbearer offered, but insisted that I fetch her water from the kitchen pump myself. Nor would she avail herself of any of the morsels offered her before Girolamo arrived.

Instead, she sat listening to the argument in the next room between her husband and some unfortunate aide. Her pregnancy had not yet changed her body, though it left her cheeks pale and her appetite uncertain. She had not yet revealed it to her husband, as she wanted Gerard's kiss to be long forgotten before she announced the coming child.

A quarter of an hour later, Girolamo arrived in a foul mood. In the months since his wedding, the count had gained weight; his long, equine face had fattened, too, evoking the bloated features of his father, Pope Sixtus.

Caterina rose and curtsied to him. "How do you fare this evening, my lord?" she asked cheerfully.

"Well, I suppose," Girolamo answered sourly, and gestured impatiently for her to retake her seat as he settled at the table. "And you?"

"Quite well." Caterina picked up her goblet while Girolamo's cupbearer stepped up to fill his, and said, "To your health, my lord."

"To your health," Girolamo echoed unenthusiastically, and drank. When he set his cup down and signaled for it to be refilled, he sat back and narrowed his tiny eyes at Caterina.

"To what do I owe the honor of your company this evening?" the contessa asked brightly.

He tensed in his chair and lifted his long chin with faint defiance. "Do I need a reason to want to have dinner with my wife?"

"You do not, my lord. I'm simply happy to be with you this evening."

The conversation continued in this awkward fashion until the first course—a *minestra*, consisting of pasta in temperate veal broth with vegetables—arrived. Before dinner, I had gone to the kitchen with a taster, who tried all the different dishes and remained in the kitchen to guard the portions set aside for our mistress. Caterina's pallor and the beads of sweat on her brow indicated that she was sorely nauseated, but she forced down a few spoonsful, all the while keeping her attention on the count.

Girolamo could not control his impatience for very long. Before the first-course dishes were taken away, he leaned across the table and stared piercingly at his wife.

"So," he said, with poorly feigned casualness, "an acquaintance of ours was recently murdered."

Caterina lifted her brows in surprise and crossed herself. "How dreadful! Who was it?"

She made a point of taking another spoonful of *minestra* and chewing it slowly, calmly, while she awaited her husband's reply.

"It was the senior aide to the French ambassador—Jean or Jacques de Montagne, I think his name was." Girolamo eyed her with hawkish intensity.

Caterina wisely failed to correct the name.

"Oh, my," she responded with mild interest, as if this news made for interesting dinner conversation. "Wasn't that the rude young man who . . ." She paused, lowering her gaze. "Well, *you* know."

"Yes," Girolamo answered flatly. "*That* rude young man."

Caterina lifted her fearless gaze to her husband. "How was he killed?"

"Poison," Girolamo said, in a tone that conveyed, *Let that be a lesson to you.* Caterina reacted not at all. "Do they know who did it?"

Now it was her turn to scrutinize her spouse's reaction. Girolamo shrugged his shoulders and dropped his gaze as he said, "Not yet."

The uncertainty in his demeanor broke the tension and fed Caterina's confidence. "It must be very dangerous to be a diplomat in Rome," she said. "Do you think the ambassador might have been the target?"

"I doubt it," the count said nastily. "I say good riddance to the bastard! He deserves it for thinking he could take liberties with my wife."

Caterina directed an affectionate smile at him and reached across the table to pat his huge hand.

"I am a lucky woman," she said, "to have a husband so protective of my honor."

Girolamo and I stared at her in amazement. This was clearly not the outcome the count had imagined; most likely, he had expected Caterina to tearfully confess everything, but her poise and genuine disinterest in Monsieur de Montagne's fate stymied him. Cruel as he was, he could not imagine a woman in such total control of her emotions that she would not cry upon hearing of her lover's death.

The supper continued on for less than an hour, at which point Girolamo excused himself, citing pressing business.

By the time she reached her bedchamber, Caterina was triumphant and gloating. It apparently did not bother her that her husband was capable of poisoning a man for no more than suspicion.

The Frenchman's death troubled me greatly, but not in the manner I suspected. I spent little time worrying over whether Girolamo would strike again, unexpectedly, by poisoning Caterina now that he no longer suspected her of infidelity.

Instead, I spent my nights staring into my dying brother's face; my days were spent distracting myself from the raw grief that hovered nearby, ready to consume me should I allow an instant of weakness. Dark memories swallowed all the joy I had felt on account of my recent encounter with Luca, so that when he appeared suddenly at places I did not expect to find him, I could only smile wanly and excuse myself.

During this time, Caterina shocked me by announcing there would be a lone visitor to supper: Rodrigo Borgia, the Spanish cardinal. Girolamo would also be attending, although the idea had been strictly Caterina's; she had convinced her husband that Borgia, having served as chancellor to several popes, had accumulated a great deal of political knowledge and would make an excellent ally. Girolamo agreed with reluctance, which he childishly displayed throughout the intimate supper for the three of them. It soon became clear that Girolamo and Borgia disliked each other too intensely for there to be any hope of a real alliance; the count excused himself early from the meal, claiming to have forgotten to tend to some emergency business.

Borgia appeared to take no offense, and remained at table with the contessa, who conversed amiably with him, as if the humiliating encounter at his secret palazzo had never taken place. I remained in attendance, but only ten minutes after Girolamo's departure, my mistress turned to me and said, "Dismiss all the others, Dea, and leave yourself. You may wait out in the corridor."

A rush of heat pricked the skin from my collarbone to my cheeks; I shot Caterina a look of utter disbelief. What was she thinking, asking to be alone with the infamous womanizer? Now, under her husband's roof, while Girolamo was nearby?

She ignored my startled gaze as she shooed me off with her hand.

I motioned for the others to leave, then went myself, not without first making sure that Caterina noticed my disapproval.

She and Borgia remained alone together for the better part of an hour. I was so distressed that I pressed my ear to the door, not caring whether I was caught. I heard no unsettling pauses, no rustling of fabric or hints of physical movement—only earnest, intense conversation, too soft for my ears to decipher.

When dinner was over and the two of them emerged, Caterina escorted

Borgia solemnly to the front entrance. There was a new, easy camaraderie between them, and when Borgia caught Caterina's hands as he wished her a good night, he kissed her cheeks as an old family friend would. She returned the gesture, rising onto her toes to solemnly press her lips to his olive skin.

When the guest had departed, I hurried over to my mistress and followed her up the stairs to her apartments. "Madonna," I hissed, half a step behind her. "What are you thinking, being alone with him like that? Your husband just killed a man out of jealousy! And here you are dining alone with Borgia, of all people!"

She stopped abruptly on the staircase so that I could come alongside her. "I simply wish to understand the workings of the Vatican. Borgia knows much that is of help to my husband. If Girolamo walks into the room, he will see that nothing untoward is happening."

"Borgia is a lecher, Madonna," I began, but Caterina silenced me with a sharp gesture and began moving again.

"He is a resource. I do this for the House of Riario. I want to see it increase in power; Sixtus won't live forever. Then what becomes of Girolamo—and more important, of me and my child?"

I stared at her in amazement. She was newly pregnant and not even fifteen, of an age when some girls were only beginning to think about marriage. But Caterina was more concerned with her political fate.

Two days later, when Girolamo was traveling again on business, Borgia arrived again and dined alone with Her Illustriousness. As before, I attended Caterina during the meal, but was dismissed from the dining chamber once she and Borgia had eaten. This time, their conversation lasted two hours; again, I kept my ear to the door and heard nothing but incomprehensible murmurs.

The day after her meeting with Borgia, Caterina invited his nemesis, Cardinal Giuliano della Rovere, to a private meal while Giuliano was still traveling. Della Rovere was in his thirties, with a tall body of muscular build, a square, handsomely sculpted jaw, and wavy chestnut hair. His speech marked him as an extremely well-educated, ambitious man; his eyes held the same wily intelligence I had seen in Pope Sixtus's. Although he seemed strong and hale, he carried a gold-handled oak walking stick with him.

Della Rovere had spent his youth in Rome as his uncle's altar boy, and had been accorded no fewer than eight bishoprics and the archbishopric of Avignon, so that he might one day ascend the papal throne. As a result, his cousin Girolamo was extremely jealous of him; della Rovere did not attempt to hide his dislike and disdain for his crude relative.

Yet the cardinal accepted Caterina's dinner invitation graciously, on short notice. He arrived at the Palazzo Riario wearing a tailored robe of scarlet silk, trimmed with matching velvet, and a red skullcap that covered his shaved crown. Caterina dressed more sedately than usual for the occasion, in a plain gray silk gown with a white veil over her coiled braids; apparently, she had decided not to use her physical charms against della Rovere. I understood why when the cardinal arrived and proceeded to ignore every female attendant while carefully scrutinizing the males.

In the dining chamber, I took my place a step behind Caterina's seat at the table, so that I faced the cardinal, who carefully propped the unused walking stick beside the adjacent chair. After an exchange of pleasantries and a cursory prayer by His Holiness, the meal commenced. Caterina had made sure that della Rovere was presented with some of his favorite dishes, including plates heaped high with glistening, dark lamprey eels in savory sauce and a roast suckling pig.

Caterina drank copious amounts of watered wine, but ate only sparingly and avoided the eels altogether; at the smell of them, she turned her face discreetly away.

"Are you unwell?" della Rovere asked. "You seem pale, Madonna."

Caterina managed a faint smile. "The heat disagrees with me these days."

Della Rovere shrugged, and managed, without pausing for conversation, to devour the entire platter of eels and top it off by downing a full glass of wine. He held his empty cup up and waited—and when, four seconds later, it had not been filled, he reached with his free hand for the walking stick. When the servant attending him realized that His Holiness needed more wine and reached for the cup, della Rovere turned in his chair and landed a sharp blow on the lad's shins with the heavy stick.

As the lad cried out in pain, della Rovere snapped, "Laggard! Maybe this will help you to remember to watch!"

In the next instant, as his cup was being filled by the trembling servant, della Rovere turned smoothly to Caterina and said, "Really, it takes some time to train them properly. If he makes another mistake, I'd recommend a thrashing for him."

Caterina responded with a small smile and a question about the cardinal's education in France. By this time, della Rovere was tucking into the roast pig.

"I was trained in science," he answered, "but what I loved most was the military training. I would have preferred a soldier's life, but my uncle had already decided on a different destiny for me."

"A warrior!" This time, Caterina's grin was genuine; she leaned a bit closer over the table. "Had I not been born a woman— Well, I must admit, I am never happier than when I am practicing with my sword."

Della Rovere frowned. "A woman with a sword? That is unnatural, surely!"

The contessa glanced down. "It's just that I admire warriors so. It is a noble aspiration . . . for men, of course."

At this, the cardinal bloomed; a faint smile played on his lips. "Yes. At times, I dream that I am a general, fighting against the Turk. We must never forget that the Crusade failed. It is high time we began another."

"Absolutely," Caterina said, with starry-eyed eagerness she did not feel. "You are a man of true mettle; if anyone could succeed against the sultan, you could."

Della Rovere took her worshipful attitude at face value and grinned, then picked up his cup with greasy fingers and took a long drink. This time, the servant attending him refilled it the instant he set it down.

After a pause, the contessa changed the subject. "I have heard tell that Rodrigo Borgia is not a man to be trusted. Yet he seeks my friendship, and I am eager for advice that might help my husband to secure his position in the world."

"Borgia!" Della Rovere sneered as he picked up his meat and began to chew on it again. His voice was partially muffled by food as he continued, "You'd be wise to have nothing to do with him. He is a dangerous man, not to be trusted."

Caterina's dark blue eyes widened in feigned innocence. "But why, Holiness? I've heard he's the wealthiest, most powerful man after Sixtus. He has been vice-chancellor of the Curia for so long that he has amassed a fortune, as well as a great deal of influence over the other cardinals."

Della Rovere's lip curled. "He has no influence over *me*. You must understand, Caterina, that as a lovely young woman, you are a target for his flattery; he would tell you anything in order to seduce you."

The contessa pretended to be shocked. "But surely he's not lying about his wealth."

The cardinal shook his head at the very thought of Borgia. "He is wealthy, true, and his position as vice-chancellor has put him in the perfect position to accept bribes. But..." He paused to take a long drink of wine, and looked at Caterina with a smug, arrogant smile.

"I do not boast," he said, "but merely state the truth. I receive more income from my benefices in one year than Borgia could ever hope to make in five. And as for power... Because Borgia is an able administrator and politician, those of us in the Curia support his remaining in that position. But would we support his election as pope? Never!" He lowered his voice and leaned across the table. "You must know, Caterina, that while he can get along well with his colleagues, all of us know that he is given to schemes and criminal behavior. He is too corruptible and dangerous to be entrusted with the papacy."

"Dangerous?" Caterina was listening earnestly now. "How exactly so?"

By this time, della Rovere had set down his food and stopped chewing. "He has murdered men who stood in his way."

"Who?"

The cardinal lifted his eyebrows. "I know, but I will not say."

Caterina persisted. "How did he kill them?"

"This is hardly an appropriate topic for the dinner table," della Rovere answered disapprovingly, "nor for a sheltered young lady such as yourself."

Caterina again dropped her gaze so that the cardinal could not see her irritation. "Cardinal Borgia has been a frequent guest at our dinner table. I thought it would be wise for my husband to learn what he could from him. But if His Illustriousness is in any danger... or if *I* am ..."

"You are in no danger," della Rovere replied flatly. "Borgia would never harm a woman or child. But had he a reason, he would not hesitate to kill your husband."

Caterina looked so stricken that della Rovere reached across the table and patted her hand.

"Forgive me. I did not come here to upset you," he said with faint affection. "We will change the subject to happier things."

Caterina nodded. "Of course, we all pray for the Holy Father's health and wish that he could live forever. But I have heard that, should the throne of Peter become vacant, you are well positioned. And with good reason. You bring wisdom, experience, superlative judgment, and a steady temper..."

At this last, I had to restrain myself from rolling my eyes, given the cardinal's quick use of his walking stick.

Caterina continued, "Clearly, you have learned much from your uncle over the years. In any case, I would encourage my husband to support you fully in a bid for the papacy."

Della Rovere eyed her carefully; in the end, his boastfulness overcame his desire to be cautious. He smiled smugly. "I would be a liar to say I was not ambitious. And I would appreciate the support very much. But unless my dear uncle lives at least another ten years—and we all pray he will, of course—I have little chance of being elected."

"Why?" Tired of pretending to eat, Caterina folded her arms and looked across the table with an expression of convincing guilelessness.

The cardinal gave an annoyed shrug and reached for a pigeon pie. "The older cardinals feel they have more right than I, as they have served longer in the Curia. They are jealous of those who are younger yet also wealthier and more powerful than they have managed to become."

"You are such a brilliant man," Caterina responded, "that I am not surprised that they're jealous."

Squaring his shoulders with pride, della Rovere confessed, "I *do* have the backing of the King of France. And many of the French nobles."

I stood at an angle so that I could see Caterina's expression; it remained slavishly admiring, but her eyes narrowed at this important fact.

"How wonderful!" she breathed. "I am honored to be sitting in the presence of a man who will one day ascend the throne of Peter." Her tone became confidential. "I know that my husband is sometimes a difficult man, and I appreciate your tolerant attitude toward him. I shall do everything in my power to influence his attitude, so that he comes to realize how fortunate he is to have you as a cousin."

Della Rovere beamed at her. "You are sweet, Caterina, and very observant for a woman. Girolamo is lucky to have you on his side."

A messenger came from Girolamo's traveling party to say that he would be gone longer than originally intended. Caterina took advantage of her husband's absence by inviting Borgia and della Rovere on different days to the Palazzo Riario. I was allowed to be present for her discussions with Cardinal della Rovere, which were all directed toward learning about the political machinations of the Holy College. But I was barred from the after-dinner discussions with Borgia.

Other respected cardinals were invited, one at a time, to dine with Caterina. Two Spanish cardinals paid their respects, as well as a Greek named Cibo, and a distinguished Frenchman by the name of Charles de Bourbon. I was able to overhear some of the conversation, which generally centered around Borgia's and della Rovere's rivalry and chances for the papacy. While Borgia was well respected for his administrative skills and intelligence, he was not trusted; della Rovere was also regarded as highly intelligent and capable, and more likely, thanks to his political connections and his wealth, to become pope. But all agreed that his arrogance grated.

In addition to these guests, over the course of three weeks, della Rovere dined at the Palazzo Riario thrice; Borgia, no fewer than six times. With each successive visit, Borgia and Caterina grew more familiar with each other, until, upon the sixth visit, Caterina inadvertently called the cardinal "Rodrigo" in my presence.

Borgia's seventh visit took place in the midafternoon, when Caterina invited him to a late luncheon, despite the fact that the cardinal had already dined with Sixtus at the Vatican. The table was set in the private dining quarters in the contessa's apartments, and Caterina asked that the sword Borgia had given her be placed in the room.

Borgia arrived in fine spirits, freshly shaved and exuding aromas of lavender and orange blossom. Caterina awaited him in the dining chamber, and when he was ushered in, she rose and hurried to him as if he had been a long-lost friend. He took her hands and bent low to kiss them.

I turned my face away, sickened.

"Come, my friend, and sit with me," the contessa said, holding on to the cardinal's hand and leading him to the chair across from hers. I followed my mistress and moved to take my place behind her, but Caterina gestured to me.

"Send all the servants away," she ordered in a low voice, her gaze still on the smiling Borgia. "But first, see that we are left carafes of water and wine, and the first three courses."

"But who will serve you?" I asked, puzzled.

The contessa favored Borgia with a cryptic smile. "We will serve ourselves," she said, lifting her arm to give a sharp flick of her hand, the signal that I was dismissed and disagreement would not be tolerated.

I directed the servants so that all was done in accordance with Her Illustriousness's wishes; the serving maids were all sent back into the kitchen, with instructions that they were not to return until Madonna rang for them. I exited through the main doorway, out into the corridor.

"Close the doors, please, and make sure that we are not disturbed," she called after me.

I did so, and began to pace nervously in the corridor. After twenty minutes of unhappy deliberation, I stopped in front of the door and pressed my ear to the wood to hear what sounded like normal, muted conversation. Vaguely relieved, I continued my pacing, more slowly this time, nodding at a chambermaid as she passed by, soiled linen in her arms. Another ten minutes, and I heard a soft clatter beyond the door as the platters were being rearranged on the table.

A few minutes later, there came a loud crash and the sharp ring of metal against marble.

I threw open the door and ran inside.

Caterina lay lengthwise on a cleared section of the dining table, her bare buttocks upon the table's edge, her bare legs dangling down, her slippered feet a hand's breadth above the floor. Her blue brocade skirt and petticoat were bunched up around her waist, pooling out over the table's surface. Her arms stretched out over her head as if she were clawing for purchase; at the

instant I entered the room, her face was slack with ecstasy. She had accidentally knocked one of the platters from the table in her excitement; a stuffed,
roasted capon lay upon its side atop a scattering of broken shards and
braised mushrooms.

Her large white breasts, newly swollen by pregnancy, the nipples darker
and larger than before, had been pulled up out of her flattening bodice,
which now pushed them up so that they looked even fuller.

Borgia's large hands cupped them reverently. He had unclasped the front
of his scarlet gown and pulled down his matching leggings to expose pale,
muscular thighs; now he stood at the edge of the table, his hips pressed fast
against Caterina's as he thrust between her dangling legs. So powerfully did
he strain against her that, with each thrust, he pushed her farther up the
table and was obliged to slip his hands beneath her shoulders and pull her
back down to him.

I stood in the doorway just long enough to take in the scene, and for
Caterina to turn her head languidly in my direction.

I shut the door and retreated into the corridor again. This time, I sat
down upon the cool marble, folded my arms atop my bent knees, and lowered my face into the void.

Nineteen

I kept my head buried in my lap until the muffled groans of pleasure on the other side of the door eventually gave way to silence. Some thirty minutes after the plate was shattered, the door to the dining chamber finally opened. Caterina emerged first, looking far less disheveled than I expected; Borgia followed, his skullcap neatly in place, his scarlet robe scarcely wrinkled. Both were flushed and smiling.

I got to my feet immediately, but my disgust would not permit me to meet the eyes of either lover. I followed dutifully as Caterina led her guest downstairs to the front entrance; he kissed her hand in parting.

As soon as we were back in Caterina's chamber and I had shut the door behind us, I whispered, "I cannot believe what you have done, Madonna! What are you thinking, engaging in such vile, insane behavior?"

Her lips pursed into an angry bud, but she composed herself. "Vile, perhaps. But far from insane."

No longer hiding my agitation, I countered, "I did not approve of your affair with Gerard de Montagne, but I at least understood it. But *Borgia*, of all men . . . The thought of him makes my skin crawl! I will never be able to protect you from your husband if any man in Rome can seduce you!"

"He is a talented lover," Caterina said slyly. "And very discreet. You never would have caught us if I hadn't lost my mind today."

Aghast, I stared at her. "Today is not the first time?"

She smirked. "Only the sixth."

I shuddered. "I am not angry, Madonna . . . I am *afraid*. How can you not be? Your husband poisoned Gerard; was that not enough of a warning for you? Why put yourself in such a dangerous situation?"

"Far more dangerous than you realize," she said, studying me. "Girolamo did not kill Gerard."

"Then who—" I gaped at her a long moment before finally whispering, *"Borgia?"*

Caterina nodded. "I don't love him, but I admire his cunning. And I will learn what I can from him. He thinks he is smarter than I. I intend to prove otherwise."

"My God," I said softly. "You know him to be the killer for a fact, Madonna? Why, then, do you invite him here, and lie with him? Why do you look for danger?"

"I am looking out for myself," Caterina answered defiantly, "and for my son." She rested a hand upon her still-flat stomach. "Because if I do not, my husband will soon fall from power. I will *not* return in disgrace to that boring little pasture called Imola, to rule over a score of peasants."

"You're barely more than a child," I protested, "and you think to outsmart Borgia? He has far more experience at treachery! How does sleeping with him protect you? And what sort of—"

Caterina put up her hand. *"Stop,"* she said fiercely. "I can tell you no more."

"Why not? I've seen the worst."

She put a gentle hand upon my forearm. "Because," she admitted shyly, without meeting my gaze, "of all the souls on earth, you're the one I want most to protect. You're the only person I trust."

My expression softened at this unexpected show of affection; Caterina saw it, withdrew her hand, and shrugged.

"Besides," she added offhandedly, "you're my talisman. If anything should happen to you, I am lost."

. . .

In the morning, two gifts were delivered from the Palazzo Borgia directly to my mistress's chambers: a large ruby pendant, encircled by tiny diamonds, and a small silver perfume vial inlaid with shimmering mother-of-pearl. Borgia's messenger refused to hand over the items to anyone other than Caterina herself; and when she arrived in her study to accept them, the messenger went down on both knees and bowed so low, his nose grazed the floor.

"As I bow before your beauty, my master bows, too," he recited, "and begs you to accept these gifts, which cannot do you justice. He says, 'The Illustrious Madonna Caterina is the bravest, the most amazing, woman I have ever met.'" As an aside, the messenger added, "He means it sincerely, Your Illustriousness; I have never seen him so enamored."

As the servant lifted his face, Caterina favored him with a gracious smile. "Let one of my ladies escort you to the kitchen; tell them to give you a glass of our best wine. Wait there until I summon you. I am preparing a response for your master that you will take back to him."

She signaled to Teodora, who led the messenger off, and then she turned to me. "There is no time for cipher. I will send a letter, written in your hand."

I sat obligingly at the desk, and took up the quill as Caterina dictated:

To His most esteemed Holiness, Cardinal Rodrigo Borgia,

I have appreciated our talks and your candor, and shall always consider you a dear friend. However, I have recently discovered that I am with child. Political discourse no longer holds any attraction for me; my focus must now be on my heir, who will need his father and his mother, as well as the support of his relatives, including Cardinal della Rovere and, of course, the Holy Father, Pope Sixtus.

Forgive me for being too indisposed to continue our discussions. I am returning the ruby pendant herewith; as for the other gift, I will guard and treasure it always.

Respectfully,

Her Illustrious Highness, Contessa Caterina Sforza

The unhappy messenger returned to his master with the ruby and Caterina's letter within the hour. Borgia would be angry, but he would not kill a woman, according to everyone in Rome. That night, I lay my head upon the pillow, greatly relieved that I should no longer have to be party to clandestine meetings with the Spanish cardinal.

My relief lasted only one day.

The following morning, I awoke before dawn to the sound of Caterina retching in the basin left for that specific purpose on her night table. I roused one of the chambermaids sleeping across the hall, and sent her to fetch bread and salt. Caterina continued to heave for a good half hour, by which time she was exhausted. I washed her face and hands and helped her change into a clean dressing gown, then propped her up in her bed, where she remained, nibbling tentatively on the salted bread.

The sun rose on a blistering, humid morning, one that Girolamo, who despised Roman summers, was still spending in the more forgiving clime of the Romagna countryside. Not an hour later, one of the guards at the door called at Caterina's bedchamber door to announce that Cardinal Borgia had arrived and was quite determined to see her.

"Send him away," Caterina groaned. "I'm ill. Tell him I will accept a letter from him, but I cannot meet him in person. And if he will not go, notify my bodyguards that he should be removed, forcibly if necessary, from the grounds."

The effort of speaking made her queasy, and I laid a damp, cool washcloth upon her forehead as the servant replied, "Yes, Your Illustrious Highness."

He had barely spoken before we heard a disturbance out in the corridor: The servant was arguing with another man; sounds of a slight physical scuffle entailed.

Suddenly, the door swung open and Rodrigo Borgia appeared upon the threshold. With his right hand, he held off the slighter, shorter servant with ease. As the smaller man vainly swung his fists at Borgia, the cardinal gazed intently at Caterina. His coldly composed features could not entirely hide his rage, revealed by the taut, faintly twitching skin just beneath his narrowed eyes.

"Forgive my rudeness," he said to Caterina. "But this matter requires me to be bold."

"Stop," Caterina ordered the servant, who dropped his fists, at which point Borgia released his hold.

"You can go," Caterina told the red-faced servant. "Only remember what I asked for."

The servant bowed and ran off. Borgia entered the bedchamber and nodded at me. "She must leave, too."

Caterina replied defiantly, "She will stay! You cannot barge into a lady's bedchamber and insist on speaking to her alone. Besides, I told you I was ill."

Borgia loomed over Caterina, and stooped to bring his face down to her level as his large hands clutched the edge of the mattress. I stayed beside my mistress and put my arms upon her shoulders.

"You have played me for a fool, Madonna," he whispered hoarsely. "Such a deceitful little creature you are! I thought you actually cared for me."

Caterina scowled obstinately at him, but her answer was unexpectedly soft.

"I *do* care for you, Rodrigo. I admire your brilliance and ambition. I thought you realized that you were dealing with someone like you."

He straightened and moved a step back. "You do flatter yourself, my dear. How did you expect me to react to your flagrant deception?"

Caterina's tone turned coy. "What deception?"

Borgia caught hold of Caterina's forearm. "Give me the vial," he warned.

"Let go of me," she snarled.

"I trusted you with my greatest secret," Borgia said, "and you have betrayed me."

He shoved me backward; I lost my hold of Caterina, and struck the wall with my back. With the other arm, he jerked Caterina from the bed. Her bare feet became tangled in the bedding; she fell to the floor on her knees, vomiting on the way down, and splattering the front of his garment.

Borgia recoiled, startled but not squeamish. He made way as I rushed to the kneeling Caterina's side and held her hair back as she retched again, this time onto a fine Persian carpet she had brought from Milan.

"She *is* pregnant, isn't she?" he asked in wonder, his tone suddenly gentle.

I nodded. To my amazement, he fetched the basin from her night table, and brought a towel so that I could clean her face.

Angered, Caterina pushed away the towel. "I did not lie about that!" she gasped, and pushed herself into a sitting position. "Or about my admiration for you. I swear I will not harm you—but I must protect myself. I'm going to have a child, who may or may not be yours."

Together, Borgia and I helped her back onto her bed.

She sighed as she closed her eyes and lay back upon the pillows. "I thought at first I had eaten something that disagreed with me. But now there is no doubt that I am with child. I cannot carry out our plan now. I cannot jeopardize the baby. He will need a father to take care of him."

"If it is mine," Borgia responded urgently, "then we will know when he is born and grows old enough to favor his sire. And if it *is* mine, Caterina, I will find a way to raise him as my own."

The sound of rapid, heavy footfall on the distant stairs made him lift his face to listen; the guards were coming. Quickly, he added, "I will not harm you, and if you give birth to my child, we will talk again, most seriously. But if it is *not* my child, hear my promise: the day will come when I seek recompense for what you have taken from me. And should you ever share it with another . . . You will deeply regret what you have done."

The guards arrived and knocked upon the door; Caterina called for them to enter. A trio of armed men escorted Borgia out of the palazzo, "with full courtesy," as Caterina demanded.

Once more, I was relieved to be rid of Rodrigo Borgia—but again, the respite would be only temporary.

Summer gave way to a temperate autumn, followed by a winter so sunny and mild that I swore I would never spend another winter in Milan. Girolamo returned from "military business" in the Romagna just in time to enjoy the improved weather. Caterina's morning sickness eased after another month, by which time her pregnancy showed, and she demurely announced to Girolamo that, God willing, she would give birth to his son in the spring. He received the news with only a bit of suspicion, which soon wore off as he considered the advantages of having an heir to pursue the family interests. Eventually he became quite indulgent of Caterina, for she wisely gave up her social life and stayed at home, entertaining no one save those pertinent to Girolamo's political interests, which included Girolamo's disapproving cousin, the powerful and wealthy Cardinal Giuliano della Rovere.

As for me, I spent my days attending my increasingly cross and bored mistress. Over the months, as the trauma of Matteo's violent death eased again, I found it easier to smile and speak briefly to Luca, the scribe, when he went out of his way to encounter me.

Our first Christmas in Rome passed with such pageantry and pomp that Caterina survived the gloominess that overtook her with the season, as her father had been murdered only one year ago during the holidays.

At last, the New Year, 1478, arrived. In March, Caterina's first child was born: a daughter, whom she named Bianca after Duke Galeazzo's iron-willed mother. Fortunately, Bianca arrived a month late by our calculations, enough to convince Girolamo (and Caterina) that she was his daughter.

Caterina had borne the pains of labor with amazing courage for a first-time mother; to everyone's relief, the child was well-positioned and the birth an easy one. In the moments after Bianca emerged from the womb, the midwife cleaned the baby, swaddled it, and laid it on the chest of its exhausted mother, in hopes that it would suckle.

Caterina stared down at it. "It *is* a boy, isn't it?" she demanded of the midwife, who shook her head.

"It's a girl, Madonna, but such a beautiful girl! Ser Girolamo will still be pleased."

Caterina turned her face away from the baby. "Take it to the nursemaid," she said flatly.

I reached for the baby first, and scooped her up. She was beet-faced and misshapen from the trauma of birth, so that her features gave no hint as to her paternity. She had been born with a surprisingly thick tuft of hair, dark gold like her mother's, although, to my and Caterina's giddy relief, it was wavy, not tightly curly.

After an initial fit of squawling, she quieted in my arms. It was I who took her to the nursemaid, at Caterina's insistence, and I who visited the nursery three times a day to hold her and coo to her in the months that followed. Unlike her mother, the child had a sweet, quiet disposition.

Caterina's total lack of interest in the child disgusted me, especially when I considered that, although he had been unable to attend the christening, Rodrigo Borgia sent the baby a pair of tiny ruby earrings and a beautifully engraved silver rattle.

Two months passed. By the first of May I felt housebound and restless; I had not left the palazzo for weeks, as I spent my days not only caring for Caterina, but also constantly checking on little Bianca and giving my lady reports on her baby's progress, whether Caterina wanted them or not. She listened to them with a distant expression, and had little to say in response.

Girolamo, on the other hand, was a far more attentive parent, and every night before supper, he came into the nursery and played with Bianca, who adored him. I was often there at the same time, and, watching Girolamo make funny faces for his giggling daughter, came to see him in a different light.

On an early May afternoon, after working very hard to care for my two charges, I received permission to go for a stroll out in the strong sunshine. The weather was delightful as I made my way out into the east garden. Within minutes, I arrived at the little glade where Caterina first experienced ecstasy with the dead Frenchman. At the sight of the scribe, Luca, I stopped in my tracks.

He sat on the bench, bent halfway forward from the waist, his breathing labored, his arms wound around himself, as if he were struggling to keep something dangerous from bursting out. At the sound of my steps, he looked up immediately, his eyes wild with horror.

"Luca," I gasped, and went to his side. "Luca, what's wrong? What has happened?"

He closed his eyes and shook his head. "Leave me, please," he said in a very low voice. "I must get control of myself. There is still a chance the count might need me." A grimace of what seemed to be physical pain twisted his lips and brow; he bent farther forward and tightened his grip on his arms.

I moved to stand beside him. "No," I answered gently, and lightly rested my palm on his shoulder. "I cannot leave you like this. Not until I'm sure you'll be all right."

"I can't," he said desperately. "I *can't . . .*"

He covered his eyes with his hands. Several deep, hitching gasps made his shoulders shake; the movement was accompanied by short moans of pain.

I sank down onto the seat beside him. "Oh, poor Luca," I murmured. "You're crying."

He turned his face toward me; there were no tears in his eyes, but his expression revealed grief. His words came in a fevered rush.

"I did my best to warn him," he whispered. "But Lorenzo has always scoffed at the need for protection. No one would dare lay a hand on him in Florence, he said. He would take care, would keep an eye on Archbishop Salviati . . ."

"*No!*" I cried out. "No, Lorenzo cannot be dead!" Along with sorrow came an all-consuming burst of rage against Count Girolamo; I wanted to kill him. I began to weep, but Luca caught my elbow.

"Lorenzo is only wounded," he said gently. "He will recover."

"Thank God!" I said.

"But his younger brother, Giuliano . . ." Luca began. He could not continue, but instead produced more harsh, staccato sounds—sobbing, I realized, without tears. If his eyes were red-rimmed, the count would grow suspicious. Luca's life now depended on his ability to hide his grief.

The scribe gathered himself and haltingly told the tale:

Girolamo and Sixtus had left the actual assassination in the hands of one Archbishop Salviati, who recruited Francesco de' Pazzi, the Medici's most powerful banking rival, to help with the attack. They agreed that both Lorenzo and his brother, Giuliano, had to die, since the Florentines would rally around the survivor should only one be killed. And the archbishop, bereft of all decency, arranged for the attack to take place in Florence's great cathedral, in the middle of mass, when both brothers were distracted.

Giuliano and Lorenzo were in separate areas of the sanctuary, but each was unwittingly surrounded by different assassins. When the priest raised the chalice to bless the wine, the killers struck. Young Giuliano was unarmed and standing next to Archbishop Salviati and Pazzi at that instant; both drew knives and slashed the young Medici mercilessly, then left him to die in a pool of his own blood.

His older brother fared better. Perhaps Luca's repeated warnings had kept Lorenzo alert, for the instant his would-be killer struck at him from behind, Lorenzo drew his own sword and whirled on the attacker. A short battle ensued, but Lorenzo's friends soon surrounded him and pushed him into the safety of the sacristy—away from the assassins and the sight of his dying brother.

"Count Girolamo and Sixtus underestimated the loyalty of the Florentines," Luca said grimly. "Salviati and Pazzi had both convinced them that the assassination would cause the citizens to rise up against the Medici and rally behind the Pazzi family, who are Sixtus's puppets. Quite the opposite happened. Within hours of the attack, the people seized Salviati and Pazzi and hung them from the upper windows of the government palace.

"Count Girolamo received the news not an hour ago. He is furious, and trying to figure out how to break the news to the pope. This will not end well. There will be war between Rome and Florence."

"Poor Giuliano," I murmured, as tears filled my eyes. But at least his suffering was over. His older brother's grief and guilt would haunt him the rest of his days.

"How can you bear it," I demanded of Luca, "knowing that you are working for the man who murdered Giuliano? A man who cannot wait to kill Lorenzo? How can you not want revenge?"

Luca leaned forward, elbows on his knees, and shook his head sadly. "Don't you see, such hatred only leads to more bloodshed. And the vendetta continues...."

"But they killed Giuliano because they were greedy and wanted Imola!"

"It goes far deeper than that," Luca explained. "Count Girolamo and the Holy Father want to kill Lorenzo because they believe Lorenzo poisoned Sixtus's favorite son, Pietro Riario. Pietro was the most powerful, shrewdest young cardinal in Rome, clearly destined to become pope. Sixtus sent him to talk to Lorenzo about the acquisition of Imola. Within a day of returning home from the unsuccessful negotiation in Florence, however, Pietro died suddenly. Sixtus and Girolamo are convinced that Lorenzo is to blame. No amount of reason will convince them otherwise."

"Did Lorenzo kill him?" I whispered.

Luca looked at me as though I had struck him. "Of course not! We obey a power holier than the Church."

I turned my face away, unable to keep tears from spilling down my cheeks. "I'm a fraud," I said. "I wasn't worthy of Matteo's company, or of yours. I see what is to come in the triumph cards, but I was never able to make contact with the angel. I only want to find the man who killed my Matteo. I'm a wicked person."

He put an arm around my shoulder. "It's all right," he soothed. "Just let go of it, Dea, and trust the angel."

"But I *can't* let it go!" I struggled halfheartedly to pull free of him. "I can't! If you had seen how Matteo suffered at the end..."

"I did." Luca's tone was firm and calm.

I turned on him angrily. "Then how can you forget it? How can you tell me that a person as saintly as Matteo should have suffered so? Should have died so young, with his killer never being punished for the crime?"

I still do not remember clearly what happened next. I believe I tried to push Luca away, but the outcome was unexpected. Luca caught my hands, and I pulled them free, only to discover that they quite naturally moved to his face, and pulled it toward mine. Once I pressed my lips to his, I did not want to stop. I found the strong muscles between his shoulder blades, and dug my fingers into them as I pressed my breast to his.

His lips brushed softly over my skin: my mouth, my cheeks, my eyes and brow. I did the same to him; his skin was warm and firm, indescribably male. He murmured swiftly, breathlessly at me.

"From the moment I saw you—that first, horrible moment when I brought Matteo to you—I knew even then that you were the one. He told me to take care of you, Dea. I made a solemn vow to him. When I saw you again, in Rome, I knew it was destiny...."

"You are so beautiful. You have my heart."

Astonishing, to hear those words. Even more astonishing was the sound of my own voice, declaring the truth I had not admitted even to myself.

"I love you, Luca."

I lingered in his arms for several minutes. I might have remained there for hours, had it not been for the shout from Caterina's balcony. I was needed.

I touched my fingers to his cheek and reluctantly rose. Grief was still subtly writ upon his features, but beneath it was an incandescent glow, one I did not doubt emanated from my own face.

Without another word, I turned and hurried back to my demanding mistress.

Twenty

When I returned to the contessa's chamber, Caterina informed me that she was leaving with Girolamo that afternoon to drill papal troops in the Castel Sant'Angelo. I was surprised at the count's acquiescence to her request to accompany him, though not surprised that Caterina had asked. Now that Girolamo was spending more time at home with his new daughter, making a new affair for the contessa too dangerous, Caterina was physically restless. Not long after the baby's birth, she began begging for Girolamo to take her to see the fortress and his soldiers.

My father the duke took me with him when he drilled his troops, she had told him, *and he also took me to watch when he trained my older stepbrothers to ride, to use cannon, to drill with pikes and swords. He was a talented soldier, and that talent has passed to me.*

Girolamo was skeptical, but Caterina was so persistent that he yielded, thinking to prove to her that no woman could possibly grasp such a manly art. She was so excited by the prospect that, as I helped her strap on her leather hilt and sheath the Toledo halberd Borgia had given her, she did not notice my red-rimmed eyes or unsettled demeanor. I said nothing of Giuliano; she would hear of it soon enough, from someone else.

Girolamo took her to the Castel Sant'Angelo that afternoon—perhaps to distract himself from his fury over Lorenzo's survival—and let her watch while he shouted commands from a rampart down to some three hundred men in the walled-in yard below. They drilled first with steel-covered pikes, each taller by half than the man who wielded it; with sustained effort, Girolamo managed to get the troops to form three equal rows, and to march around the circumference of the yard.

Then, no doubt still in an ill mood and thinking to humiliate his wife, the captain of the papal army turned to her and, gesturing at the men below, said, "Well, Madonna? They are now yours. Let us see what you know of soldiering."

Caterina gave him a small smile, then called to the troops in a voice as strong and authoritative as Galeazzo's. *I never doubted,* she said to me that night as she recounted the tale, *that they would obey me.* With a few barked commands, she persuaded the troops to merge into one long row and face outward in a circle, ready to intercept any invaders. Then she made them split again into three rows, then two, and line up in front of the nearest entrance, spears at the ready.

Girolamo was astonished into speechlessness. When he recovered, he dismissed the troops and took her down to the training yard himself. His aim was to embarrass her. To that end, he had her draw her sword and execute certain maneuvers with it, with the hopes that she would be entirely ignorant of the terms he used. Alas for him, Caterina knew them all, nor could Girolamo succeed in physically tiring her.

By the time they returned home from the Castel Sant'Angelo, Girolamo's attitude toward his wife had dramatically shifted. He was jealous of her, true, but he was also impressed, and when Caterina confessed that she wished to use her talent only to help further the aim of her husband and his future sons, he was won. It was then that he shared the news that Lorenzo's brother had been killed in Florence by "unknown assassins." Caterina expressed mild sadness—her father had always been Lorenzo's staunch ally—and Girolamo, the liar, echoed her regret.

From that day forward, the count began to share something of his military world with his wife, and allowed her occasionally to accompany him when he reviewed the troops. Caterina even designed special drills, for which purpose she convinced Girolamo to provide her with a map of the fortress's interior. In time, she became a favorite with the troops, and her husband grew so proud of her support that he presented her with a steel cuirass, its breastplate curved to accommodate her womanly form, and the combined emblems of the Riario and Sforza—the oak and the basilisk—engraved over the heart.

As the seasons changed, the baby Bianca flourished; amazingly enough, her eyes changed from blue to brown and came to resemble Girolamo's, a fact that brought Caterina and me no small amount of relief. Borgia, of course, no longer came to the palazzo, but Cardinal Giuliano della Rovere remained a frequent visitor, and often conferred privately with Caterina when Girolamo was gone on business.

By then, Luca and I had ceased relying on chance encounters and met regularly at dusk, after the heat broke, at the stone bench where Caterina had surrendered herself to Gerard.

Luca was not the same after Giuliano's murder; guilt had carved a permanent line between his brows, and left a lingering sadness in his eyes that romance could not dispel. Each day when we first greeted each other in private, he always began by sharing the latest news from Florence. And there was always news. Pope Sixtus, enraged by the spontaneous execution of the conspirator Archbishop Salviati, excommunicated Lorenzo and placed Florence under interdict, thereby denying her the ability to do business with all other Christian city-states—until her citizens agreed to turn over Lorenzo. To their credit, the Florentines rebelled against the pope and rallied behind Lorenzo. Furious, Sixtus convinced the King of Naples to declare war on Florence.

After relaying the day's somber news, Luca nonetheless took me in his arms, and we kissed each other until half an hour had passed, by which time I was obliged to return to the contessa's service. I had forgotten what it was like to be tormented by unfulfilled sexual desire; I had not lain awake, simmering, since I had shared a bed with Matteo, not knowing then that he was my brother.

As the weather warmed, so did our passion, and we grew dissatisfied with mere kisses. When Luca one day reached for my breast, I let him free it from the restraint of the bodice, and kiss it; and when, one day, I grew bold enough to reach between his legs and for the first time touch a male organ, he did not recoil. Nor did he pull away on the steamy August day that I finally pushed away the cotton lawn covering it and took it in my hand, marveling at the sheer strangeness of it, so hard and unyielding, yet covered in skin that was velvety soft to the touch.

At his urging, I began to move my hand up and down over the shaft, catching the velvety skin and bringing it up over the pink-brown toadstool tip. This made him groan with pleasure; encouraged, I increased the pace, though in retrospect, my technique was certainly clumsy.

"Stop," he gasped. "I can't bear it any longer. I must have you, Dea. Please . . ."

By then, reason had deserted me. "Only tell me what to do," I said. I lifted my skirts, as I had seen Caterina do too often, and waited, pulsing with lust, yet also abruptly nervous.

"You know," he whispered, and at my silence, paused to glance up at my frightened expression.

"My God," he said finally. "You *don't* know, do you?" A look of under-standing crossed his features. "Of course. He was your brother; the marriage was never consummated. You're a virgin. . . ."

"I don't care," I answered defiantly.

"Well, I *do*," he countered, and reached forward to gently lower my skirts. "You deserve better than this for your first time."

"But I want to please you." Stubbornly, I reached for him again.

He caught my hand tenderly, and whispered in my ear. "All you need to do to please me," he confessed, "is what you were just doing. *If* you're sure you still want to."

I took him in my hand again, and a moment later was startled when a pale, warm substance—thick as the white of an egg, but opaque—spurted out from the tip, filling my hand and dripping onto my skirt. Immediately, the shaft shrank, and the pinkish tip disappeared back into dangling, wrinkled skin.

Amazed, I drew back to examine the odd-smelling contents of my palm while Luca sat gasping, eyes closed and mouth open. Clearly, he was spent, though I was even more eager to lose my virginity.

"I'm sorry," he breathed. "So sorry . . ." His eyes flicked open; he reached for a kerchief tucked into his belt and handed it to me as he glanced at my skirt. "You'll want to wash that spot out soon, or it'll stain."

I went over to the nearby fountain and washed my hands in the scallop-shaped stone basin. I dipped his handkerchief into the water; while I was dabbing at the dark viscous spot on my skirt—awkwardly situated near my lap—Luca came over and kissed me.

"I'm sorry," he said again. "Now I am satisfied, but leaving you wanting."

I smiled faintly. In those days, I had no notion of how to satisfy myself; I had always been wanting. Today would be no different from all other days. But I was very pleased to have made Luca happy, and I told him so.

He grinned, but almost immediately grew somber. "There's something I've wanted to speak to you about. Something I've been thinking about for a long time."

His tone was so earnest that I stopped my effort to clean the stain and looked at him. His dark complexion was thoroughly flushed and streaked with sweat; he dropped his gaze, unable to meet mine, and stared down at the fabric still gathered in my hand.

He was nervous, and the realization unsettled me.

"I have not spoken to the count of this," he began, "and there is no guarantee that Her Illustriousness would allow it, either. But I would like— That is, Dea would you consider . . . if we can get the approval, that is . . ." He paused helplessly as anxiety swallowed his words.

Out of pity, I stepped into the gap. "Of course I will marry you, Luca," I said.

I returned in a thorough daze to the contessa's apartments, where Caterina was being dressed for supper with the count and Cardinal della Rovere. The day had been uncomfortably hot, and Her Illustrious Highness was irritated by the prospect of wearing a gown and heavy sleeves over her lawn chemise. She stood in front of the full-length mirror near her closet while Teodora laced heavy, bell-shaped sleeves to the shoulder of her silk overdress.

As I entered, she scowled piercingly at me; as I curtsied, she demanded, pointing: "You didn't have that stain on your gown when you left. What happened?"

I looked down at the incriminating damp area on the blue silk. To my horror, I saw a spot I had missed, where Luca's seed had dried into a crusting white pearl.

Caterina's brow furrowed more deeply as she followed my incriminating gaze to the pearl, at which point she erupted in laughter.

"Why, Dea!" she exclaimed, when she caught her breath. "You've been to see a gentleman, haven't you?"

I could not look at her or the giggling Teodora, but directed my blushing face toward the marble floor and mumbled, "Please, Madonna, may I speak to you alone?"

"Of course," she answered, jolly and grinning as she nodded to Teodora, who bowed and hurried into the corridor, shutting the door behind her.

Before I could utter a sound, Caterina said happily, "I hope, for your sake, that he is an excellent lover, though it seems his aim is less than true. Honestly, Dea, I was beginning to worry about you. It has been far too long since you have been with a man."

"Your Illustrious Highness," I began, as she lifted her eyebrows at my uncharacteristically formal tone, "I was not going to trouble you with a request until tomorrow, but since you have broached the subject of . . . gentlemen . . . there is one in particular who has asked for my hand. I cannot give it, of course, without your consent and the count's."

Her cheer faded at once. "Who is the man?"

"One of the count's secretaries. His name is Luca da Siena."

"And his family?"

"He is an orphan like me, Madonna." My knees felt suddenly unsteady. "One who was fostered and given an excellent education. Count Girolamo hired him because of his talent and discretion. He is a kind gentleman—noble of heart, if not blood."

Caterina's expression grew opaque; she folded her arms tightly over her chest—the left arm covered in heavy gold brocade, the other in voluminous, gauzy white cotton, gathered at the wrist. She turned from me and her mirror, walked toward the open French doors leading to the balcony, and stared out past the garden at the darkening Roman skyline.

When she spoke again, her back was to me. "I assume," she said slowly, "that you care for this Luca da Siena."

"I do." My answer was barely louder than a whisper.

She wheeled about, her expression unguarded, her arms still folded tightly. "What is it like?"

I shrugged, perplexed. "What do you mean, Madonna?"

"To love someone," she said. "I can tell from your face that you love this man, and you loved your husband, too. What is it like?"

"It is . . . wonderful," I replied. "It gives me a reason to wake up every morning. When he is happy, I am happy; when he is sad, I want only to cheer him. It is the best thing in life; nothing else comes close to it." A wave of sorrow washed over me at the memory of Matteo. "And there is nothing more horrible in all the world than losing the one you love. So I suppose it can also be the worst thing."

"Then it is dangerous," Caterina said softly.

"Yes." I imagined losing Luca, too, and closed my eyes at the pain. "Very dangerous. Once you have lost someone, loving again takes courage."

She tilted her head, thoughtful. "How do you know whether you love someone?"

"You will know when it happens, Madonna."

She nodded slowly, her expression faintly wistful; I watched it harden as she spoke again, all earnestness replaced by stern defensiveness.

"There are certain conditions," she said. "You must still sleep in my bed at night—although you may retire much later, if you wish. And I must know where you are at all times. This Luca da Siena has no rights to you except those I choose to grant him. I will be lenient with you both, but I will not lessen your duties. And God forbid you get pregnant and have whiny little children who will also demand your time."

"Thank you, Madonna, thank you," I babbled. "You are so generous, so kind . . ."

Her lip twisted scornfully. "Stop sniveling. You have yet to gain the count's permission."

At sunset the following day, I went for my walk in the garden and found Luca in our customary place, sitting on the stone bench near the fountain. He was slumped forward, head bowed, his elbows on his knees, his hands clasped tightly as if in urgent prayer. He looked up at the sound of my footfall, and the instant I saw his mournful face, I let go a moan of disappointment.

Too late, Luca composed himself and assumed an expression of vague cheer. "It's not so bad," he sighed, catching my hand and pulling me to sit beside him. "I should have known better than to ask at this time. Girolamo is so preoccupied these days with the war against Florence that he has more need of me than usual lately. He told me not to vex him with such matters now." He lowered his gaze as his voice dropped to a near whisper. "Perhaps it's for the best. Lorenzo needs my services more than ever."

For Luca's sake, I held my tears, and told him of Caterina's response; he was surprised to learn that she was superstitious about being away from me for long, as I had protected her during her father's assassination.

We sat in the deepening twilight and spoke quietly about the Medici and the war, including the depressing fact that the King of Naples, aided by Girolamo's forces, had a much larger army than Florence. She was under siege, but her citizens still remained loyal to Lorenzo, who repeatedly offered to turn himself over to Rome in order to spare the city, to no avail.

"Even Lorenzo doesn't see how he can win this war," Luca confessed. "If Girolamo wins . . . I don't know how I can pretend to be joyful."

I stroked his cheek, and we wrapped our arms around each other as we talked. When the waning light turned to darkness, I kissed him, and returned to Caterina.

Twenty-one

Girolamo's refusal did not weaken the love I shared with Luca; to the contrary, it strengthened our resolve, though our frustration at being denied each other grew.

I argued that we might as well engage in the nuptial act. We ached for each other unbearably, and even if I became with child, would that not give Girolamo a compelling reason to let us marry?

But Luca would not. Instead, he taught me to please him with my hand and mouth, and one afternoon in late autumn, he introduced me to ecstasy.

That day was unexpectedly chill, with a drab sky, steady drizzle, and gusts that made the trees bow, too inclement for a rendezvous in the garden. Luca found me in a corridor in Caterina's apartments and whispered that I should meet him in the storage room just outside his office.

When the sun slipped low in the sky, I asked Caterina permission to take "my walk" as usual.

"Hardly the weather for walking," she said slyly, smirking. At my stricken expression, her smirk transformed to a frank grin. "Go ahead, but don't get wet."

I murmured something about walking the corridors, then curtsied and hurried from my lady's apartments toward the count's, and the haven of the storage chamber adjacent to the scribe's office. It had been a long time since I had visited the dim closet of a room, but little had changed: the shelves still held stacks of clerical supplies. There was just enough floor for two people to lie down side by side, but not enough for either of them to stretch out an arm.

But there were a few significant differences: for one, Luca was standing there, with a lit lamp, and for another, there was a dark blue woolen cloak that had been spread out to cover most of the cold floor. When I opened the door and entered, Luca hurried to set the lamp upon one of the shelves, and quickly locked the door behind me. Only then did we embrace.

As he kissed me, he pressed his lean, trembling body so hard against mine that I had to take a step backward, lest I fall; I kissed him back, pushing with equal fervor. All the while, I was distracted by the wool cloak on the floor. Was this a sign that Luca had decided to deflower me? I reached between his legs, but he pushed my hand away.

"Not for me today," he breathed into my ear. "Lie down, Dea."

I lay down upon the fine blue wool, my head toward the count's gardens, my feet pointed at the locked door. He knelt beside me and tenderly drew up my skirts and petticoats to expose my legs and hips.

"Don't do anything," he whispered. "Just lie back."

As he spoke, he began to lightly run his hands outside my legs and over my abdomen, which made me tremble. I forced myself not to move and closed my eyes.

Luca's hands caressed the outside of my legs again, then moved between them. I parted them at once, and moaned softly as he ran his fingers and palms over the skin of my inner thighs, up and down, featherlight. Deftly, he insinuated his body between my legs; I tried to pull him up so his face was even with mine, but he waved my hands away, his face so close to the mound of my pubic hair that I could feel his warm breath.

He stroked the inside of my thighs again, then slowly moved to the delta of hair, and gently put his hand upon it. I squeezed my eyes harder shut and tried not to think of Bona or be ashamed. Instead, I lost myself in the sensation of fingers gingerly touching my most private part; as I began to relax, letting my mouth open as my breath came faster, I felt his fingertips slowly circle from my uppermost thigh around the delta, across my abdomen, then down again.

Just when I felt I could bear the mounting desire no longer, the fingers went lower, and parted the lips between my legs; I gasped when I felt Luca's tongue there, teasing the small bump of flesh hidden within the folds. Then he raised himself up, put two fingers upon the sensitive flesh and massaged it in a circular fashion, an act that made me squirm with delight.

Afterward he let the tip of his finger linger sensually at the opening to my womb, then slid it in to the first knuckle, then the second, and plunged his finger entirely inside me.

He moved his finger, slowly at first, then with increasing force and speed; I ground my hips into the floor and moaned. I wanted him badly, but before I could speak, he began to massage two fingers on my most sensitive flesh, while at the same time plunging his finger in and out of me.

I was lost to pleasure. I writhed on the floor, not caring whether we were discovered, not caring about anything other than the magic Luca's hands were creating. In the midst of this, he lifted his head to look at me and removed one hand. Something soft and white struck my face: his handkerchief.

"You must be as quiet as possible," he whispered. "Put the handkerchief in your mouth, and when the time comes, bite down hard on it so that you don't scream."

I frowned, perplexed. "Scream?"

He lifted his face higher, so that I could see his wicked grin. "You'll understand when it happens. Just try not to make any noise."

I dutifully wadded up the linen kerchief and put it in my mouth. Luca's fingers returned to the exquisitely sensitive mound of flesh and my womb.

Soon there was nothing but the pleasure. My body and mind transcended all external circumstances, all time; no wonder Caterina had been willing to risk everything for such bliss.

I sensed imminent dissolution, no distance between me and the rest of the entire world; my legs went rigid and my backed arched as if I were in the throes of lockjaw. A wave of ecstatic energy coursed up from my feet, through my legs, and exploded when it reached my pelvis. My womb contracted around Luca's finger—again, again, again—and with it came the most pleasurable sensation I had ever known.

At the last instant, I remembered to bite down hard upon the kerchief to keep from howling, though I surely made noise; when I came to myself again, Luca was bending over me, begging for quiet.

The year that passed was bittersweet, as Luca and I had little time to spend alone with each other. The war between Florence and the Naples-Rome alliance continued, and the Florentines remained staunch in their support of Lorenzo, although it grew harder with each month to keep a supply of food coming into the city on the River Arno.

Christmas passed, and the New Year, 1479, arrived. In late January, Caterina announced that she was pregnant again, though her condition did not prevent her from occasionally drilling the troops with Girolamo; eventually, Girolamo trusted her enough to lead the entire drill while he sat back and watched. Rumors began that the soldiers were more loyal to Caterina than to their impatient, hotheaded captain.

During the long months of her confinement, Caterina did not pamper herself, but instead recruited one of Girolamo's commanders to teach her how to handle her sword and shield while on horseback. Even as her belly swelled, her arms and legs grew more muscular and lean, and her strength grew formidable.

By the time she gave birth again, in August of 1479, she was so strong that the labor itself lasted only four hours, and she expelled a robust, healthy child. At the sight of the baby's tiny male member, she laughed softly, pleased.

"A son," the midwife crowed, and we all smiled.

"His father and I have agreed to name him Ottaviano," Caterina announced, her voice an exhausted whisper, her mood exultant. She laid her head back down upon the pillow and sighed as the wailing child was set upon her breast.

"Ottaviano," I echoed. The name of the first Roman emperor; Caterina and Girolamo clearly had high expectations for their little son.

"A son," Caterina repeated. "Perhaps, someday, I will rule as his regent."

She smiled faintly at the thought, while the midwife and I shared a fleeting look of concern at my lady's words. Caterina could rule as regent in place of an underage son, but only if Girolamo died first; what an ill omen, to speak of the father's death only moments after the son's birth!

The boy's arrival caused much more of a stir than baby Bianca's had. He was christened by Pope Sixtus himself, and an army of well-wishers trooped through the palazzo the week after Ottaviano's birth to deliver gifts and fawn over mother and infant. Rather than receive her guests in bed, as was the custom of most noble mothers, Caterina insisted on sitting up in a lavishly appointed reception room, the boy in her arms. Even Cardinal Borgia came. Girolamo was ecstatic with pride.

Little Ottaviano's appetite was voracious, and the baby swiftly grew into a miniature version of Girolamo, with the same long limbs, equine features, and overpowering jaw . . . and the same faintly hostile dullness in his eyes. His sister, Bianca, was more than a year older, but even before Ottaviano could walk, he had grown larger and longer than she, and much fatter. Yet unlike his sister, he was slow to develop mentally; I visited him and his sister almost every day in the nursery, and while Bianca was an affectionate child who loved to be held, Ottaviano squirmed and whimpered and fought his way out of my arms.

As the months passed, Girolamo went from being exultant—victory against Florence seemed assured, as the Neapolitan army had succeeded in blocking all supplies from coming into the city—to being furious. By the time Ottaviano celebrated his first Christmas, Girolamo had learned of Lorenzo's secret gambit.

Unable to bear the sight of his people starving, yet unwilling to surrender them to Girolamo and Sixtus's despotic rule, Lorenzo somehow escaped Florence and the armies surrounding her. Alone, he rode for more than a fortnight before reaching Naples. There, he offered himself to King Ferrante, asking only that the king first speak with him about the Florentine people before executing him or sending him on to Rome.

Lorenzo's courageous act and his genuine respect for Ferrante so impressed the Neapolitan king that he ordered Lorenzo be treated as a guest, free to roam the palace grounds. Ferrante entertained and dined with

Florence's first citizen, discussing everything *except* the war. After weeks of being pampered and showered with gifts, but not allowed to plead on behalf of his people, Lorenzo finally returned home.

But his gambit worked. Food began to find its way into Florence, and by the early spring of 1480, King Ferrante provoked the pope's wrath by calling his army home to Naples.

Outraged over the "loss" of Florence, Girolamo and Sixtus turned their territorial ambition to the Romagna, the rolling fertile countryside that lies just northeast of the Medici stronghold of Tuscany. The city of Imola was not enough for Girolamo; he lusted after the nearby towns of Faenza, Pesaro, and Forlì.

His machinations to take Faenza failed, however, as King Ferrante made it clear that Naples would protect Faenza at all costs. Nor did he dare invade Pesaro, as the Milanese promised war if Pesaro were attacked.

Forlì was especially attractive as its ruler, Pino Ordelaffi, had just died and left no immediate heir other than a sickly, illegitimate fourteen-year-old son, Sinibaldo. True, there were two healthy male cousins eager to claim Forlì, but the pope shrewdly chose to back Sinibaldo, who was far too ill to live long. Sinibaldo happily signed the papers that made him a papal protectorate; should he die without heirs, Forlì would become property of the church.

When the Ordelaffi cousins, Antonio Maria and Francesco, invaded Forlì, however, they quickly routed Sinibaldo's forces; during the struggle, the housebound Sinibaldo died of "mysterious causes." Immediately, Girolamo led an army of eight hundred men into Forlì. The Ordelaffis' small army could not hope to survive the onslaught. At the news of the approaching enemy, Antonio Maria and Francesco fled. On August 9, 1480, Girolamo claimed the town of Forlì for the Riario family. But his dream of possessing a huge swath of Italy—Tuscany and most of the Romagna—was dashed. Nonetheless, we celebrated in the Palazzo Riario in Rome when news came that Forlì, too, was ours—although Caterina was sour at the notion that, instead of taking the full cluster of grapes, her inept husband had managed to pick only two small, rural ones.

Only days after she learned that Forlì was hers, Caterina gave birth to a second son, also named after a Roman emperor: Cesare.

. . .

November of that year brought Caterina distressing news: Her stepmother, Bona, who had always been kindly disposed toward her, was removed from power in a bloodless takeover by the late Duke Galeazzo's younger brother, Ludovico, known as il Moro, "the Moor," because of his jet-black hair and swarthy complexion.

Caterina's twelve-year-old half-brother, Gian Galeazzo of the long, flowing blond curls and delicate constitution, was still given to childish tantrums and showed no interest in the affairs of the state he was bound to inherit. He had always resisted Bona's attempts to educate him in such matters, preferring instead to dedicate himself to the pursuit of pleasure. Perhaps, Caterina suggested halfheartedly, Ludovico would force Gian Galeazzo to become more serious about his responsibility to Milan.

But those of us who had come with her from Milan knew exactly what would happen. Ludovico had been an infrequent visitor to Duke Galeazzo's house because the duke had always feared his younger brother would steal his kingdom. In public, Ludovico was far more affable than his late brother, but the private man was just as capable of murder and deceit.

Caterina was depressed for weeks over the matter, especially after she reluctantly penned a letter of congratulations to Ludovico and expressed her support for him. In response she received a brief, perfunctory response that Milan was always at her service.

This failed to relieve her worry. Ludovico had never known his niece Caterina very well, nor had they ever developed a bond of affection. In the end, il Moro would show where his true loyalty lay . . . and it was not with Caterina.

He would become the first crack in the cornerstone of the Tower.

The father of the little emperors, Girolamo, became obsessed with stripping Lorenzo of Florence, so virulent was his hatred of the man. When the summer of 1481 arrived, Girolamo announced to Caterina—then five months pregnant—that it was high time she accompany her husband on a pleasure trip, first to glorious Venice, and then to the Romagna and Imola and Forlì, where she would be welcomed by her new subjects. The fact that she would miss the hottest days of the Roman summer made the prospect even more attractive.

Caterina was elated and immediately ordered new gowns. Luca relayed that the count "needed him especially" on the journey, so my beloved would be joining us; I had never been to Venice, and began to grow excited about the notion. Since we would be gone for months, packing for Her Illustriousness took days, as it was necessary to pack for the coming infant as well. The plan was for Caterina to give birth in Forlì, if all went well, for nothing would win her subjects over more quickly than celebrating the arrival of a new child.

Two nights before we were to leave, Caterina arrived back at her apartments quite late after a private dinner with her husband. The chambermaids had retired but I was still dressed, with the light on, sitting alone in front of the flower-filled hearth and shuffling the triumph cards. I had thought to leave them behind, but some instinct prompted me to pull them out and consider putting them in my half-packed trunk.

I looked up as the door to the room opened; Caterina entered, her head down, her face averted. Her expression made me ask, "Madonna? Is everything well with you?"

She shook her head as I set the cards aside and rose. Her lips were pressed together so tightly as to be invisible and her brow was furrowed. She moved toward me and silently thrust out her arm, a demand that her heavy sleeves be removed at once.

I immediately began unlacing one of them, and as I unraveled the silken cord that held the brocade in place, I said softly, "You are troubled, Madonna. How can I help?"

She let go a long tremulous sigh as I pulled one sleeve from her arm, then folded it and set it upon my chair; as I crossed to unlace the other one, she said, her voice breaking, "The bastard. The goddamned *bastard!*"

I finished unlacing the second sleeve and set it down with the other. "I'm so sorry," I said, mystified until a sudden explanation for this behavior occurred to me. "Oh, Madonna, don't tell me that the count has canceled the trip!"

"It's worse than that," she said, her face contorting. "I still must go. But Dea, *you* cannot come!"

With that, she put her hands to her eyes.

I took her wrists gently, and pulled her hands from her face. "There must be a mistake," I said. "Why would he not allow *me* to come?"

"He says only those he chooses can accompany me. I am only to have one lady, a della Rovere, in my entourage. I am not allowed to bring anyone from Milan! He is bringing one trusted secretary. He says it is because we are going on a 'sensitive diplomatic mission.'

"Nothing I can say will make him change his mind. I told him if I could not bring you, I would not go at all, but he says that he will use force to take me." Her eyes filled with tears. "I'm afraid, Dea! If I leave you, something awful will happen! I will die in childbirth, or be assassinated, or be set upon by brigands . . ."

"Hush," I said, with such confident calm that she did. "Let us get you undressed first, Madonna. Those clothes must be so hot. . . . See, your neck is sweating."

She raised her arms so that I could lift off her overdress. I removed her headdress, uncoiled her braids, and brushed them out.

As I did, she began to speak again. "Girolamo is going to meet with the Doge himself. Something political is going on; I don't know what it is, but Girolamo is very excited about it." Her face crumpled. "I cannot be without you, especially if I'm going to give birth."

I finished brushing her hair and bade her slip out of her damp chemise and step into a linen nightgown. "You will be fine without me," I said firmly, hiding the disappointment I felt at being separated from Luca for such a long time. "You're a grown woman now, and too old for such a silly belief."

Her gaze locked on the triumph cards stacked neatly on my chair, upon their black silk cloth. "Am I?" she said. "Let's see what the cards have to say about the journey."

I sat back down in front of the hearth and she sat in the chair beside mine. I shuffled the cards, then handed them to her and let her shuffle and cut them.

When she was satisfied, she gave them back to me. Instead of setting the deck down, I fanned them out in my hands, the backs of the cards facing her.

"Pick one," I said. "Just one. That's all we'll need."

Impulsively, she reached for a card, but hesitated at the last instant before her fingers touched it. Finally, she squared her shoulders and drew in a breath, then pulled the card free and showed me its face: the Hanged Man.

I kept my expression carefully neutral as a wave of fear washed over me; I did not forget that I was speaking to an overwrought pregnant woman.

"The Hanged Man," I said coolly. "We have seen this before. It has to do with sacrifice." I looked away, unable to meet the terror in her gaze.

"But what does it mean? Will someone die? Will *I*?"

"I don't know," I said honestly, though I, too, was frightened for her. "But remember, this sacrifice always leads to a wonderful result. In the end, great things are accomplished." I forced a small smile. "Who knows, Madonna, maybe the sacrifice is leaving me behind, so that you can learn to be confident when I am not with you."

"Do you think so?" she asked wistfully.

I nodded. She calmed herself and, exhausted, climbed into her bed. I undressed myself, extinguished the lamp, and finally crawled in beside her.

She was not yet asleep. In the darkness, she whispered, in a small voice that belonged to a much younger, less confident girl, "Dea? Could you hold me, just until I fall asleep?"

She had not asked this of me since her father died; the timbre of her voice reminded me of the terrified girl in the cathedral of Santo Stefano whose father had been murdered in front of her eyes.

"Of course," I answered tenderly.

She rolled onto her side, her back to me. Full of pity, I rolled toward her, facing the same direction, and put my arm over her shoulder. Not three minutes later, much to my gratification, Caterina began to snore.

The day before the count and contessa's departure, all in the Palazzo Riario worked feverishly to prepare for the months-long journey. By dusk,

I had only a few minutes to spare to see Luca; we met in the garden and I kissed him farewell.

He wanted to see me again before dawn to say our final good-byes, and to linger in my arms a time that night, but I was in no mood for either. I wanted to be swift, partly out of a desire to spare myself extra tears.

I resisted all his efforts to make me stay with him as I wished him a safe journey. He was disappointed but understanding.

I resisted weeping that night, although I slept fitfully, wakened by forgotten nightmares that left me with a sense of dread. Someone, I knew, would die as a result of the journey—perhaps Caterina, or even my darling Luca. Either way, the death would lead to transformation, and the birth of an unexpected future.

Twenty-two

With Caterina gone, my days were filled with playing with little Ottaviano, Bianca, and Cesare in the nursery, as well as replying to correspondence for Caterina with a brief note explaining that Her Illustrious Highness was traveling and could not respond to any requests until her return. These slight duties left me with far too much time to worry about Luca and my mistress.

I received my first letter some two weeks after their departure.

6 August 1481

Dearest beloved,

The count's bodyguards are reading every letter before it is sent; therefore, I shall keep this brief and try not to disgust them overmuch with my declarations of love. Count Girolamo bids me remind you that you are to show this letter to no one, not even those in the Riario household, and again, to tell outsiders who ask after his destination that he is in the Romagna visiting his new city, Forlì.

At this moment, it is no lie. We arrived in Forlì yesterday. It took us a bit longer than usual to make the journey, as Count Girolamo chose not to take the main road that runs through Florence, but a narrower, less-traveled road leading through the heart of the Romagna.

As we approached Forlì, the terrain grew sweeping and flat; no wonder they grow so much grain here. We passed by field after field of wheat, golden and almost ready for the harvest. The town is small and most definitely not Rome.

Even so, the contessa has charmed the inhabitants thoroughly. In this respect, she is a great help to her husband, who is less comfortable in social situations. The night we set foot in Forlì, there was a fire in one of the kitchens in the royal palazzo. A bad omen, the locals say. Who knows whether they will be right?

There is so much more I could tell you, but I must wait until the happy day I return home to you, and can put my arms around you at last.

Until then, my beloved, I remain your servant,

Luca

8 August 1481

Dear Dea,

We arrived in Forlì a few days ago. The land here is exceptionally flat, but I am looking from the western window of the former duke's palace at the beautiful Apennine Mountains.

Although the city is rather small, the people here are enthusiastic, and did their best to greet us in a proper manner. We rode through the city gates while young men, all dressed in white, waved palm fronds to welcome us, as though we were Christ entering Jerusalem. By then it was sunset, and most of the citizens lining the narrow streets held up candles, to lovely effect. I wore my new gold brocade dress with silver embroidery, which caught the light nicely.

We were taken to the Church of Santa Croce. A group of Forlivese nobles carried Girolamo from his horse to the altar, where he was duly blessed. Then it was on to our new palazzo, where we were obliged to sit through a sermon from a priest. Only then did Girolamo stand up and announce to all those gathered that he would govern them "as a good father would," and that he would never require them to pay taxes (since we can live quite comfortably without the revenue).

This provoked cheers from the people inside the palazzo's chapel with us; the news spread like wildfire in seconds to the commoners standing out on the street below. Their roar of approval was deafening; only a shower of sweetmeats and pastries from the palace windows quieted them a bit.

After that came a ball. I danced for hours while Girolamo sat and watched. Perhaps I danced too long, for I was so tired the next morning, I could not rise until midday. I do not know why this particular pregnancy saps my strength.

Forlì is all right, although I would never want to settle permanently here. I am too used to the pleasures big cities provide, and cannot wait to see Venice. Let us pray that my lord Girolamo has not made his last conquest. I would prefer to rule over larger territory, one with a grand city as its capital.

Please respond at once. I think that a letter written in your hand would soothe my nerves better than anything else; I would wear it on my person during this journey, and be comforted by it.

   With affectionate regard,
   Caterina
   Countess of Imola and Forlì

I wrote back to Caterina at once, telling her of her children's antics and complaining about the beastly hot weather in Rome. I instructed Caterina to "believe that this letter will keep you from harm, and it will do so." It was a small lie meant to comfort her.

With the lord and lady both gone, the Palazzo Riario hosted no visitors. Evenings were quiet. I spent them alone in my lady's bedchamber, pining for Luca while I brought out Matteo's little diary and tried in vain to decipher it.

I worried, too, about Girolamo's secret meeting with the Venetians. There could be little doubt that he, too, was not satisfied with such a small, rural possession as Forlì, and sought to use Venice's military might to further his ambitions.

1 September 1481
Dearest beloved,

   Tomorrow we set off on the weeklong ride to Venice. As always, His Illustriousness forbids you from mentioning his destination to anyone.

   Out of the entourage that accompanied us from Rome, I alone have been invited to go with the count. Only Her Illustriousness, the Forlivese archdeacon Matteo Menghi, and Ludovico Orsi, an assessor from Forlì, will be allowed to go with us. No one else has been told of our departure.

   His Illustriousness obliges me to attend a special feast for the town's mayor, Luffo Numai, but I have no heart for it. I am well physically, of course, but can think of only you, for I love you more than anything else in this world. Fear not, I will return to you safely, though it will probably not be until the following spring; the contessa was quite uncomfortable during the journey. She now swears that she will not make the entire arduous trip back to Rome, but will instead stop again in Forlì to give birth.

How I love you! I am smitten and can think of nothing but you, and the moment we will be in each other's arms again.

10 September 1481
Dear Dea,

At last! We arrived in Venice today. I am exhausted, but so excited that I cannot yet sleep, so I am writing this letter to you in my own hand as I recline on a featherbed more luxurious than my own.

The city is like nothing I have ever seen; it is true what they say, that it sits upon the sea. To enter it, we were obliged to leave our horses and wagons behind, and board a boat garlanded with flowers and draped in gold fabric. This took us in style to the Grand Canal, and the heavily colonnaded palace of the duke—or Doge, as the people here call him. One side of the stone palace faces the street; the other, the sea, where the water laps at its feet. I do not know how they survive here, as it seems that one large ocean wave could easily carry the whole city away.

At the palace, Girolamo and I were received with as much pomp and celebration as when I first entered Rome. The Doge was waiting to greet us. His demeanor is quite handsome and graceful, and his agility belies his years, but his face, alas! I have seen but one homelier, belonging to that man from Florence who must not be named. To mark his status, the Doge wears a tight golden cap that rises up from the back of his head to form a blunt, fat horn.

The journey here was arduous; perhaps the rocking of the carriage brought it on, but the child in my belly feels exceptionally heavy and has left me more tired than usual. Tomorrow Girolamo has an important meeting and I will spend the day being entertained by the city's prominent gentlewomen. I hope to see the church and square of San Marco, which is not connected to the city by roads, but stands alone, surrounded by nothing but sea.

The buildings are all very pretty, but they cannot compare to the cardinals' palaces in Rome. The most beautiful aspect is the play of the light upon the water, which fills the streets with a soft, romantic glow—especially at dusk, when the pale palaces reflect the sunset, bathing all of Venice in golden pink light.

Please respond at once. I feel a sense of foreboding and would be reassured to have another letter from you. I miss your company.

I must sleep now.

With affectionate regard,

Caterina

Contessa of Imola and Forlì

P.S. Girolamo insists I remind you that this letter must not be shared with anyone, including those in our own household, under pain of death. And, of course, when visitors inquire after us, they are to be told that we are in the Romagna. No mention of Venice.

Lonely weeks passed, punctuated by love letters from Luca that I read again and again in private.

Dearest beloved, how I yearn for you . . .

Although heartwarming, his letters were brief and held little description of Venice, with good reason: Count Girolamo kept him enormously busy, which suggested that His Illustriousness was negotiating a contract with the city on the sea. War was surely in the offing.

28 September 1481

Dear Dea,

Back in Forlì again. The respect and goodwill shown us by the Forlivese has been replaced by an air of distrust and unease. Girolamo believes some of them are still plotting the return of the Ordelaffi, Forlì's former rulers.

As for Venice: I am too tired to describe everything; it shall wait until I see you again . . . if I see you again. Suffice it to say that Girolamo was given numerous awards and privileges, as well as the key to the city. It was hard to leave a grand city for grim little Forlì, but whatever business Girolamo had with the Venetians was resolved to everyone's satisfaction. I have never seen my husband so cheerful.

Meanwhile, there is the problem of Forlì. In all honesty, I do not feel strong enough to travel; the child inside me seems to drain the life from me, so I am quite inclined to remain and give birth here.

However, neither Girolamo nor I feels safe in Forlì. The day before we were to reenter the city, we were intercepted on the road by a messenger from the mayor, Luffo Numai, and warned to take special care. It seems that certain reprehensible men were planning to slaughter us as soon as we passed through Forlì's gates.

Girolamo is furious. He wants to capture and torture the assassins, then make their execution a public spectacle. I barely managed to convince him that now was not the time to make an example of any Forlivese, since we have not yet won their hearts. At my suggestion, Girolamo instead announced that food and wine would no longer be taxed.

Privately, though, my husband still chafes; he suspects Lorenzo de' Medici of being behind the conspiracy to murder him, and he wants to leave Forlì at once. I feel differently; I am no more than six weeks from giving birth, and in truth, I have felt unwell throughout the pregnancy and feel even more so now.

I will try to convince him to remain here, and to let you come at once to assist me during labor. Otherwise, I fear what might happen.

Pray for me.

Caterina

Contessa of Imola and Forlì

The mention of assassination filled me with fear; the triumph cards had indicated that innocent blood would be spilled. I worried terribly as well about Caterina's health; outside of occasional bouts of morning sickness early in her pregnancies, she had never "felt unwell" when with child.

A fortnight passed without my receiving a letter from anyone; and then, one cold, rainy evening in early November, a messenger arrived and started pounding upon the kitchen door. He sent the scullery maid to fetch me, "owing to an extremely urgent manner regarding her mistress."

I flew down the stairs and found the messenger standing in the sitting room, his soaked cloak dripping onto the carpet, his hands gripping his equally wet red wool cap.

It was Luca, his hair slicked by the rain and hanging in soggy strands around his face, sunburned and drawn with fatigue. At the sight of him, I cried out in joy and ran to him. We embraced briefly, and he pulled away, his expression somber.

"I have summoned Her Illustriousness's physician, as well as the midwife. The contessa will arrive in an hour or so," he said. "You should prepare her bedchamber with water and towels and whatever else women need at such times."

I put a hand to my heart. "Is she in labor?"

"We have asked her, and she tells us that she does not think so," Luca answered grimly, "but she is in such severe pain that she cries out from time to time."

Despite my joy at seeing Luca, I summoned Teodora and we readied the bed, covering the mattress with several old blankets. Luca brought the birthing chair up from storage, as well as a large iron kettle from the kitchen while Teodora and I stoked the hearth and filled the bedside pitcher and goblet with water.

As Teodora was finishing up, I stepped outside to speak with Luca.

We clasped hands as I whispered, "Caterina was feeling poorly and wanted to have the child in Forlì. What happened?"

His expression darkened. "Count Girolamo. He was convinced that, if they remained, he would be assassinated. It was clear that the contessa was too ill to travel, but Girolamo ordered her to come. She rode half the way on a mule, until she could no longer bear the pain of sitting. We put her on a litter, but she was still horribly uncomfortable." He shook his head at the memory. "I pray God she survives and doesn't lose the baby."

"Bastard," I whispered as my eyes filled with stinging tears. I closed them as Luca responded:

"The count feared for her safety as well. He believed that if she stayed, both she and her child would die. He was solicitous of her during the journey, but you know the contessa; she treated his order as a physical challenge, and would not complain. He and I rode beside her. By the time we crossed the Apennines, she was white and trembling, and a day later, she groaned and slumped in her saddle. She would have fallen to the ground had Girolamo not hurried to catch her."

I could find no words. We held each other and Luca whispered in my ear of his journey, of the Doge's proclamation that Girolamo was now an honorary citizen of the realm. Venice would provide troops to help Girolamo wrest Florence from the Medici while Girolamo would provide troops to help Venice seize nearby Ferrara.

In time, the fat, white-haired doctor and somewhat younger midwife arrived and were escorted to Caterina's chamber. An hour passed. Because of the rain and closed windows, we could not hear the hoofbeats as the caravan neared the Palazzo Riario, but when a distant door slammed downstairs, I ran to the third-floor landing.

From below came Girolamo's gruff bass, and a babble of excited voices. I ran down to the second-floor landing and stopped.

Girolamo was ascending the steps. Like Luca, he was bedraggled from the rain, his cloak and cap and hair dripping water, and his face revealed grim, uncommon determination. He took the stairs two at a time while a group comprised of soggy travelers and servants struggled to keep pace with him.

In his huge arms he bore Caterina, limp in his grasp. Her eyes were closed, her lips parted and gray.

I quashed my instinct to run to her, and stepped aside so that the count could make his way swiftly up the third flight of stairs.

I ran after him and arrived just as he set Caterina down on her bed. She was shivering; her belly was hugely swollen, as were her feet and ankles, and her face was bloated.

"Madonna," I murmured to her. "It's I, Dea. . . . You're home at last."

Her eyelids fluttered, then opened a slit. "Dea," she breathed, and weakly gripped my wrist to draw me closer. "Dea, it's really you, isn't it?"

"It is," I confirmed, "and everything will be well now."

She sighed with relief and closed her eyes again, but a second later grimaced and put a hand to her ribs, then let go a piteously weak laugh.

"He loves to kick, this one," she whispered, rubbing the spot. "He has not given his poor mother a moment's rest. I think he will take after her."

Those few sentences exhausted her, and she said nothing more as I stripped her of her damp clothes and slippers, only to find a bundle of my letters to her hidden inside her bodice. The sight of them made me want to weep. How could I have deserted her? I brushed the tears and guilt aside, and steadied myself as I called for a clean chemise.

As soon as I had dressed her, the doctor elbowed me aside.

"I must conduct an examination," he said pompously, shooing us away from the bed. By then, there was no one else in the room except Caterina, her husband, the doctor, the midwife, and myself. Three of us watched as he put an ear to my lady's heart, laid a palm upon her forehead, palpated her stomach, and tented the sheets so that he could examine her privates.

When he emerged, Girolamo demanded anxiously, "Well? Is she in labor?"

The physician's expression was less than reassuring. "She shows no signs of other illness. I must assume that this is part of the birthing process."

We all looked down sharply at the bed as Caterina, with great effort, whispered, "No physician. Only the midwife."

"Her Illustriousness has no fever," the doctor countered, with polite disdain, "but she may still be delirious."

The midwife—lean, iron-haired, and clearly distrustful of the doctor—curtsied to Girolamo. "Your Illustrious Highness," she said, "if I may please examine your wife."

Ignoring the physician's scowl, the count turned, faintly hopeful, to the midwife, and nodded.

"If the men would give us some privacy . . ." the midwife said politely. She was most likely a merchant's wife or daughter, decently dressed; though weathered, her features were fine enough to be deemed still pretty. She was a small creature, with fine, delicate hands, the nails clipped to the quick.

Girolamo caught the clearly irritated physician's elbow, led him out into the corridor, and closed the door.

The midwife turned to me. "Would you kindly lift the lamp, Madonna? I will need your assistance to examine her properly."

I did so, eager to be of help.

The midwife leaned over Caterina and said, "Your Illustrious Highness. My name is Flora, and I shall do everything possible to bring your child safely into this world and make sure you remain in it. But first, I must examine you. It will be painful at times, but I will warn you first."

Caterina opened her eyes and listened, then nodded in agreement. She closed her eyes again as Donna Flora's deft fingers touched her belly, gently probing; the wool at Caterina's waist jumped suddenly, and Flora laughed.

"Your child is strong, Madonna. He is knocking at the door and asking to be let out. How many months have you been pregnant, Madonna?"

"Almost ten, I think," Caterina whispered.

"Don't worry, Madonna; we have ways of dealing with laggards." Flora lifted the hem of my lady's wool chemise, speaking at the same time in a tone designed to soothe. "Now I am lifting your chemise, Madonna. . . ."

The midwife gestured for me to lift the lamp higher; narrating all the while, Donna Flora spread Caterina's white legs quite wide, and slipped a pillow under her hips.

"Now," Flora said, "here is where a bit of bravery is called for. I shall start as gently as possible, but I must put a hand inside you to feel how the child is situated. It will help if you bend your knees."

Caterina did so as Donna Flora opened a jar of sweet-smelling unguent, which she rubbed thoroughly over her hands. She bent down to look between Caterina's legs, beckoning me to bring the lamp even closer.

Donna Flora's touch was skilled and smooth. She performed a shallow examination, then looked to Caterina, whose eyes were squeezed shut.

"Now you must prepare yourself for some pain," Flora said, at which point my lady squinted harder and set her jaw.

Flora's slow, careful examination took long, arduous minutes; Caterina groaned, then gritted her teeth.

With her hand still in Caterina's womb, Flora said, "Your water has not yet broken, but the baby has dropped. Unfortunately, his head is not down as it should be; he wants to come feetfirst. Once your water has broken, I can try to move him into proper position. Even if that fails, you should know that I have delivered dozens of breech babies safely. It is just a bit more work for us all. If you are ready for labor, Your Illustriousness, I can help bring it."

Another spasm seized Caterina; her face contorted as she gasped, "Hurry!"

At that, Flora set to work. The kettle was on the hearth, and once the water began to steam, Flora fetched some herbs from her large black pouch, which she had set in a corner. She set the herbs into a cup, and ladled hot water over them.

Caterina sipped the brew slowly. Some ten minutes later, when she had finished the entire cup, Flora took it from her.

"Lie down again if you would, Madonna," she said, and the two of us helped Caterina to squirm back down onto the mattress and part her legs. "This will hurt," Flora warned.

It did, indeed. Flora put her fingers inside the contessa and made an abrupt circular movement with them that made Caterina scream. Not yet content, the midwife moved her fingers a second, then a third time.

"There," she said, satisfied. "I am sorry to hurt you, but this will hurry things."

She made Caterina another cup of tea; by the time my lady finished it, she was obviously inebriated and in less pain.

"Now," Flora said cheerfully, "we walk."

Together, we lifted Caterina from the bed and onto her feet. With her one arm over my shoulder and the other over Flora's, Caterina was able to stagger all the way from her bed to the closed French doors, then back again, pausing several times when much stronger contractions struck.

We turned and headed back for the bed; as we neared it, Caterina pleaded, "Let me lie down now. I can't walk anymore. Just let me rest. . . ."

"*One* more time," Flora said firmly.

Her insistence was justified. We had turned back toward the French doors and taken only two steps when Caterina stopped in mid-stride and stiffened.

"It's running down my leg," she said, wide-eyed.

Flora knelt down at once to peer under my lady's undergown; she re-emerged smiling. "Your water has broken, Madonna. Now I can safely turn the baby. Back to the bed," she said. "Now comes the hardest part."

Once again, Caterina lay down, spread her legs, and bent her knees, and I held up the lamp for Flora, whose expression was determined. Caterina bit her lip as Flora's entire hand entered her, and stiffened her legs as it moved deeply inside her. The midwife's lips and brow were pursed as she tried, again and again, to move the unborn child. At last, she glanced up at me.

"Make Madonna another cup of tea," she ordered, "and make it strong. Your Illustriousness, I am sorry, but I cannot turn this one without using both hands. Let us try to make you a little more comfortable."

While Flora made encouraging small talk, asking after Caterina's other children, I watched as Caterina's pupils gradually grew larger and larger until her eyes were more black than blue.

After several minutes, Flora said, "All right, Madonna. When the pain comes over you, breathe out as hard as you can."

Impossibly, Flora insinuated her other hand inside Caterina, and when the midwife's arms moved ninety degrees, in a half circle, Caterina screamed.

Flora was gasping; her work apparently required not just delicacy, but great strength. She repositioned her hands and made the half circle motion again and again, while Caterina cried out piteously.

At last, Donna Flora drew her hands out. "I believe the baby's head is in the correct position now, Madonna," she told Caterina. "It's time to walk again."

We walked. This time, Caterina reported that true labor pains had come upon her. Heartened, we spent the entire night walking back and forth, stopping only when Caterina was too exhausted to take another step.

By dawn the next day, Caterina was so weary that she could no longer sit up. She had already borne three children, and had never been in labor more than six hours. Now more than a dozen had passed, and she had not even crowned. Worse, the baby had become still.

"Mine was a difficult birth," the contessa breathed. "Don't fret, Dea. This is simply more proof that this child has as much spirit as his mother."

But now, even the stoic Flora was beginning to look concerned. Another examination brought Caterina more agony, but no good news. The child's head had not shown itself because one arm was flung upward, as if it were shielding its face. Grimly, Flora confessed that Nature had designed a woman's body to be just wide enough for the head to pass, but not both a head and arm. I put my hand upon Caterina's shoulder, and she put her own hand atop it.

"What can be done?" I asked, to spare my tired mistress the effort speech required.

Flora hesitated. "I must catch the child's arm and push it back down so that it rests alongside his body. This will be extremely painful for you, and I might break the child's arm, or worse, cause you to bleed. But we must do it now, and quickly; the baby needs air."

"This one is destined for great things," Caterina whispered. "I know it in my heart." She turned her pale, sweat-slicked face toward mine. "Make sure he survives, even if I do not."

"He will survive," I answered, my voice husky, "and you will, too, Madonna."

"First," Flora said, "I must make you some fresh tea." She retrieved a different concoction—this one a pale powder—from her black bag in the corner. This she mixed with hot water from the kettle, and handed it to Caterina.

Caterina made another face, but in a show of valor, threw back her head and swallowed the entire cup. Within twenty minutes, her head began to loll, and the blacks of her eyes were now as small as grains of sand. She had endured nine contractions during this time. The baby was desperate to come, but his crown had still not appeared.

"You are drowsy," Flora said loudly, leaning over her, "and for now, do your best to relax. I will let you know when we need your help."

I crouched beside the bed, my face near Caterina's, and took her hand. Morning light now filled the chamber, and the midwife had no need of the lamp; all my attention was focused on my mistress.

Flora stood with her feet on the ground, and leaned the upper half of her body onto the bed, between Caterina's legs. My mistress started when Flora's slender fingers entered her again, and remained tense as the midwife slowly slid her hand into the birth canal. I watched Flora's intent expression as she did her best to enter smoothly, without hurting Caterina, and I saw her lips curve upward when her fingers found the baby.

"There is the crown," she said reassuringly. Her hand moved again. "And there the little arm. Madonna, brace yourself."

Flora turned her own arm sideways; her eyes lit up with triumph as she caught hold of her target and pushed more deeply into the contessa's womb. Caterina howled without restraint, her bent legs writhing and striking the midwife. It took a full excruciating minute for the midwife to complete her work. At last, Flora slowly withdrew; Caterina's entire body relaxed as she let go a sigh of profound relief.

Her Illustriousness gritted her teeth and cried out again; when the contraction waned, she let go a loud, surprised gasp, and pushed herself up on her elbows. "It's coming!" she called, eyes wide, to Flora. "It's finally coming!"

Together, Flora and I lifted Caterina from the bed and settled her into the birthing chair. I held on to her shoulders as she endured several more strong contractions while Flora knelt at her feet. In the end, Caterina grasped the handles on the seat and bore down hard, her face an alarming shade of red as she let go a guttural roar that could be heard throughout the east wing of the palazzo.

I heard a wet, slithering sound, and looked beyond Caterina's shoulders and lap to see something small and yellow drop into Flora's waiting arms.

"A girl!" Flora called jubilantly. She used her fingers to tenderly clear the infant's mouth and flattened nose, then called for the basin and warm water.

I delivered both to her immediately and knelt beside her as Caterina dozed, slumped over, in the birthing chair.

I was used to the sight of newborns, and therefore was not surprised that its face was covered with pale yellow birth cheese and streaks of dark blood; nor was I disappointed when Flora swiftly and expertly cleaned the mess away to reveal a crimson, irregularly shaped face with slits for eyes, a bruised forehead, and a completely flattened nose. What unnerved me was the deep bluish tinge of the infant's chin, mouth, and fingertips.

Flora was concerned as well; instead of continuing to remove the birth cheese so that the baby could be presented to its mother, she immediately turned it over and firmly thumped it on its back to encourage it to draw its first breath. The child's tiny limbs flailed weakly, but it did not attempt to breathe on its own.

"Give her to me!" Caterina demanded, suddenly alert; she reached for the baby in Flora's arms.

Flora ignored her, instead thumping the child again; this time, the child coughed up a plug of birth cheese and dried blood, and sucked in an audible breath.

Caterina and I immediately smiled at the sound. Flora, all business, demanded a damp towel and the swaddling blanket, which I fetched at once. Soon the child was clean and tightly wrapped in its blanket before being presented to the worn but jubilant mother.

Caterina looked down at the tiny girl in her arms with something very like affection. "I shall name you Galeazza Maria, after my father," she whispered to the baby, "and will train you to be a prince and a soldier, just as he was."

She kissed the child's face and rocked her while Flora, smiling proudly with accomplishment, gently examined and cleaned Caterina and the mess beneath the birthing chair. I, too, was grinning as I removed the soiled blankets from the bed.

When the bed was ready for mother and child, Flora and I moved alongside Caterina. Before we could lift her, Caterina looked up at us, her eyes wide.

"Her muscles are jerking very hard, despite the swaddling," she said, her tone rising with alarm. "I think she is having a fit."

I looked down. The baby's face was contorted; a desperate gurgling sound emerged from its lips, now a deeper shade of blue.

"She needs air," Flora said, snatching the child. After clearing its mouth and nose with her finger, Flora moved toward the fireplace and turned the baby on its stomach again, her one hand gently supporting its midsection while the other thumped its back.

When the child still failed to draw in a breath, Flora stepped up to the hearth and unswaddled the child so that it was naked. Grasping both of its little ankles, she dangled it upside down in front of the warm fire, and struck its back again. The impact caused one of its feet to kick free of Flora's grasp; the freed little leg bent at the knee, and the ankle fleetingly crossed over the opposite leg, forming a near-perfect 4.

It was the image of the Hanged Man.

Flora caught the baby's errant ankle, and again swatted the child on the back. It let go a mortal strangling sound that brought Caterina to her feet.

"Don't die!" she shrieked. "Don't you dare die!"

Flora gave the child one last blow. In the profound silence that followed, her shoulders dropped suddenly, and her head inclined toward the fire.

"No!" Caterina screamed. "Give me my baby!" Clawing the air, she fought to rise from the chair.

I quickly took the infant from the unresisting Flora, and wrapped it in its blanket again before presenting it to Caterina. She sank back down in the birthing chair, cradling it in her arms. Its features looked peaceful, although its little blue lips gaped open; when Caterina closed its mouth, it looked as though it were sleeping.

"Get her out of here," Caterina demanded, her voice raw with emotion. "Get her out of here, and let me never set eyes on her again! She killed my baby! She killed my Galeazza!"

Twenty-three

Caterina refused to eat or drink anything that day, saying bitterly, "This is too cruel. What kind of God steals babies from their mothers' arms?"

"The same God that causes them to be born," I answered gently. I could not fault her for the question; I had asked a similar one myself, when I lost Matteo.

"*Damn* God!" she cursed. "Why let them be born in the first place?"

I pulled a chair to her bedside and sat down. "Before you left for Venice," I began softly, "do you remember the triumph card you chose?"

She would not look at me.

I continued calmly. "It was the Hanged Man. Sacrifice. Do you remember what I told you, that something terrible would occur—"

She interrupted. "You didn't say then that it would be so horrible."

"I didn't know what exactly would happen, Madonna. But remember, I also said that marvelous good would come of it."

"My baby's death?" She turned toward me at last, filled with exhausted rage. "What good can come of such a pitiful tragedy?"

I drew a breath to reply, but she began speaking swiftly again.

"I tried to be brave like you said, Dea; I tried to begin to care about people. This child . . . my little Galeazza," she said, swallowing a sob, "she kicked harder than any of my others. She was so strong I thought she was a boy, and I knew she would become a great soldier. I began to whisper to her, to tell her of her heritage—of her grandfather, the duke of Milan, and her Riario ancestors, and how I would train her myself in the martial arts. How she would never need to fear anything, how she would become the greatest of all the Sforza and Riario."

Tears streamed silently down her cheeks. "It made me happy . . . and I began to love her. But what is the point of it? She took her first breath and died. She fought so bravely just to enter the world . . . and she was defeated."

Her face contorted as she held back another outpouring of grief; ultimately, her stubborn pride triumphed, and her features hardened into a bitter mask.

As I watched that terrible transformation, realizing that little Galeazza's death could well cause her mother's heart to grow even colder, my foggy thoughts took on a sudden clarity. I heard no inner voice, felt no unnatural sensation, but I knew without doubt why fate had placed me with Caterina at that dreadful moment, and what I had to do.

I rose from the chair. "With your permission, Madonna. I should like to fetch the triumph cards."

She shrugged. "Why? To tell me of further sorrows to come? I already know my end . . . the Tower, just as my father. Whatever kingdom I have on earth will shatter around me."

But she did not stop me from going into the closet and retrieving the black silk bundle from my trunk. I sat down in the chair beside her, unwrapped the bundle, and spread the black silk atop the mattress, just next to where she lay.

I shuffled the gilded cards atop the silk and pushed them toward her hand. "Take these, Madonna," I said, "and shuffle or cut them as you wish."

She pushed herself to a half-sitting position and with great reluctance, cut the cards into four stacks.

I told Caterina to turn the top cards of each pile over, one at a time. The first she turned over was the Knight of Chalices, and I gestured for her to wait before revealing the others.

"This is the future that results from the Hanged Man," I said, listening to the words issuing from my mouth as if they were being said by another.

"See here the Knight of Chalices." I pointed at the card, which showed a handsome man astride a golden horse; in his hands, he carried an engraved golden chalice.

Caterina looked down at the card with dull resentment; had she possessed any energy, she might have hurled the cards to the floor.

I spoke swiftly, soothingly. "This is a real man, Madonna, one who will come to you bearing gifts, and much more. A chalice holds feeling: sorrow or happiness, love or hatred. I am not yet sure what he brings, but I know that he will be an ally."

Caterina shrugged, though I saw a glimmer of faint interest in her eyes. "When will he come?"

I stared down at the card; years would pass before this man appeared in the flesh. "In time," I said finally. "I will know more when the other cards appear."

Caterina turned over the second card.

Against the card's white background, surrounded by scrolling green vines and flowers, were two great goblets, representations of the gift that the Knight of Chalices would bring. Filled to the brim with emerald liquid, one cup stood above the other, and between them was a white banner that read *amor mio. My love.*

Despite the horror of the preceding day, I managed a wan grin. "I believe you can read the banner, Madonna. See the green liquid? It represents love and fertility—most specifically, love between a man and a woman." I paused and said with honest cheer, "I do not exaggerate, Madonna. The cards are clear: your true love, the Knight of Chalices, will come to you."

I glanced up at Caterina, whose eyes were wide and focused on the Two of Chalices. Her brow was furrowed and she was breathing heavily, as if trying to hold back tears; at the same time, her gaze was wistful. Her fingers were unsteady as they flipped over the third card.

Against a gilded background, a young warrior, clad in full body armor and bearing shield and halberd, rode astride a caparisoned white stallion. The warrior's shield was lowered; he was not at war, but placid and content to recall his past successes in battle.

He was the Knight of Swords, and he was oriented so that he and the Knight of Chalices stared at each other, with the Two of Chalices between them.

"The father," I said, gesturing at the Knight of Swords, "and the son." I pointed at the knight in armor, and my voice dropped in amazement. *"Your* son, Madonna. A great warrior, courageous and skilled in battle. If you are willing to open your heart."

"You would not lie to me," Caterina said tremulously.

I took her clammy hand and stared into her eyes. "I would not. And I have never. You cut the cards, not I."

"It's hard now to believe fate could ever be kind. My father and my baby, gone . . . and Bona banished; I have lost Milan now, too." She looked down at the last card mistrustfully. "What if it is the Tower, or the Hanged Man, or something worse?"

She let her long fingers hover above the card for a moment before finally turning it over. It was the Six of Batons, three golden scepters crossed diagonally over three identical ones. Caterina looked anxiously to me for an explanation.

"Victory," I said, smiling with relief. "Victory, Madonna! See, these are scepters. This child will be very powerful, and his acts will lead to great success. He will be known throughout the world."

She scrutinized me for several seconds, and apparently grew convinced of my sincerity, as the furrows in her brow melted away. The sorrow in her eyes eased slightly.

"I am very thirsty," she said, "and still in pain. But I should like to bathe before I make use of the midwife's powder."

By spring of 1482, the papal army and Venice had begun their war against Naples and Ferrara. Pope Sixtus demanded that those who had earlier fought with Naples's king against Lorenzo return at once to Rome to pledge their loyalty to the papacy. The Orsini clan obeyed, but most of the powerful Colonna family sided with Naples, as did Florence, Urbino, Mantua, Bologna, Faenza, and, to Caterina's dismay, Milan, under her uncle Ludovico. Caterina's ties to Milan were frayed almost to the breaking point, as was her usefulness to the Riario clan. She had grown up without coming to know Ludovico, so the two were near strangers, without a bond of affection to guarantee familial loyalty.

Naples responded by sending a massive army northward to Rome, so quickly that Girolamo could not lead his troops to Florence, but was obliged to fight to hold papal territories perilously close to Rome's ancient walls.

At first, Girolamo was victorious against the Neapolitans, until Lorenzo de' Medici shrewdly sent an army directly to Forlì, overwhelming the town's defenses. He read his enemy well: Girolamo immediately sent a large contingent of soldiers—one he could not spare—to Forlì, as he could not bear the thought of losing his tiny domain.

Although Girolamo managed to hold on to Forlì, the army that remained with him in the Roman countryside could not withstand the mighty Neapolitans, who soon captured fortress after fortress outside of Rome.

By December 1482, winter had called a temporary halt to hostilities, and a restless, sullen Girolamo returned home to his wife. Pressing their strong advantage, Naples, Florence, and Milan announced that they intended to prosecute Sixtus for various crimes, including the murder of Lorenzo's brother.

Sixtus had no defense for several of the charges, and there were far too many witnesses to his conspiracy against the Medici. Disgusted, His Holiness agreed to a truce, although it destroyed his hopes of gaining power and stability for his son Girolamo.

During all this time, Caterina refrained from any affairs, instead spending her free time with her children. She was awkward around them at first, and they around her, for they did not know each other well. But Caterina persisted, and soon became the children's favorite, for she had a gleeful imagination and created games to occupy them. She often visited Sixtus as well, as he was in ill health, and met Cardinal della Rovere—Sixtus's choice for his successor—whenever possible.

The year 1484 began with dire warnings from horoscopists: the stars and planets were moving into positions that augured major disasters, war, and the deaths of prominent persons. Not soon after, Sixtus suffered an attack that left the right side of his face immobile. His speech became increasingly slurred, and he could no longer swallow solid food without choking; in addition, his gout had become so painful that he could not take a single step unaided. Most times, he relied on a litter and was carried about the Vatican.

Caterina responded by visiting Sixtus more frequently; the old man adored her company, not just because of her beauty, but because she regaled him with stories that made him laugh and was so vehemently cheerful that the mere sight of her made him smile, despite his physical misery. Cardinal Giuliano della Rovere, Sixtus's favorite, often joined the two. Her insistent friendship with the cardinal suddenly made sense to me, especially now that she could not count on political support from Milan.

On one such informal occasion, Caterina met with His Holiness in early spring, on an unusually cold afternoon. The contessa was pale that day; she had been unable to keep her breakfast down, and refused lunch. Both she and I suspected pregnancy, though it was far too early to be certain. Yet by the time she entered the sitting room in the papal apartments, her gaiety and energy seemed genuine.

The former Francesco della Rovere sat in a high-backed, thronelike chair with extra padding for his aching bones. His huge bare feet—an alarming shade of violet, and so grotesquely swollen that his ankles had disappeared— rested on an ottoman topped by two feather pillows. The ottoman was placed next to a blazing hearth that made the room oppressively warm, but His Holiness still shivered, despite being wrapped in a heavy fur throw. His girth was now so great that his throne had no arms, lest his massive bulk should become stuck in the chair; instead, it hung over the edges of the seat. The keen, jaded look in his eyes was gone, replaced by one of vague, anxious impotence. Cardinal Giuliano della Rovere sat opposite him, and got to his feet when we entered.

"Caterina, my darling," the pope said weakly. Though I always accompanied the contessa on her visits to the Vatican, Sixtus viewed me as a servant, not a family member, and ignored my existence.

Caterina knelt beside him, where the arm of the chair would have been. "I will not ask to kiss your slipper, Holy Father," she said.

One of Sixtus's talonlike hands obligingly appeared from somewhere inside his fur covering; he held out the gold Ring of the Fisherman for

Caterina to kiss. "Such formality," he sighed. "Will you never call me Uncle Francesco?"

Caterina rose gracefully and kissed his ponderous cheeks. "I call you Father," she said, "because that is how I love you, as I would my own father; and I say Holy in order to show the respect I have for you and the office you bear."

Sixtus grinned, pleased, as did the handsome Cardinal della Rovere, who embraced Caterina as a relative, with a solemn kiss on each cheek.

"Shall I remain?" he asked Sixtus politely. Obviously, his had been a friendly, not political, visit.

"Of course, of course," Sixtus replied. "I am always happy to see family. I have nothing better to do these days, thanks to this accursed gout." He frowned down at his glaringly red feet. "I would as soon cut them off; they pain me so that I cannot bear the weight of the sheerest linen upon them." He looked up at Caterina and the cardinal, and waved an impatient hand at them. "Sit, sit! Formality is pointless; look at me, with my bare feet! Sit and talk with me, Caterina."

Della Rovere pulled another chair close to the pontiff, so that Caterina could sit next to Sixtus while the cardinal returned to his own chair in front of the hearth. I unobtrusively edged my way back toward the door, knowing that the offer did not extend to me, and watched the group from a short distance.

Caterina proceeded to deliver a lively monologue about her children—Sixtus's grandchildren: Bianca was six now, very studious and good at her letters; the best that could be said of Ottaviano was that he was five and looked almost exactly like his father. Four-year-old Cesare had a great fondness for his mother's hunting dogs and loved to play with them.

His Holiness drank it all in greedily, but when Caterina began to speak of the war against the Colonna, and her hopes for Girolamo's success and safety, Sixtus's expression darkened.

"Damn the Colonna!" he interrupted, his yellowed eyes narrowing. "They are nothing but traitors deserving of excommunication!"

Just as the pontiff let go his exclamation, I became aware of a charming little girl standing in the doorway. She could not have been more than five years old, at most, and was as dainty as a doll. Long, perfectly crimped golden curls spilled over her shoulders, covered by a miniature brocade gown of light blue. Both of her little hands gripped a woven basket so large she could scarcely manage it; inside the basket was a spray of delicate purple irises.

As everyone's gaze turned to her, she performed an impressive curtsy; as she rose, she asked, in a high, sweet voice, "Holy Father, may I have permission to enter? They say you are sick, so I have brought you some flowers."

Sixtus clapped his hands in delight. "Enter, my child! What a lovely little sight you are."

The girl entered with faint timidity, and paused in front of Sixtus's swollen feet. Laughing, he proffered his ring for her to kiss, which she could manage only standing up, but once she had kissed the ring, she stepped backward and knelt.

"Stand up, my darling! Stand up! I know you, of course, but I have forgotten your name."

"Lucrezia," a deep male voice said from the doorway, as Rodrigo Borgia stepped into my line of sight. He met first della Rovere's, then Caterina's gaze with one that was faintly menacing. "Forgive me if she has offended you in any way, Holiness, but she was very troubled to hear you were not feeling well, and wanted to do something to cheer you."

Borgia's hands rested on the shoulders of two boys, a few years apart in age, who stood in front of him. The elder was markedly taller, and would clearly grow into a very handsome man; he stood straight and eyed the adults directly but courteously. The second was less impressive, and could not bring himself to look at anyone, but hid his face in his father's scarlet robe. Both boys sported their father's dark hair and eyes.

"She is delightful," Sixtus said, motioning for little Lucrezia to rise. I stepped forward to take the basket from her, and set it on a table near the pontiff, where it could be properly displayed. "And these are the boys?"

"Juan," Borgia said, patting the shoulder of the shy boy, "and of course, my eldest, Cesare, who is almost nine now. They, too, are concerned for you."

Juan continued to hide his face, while Cesare executed a perfect courtier's bow. "May I address you, Your Holiness?" Cesare asked. He was extremely precocious for his age; his diction and intonation were those of an adult.

Sixtus nodded, smiling.

"We pray for your health every morning and every night, Your Holiness. I am sorry to see you unwell and hope you are restored quickly to robust good health. As for my brother . . . please forgive his behavior. He was born bashful, but he has expressed to all of us his good wishes for you."

At that, Juan reached out and punched his brother in the ribs; Cesare let go a gasp, but regained his composure immediately, and did not retaliate.

"Juan!" Borgia hissed sharply. "Have you no manners at all?" Aware that he was losing control, the Spanish cardinal tightened his grip on his younger son, and with a bow, addressed Pope Sixtus.

"Forgive me, Your Holiness, but I think it is best the children and I leave now. One in particular is growing rather restless." He shot Juan a dark look just as Lucrezia let go a whine of disappointment.

"Come, Lucrezia," Borgia commanded; after another curtsy to Sixtus, the little girl ran toward her father, her long golden ringlets bouncing.

Just before she could take Borgia's outstretched hand, Juan stuck out his foot diagonally, tripping Lucrezia so that she fell hard against her father. Borgia staggered backward; Lucrezia would have struck the floor, had Cesare not caught her.

In a thrice, he set Lucrezia out of harm's way and slapped his younger brother. "Don't hurt her!" he shouted, with true anguish. "Don't you ever dare lay a hand on her!"

Borgia had to hold him back. "With your permission, Holiness," he said grimly, his black brows knit together with barely repressed paternal rage.

"Children are so unpredictable." Sixtus sighed, and dismissed the four of them with a careless, backhanded wave; they disappeared noisily down the corridor.

"Dea," Caterina asked softly, casually, "could you find a vase and some water for the flowers before they fade?"

I nodded, although Sixtus could easily have rung for an attendant. As I stepped from the chamber, I heard someone arguing in the alcove at the end of the corridor, perhaps a dozen paces directly in front of me. Out of courtesy I paused and stood, silent and unobtrusive, against the wall, praying the parties involved would soon leave so that I could continue in their direction.

Rodrigo Borgia faced his children, who were lined up opposite him. Surprisingly, he was not chastising Juan, but Cesare. The cardinal had seized his elder son's wrist with such force that the boy winced at the pain.

"Why must you always fight your brother?" Borgia demanded, in a tone that threatened violence; the fury in his eyes terrified even me, an observer.

He bent down and thrust his face into his son's, tightening his grip on Cesare's wrist. The boy paled and pressed his lips more tightly together, though he would not cry out. Beside him, little Lucrezia wept softly while on his other side, Juan smirked.

"Because he hurts her!" Cesare shouted angrily; he did not shrink from his father's fury, but instead glared back at him with pure hatred. "She's only a baby, and my sister, and I will not tolerate her being hurt any longer by *anyone!* Do you understand me, Father?"

Murderous rage flared in Borgia's eyes. He crushed Cesare's wrist until the boy cried out; with a swift, violent movement, Borgia used his powerful grip to push the boy onto his back against the hard marble floor. Lucrezia let go a shrill cry and threw herself upon her brother.

"Don't hurt him," she sobbed. "Please, Papa... Cesare, are you all right?"

"I have put all my hope in you," Borgia hissed at his fallen son. "I will give you the world—only do not disappoint me. You must never behave so in front of any person of import, much less the pope!"

In reply, Cesare struggled to his feet, and took his sister's hand; Lucrezia peered up at him with slavish adoration. In a voice just as deadly as his father's, he vowed softly, "I will kill whoever harms her again, I swear."

Clutching Lucrezia's hand, the boy turned his back to Borgia and stalked off rapidly. Juan sniggered, and Borgia raised his hand as if to strike him, which immediately turned Juan's expression to one of respectful somberness.

The cardinal grabbed Juan by his elbow and hurried off after the other children. I did not move until they were all out of sight.

I confess, I felt a certain kinship with Cesare that day; I knew what it was to love a sibling desperately, and to want to kill those who would hurt him. I hoped that, unlike me, Cesare would find a way to protect the sister he so adored.

Unlike his wife, Girolamo was so undone by the possibility of his father's death that he rarely appeared at the Vatican. The papal captain's discomfort had little to do with sorrow over losing his father and mentor, but rather with ambition: Girolamo could not bear the thought of losing all his power and returning to his embarrassingly small fiefdom of Imola and Forlì.

Over Sixtus's weak objections, Girolamo goaded the Orsini into fighting with the papal army against the Colonna, in hopes that he might obtain many of the Colonna's grand palaces and fortresses outside the city, in the Roman countryside, before the inevitable occurred.

I secretly pitied the Colonna, who did not deserve to be destroyed simply because they had disagreed with Sixtus. Caterina—aware, like Girolamo, that the time had come for the Riario to grab as much power and land as possible—supported her husband thoroughly in the war. Even though she was by this time obviously pregnant, she expressed hope that she could join him at the battlefront.

Count Girolamo, however, instructed her to remain home with the children. And when the rains ceased and the weather turned pleasant, he led the papal army, along with the fighting force of the Orsini, eastward, into the rolling countryside. By midsummer, he had captured the town of Cave from the Colonna and claimed it for the Riario.

The Colonna, who had not been able to muster an army strong enough to withstand the combined forces of the papacy and the Riario, surrendered and offered to make whatever apologies or reparations were sufficient to win the Holy Father's blessing again. Girolamo wanted neither, but craved land and wealth. And so he continued his war, and in July, seized the town of Capranica from its Colonna lords.

Giddy with success and the realization that he would be met with nothing but victory, Girolamo invited the patriarch Virginio Orsini, Caterina, and even the children to camp with him and his army outside of his next target, Paliano.

Caterina was determined to go, despite being seven months pregnant by this time. I scolded her, but she pointed out that she felt robustly healthy and had no cause for concern; I accompanied her reluctantly, making sure that our company included a midwife.

I had no taste for war or camping with soldiers in the mud, but Girolamo surprised us all. In the lush countryside outside of Paliano, he had set up huge silk tents adorned with banners and filled with all manner of comforts, including real chairs and beds, a freshwater well, and four private wooden privies. These were situated atop a hill, above the soldiers' encampment and the oxen and horses, so that we were not exposed to unpleasant sights or foul smells. At first sight, it seemed more like a joust than war.

One large tent housed Virginio Orsini and his sons, another Caterina and the children, and a third Girolamo and his closest aides—who, to my utter joy, included Luca, whom I had not seen since his master went to war. Later, after night fell, both Luca and I wandered out of our tents in search of each other, and went into the forest for a few hours of talk and pleasure.

Girolamo remained certain of an immediate victory; Caterina and Virginio Orsini, along with two of Girolamo's captains, were not so sure. Paliano was larger and more fortified than either Cave or Capranica, and scouts had reported that it had recruited more fighting men, too.

But Girolamo was stubborn. On the third of August, he began the attack on the city. To his surprise, the Colonna were ready for him, and by the end of the very first day, had fought their way to into the papal camp in the valley below us. On the crest of the hill, Caterina stood with her protective arms around her sons Ottaviano, then only five, and four-year-old Cesare, as she pointed out to them the invaders below and explained their battle technique and how Girolamo's soldiers responded.

On the second day, the Colonna's army managed to push our encampment back, obliging our men to move our tents back one ridge, under cover of night. By then, Girolamo was glum, and Caterina and the canny old warrior, Virginio Orsini, convinced him of the need for more supplies; I stood beside Caterina and watched as Luca, writing at impossible speed, penned a letter to His Holiness detailing what was required. Caterina remained confident and cheerful—for the sake of the children, perhaps, or because, like Girolamo, she could not countenance defeat. I found it more difficult to summon optimism; for each time I heard cannon fire, or the shrieks of the wounded and dying, the earth shook, and I felt myself spiraling headfirst, down among the shattered fragments of the Tower.

After eight days of fighting, Girolamo had still not received the requested supplies, and his army had been pushed farther back into the countryside by the Colonna's superior forces.

"If things do not turn in our favor by tomorrow," my lady sighed, "I will join the fighting myself."

She said this in the late afternoon, before our soldiers had returned. We sat in our tent looking at the hill before us, which blocked any sight of the war being waged just beyond it. One of the children's nurses had taken them back to the bedroom, separated from us by a white silk flap.

Nearby, one of Orsini's sons, twenty-year-old Paolo, was reclining on a sofa beside a pile of armor. At midday, he had fainted in battle because the weather had turned miserably sultry, and a friend had rescued him and brought him here to safety. After Caterina's ministrations of water and cool compresses, Paolo had recovered enough to consider rejoining the fighting, but she dissuaded him, with good cause: it was late afternoon, and the temperature had soared even higher. A short jaunt to fetch water beneath the unrelenting sun had convinced me to seek shade as soon as possible.

"Rest here," Caterina cajoled him, "in the comfort of our tent. By the time you put on your armor, it will be dusk anyway, and the fighting will be over."

As we sat, indolent from the heat, hoofbeats thundered up the hill toward our tent. Paolo took up his sword and went outside to investigate. He returned with a young rider, rumpled and forlorn, who looked as though he had not slept in days. He was covered in dust, and had ridden so fast he had lost his cap.

He bowed to both of us ladies, and said, "I bear a message from Rome for Her Illustriousness, Caterina Sforza." His hand went to the leather pouch slung over his shoulder, and brought forth a sealed letter.

Caterina rose, frowning. "I am she."

The lad genuflected as he handed over the letter.

Caterina broke the seal as the three of us watched. Her glistening face was brown from the sun, and her eyebrows bleached almost white; I watched the latter rush together above the bridge of her nose, but she remained calm and otherwise expressionless. I remember thinking that Sixtus must have denied us the desperately needed supplies, and that she was taking the news remarkably well, when she glanced up from the parchment and nodded at the messenger.

"You have done well," she said briskly to him. "Go to our kitchen—two tents away"—she pointed—"and get yourself and your horse food and water. When you see my lord Girolamo, relay this to him."

She returned the letter to the courier, and disappeared behind the flap to go in the bedroom and speak softly to the nurse. In the next instant, she was back.

"I must leave immediately for Rome," she told Paolo. "But it will be very dangerous, and I am in need of your protection. Will you come?"

Paolo nodded; he could hardly refuse his captain's wife.

Caterina then turned to me. "I will not order you to attend me—though of course, you know why I want you to. The choice is yours."

"To go to Rome?" I imagined that she was going to confront His Holiness to demand the supplies.

She gave the curtest of nods, and said, with perfect composure, "Sixtus is dead. The fate of the Riario now rests in my hands."

Twenty-four

We would not learn the full story until much later: Caterina's uncle Ludovico became fearful when he learned that Venice was urging the powerful duke of Orleans to bring an army down from France to invade Milan. Ludovico had immediately contacted Florence and Venice and negotiated a truce with them, finally ending the Venetian war that Sixtus had launched so long ago. Venice received a small but succulent plum, the fertile northern region of the Polesine; Florence was given nothing, but a blind eye would be turned to its efforts to capture the fortress at Sarzana and the city of Lucca.

Ludovico revealed his true feelings for Caterina, or rather, the lack thereof, by not negotiating with Sixtus; the papacy and the Riario received nothing. Once His Holiness died, there would be nothing for Girolamo save two towns in the bucolic Romagna.

Sixtus received news of the truce on the eleventh of August. He responded by furiously shaking his fist in the air and shouting at length about the peace he called "shameful and ignominious." He was inconsolable, much to the despair of his attendants and physicians, who feared for his health.

Their concerns were justified. By that afternoon, Sixtus was ill with one of Rome's deadly summer "fevers," and before dawn the next day, on the twelfth of August, the pope was dead.

Rome lay a long, hard day's gallop from Paliano. Caterina did not believe I was capable of defending myself, and insisted that I be her passenger on her horse. She was ready for battle: a heavy breastplate was strapped over her swollen midsection, and her shield tied to her steed. She wore a broad-brimmed French hat with huge white plumes, tied beneath her chin, into which she tucked her golden hair; around her waist was buckled a velvet moneybag, heavy with gold, and a thick leather belt that held her current favorite weapon, a huge curved scimitar.

Paolo Orsini, good soldier that he was, posed no questions, but as I fastened a canteen to my belt, I asked, "Where are we going precisely, Madonna?"

She swung up easily onto her horse and looked down at me as if I were a simpleton.

"To the Castel Sant'Angelo," she said brusquely, as if it should be obvious, and gestured impatiently at me.

I climbed up behind her to sit on the mare's blanketed back, and wrapped my arms around Caterina. My grip was at first ginger; later, as we reached breakneck speed while tearing through the countryside, it grew desperate.

When night fell some four hours later, our wild ride stopped; I expected to encamp and continue at dawn. But Caterina had a different plan. I returned from relieving myself in the woods to discover that she and Paolo Orsini had lashed lanterns to the shoulders of their horses, and intended to continue riding until we reached Rome.

"Too much time has already passed," she said, ignoring my complaints about my aching backside.

Again we rode, this time at a slightly reduced speed. I tried to make sense of the tiny strip of terrain rushing toward us, illuminated by the lanterns' wavering arcs of yellow light, but it left me dizzy; I closed my eyes and clung fast to Caterina. After a time, the land flattened out, and our way grew easier as we took the more-traveled paths to Rome. I remember passing through the countryside and hearing distant church bells announcing the hour of Compline, when good Christians said their late-night prayers before retiring.

By my calculation, we arrived at the walls of the city near midnight. Orsini and Caterina both agreed that we should enter via the southwest, as a small contingent of Girolamo's soldiers had encamped near the gate, at the Church of Saint John of the Lateran. They could provide us with enough protection to cross to the other side of the city and the Castel Sant'Angelo.

We approached the main gate known as the Porta Maggiore to perceive, just inside, the flare of torches and shouts of men, as a few members of the papal army tried to disburse some two dozen ruffians. The crowd's chant rose on the air:

Colonna! Colonna! Death to the Riario!

I could not see Caterina's face, but at the sound, she wheeled her horse about. Paolo Orsini did the same, and followed as Caterina's mount thundered southward along the city wall. Soon we came upon a second, smaller gate—the Porta Asinaria—which was not only deserted, but also located very close to the Church of the Lateran and the papal barracks.

We rode through the gate, staying close to the city wall, under the cover of the trees that lined it. The air was hazy with dark smoke that made my eyes stream; Rome was burning, or at least parts of it. To the north, the sky glowed an unnatural pink-red. Closer by, through the branches, the monastery and basilica of Saint John could easily be seen; the huge windows of the church were brightly lit, as were half the windows in the monastery. The tents that once housed members of Sixtus's army were gone, replaced by a dozen infantrymen and half as many mounted guards, all of whom patrolled the perimeters.

We were fortunate to have entered a zone protected by the army, but the city's hills before us flickered with torchlight, and the streets beyond echoed with the shouts of rioters, eager to take advantage of the political chaos following the death of a pope.

One of the infantrymen spotted our torches at once, and cried, "Halt! Who goes there?"

Followed by Orsini, Caterina emerged from the shelter of the trees; two mounted soldiers approached her at once.

One of them, a commoner as large as the count but twice as fat, gawked at her in surprise. "A woman!" he called to his companion, with a hint of lasciviousness in his tone. "*Two* women."

Orsini rode up alongside Caterina, which caused the riders to reach for the hilts of their swords. "I am Paolo Orsini," he said sternly. "And these are not women, but *ladies.*"

Before he could say another word, Caterina pulled off her hat to display her golden hair. "I come from my lord and husband, Count Girolamo."

"Your Illustriousness!" The other soldier, a younger man whose speech marked him as higher born, bowed immediately on his horse; the heavy man followed suit.

"And your name is?" Caterina demanded of the younger.

"Antonio da Fiorentino, Your Illustriousness."

"Antonio," she said, "I charge you and your compatriot to escort us safely to the Castel Sant'Angelo. Count Girolamo has ordered me to secure the fortress in his stead until he can arrive."

Caught in the light from the torches lining the exterior of the basilica, Antonio's sharp features revealed temerity.

The heavier soldier said, "We cannot, Madonna. It's far too dangerous! The streets are filled with enemies of the Riario, especially near the Vatican!"

Antonio waved his companion silent. "Of course we shall obey, Your Illustriousness. But you shall need more than Sandro and I to escort you. Let me bring more men at once."

We rode alongside Paolo Orsini, with Antonio and Sandro flanking us on either side; an extra swordsman rode alongside Antonio, to afford us women more protection. Two soldiers armed with pikes rode ahead of us, and two behind. Caterina wisely chose to avoid the populous areas of the city, instead taking narrow side streets to the birthplace of Romulus and Remus: the Palatine Hill, inhabited by pines, overgrown Roman ruins, and flocks of sheeps and goats who grazed the area during the day. I stared at the crumbling, roofless skeletons of two-thousand-year-old palaces, rendered ghostly by wisps of smoke and the ever-increasing reddish glow from the fires in the wealthier districts.

From there we passed down into a quiet, sparsely peopled area, where we kept to wooded areas before entering the Trastevere, where the working commoners dwelled. There we were forced onto narrow streets, past homes guarded by their owners; more than once, menfolk noted the papal uniforms and stuck their heads out of the windows to cry out, *Death to the Riario!*

At last, we made it to uninhabited marshes, and as the horses picked their way through the vile-smelling muck, Caterina questioned Antonio, who rode beside us. Most of the news was not good: our home of several years, the Palazzo Riario, had been destroyed, and all the belongings stolen or burned. I let go a cry of loss and indignation at the revelation; Caterina listened silently.

"We are sorry, Your Illustriousness," Antonio said. "With so many of our forces gone with Count Girolamo, and the rest protecting the Vatican, we did not have enough men to protect his palazzo. The crowd moved so quickly . . . the servants barely escaped with their lives. What the servants did not take, the crowd did, and what they did not want, they set afire. I'm afraid that many of the fine palazzi have been completely destroyed."

Caterina's tone was grim. "What has become of the cardinals? Are they in conclave to elect a new pope? I am concerned for my husband's cousin, Giuliano della Rovere, of course. And I hear that Rodrigo Borgia has made many enemies."

Antonio shook his head. "They are all well, so far as I know. Most are in conclave at the Vatican, under heavy guard. But I have heard that Borgia and della Rovere are communicating with the conclave via messenger; neither one dares leave his palace. Borgia has several cannon trained on the street, and della Rovere's palazzo is similarly well guarded." He paused. "Unfortunately for the Riario, Cardinal Colonna has been freed from prison and has joined the conclave. He is surely doing everything in his power to ensure that Cardinal della Rovere is not elected."

"And the Castel Sant'Angelo? Who holds it?"

"Our troops. Though I must say, Your Illustriousness"—Antonio lowered his voice confidentially—"that the fortress has been attacked several times during the day by an organized, trained militia. My fellows have fought them, and say that some have been seen wearing Borgia's colors."

"I am not surprised," Caterina said drily, turning her attention back to the swampish ground ahead of her.

We followed the snaking Tiber until the ground grew more solid, and we came upon the carefully maintained Vatican gardens. From there, we rode eastward alongside the massive southern façade of Saint Peter's, its high, narrow windows aglow. Our soldiers reassured us that we would be safe crossing through the square; indeed, we passed through one of the archways into the plaza to find it surrounded on three sides by armed papal guards. On the steps leading to the atrium in front of the basilica, and at the northern archway leading to the Vatican, were several cannon, their muzzles trained on the passage leading out to the street.

Guards lifted their swords at the sound of our approach; Antonio called to them, and quickly explained our need to reach the nearby Castel Sant'Angelo.

"Take care," called one of the artillerymen. "We can protect you here in the square, but not beyond. You will have to pass through a dangerous area."

"Then give me more men," Caterina demanded indignantly, "for I must obey my husband's command!"

"Forgive me, Madonna," the weary artilleryman replied with a bow. "With all my heart, I would follow Captain Girolamo's order. But we are too few; if any of us desert our posts . . . Well, His Holiness's fleeing servants stripped his apartments of many valuables already, which is bad enough. But if the crowd gets into the basilica or the Vatican, they will steal everything and desecrate what is left."

Caterina could not argue with the man's logic. We made our way across the square, and paused at the archway leading out into the street. The Castel Sant'Angelo was only a five-minute ride straight ahead, down through the narrow street that cut through the heart of the neighborhood known as the Borgo.

I peered over Caterina's shoulder through the archway at what lay before us. The night was black and the way unlit, save for the sweep of torchlight from those fighting in the street. Darkness alternated with shards of yellow light that revealed a glimpse of a contorted face, the fleeting gleam of steel. Amid the groans and screams came battle cries:

Colonna! Death to the Riario!

Orsini! Orsini! Girolamo!

Our protectors closed ranks around Caterina, who drew her scimitar and ordered, "Onward!"

I held tightly to Caterina as we cantered into the chaos. Our lanterns revealed a swarm of men fighting on foot in the near distance in front of the fortress, its exterior lit by sconces encircling the second floor. The muzzle of a cannon peeked out from each upper battlement.

Unfortunately, our lanterns also revealed our presence. As our horses' canters became full gallops, some of the fighters turned from battle toward us. Our soldiers' uniforms revealed our loyalties, which caused fresh chanting: Colonna! Death to the Riario!

A few of those who took up the cry ran directly at us with long swords. In the tumult, the two pike-bearing soldiers guarding our front were forced to veer off to one side in order to fight off the attackers. In the next instant, the two at our side were forced to engage in swordplay.

A great brute bearing a monstrous longsword rushed toward Caterina, crying with delight, "It's her! The contessa—Girolamo's wife! Get her!"

He reached with an impossibly long arm and grabbed her right stirrup; the horse reared, and I slipped from its backside directly onto the brick paving. It knocked the breath from me, and I lay stunned, watching as the brute tried to seize the horse's reins. He nearly succeeded, but Caterina caught them first, and when the horse brought its front legs down, she leaned forward over the horse's neck, balancing her heavily pregnant body with grace, and brought the scimitar down on the brute's bald head.

A faint red mist sprayed upward from his crown as the blade sank into his scalp; there came a muffled crack as the steel bit into his skull. As Caterina pulled the scimitar up, ready to strike again, blood gushed from the wound with such force that the brute's face was immediately covered with blood. He dropped to his knees.

Only then did Caterina turn. "Dea!" she shouted, scanning the dark ground for me.

I found myself able to breathe again, and exhaled a scream as I struggled to my feet. Antonio was beside me, and reached down to pull me up into his saddle. As he did, one of our troops retook his place in front of us, and used his boot heel to push the impaled body of one of our enemies from his pike.

The group that had proclaimed itself loyal to Girolamo and the Orsini surrounded us, fighting off our attackers and allowing us to make our way quickly up to the cylindrical fortress. We rode up a walled-in spiral ramp that led to an impenetrably thick metal gate, and as our protectors worked the brass knocker, Caterina cupped her hands about her mouth and bellowed, "Girolamo! Girolamo! I come with orders from Count Girolamo!"

A man's face appeared at one of small, barred windows two floors above us. "I am the castellan, Vittorio de' Lampugnani. Who calls?"

Lampugnani had been the surname of Duke Galeazzo's assassin, but Caterina did not flinch. This man was no relation.

"I, Caterina Sforza. I bring orders from Captain Girolamo!"

The face disappeared at once. As we waited, one of the pro-Orsini street fighters ran up the ramp behind us. His sword was sheathed and he held out his empty hands to show he meant no harm.

"Your Illustriousness," he called to Caterina. "Is it truly you?"

"It is," Caterina said, impatiently glancing up at the fortress window.

"May I have a word with you, on behalf of my master? My name is Luigi da Volterra."

The soldier Antonio put a hand on his hilt. "And who, pray tell, is your master?"

Luigi, a broad-chested young man, looked to Caterina. "I would prefer to share that with Her Illustriousness. Perhaps she might understand why—"

"Let him come to me," Caterina told Antonio and the others as she dismounted and tossed her reins to the nearest soldier. Our men moved their horses only a few steps away in order to let Luigi pass. As they did, I dismounted from Antonio's horse and went to stand beside Caterina. Antonio did not trust Luigi, either; he kept the point of his sword aimed directly at Luigi's back.

Caterina waited until Luigi was close enough to hear her whisper, "Who is your master?"

"Your cousin, Cardinal Giuliano della Rovere. On the day the Holy Father died, our forces arrived here at the same time as Borgia's; thus far, we are at a stalemate because my master did not anticipate that so many men would be needed to guard the palazzo. But while your husband's forces have kept Borgia's men at bay, they will not let us enter to claim the fortress." He blinked at the contessa's swollen belly. "May God protect you; you are with child, yet you ride on such dangerous streets?"

Caterina's expression was opaque. "Tell your master I thank him for the protection he provided me tonight. Reassure him that I will keep the Castel secure until a new pope has been elected. But tell Cardinal della Rovere that he should use his troops for his own protection. Let him tend to his business, and I will tend to mine.

"In fact, you must tell his men to retreat and leave the square at once, for I intend to disperse Borgia's men most forcefully."

Luigi blinked rapidly; his lips parted in surprise. "But Your Illustriousness, it would be an enormous advantage to my master if we gain the fortress. . . ."

"I will cede it to him after he is elected," Caterina hissed. "Otherwise, he will draw the ire of everyone in the streets who now hate the Riario, and his election will not seem legitimate. In the meantime, I will hold the Castel safely for him. Now tell your men to retreat. I have given you fair warning."

Luigi had no chance to reply; as the contessa finished speaking, the great gate rumbled open before us, revealing the castellan, Ser Vittorio, surrounded by a score of armed soldiers. Behind them was a poorly lit, dank-smelling dungeon.

As Luigi ran back to the fighting, the rest of us hurried inside the fortress and the gate behind us rumbled shut. Our protectors rode on, their steeds' hooves ringing against the stone until they found their way outside to the stables.

Caterina stepped up to the grizzled Vittorio, who eyed his new commander: a twenty-one-year-old woman wearing a French hat with plumes bedraggled by the hard ride, a fine beige silk gown, and an ill-fitting breast-plate, from beneath which the lower half of her heavily pregnant belly protruded. Another man might have laughed, but Vittorio and his men had been drilled by the contessa many times, and knew that she would not toler-ate disobedience.

"Your Illustriousness," Ser Vittorio said, as he and his troops bowed to her.

"For now," Caterina told them, her voice loud and echoing off the an-cient stone walls, "I am your captain, by order of my lord Girolamo. You are to obey me as you would him."

There followed a palpable pause; some of the men shifted their feet and looked uncertainly to Ser Vittorio, who was already locking the bolts. "We are obliged to carry out our lord's orders until a new papal captain has been appointed," he said firmly.

Caterina returned to face those remaining, and pointed the tip of her scimitar's blade to the sky.

"Let there be no question of motive," she told the troops. "We will hold the Castel Sant'Angelo safely for my lord and husband until order can be restored! Let us allow no invader to seize the fortress and impose his will upon the papal election!" She drew a deep breath, and shouted with irre-sistible ferocity: "Girolamo, Girolamo! Success to the Riario!"

"Girolamo, Girolamo!" Ser Vittorio roared in reply, lifting his own weapon; his men took up the cry, their reluctance transformed into enthu-siasm.

I cannot forget Caterina's expression at that instant: triumphant, tran-scendent, fully alive. Until that moment, I had not fully believed her claim that she was born to lead in battle, but the proof was there, in the soldiers' cheers, in the utter joy illuminating my lady's face.

I smiled, but did not join in the chanting; the contessa's happiness would be at best fleeting. Like the Palazzo Riario, the life that we had known in Rome was lost forever. We had entered, for the first time, the world of the Tower.

Twenty-five

That night, I followed dutifully as Ser Vittorio escorted Caterina around the Castel, explaining the military situation: only three hundred troops currently inhabited the fortress, which held adequate food, weapons, and ammunition to last a month, by which time a new pope would surely have been chosen; all of the men were trained in artillery and swordsmanship, save for some twenty experienced archers.

The fortress itself had three distinct sections: a vast dungeon below ground level, the soldiers' quarters on the first three floors, and the grandly furnished papal apartments on the upper floors. The ground level led to a large open courtyard where the troops drilled. The soldiers' area consisted of endless low-ceilinged, poorly lit rooms whose walls were stained by rust and mildew. The rooftop was equipped with a cannon at every battlement; beside each cannon were pyramids of stone cannonballs, heaped as high as Vittorio's head.

Caterina peered down from the battlements at the shadowy figures down in the street below. Apparently, Cardinal della Rovere's men had taken her advice and fled, for the fighting had stopped, and those remaining had gathered in a circle to listen to instructions.

"Rouse the longbowmen," she told Vittorio. "And have them kill as many of those men as possible. These are Borgia's troops, and at the first opportunity they will seize this fortress. Tell me the outcome, no matter the hour."

Vittorio readily agreed, then led us to our temporary quarters: the lavish papal apartments. He apologized for the fact that there were no servants to attend us, or hot water, or food beyond tasteless military fare, which he brought us himself on a scarred wooden tray, along with mead, which Caterina drank greedily while proclaiming it tasted like piss. He also brought us a bucket of water, and after I removed Caterina's armor, dress, and chemise to air them out, I poured some into a silver basin, so that my lady and I could wash away the accumulated dust and sweat of the harrowing day's efforts.

Caterina refused to retire naked, given the need for readiness; I solved the problem by finding two lawn nightshirts that had obviously belonged to someone far more ample than either of us. Once Caterina slipped one on, she crawled onto the huge bed, its gold brocade cover embroidered with Sixtus's emblem of the golden oak above the papal keys. She did not bother to climb beneath the sheets, but laid her head upon the pillow and let go a poignantly weary sigh. I lay down beside her and blew out the lamp.

"So now you understand the affair with Borgia," she said.

"What?"

"Borgia," she answered drowsily. "He told me that if I killed della Rovere and held the Castel Sant'Angelo for him when Sixtus died, he would become pope and give me all the land in the Romagna that I wanted. And a grand estate in Rome. And a secret position as his military adviser." She giggled faintly. "I am so tired . . . I should not be telling you these things."

Her words brought me back from the edge of sleep at once. "He said these things to you . . . and you agreed to them?" I asked, appalled. "You knew he was capable of murder, yet you slept with him?"

"I did," she said. "I agreed with his plan at first because I was naïve enough to hope that he would bring me such power. Once I came to know him, I realized that he would never let me have such things. He is too clever, and I knew that, should I ever displease him, I would be destroyed."

"Do you think he might still try to kill you?"

Her tone grew grim. "He would find a way to do something worse. Disgrace me publicly, strip me of my title, perhaps, but not kill me."

"Did you really consider killing della Rovere?"

The mattress shifted as she shrugged in the darkness. "For an instant, perhaps. Until I learned that della Rovere has more money and influence than Borgia. If we are lucky"—she paused to let go a yawn—"della Rovere will become pope. He promised that he would keep Girolamo as his army captain when I swore that I would keep the Castel Sant'Angelo out of Borgia's hands. But then, della Rovere also claimed that he had enough troops at his disposal to take the fortress.

"So perhaps he is wrong about being able to buy the papacy easily. And if that is the case, then it's wisest for me simply to hold the fortress until I can negotiate for more land. Otherwise, Girolamo and I are left with nothing . . . except Forlì and Imola."

Caterina hesitated such a long moment that I thought she had fallen asleep. Abruptly, she asked, "Dea . . . is this what the Tower card predicted? Am I going to fail?"

I, too, paused as I considered my answer.

"Do you remember what I told you years ago? The card spoke of an upheaval, of the destruction of a way of life. Like the Palazzo Riario being burned. Whatever happens, your life will never be the same."

I waited for a reply, and was answered seconds later by light snoring.

The next morning I woke to the teeth-chattering boom of the cannon on the roof above me. Caterina had dressed and gone. I pulled on my own clothing; as I dressed, the cannon sounded again.

I found the staircase leading up to the roof of the fortress, where the sun was already shining. By then the cannon fire had ended, although the tang of gunpowder was still in the air. As she stood near one of the battlements with the artillerymen, Caterina spotted me and walked across the roof to greet me. Her manner was brisk, but not cheerful.

"We have routed Borgia's men," she reported, "at least, those who survived the longbows last night. They won't return for some time." She paused, and her expression briefly darkened. "As for Girolamo . . ."

Her lips twisted in an effort to contain a swift-welling rage. "My lord received the news of the pope's death shortly after we did. He chose . . ."

Her voice began to shake with anger, and she paused until she could control its trembling. "He retreated," she said, clipping the words, "and ran back toward Rome. So Paliano is safely back in the hands of the Colonna, as are Cave and Capranica, the towns we conquered. All of our effort was for nothing."

She directed her furious gaze downward, lest the troops see her emotion. "Girolamo led his army to the outskirts of the city. He could easily have made it back to the Castel Sant'Angelo, but the conclave of cardinals ordered him to stay outside the city gates until the new pope was elected." She glared up at me. "And Girolamo, the idiot, is *obeying* them! He will ruin us!"

"I am sorry, Madonna," I whispered.

"My only hope is that della Rovere manages to bribe his fellows into choosing him," she replied bitterly. She paused, and her tone grew calmer. "Go down to the second floor," she said, "and eat at the officers' mess. Then go back to the papal chambers; it's safest there, and you'll be out of our way."

Before we parted, a trumpet blared in the street below.

Ser Vittorio, the castellan, peered over the battlement and cried out, "Who goes there?"

I hurried to the battlement to look down with the others.

Six men on horseback waited in the street; four of them brandished halberds, one waved a white flag, and one wore a priest's cassock. The priest shouted while all of us strained to listen.

"I bring an urgent message to deliver directly to Her Illustrious Highness, Caterina Sforza."

Caterina stepped out onto the edge of the battlement. "I am here," she shouted. "Who sends you?"

The priest executed a courtly bow in his saddle. "Your nephew, His Holiness Raffaele Riario."

I frowned. Though he had been an infrequent visitor to the Palazzo Riario, I remembered Raffaele well. He had received his cardinal's cap from his great-uncle Sixtus at a scandalously tender age, and had unwittingly accompanied the late Archbishop Salviati to Florence on the failed mission to assassinate Lorenzo de' Medici. After his brother Giuliano's murder,

Lorenzo had taken pity on the terrified young Raffaele, and sent him safely back to Rome with an armed guard.

"What news?" Caterina demanded curtly. She had never been fond of Raffaele, whom she considered cowardly.

"He fears for his aunt Caterina's safety, and that of her unborn child," the priest called back. "And he urges you to come discuss the holding of the fortress with him. We are here to escort you to a protected place where you can meet him."

"Witless dolt," Caterina muttered under her breath, then raised her voice again. "I cannot leave the Castel Sant'Angelo until we have a new pontiff. I invite my nephew to come inside the fortress, where I will be happy to discuss whatever he wishes. I guarantee his safety."

After a pause, the priest responded, "Please, Your Illustriousness. You are with child, and this"—he gestured sweepingly at the fortress—"is no place for a woman. My master begs you to go to your husband. He and the other cardinals intend to deal most generously with you and your family."

Caterina laughed heartily. "Tell me, Father," she shouted, grinning, "does Raffaele believe me to be completely stupid?"

The priest answered with perplexed silence.

Caterina leaned forward, hands resting upon her thighs; her smile vanished at once, replaced by honest fury. "Answer this, then: Do you know who my father was?"

The priest and his fellows looked at each other in confusion. "Galeazzo Sforza," the priest called, "Duke of Milan."

"One of the most intelligent men ever to grace Milan's throne," the contessa said. "I may be a woman, but I have my father's brain! I am not fool enough to leave the fortress. Go tell your master *that!*"

With that, she turned her back to him, and climbed down from the battlement.

The days grew tedious. The heat was sweltering, the food and drink disgusting, and the news less than encouraging. Tired of camping with his men outside the city gates, Girolamo decided to passively await news of his fate in

the nearby Orsini stronghold of Isola, where he and his children were luxuriously housed and fed. He sent his wife a letter commanding her to join him;
furious, Caterina secretly fed the letter to the lamp's flame and lied to her
troops.

Meanwhile, she and I listened to distant battles in Rome's streets as cardinals and clans struggled for power. On our eleventh day in the fortress, we
watched as a fresh army of five hundred marched through the Porta Maggiore into the city. For a glimmering instant, Caterina hoped that Girolamo
had finally found his courage, but as the army neared, its brilliant red and
yellow banners came into view. It was the standard of the Colonna, with a
golden crown topping a large white Roman column. My lady cursed her
husband beneath her breath as the Colonna troops encamped on the other
side of the Tiber.

"He could have taken the Castel Sant'Angelo," she said angrily. "I told
him again and again that we had to be ready to take it, in the event of Sixtus's death, but he would never respond to me. Now . . ." She could not
bring herself to continue.

On the following day, the twenty-fourth of August, came the worst news
of all. Girolamo had signed a contract with the Sacred College, forfeiting his
position as captain of the papal army and surrendering the Castel Sant'Angelo
in exchange for four thousand ducats, restitution for his destroyed palazzo,
and a guarantee that the future pope would recognize him as the lord of
Forlì and Imola.

"At the very least," Caterina said, "my husband could have supported
me, could have sent more troops. And we could have negotiated with the
new pope, whoever he might be. Now it's ruined."

Cardinal Giuliano della Rovere had been one of the architects of the
agreement. His dislike of Girolamo had clearly outweighed any familial
loyalty or promises to Caterina.

In bed that night, Caterina told me that Borgia had at least been honest
about his aims and truly smitten by her boldness. "I should have thrown in
my lot with him," she moaned, and sat up suddenly to cover her face with her
hands. She did not weep, though she had every right to. Late pregnancy left
her exhausted and physically miserable, yet she had pushed herself past the

limits of endurance, surviving on little sleep and poor food; worse, her amazing efforts had all been for nothing.

When she could speak again, she confessed, "I cannot hold the fortress. Girolamo's letter warned that Florence and Siena are gathering troops to force me to surrender. And it's only a matter of time before the Colonna's army attacks us."

Caterina did not sleep at all that night. By dawn, she had written two letters, one to Girolamo and one to the Sacred College. By noon, she had received replies from both, which included permission to take one hundred and fifty armed men as her escort through the streets of Rome, back to her children. Her husband was already in the city, settling his monetary accounts.

I rode on horseback beside my mistress, who held herself with regal poise as she rode through the restless streets on a great white palfrey. There was no self-pity in her aspect when she gazed for the final time upon the Castel Sant'Angelo, the Vatican, or Saint Peter's, nor did she so much as glance in the direction of the rubble that had been the Palazzo Riario. But as she passed through the gate of Porta Maggiore and out of the city at last, her features hardened into an expression of bitterness.

PART III

Forlì

1484–1500

Twenty-six

The road back to Forlì was a bitter one, paved with Girolamo's sullen defensiveness and Caterina's simmering fury over his monumental failure. The two would not look at each other when our small caravan came to rest. Girolamo had left the city with little more than forty-four hundred ducats—less than the cost of Caterina's wedding gown, which had perished in the fire.

I, however, was ecstatic to find Luca whole and healthy, and with Caterina's glum permission, I rode beside him on a mule; we talked much of the day, and always at night, when we had encamped and the others were sleeping, we stole from our tents and held each other beneath the starlight.

Three days into our journey, a messenger from Cardinal Giuliano della Rovere intercepted us. *"Habemus papum!"* he cried as he galloped up to Girolamo, who was astride his horse.

The count ordered our caravan to stop. Caterina, who had seen the messenger arrive, jumped out of her carriage and ran as fast as eight months of pregnancy would permit.

To her relief, Borgia had not been elected pope, but neither had Cardinal della Rovere. Their fierce battle over the papacy had created such turmoil in the Sacred College that none of the others would vote for either of them.

Instead, della Rovere's message claimed, he had suggested that his supporters elect his protégé, an Italian-born Greek named Cardinal Giovanni Bat-
tista Cibo. Cardinal Cibo, now Innocent VIII, was an affable man who had
given no one reason to dislike him; even Borgia had been persuaded to vote
for him. And, della Rovere gloated, Cibo would do exactly as he was told,
for it was della Rovere who had persuaded Sixtus to give Cibo his red hat.

Girolamo received such news with a faint smile; at least a della Rovere
was behind the Throne of Peter. Caterina turned away without comment.
Della Rovere could brag all he wanted to, but he had lost the papacy and
refused to help Caterina in her darkest hour.

Even Forlì failed to celebrate the arrival of the count and contessa. We
passed through the gate in the city walls, where not a soul waited to greet
us; as we rolled past streets lined with the drab, sturdy cottages of the work-
ingmen, people stared at us from open doorways but did not cheer. As we
made our way into the largest square in the center of town, past a small but
bustling marketplace, merchants, farmers, and housewives grew still and
watched us silently.

Not until we reached the wealthiest neighborhood and the house of the
mayor, Luffo Numai, were we received with anything resembling hospitality. Numai's house reminded me of the Palazzo Medici in Florence; it was
three stories high, with rows of tall, evenly spaced rectangular windows set
in pale brown rusticated stone. Like the Medici palace, Numai's dwelling
was bare of any adornment—a dreary sight for those used to the glittering
façades of the palazzi in Rome.

A scullery maid with a filthy apron answered Girolamo's knock. So unnerved was she by the Lord of Forlì's appearance that she turned her back
to him and left him standing outside the open door while she shouted up
the stairs for her master to come.

Luffo Numai had been the chief political adviser and go-between for
Pino Ordelaffi, then his son, Sinibaldo, until it became clear that Girolamo
would succeed them. At that point, he switched loyalties to the new Lord
of Forlì so convincingly that Girolamo had entrusted him with the key to
the Riario's new palazzo in Forlì.

My first glimpse of Ser Luffo came as he ran from the staircase to the
doorway and clapped his hands in an overly dramatic display of joy at

the sight of Forlì's newest permanent residents. So grand and exaggerated was his bow that, had I and the others not been so exhausted and disheartened, I would have giggled at the sight.

Numai ran back up the stairs and returned with a ring of keys, which he pressed into the count's palm. As Girolamo headed back to his mount, Numai ran to Caterina's carriage.

Ser Luffo was dressed like a merchant in a tunic of crude gray silk over plain black leggings; he wore no gold, no jewelry. He was completely bald to his mid-crown, where a shock of thin, dark hair began and fell to his shoulders. He wore round spectacles, which he kept unconsciously adjusting. I judged him to be late in his fifth decade.

"Oh, Your Most Illustrious Highness!" he exclaimed, clasping his hands as if overwhelmed, as Caterina leaned out the window of the carriage. "I had forgotten your dazzling beauty! Each time I see it, it amazes me even more! Please, please, will you do me the honor of dining with me this evening? Your husband our lord the count said I should ask you for an answer. I should so like to welcome you properly to our city!" All of this was punctuated with sweeping, obsequious gestures.

Caterina gave a slight, insincere smile and nod. "Ser Luffo," she said wearily, by way of greeting, and retreated from the window.

Our caravan set off again; within minutes, we had arrived at the new Palazzo Riario. Barely larger than Numai's house, it was a long rectangle built of unevenly sized bricks in shades of orange, white, and gray, all bleached pale by the sun. The front façade was broken by two rows of a dozen tall identical arched windows, six on either side of the wooden door; a third row of small circular windows marked the top floor.

I went with Caterina, the children, and the nurse, Lucia, into the house in search of the nursery. There were no sweeping marble floors or staircases, no walls covered with glittering thread-of-gold tapestries, only uneven wooden floors that creaked, covered for the most part with worn, dirty carpets. The walls were grimy stucco, cracked and clumsily plastered; as we headed up the stairs, the wooden railing wobbled alarmingly. Here and there were whispers of our former life—a portrait of Caterina, a priceless vase, golden candlesticks, a fine bedspread—but for the most part, the house seemed common, old, and grim.

Caterina had lived here for a few months some years ago; her letters from Forlì had held no complaints about the residence. Perhaps, I told myself, the new Palazzo Riario had seemed quaint and rustic then, an acceptable place to visit so long as one could always return to Rome.

I helped the nurse, Lucia, find the children's things and get them settled for the night. Afterward I made my way down dark, narrow halls in search of my mistress's chamber. Unfortunately, I encountered Ser Luffo, who had brought two servants who knew where everything was kept in the house, and were happy to assist us for the first week at no cost.

He had presented them to Girolamo, and was now wandering about the house alone and unescorted in search of the Lady of Forlì, ostensibly to remind her of his invitation to supper. We were headed toward each other at a quick pace in the dim light, and almost collided.

"Ah!" he said, recoiling slightly. "You I have not seen before." He pushed his spectacles up his nose and leaned toward me, squinting. Behind the lenses, his magnified eyes crinkled lecherously at the corners. "And what a comely one you are, too. Are you one of Madonna Caterina's ladies?"

Before I could answer, his hands attached themselves to the front of my bodice and squeezed, as if they were testing the ripeness of plums. Ser Luffo stepped up to me, the front of his body touching mine, and whispered in my ear.

"Your mistress is famed for her loveliness, but I tell you, you are more beautiful by far. Your black hair and eyes, your nose and lips . . ."

He tried to worm a hand beneath my bodice. I drew back and slapped him with all my strength, sending the spectacles flying.

"*Bitch*," he gasped, more out of surprise than anger. He dropped to his knees and began groping the thin carpet in search of the lost spectacles.

I could see them clearly, but was so exhausted by the events of the past two months that I did not care what the second most powerful man in Forlì thought of me.

As he scrabbled about on the floor, I said icily, "I am Her Illustriousness's sister, raised with her at the court of Milan. And you will never lay a hand on me again."

He patted the floor as I spoke, and discovered the glasses. At my former statement, he put them on, still sitting on the carpet, and looked up at me in disbelief but, surprisingly, no anger.

"Ah," he said, scrutinizing my face with an eerie reverence. "I see it now. You are unmistakably Duke Galeazzo's daughter."

"Duchess Bona adopted me," I snarled. "Now let me pass."

An odd, excited light shone in Ser Luffo's eyes as he touched his fingertips to his offended cheek. "What a strong thing you are! I will not harm you, my dear. And I apologize thoroughly for upsetting you. Only . . ." He pitched himself forward, his face pressed to the floor in craven submission. "Only pray tell me your name! It shall be on my lips always!"

He crawled closer on his elbows and knees until he found the tip of my slipper, and kissed it.

I was too taken aback to say anything but the truth. "Dea."

He gazed raptly up at me. "Dea," he murmured. "I should have known; you are indeed a goddess!"

I flushed. "Ser Luffo, please rise and make way." These were not the halls of Rome; the corridor was too narrow for me to step past his huddled body.

"I will, I will, most beautiful goddess! But . . . perhaps you will have to kick me before I am able to rise."

"Please," I hissed. "Get up."

Ser Luffo responded by pressing his face into the carpet again and cradling his head in his arms in preparation for the blow.

I was tired and impatient, eager to find Caterina and make sure her bedchamber was arranged so that she and I could lie down upon a real mattress after a week of travel. Although it went against everything Bona had ever taught me, I timidly tapped Ser Luffo's knuckles, laced over his bald crown, with the toe of my slipper.

"Harder," he urged, his voice muffled.

I kicked him again, this time with moderate force.

"Harder," he begged again, and the third time, I delivered, kicking him hard enough to make him list to one side.

"Now get up at once!" I ordered sternly.

Ser Luffo rose, panting with desire. "Dea, my darling Dea, I shall dream of you tonight! The day will come when you desire my help, or have need of something. And when you come to me, behaving as you did just now, I will give you anything. Anything! Only ask it . . ."

He lurched at me as if to seize me again, but I raised my hand in warning, and he stilled.

From the corridor behind him came a muted giggle. I looked in its direction, as did he, to see Caterina standing four paces away.

She smirked at Ser Luffo as he scrambled to his feet and told her that he had only come to deliver the servants, and that he could see she was quite tired. He promised to deliver the banquet to our palazzo rather than require us to come to his house that night.

With that, he retreated swiftly; Caterina grinned as she watched him take flight. "I see you have met Ser Luffo," she said. "He has a certain weakness, which you can certainly turn to your advantage."

For the first time in a month, she and I laughed together.

She led me back to her bedchamber, where Marta—an older woman, who in Rome had overseen scores of chambermaids for the Palazzo Riario— was helping my lady unpack. Of the hundreds of servants, aides, secretaries, cooks, and laundresses who had previously comprised the Riario household staff, we were obliged to make do with twenty. The children now had one nurse, not three, and Caterina no longer had a dozen chambermaids to attend her, but only Marta and myself.

At the end of a very long day, Caterina and I fell exhausted into bed, which happily was covered in a fine spread and pillows and linens from Rome. It was only then that Caterina finally permitted herself to cry after the bitter disappointment of being forced from the Holy City. Once she began, she found it difficult to stop, and I held her in my arms like a child.

Three weeks later, Caterina gave birth to a healthy son, Giovanni Livio. It should have been cause for the father, Girolamo, to rejoice; with three sons, the Riario-Sforza lineage would clearly continue for at least another two generations. But, shattered by the loss of wealth and prestige, Girolamo had taken to drinking and gambling all day in his dining chamber, ignoring the fact that he now had no income at all, since his subjects paid no taxes. He left all governing and financial affairs in his wife's capable hands, though she was far too busy overseeing the repairs of their new residence. At the same time, Girolamo resented her deeply, for her courage served to underscore his cowardice. Yet he let her have her way in almost everything, perhaps because he secretly admired her brave attempt to hold the Castel Sant'Angelo; this fact eventually brought me great joy.

All the secretaries, scribes, and personal attendants who had served Count Girolamo in Rome had been paid for by the Vatican, with the exception of four: an aging valet named Niccolò, a chamberlain, a cupbearer, and Luca. Now that his master had given up politics and correspondence to spend his days at the gaming table, Luca had a great deal of free time, which he spent helping his three peers. When his assistance was not required in the count's wing, he spent it doing odd jobs for the contessa, which meant that he spent more time with me.

Perhaps Luca's presence reminded Caterina of his love for me, or perhaps she noticed the glances Luca and I shared. I prefer to think that I had simply underestimated my mistress.

One day I was helping the aged Marta change the linens on my lady's bed when Caterina entered the room. She had given birth only a fortnight before, and was still tired; worse, she had just been to see her husband, who before midday was already drunk and playing dice with his new noble friends, the dissolute Orsi brothers and the hotheaded Ludovico Pansecco. Girolamo had put a gaming table in his private upstairs dining room, which he dubbed "The Hall of the Nymphs" for the mural of naked demigoddesses upon the walls. Usually, after such encounters with her husband, Caterina was scowling and irritable, but that morning, I looked up from the linens to see her trying to suppress a smile; her eyes were unusually bright.

"Dea," she said liltingly, "I would speak to you alone."

She looked pointedly at Marta, who departed as quickly as her aching bones permitted. I tucked in a sheet and, after smoothing it with my hand, walked up to my mistress.

"My husband," Caterina began, "is not comfortable discussing the Castel Sant'Angelo, but I believe he has finally come to see just how great a risk I took for him—a risk that deserves to be repaid. As a result, he has granted one of my most persistent requests." She paused for dramatic effect, study-ing me carefully to see whether I understood her.

I waited silently, politely, for her to go on; my mind was already moving to the fact that the children's bedclothes also needed washing, and that the nurse, Lucia, could not possibly watch her four charges while taking the soiled linens down to the overwhelmed laundress.

Seeing how distracted I was, Caterina sighed and stated her surprise bluntly. "Dea, can't you guess what I am saying? Girolamo has agreed that you may marry Luca."

I stared blankly at her, trying to process the words, and, finding them too incredible, could not. "What?"

Grinning, she repeated herself.

Stunned, I sat heavily on the edge of the bed. Caterina moved in front of me and took my hands.

"Dea, don't you understand?" Her tone was giddy. "You can have your Luca! And you can choose the day."

When I could speak, I whispered, "Oh, my lady. Oh, my lady . . ."

I had not intended to move, but the next instant, I found myself stand-ing, my arms wrapped tightly about her, as if she truly were my sister. Startled by my impulsiveness, she took a half step backward, but corrected herself at once, and leaned into the embrace.

"Thank you," I said, my cheek against hers. "Thank you . . ."

"Do you not think," she said slyly into my ear, "that we should share the news with Luca, too? The count is certainly in no condition to do so."

Less than a month later, Luca and I were married in the late afternoon in the town's main cathedral, Santa Croce, also called the Duomo. Luca had made private arrangements with the priest, telling him that it would be a small affair involving household staff. He did not bother to mention that our few guests would include the Lady of Forlì, who remained heavily veiled until she was safely inside the church. Girolamo was back at the pa-lazzo, of course, well into his cups in the Hall of Nymphs.

I could not afford a new wedding dress, but made do with the best sum-mer gown—of silver silk trimmed with black lace—that I had taken with me to the battlefront at Paliano. To my surprise, Luca had also chosen a silver brocade tunic, with a fingerprint of dark ink near its hem; I smiled at the stain and told him he looked handsome, which was no lie. He had trimmed his black mustache carefully, and shaved most of his beard to leave a neatly sculpted goatee.

As we stood before the priest in the chapel, Luca's voice wavered slightly as he recited his vows; I tried, but could barely speak above a whisper. When he faced me at last to slip the thin gold band upon my finger, his hands were damp and shaking, and his eyes unnaturally wide. Once the priest pronounced us wed, however, he broke into a grin of pure relief and we sagged, exhausted by nerves, into each other's arms. When Luca's lips found mine, however, his energy returned, and I would have fallen onto my back from the passionate pressure of his kiss had he not held me fast. As it was, I was obliged to bend backward from the waist, a move that caused Caterina and the children to giggle and clap, much to the priest's disapproval.

It was November, and frost had already burned the gardens behind the palazzo. We celebrated instead in Her Illustriousness's dining chamber, a room so small that the house staff, reduced as it was, filled it. Caterina drank and dined and danced as if she were one of us, and I think, at that moment, that she was as happy as she had ever been in Rome; I was certainly happier. Luca kept refilling my goblet, and I drank a great deal of the sour local wine.

At last Luca whispered in my ear; the time to leave our little party had come. Hand in hand, we stumbled to his sterile bachelor's room, which he had earlier shared with Girolamo's cupbearer. Now it was ours alone, and as Luca swung open the door, I took it in: It was barely larger than Caterina's walk-in closet in Rome, and just as gloomy; the only light came from the small, circular window, which was so high that neither Luca nor I could look out through it. The only furnishings were a low bed half the size of Caterina's, one small night table, one unpadded wooden chair, one large cabinet, and a small trundle desk equipped with quill and ink. The furniture was crowded together, leaving little space for walking; combined with the dirty stucco walls, the effect was grim.

Yet I laughed as Luca walked over the threshold and started at the sudden crackle beneath his boot; some sly soul had scattered unhulled walnuts on the floor, an ancient tradition normally reserved for royalty, meant to mask the sounds of lovemaking. We pushed the nuts out of the way as best we could, and, after securely closing the door, began to undress each other; I unlaced Luca's heavy sleeves, and he mine. We proceeded slowly, solemnly, for we had never seen each other fully undressed and the moment seemed oddly sacred. I was fascinated by Luca's body—by the sweep of sparse dark hair across his upper chest, by the inverted *V* of hair that began beneath his navel and continued downward.

I caught his wrist, thinking to drag him to the bed, but he resisted, instead pointing out the bottle of wine and two goblets resting on the night table. There was a small note sticking out from beneath one of the goblets; surprisingly, it was from Count Girolamo, wishing us well. To our delight, the freshly uncorked bottle contained excellent wine from Rome.

"It's a sign," Luca teased, as he filled a goblet and handed it to me as I sat on the lumpy, disagreeable-smelling mattress.

I shook my head, grinning. "A sign of what?"

"A sign that I must get you drunk. You are, after all, a virgin; we must make sure you feel no pain."

I laughed as I sat back against the hard wooden headboard. "You're too late for that; I'm already drunk."

"Then we must get you even drunker." He sat beside me on the bed and we touched goblets.

We did not even finish the first cup. When Luca leaned over to kiss me, I reached past him to set down my goblet, and proceeded to kiss back. Once I began, I found I could hold nothing back, and soon he was easing himself carefully down onto me.

"Are you ready?" he whispered.

I was ready.

For all the fables I have heard about losing one's virginity, I will tell you this: I felt little pain, and what I felt was soon forgotten as we gave ourselves over to ecstasy.

Just as he had done in the storage closet outside his secret office in Rome, Luca clapped his hand over my mouth in an entirely unsuccessful effort to muffle my screams.

. . .

For the first few weeks of our marriage, I spent the nights with Luca and stumbled back to my mistress's bedchamber before dawn. Each night I fell asleep to the deeply comforting smell of iron-gall ink, male flesh, and parchment. Luca would light the lamp and carry it to the trundle desk, where, placing his cap over the lamp globe so that my eyes were shielded from its glare, he sat and wrote, just as my brother had. I never asked what he was writing, and he never volunteered any information about it.

Once, I woke to find that the lamp had gone out. Luca had opened the shutters, and stood beneath the little window with a ribbon of moonlight in his hair. I watched through barely open eyelids as, with his extended forefinger, he drew the outline of a five-pointed star in the air, before the southern wall. I lay still, scarcely breathing, as he continued drawing the circle, moving carefully from quarter to quarter, lest he collide with the furniture and wake me.

The sight filled me with love and guilt and terror: love, because I knew that Luca knew the angel, and that my husband's heart was as pure and noble as my brother's; guilt, because I knew Matteo had wanted me to come to know the angel, but I had not pursued it; and terror.

Terror, because I feared what the angel might ask of Luca.

Terror, because I feared even more what it might someday ask of me.

Twenty-seven

It is far easier never to know wealth and status at all than to have them in abundance and suffer the shock of losing them. Nonetheless, I was content those first four years in Forlì because of the joy Luca brought me; the tiny, uncomfortable room we shared was more a haven to me than any of the grand bedchambers in Milan or Rome that I had shared with Caterina. Although my lady had more need of me than ever before, she was generous, often permitting me to sleep with Luca the entire night; but there were many nights when old, dark fears overcame her and she could not forget that terrible moment when her father was killed before her eyes. On those nights, I went to her bed and remained there to comfort her.

The enmity Caterina felt toward her drunkard husband continued to increase as Girolamo, utterly undone by his fall from grace, refused to speak with her about their lack of income. She had attempted at first to restore the old palazzo and bring it up to Roman standards, yet within the first two months, she realized that there were no funds to do so. The forty-four hundred ducats from Rome were almost gone, and what remained needed to be spent on food and drink for the household.

This caused Caterina to acquire the habit of dining often at Luffo Numai's house, for she and Girolamo would be assured of enjoying free but good wine and food. Unfortunately, I accompanied Caterina to those meals, and spent most of my time fending off Ser Luffo's advances. I admit, I learned that the fastest way to please Ser Luffo was to strike him and speak cruelly to him—the crueler, the better—which reduced him quickly to a quivering mass who did my bidding. During one such encounter out in the hallway, Caterina left the dining hall in order to visit the water closet and saw us again.

"It's good that you do not entirely spurn Ser Luffo," she told me later. "I've done the same with him myself. He's far too powerful for us to make an enemy of him; the people listen to him."

Her attitude was far different from that of the spoiled duke's daughter who had done whatever she pleased in Rome; such is the price of poverty. Caterina eventually pawned most of her jewels and silverware, and found herself in the humiliating position of begging money from her relatives— Ludovico the Duke of Milan, Cardinal della Rovere, and even her disapproving nephew, Cardinal Raffaele Riario. Ludovico and della Rovere never replied; astonishingly, young Raffaele did, with true concern for his struggling relatives. He paid a visit to his aunt and uncle in Forlì in grand style, throwing silver coins to the peasants and providing a public feast for them in the town square, to show them what it meant to be a Riario. His generosity extended to his aunt; without Girolamo's knowledge, Raffaele gave Caterina a gift of several thousand ducats, knowing she would make far wiser use of it than his spendthrift uncle.

The shame she suffered over that incident propelled her to action. One morning she went to Girolamo's bedroom as he lay sleeping off the previous day's wine, and would not leave until he agreed to sober up long enough to convince Forlì's city council that, given that the Lord of Forlì was near bankruptcy, he must now impose taxes on the citizens. To his credit, Girolamo remained sober long enough to do the deed, and succeeded because of his wife's careful instructions. It was enough to fend off hunger in the Palazzo Riario, but not even a tenth of the money that had poured into Girolamo's coffers in Rome.

Yet poverty was not the greatest of Caterina's concerns: there remained the question of physical safety. Pope Innocent had formally invested the Riario with Imola and Forlì, but made it clear they could not count on Rome for protection should any other greedy soul decide to invade their little fiefdom. Once captain of the great papal army, Girolamo now oversaw the tiny local militia whose loyalty could not be counted on, as the Forlivese still perceived the Riario as outsiders. Nor did Girolamo have the money to buy mercenaries, as many rulers of small duchies did.

As a result, Caterina again penned many letters asking for military help, should it ever be needed. She received only one reassuring reply, but an important one, from Duke Ludovico: *The might of all Milan,* he wrote, *stands behind you.* We could only hope that Ludovico was as generous with his soldiers as with his words.

After two years of near-constant inebriation, Girolamo collapsed at his gambling table; one of the Orsi brothers came stumbling out of the Hall of Nymphs shouting for a doctor. Caterina found her groaning husband on the floor, doubled over in agony, clutching his ribs. Luca helped carry him to his bed.

Caterina stayed with him until the doctor came. Girolamo suffered from excruciating pain in his upper abdomen and vomiting; the very sight of food nauseated him. He also suffered from teeth-chattering chills and soaking sweats.

The doctor pronounced that the patient had a "glandular disorder," and when Caterina asked the doctor pointedly whether Girolamo would live, the physician shrugged. "Time will tell," he said. "It might get better, or worse."

For the rest of his life, Girolamo was to drink no wine or spirits or eat rich foods. In the interim, the doctor supplied him with a liquid to relieve pain, one so bitter that Girolamo would not drink it without pleas and threats.

The liquid worked; Girolamo slept. As he did, Caterina and I returned to her chamber. In private, she spoke, her tone grimly serious.

"Will you ride with me now to Ravaldino? I give you a choice because of the grave danger involved."

The fortress of Ravaldino was the single most impressive structure in Forlì; it lay flush with the southeastern wall of the city. Girolamo and Caterina were its rightful owners, but it was now held by a man named Zocho, a mercenary who had fought for Girolamo for many years. As a reward for Zocho's friendship and services, Girolamo had made him castellan of Ravaldino. Unfortunately, since arriving in Forlì, Girolamo had relied on his new castellan to loan him money to cover his gambling debts. Since the count had no way of repaying him, Zocho suggested that he be given a percentage of ownership in the fortress. After four years, the result was that Zocho had earned more than fifty percent ownership in Ravaldino . . . and he had already let the Lord of Forlì know that the fortress was now his, unless Girolamo could find a way to reimburse him for the loans.

Before I could reply, Caterina interrupted.

"If Girolamo dies," she said evenly, "I must have control of Ravaldino. There are far too many power-hungry souls who believe they can easily wrest Forlì and Imola from a poor widow. I cannot trust the Forlivese, nor can I afford an army. But if I have the fortress . . ."

She trailed off at the sight of my face; I cannot imagine what she saw, for at the moment, I was plummeting down into darkness amid the jagged stones, my eyes blinded by searing lightning. "The Tower," I gasped, though I was not speaking to her; I was in another place and could see nothing but the imprint of lightning on my inner eyelids.

I became vaguely aware that Caterina was shaking my shoulders angrily. "I have already survived the Tower!" she shouted. "I have nothing more to fear."

"Thrice you will enter the Tower, and thrice emerge," I said, frightened by the fact that I did not know where the words were coming from. "Whether alive or dead at the last is your choice. Choose well, and what you perceive as victory shall be defeat; what you see as defeat shall be your greatest victory."

She held on to my upper arms until the spell passed; without her, I would surely have fallen. When I came to myself, Caterina continued speaking, as though I had not just uttered a frightening prophecy.

"Go find your husband, Luca," she said urgently. "His is the best script, and he knows how to make an order look official."

That night, as Girolamo lay on his sickbed, Caterina and I rode on horseback to Ravaldino. We stopped at the moat and Caterina called for Zocho to appear. He climbed onto the battlement above the drawbridge; his clumsiness showed that he had already imbibed a good deal of wine.

At the first sight of him, I knew my lady's cause was hopeless. Zocho was no nobleman; he laughed scathingly at the sight of Caterina, then turned his insolent, faintly lascivious grin on her. He was tall, thin, and completely bald, dressed in a rumpled, wine-stained tunic of plain cotton. A thick raised red scar bisected his right cheek, ultimately pointing to his right ear, which sported a large gold hoop. His pointed chin bore a scraggly goatee.

"Caterina Sforza!" he exclaimed sarcastically. "The Lady of Forlì has come for a visit . . . which means, most assuredly, that the Lord of Forlì is dead. I heard that he had fallen ill."

Caterina's temper rose at his impudence, but she struggled to contain it. "I have just left my lord's side," she said. "He is recovered enough to sign this." She held up the writ Luca had so recently penned, and which Girolamo in fact had signed, though Caterina had held her hand over his as his shaking hand gripped the quill. "It is an order from my husband. You are to surrender Ravaldino now, to me. My lord has the right to seize whatever property is necessary for the protection of Forlì, debts notwithstanding."

Zocho cackled heartily at the notion that he would surrender his fortress to two women, one of them unarmed; once recovered, he squinted at the writ in Caterina's outstretched hand and shrugged. "A piece of paper. How do I know the count is not dead, and that this is not forgery?"

"Lower the drawbridge, and I will come inside and show it to you," she said. "You know my lord's signature as well as anyone."

Zocho folded his arms and shook his head. "Dear lady," he said, "I heard how you took the fortress at Sant'Angelo, and have no desire to let you inside. I will tell you this: bring Girolamo's heir, Ottaviano. If he will pay off his father's debt, I will happily turn over Ravaldino to him."

No amount of arguing would convince him. Infuriated, Caterina swung her horse about and rode away; I followed.

. . .

Girolamo did not die. Over the next week, his pain gradually eased, though he suffered for three days for want of wine. Afterward he remained too weak to sit at the gambling table.

Interestingly enough, Zocho failed to outlive his master. As he was enjoying his supper inside Ravaldino in the company of two fellow soldiers—one of whom had been inside the Castel Sant'Angelo when Caterina seized it—they turned on him with knives, and Zocho was no more. Ravaldino was now in my lady's hands, with a new castellan, Tommaso Feo, who was utterly loyal to her.

I asked no questions; I did not want to know the truth, and Caterina offered up no details.

On the night of the fourteenth of April 1488, I woke in my husband's arms to the sound of a woman screaming; the cry emanated from the contessa's apartments and was so dire that Luca and I bolted from the bed and ran toward the source immediately. Soon there came not one cry, but many, some of them triumphant. From the ground floor came the sound of intruders.

We reached the door to my lady's bedchamber just as the nurse and Caterina's eldest, Bianca, were herding the children inside to their mother. Nine-year-old Ottaviano sat quietly weeping on the bed beside his younger brother Cesare.

Caterina emerged from her closet holding two swords and a dagger; she handed one of the swords to Girolamo's old valet, Niccolò, who was trembling so badly that he could not hold on to the hilt. The other she tried to press onto Ottaviano, but he would not lower his hands from his face.

Caterina's eyes were dazed, her cheeks still damp from an earlier rush of tears, but her voice was unsettlingly calm. "Dea, help me push the furniture against the door. They will be coming for us. Girolamo has been murdered."

At this, the older children let go fresh wails; Caterina did not notice them, as her gaze fell on Luca.

"Do you know the way to Milan?"

Luca nodded.

"Go to my uncle as fast as you can," Caterina said, "and tell him I need military help at once, or Forlì is lost. If you can stop safely at Ravaldino on the way, tell the castellan that he is not to surrender under any circumstances." As Luca swiftly kissed me, Caterina added, "Be careful going to the stables. If they see you, they will kill you."

I watched, panicked, as Luca left, but I knew that his chances of surviving were actually better than ours. By then, Marta the chambermaid had arrived and helped Lucia comfort the children. With the help of Niccolò, Caterina and I bolted the door and pushed my lady's heavy wardrobe against it.

"That is all we can do," Caterina sighed, and sat down on the bed to hold her children. As she pressed her lips to four-year-old Giovanni Livio's crown, she shared a dark glance with me: we had no means of escape, and little time before Girolamo's killers would break through our pathetic barrier.

"Hush," Caterina said gently to her children. "When our enemies arrive, remain calm and be courteous. We cannot fight them with so few weapons, so no one is to strike out at them first. You are Riario; your father suffers no more, but is in Heaven now, looking down upon you. Make him proud. If they take me from you, don't be afraid. I am your mother, and I will fight to the death for each and every one of you. Do you understand?"

Ten-year-old Bianca, mature for her age and the most fearless of the group, nodded solemnly on behalf of the others.

"But I do not intend to die," Caterina said. "If I can, I shall outwit them. So don't believe anything they tell you." She put a hand upon Ottaviano's shoulder. "I will not let Forlì be so easily lost."

I hugged myself and walked rapidly to the room's single large window. *Thrice you will enter the Tower,* I had told Caterina, and decided that I had been wrong. There was no possibility we could survive; they would slaughter us here, and quickly.

The window opened onto the small square in front of the palazzo; the glass caught the golden light of torches in the street, and the cries of those below floated up into the bedchamber.

Liberty! Liberty! Long live the Orsi!

Careful to hang back in the shadows, I glanced down at the street, where Ludovico Orsi was urging on a crowd of angry peasants who swarmed like insects over a long, pale object in the dusty street. The glow from their torches caught the film of unshed tears in my eyes, dazzling me. When my vision cleared, I saw their prize: a man's naked corpse, its face and torso covered by blood. A merchant from town knelt beside it, and, lifting its lolling head in his hands, bit deeply into its scalp and pulled his face back, brown hair and blood streaming from his mouth. He spat them out, and bent down again to take another bite. At the same time, a fellow beside him used a dagger to slice flesh from the underside of the corpse's arm.

A very long arm, and a very tall corpse. I recognized Girolamo from the shape of his body, not his features, which were already crushed or cut away. I clamped my hand over my mouth and turned away.

As I faced the bed and the furniture shoved against the barricaded door, I heard the first strike of an ax against the wood. Caterina straightened her shoulders, rose, and walked calmly up to the shuddering door.

"There is no need to destroy anything else," she called. "We will let you in. Put down your weapons! There are children here!"

I hurried to help her push the furniture aside.

To my astonishment, the men led by Cecco Orsi did not kill us. Instead, they permitted Caterina to calmly kiss each of her children before leaving the room. Surrounded by a cluster of armed men, whose presence protected us from the irate crowd as it hurled curses at Caterina, we were led on foot to the Orsi palazzo. There, we were put under guard and treated civilly; even Niccolò, the elderly valet, who had been an eyewitness to the murder, was allowed to stay with us. It was then that he finally told us the tale of Girolamo's murder.

The Orsi brothers, who had been Girolamo's constant companions until his illness, knew well where the key to the Hall of the Nymphs was hidden; Girolamo so distrusted the Forlivese that he had taken to locking any room after he had entered it. That night, he had felt well enough to dine in his favorite room. When he had finished supper, he dismissed all of his attendants save one: Niccolò.

"It happened so quickly," Niccolo said mournfully. "His Illustriousness had opened the window and was taking in the night air, when Cecco Orsi suddenly appeared. Of course, he trusted Cecco with the key, and expected no harm; in fact, the count greeted Cecco, and held out his hand to see the piece of paper that Cecco was waving. Cecco was saying something about being able to pay the meat tax, and just at that moment, one of the count's military captains—Ronchi, I think his name is—came up behind His Illustriousness with a drawn sword.

"I cried out, but by then, Cecco had already buried his knife in my lord's ribs." The old man began to weep softly. "But Lord Girolamo did not fall. He ran for the door, but the captain blocked him. In despair, he dove beneath the table, but they grabbed him by his hair and pulled him out.

"By then, Cecco had completely lost his nerve, and was ready to flee; he dropped his knife and turned away while the captain quickly finished the job."

Caterina listened tearlessly, but the corner of her upper lip was curled with hatred and disgust. "Cecco lost his nerve? And where was his brother, Ludovico?"

"Downstairs, I suppose. Ser Cecco is by far the braver of the two."

Caterina's expression hardened, but I saw the faint glimmer of hope in her eye.

"Cowards," she whispered, too softly for the guards to hear. "We are dealing with cowards."

When morning came, the papal governor of the neighboring town of Cesena paid Caterina a visit. Monsignor Savelli was short, slight, white-haired and dressed in a priest's simple black frock, but he moved with the confidence of a Roman cardinal. He was also supremely polite, and greeted Her Illustriousness warmly; they had met on several occasions, and though Savelli cared nothing for Girolamo, he was quite taken with Girolamo's wife. The monsignor had taken command of the town in Pope Innocent's name, and was ferreting out the truth behind the uprising, after which he would decide whether the Orsi's request to replace the Riario had merit. The Orsi, of course, were fully cooperating with him, as they needed the pope's blessing to rule. In return, they were allowed to hold Caterina prisoner and continue in their efforts against her.

I attended Caterina and him as they sat in the well-furnished antechamber on soft chairs and the children played back in the bedroom.

Savelli paid close attention to Caterina as she told him the truth of the matter: that Cecco Orsi, who had recently collected the annual meat tax for Girolamo, foolishly spent it, then begged his lord for extra time to come up with the money. His brother Ludovico was also still smarting from one of Girolamo's tantrums. Girolamo had died as the result of a petty vendetta, not a genuine uprising; Savelli could go through the financial records himself and see how generous Girolamo had been to his people. He had never done anything to offend the Forlivese.

Savelli nodded sympathetically as he listened; when Caterina finished, he said, in the gentlest of voices, "I must apologize for intruding in this affair, but of course, you can understand the Holy Father's interest in maintaining peace in the Romagna. It's always possible that His Holiness might decide to invest your son, Ottaviano, with Forlì. In the meantime, peace would be best served if you surrendered the town, and returned to your property in Imola. There, you and your children can safely await our judgment."

Caterina's soft tone matched the priest's. "Surely you realize, Father, that if I surrender now, Forlì will be forever lost to the Riario. We have no champion in Rome."

"You have your nephew, the cardinal. He has a good deal of influence."

Caterina smiled woodenly. "Raffaele's influence does not extend to Peter's throne, unfortunately."

Savelli leaned forward and paternally patted Caterina's hand, which gripped the arm of her chair. "Retire to Imola, dear girl," he said, "and raise your children. You have just lost your husband; now is the time to grieve, not worry with politics."

A deep flush traveled from the hollow of my lady's throat to her cheekbones; her grip on the chair tightened as she pushed herself to her feet. "These Orsi are fools," she said bitterly. "They lack the wits to govern. The fact that they have let me survive is proof of it. I *will*—" she began, but stopped and with great effort, controlled herself.

Savelli stared up at her blankly, benignly. "Yes, my dear?"

Caterina took her time answering him; when she spoke, her voice was silky and sweet. "I will consider everything you have said, Monsignor. Thank you so much for coming."

The next day, we were all moved to more secure, less hospitable quarters: the stuffy room in the tower above Saint Peter's gate, where watchmen usually slept. The room was so small that the older boys and I sat upon the floor without space enough to stretch our legs, while Caterina and the younger children sat cross-legged upon the narrow straw cot. It was disheartening at best, especially as the children made constant use of the single chamberpot, and there was no breeze to carry the smell away.

But Caterina's grim mood soon lightened. The three men charged with guarding her were sympathetic to the Riario, though not enough to set us free; however, they were happy to provide the contessa with paper and quill so that she could write to her castellan, Tommaso Feo, who was still loyally holding the fortress at Ravaldino.

Even better, they were willing to deliver her letter.

The next day, Cecco and Ludovico Orsi, who were now feeling the full strain of their tentative position, came with an escort of armed guards to take Caterina away. Bianca began to cry, and the rest of the children soon followed. I did my best to comfort them, although I, too, was terrified that Savelli had secretly been offended by Caterina's angry outburst about the Orsi, and that these men had come to take her to the executioner's block.

Within two hours, Caterina was returned to us; I was frightened at first by the spot of dried blood on her neck, but she was not only well, but triumphant. "Luca!" she whispered exultantly to me, so our guards could not hear. "He made it safely to Ravaldino, and beyond!"

She sat on the cot, tucking her legs and skirts underneath her, and told the tale with relish. The Orsi brothers had taken her to Ravaldino, and dragged her in front of the fortress, at the very edge of the moat. As Cecco held a knife to her throat, he ordered her to call to her castellan, Feo. She did so. When Feo (whose name suited him, as he was unforgivably ugly) appeared, Cecco threatened Caterina with death unless she ordered her castellan to surrender.

Caterina flatly refused. Cecco insisted again, this time pressing the blade against her flesh.

"When I refused again," she said, "he pricked my throat and drew just a drop of blood. He touched it with his finger and showed it to me, thinking I would faint, I suppose. I laughed at him. The third time I refused, he began shouting at me.

"Out of pity for Cecco," she said, amused, "I finally called to Feo to surrender. Of course, Feo would not, and poor Cecco had to put the knife to my throat again. By then, both Feo and I were grinning. Cecco threatened my life three more times, then simply gave up. And here I am."

For the next three days, Cecco dragged Caterina to the fortress and repeated the farce, and for three days, the outcome was the same.

On the fourth day, our friendly guards escorted us from the little room in the tower down to the street, where four horses, a dirty wagon, Monsignor Savelli, three of his personal attendants, and the Orsi brothers awaited us. The Orsi brothers seemed bitter and downcast; Monsignor Savelli was in mildly cheerful spirits, with a faint hint of triumph in his eyes.

As two of our guards mounted horses and the third helped Caterina into the wagon, Savelli reined his steed alongside her.

After the two exchanged polite greetings, Savelli announced, "I received a messenger this morning from your castellan. He has indicated his willingness to surrender Ravaldino to me, if I will grant him one condition: a meeting with you, so that he can collect the back pay you apparently owe him. He also wants a letter praising his loyal service, so that he can obtain employment elsewhere."

Caterina lowered her gaze. "Traitor!" she growled, then looked back to Savelli and said wearily, "Without the fortress, I have no hope. I will write the letter, but I have no money. Feo can be very stubborn; he will not surrender without it."

"What sum do you owe him?" Savelli asked guardedly.

Caterina answered without hesitation. "Two hundred ducats."

The monsignor sighed, and handed Caterina a small velvet purse. "At least you tell the truth," he told her. "This is the same amount Feo asked for." He also handed her a freshly inked quill, and the letter, already written, which she quickly signed.

As Caterina blew on the ink, Savelli continued. "As for the meeting . . . Your Feo has asked that it occur inside the fortress."

"Really?" Caterina asked. "Are you not concerned that he will attempt some trickery?"

Savelli cleared his throat and shot a sidewise glance at the brooding Orsi brothers, who sat on horseback a short distance away. "Concern has been expressed. This is why we are taking you all; I have agreed to let the Orsi hold your loved ones while you are inside Ravaldino. If you do not return in three hours, the Orsi are determined to kill them." He lowered his voice. "Apparently they do not understand a mother's love. I have reassured them that, knowing your children are hostages, you will return."

Caterina looked to the Orsi and our armed guards. "Of course I will return," she echoed solemnly.

The ride to the fortress did not take long. As the wagon rocked, I felt terror combined with a keen sense of the present moment, as if I had always rattled toward Ravaldino and an uncertain fate. I looked to Caterina, whose expression was utterly impassive; the armed guards were flanking us and able to see our faces, and my lady would not meet my gaze.

A group of curious Forlivese had learned of the coming drama, and had gathered a polite distance from the fortress to watch. They made little noise as we appeared; apparently they were not partisan, but pragmatically interested in the outcome.

When we stopped at the outer edge of Ravaldino's moat, a guard swung Caterina down from the wagon while Savelli shouted for Feo to lower the drawbridge. The castellan's face briefly appeared at a battlement, then disappeared again; soon, we heard the creak of the wheel and the clank of the chain as the bridge began to lower slowly.

Caterina, purse and letter in hand, turned back to gaze at each of us in the wagon, then spoke suddenly to Savelli. "I am afraid," she said. "Feo has been loyal to my husband, but he is a soldier, and I a helpless woman alone . . ."

The monsignor nodded sympathetically. "Would you prefer that one of the guards accompany you?"

"Yes, please. Two would be even better; Feo is cunning and very strong."

Savelli looked to our three guards. "Accompany her," he commanded them all, and looked at the sulking Orsi. "You see? There is no chance of her escaping now."

The guards dismounted and went to Caterina's side. She looked at the drawbridge, now almost fully down, and back at the wagon.

"My lady-in-waiting, too," she said, staring at me. "I should not like to be the only woman there."

With a long-suffering air, the monsignor nodded, and I was helped from the wagon just as the bridge struck the earth with a thundering rumble. A sudden breeze lifted the stray, damp tendrils from my neck and made my white veil flutter as I followed Caterina and the guards over the long, narrow bridge. I was too busy watching my step to notice that, one by one, the guards slipped past Caterina to run into the open maw of the keep; I did not realize it until Caterina herself grabbed my elbow and spoke into my ear.

I could barely hear the words above the sudden murmur of the crowd.

"Quickly, quickly!" she urged. "Run!"

Startled, I did as she ordered, and ran into the dank courtyard, where the guards were climbing the stairs toward the roof; the sweating Feo—a short, wiry spider of a man—was already reversing the crank. As the draw-bridge lifted off the ground, Caterina was one step from entering the court-yard. There she turned, and, shaking her fist in the air, cried, "Death to the Orsi! Long live the Riario!"

With that, she ran up to join the soldiers on the roof, where some of the cannon were kept; I following, gasping. By the time I made it up the stairs, Caterina was already at the battlement, taunting her former captors.

"Assassins! Traitors! Remember this moment when you are being drawn and quartered in the town square! I will destroy the House of Orsi!"

Some in the crowd cheered—not so much a display of loyalty, I suspect, as one of approval that the drama had just grown exciting. Monsignor

Savelli sat astride on his horse, his hand covering his gaping mouth. Cecco Orsi was on his feet, red-faced, striking the air with his fists; his brother sat nearby, stunned into silence.

"I will kill your children!" he screamed, and drew a dagger. "Do you see me? I will kill them all now unless you return at once!" He ran to the wagon and caught Ottaviano's arm in an unsuccessful attempt to pull the wailing boy out. "I swear, I will kill him now!"

Caterina's face contorted with hatred. She bent down, caught the hems of her skirt and chemise, and in a single, swift move, lifted them to her waist to bare the golden tuft of hair between her thighs.

She pointed to it, in a gesture of ultimate contempt, and shouted down: "Go ahead! Can't you see, you fools, that I have the stuff to make others?"

And with that, she dropped her skirts and turned her back to them.

Twenty-eight

By then I was behind Caterina, and offered my outstretched hand to help her climb down from the battlement. Hers was trembling as she took the great step down from the stone ledge, and as she hopped down into my arms, her expression held no fury, no indignation, but only fear.

"Stay hidden, but watch the Orsi carefully," she begged, gripping my forearms. "The Orsi won't dare harm my children, I *know* they won't harm them, but . . ." Tears filled her eyes and she wiped them away impatiently. "I have to help Feo with the artillery now. But if it looks to you as though the Orsi really intend to hurt my darlings, call for me, and I will engage them in negotiations again."

"I will," I said.

Caterina hurried to the next battlement and crawled skillfully up the parapet to the platform, where Feo and three of his skeleton crew had finished loading powder into one of the cannons and were just dropping a bleached stone ball down the muzzle.

I could hear Caterina questioning her castellan about the precision of his aim as I stepped onto the parapet and pressed my body against the rough stone of the battlement to peer down at the Orsi, as Caterina instructed. On the other side of the moat, Monsignor Savelli's attendants had drawn longswords; they and their horses now stood between the wagon and Cecco Orsi, who had been forced to unhand Ottaviano. While his brother Ludovico sat dazed and downcast upon his horse, Cecco was still on his feet, waving his dagger and cursing the monsignor for his stupidity. In the wagon, little Giovanni Livio was crying as his nurse, Lucia, held him and attempted to shush him; Ottaviano looked just as unhappy as his youngest brother, but Bianca sat up straight and proud, a half smile on her face as she looked up at the battlement where her mother had just appeared.

The Forlivese were buzzing. Suddenly, three of them ran forward to distract Savelli's aides, and Cecco and Ludovico quickly seized Ottaviano and pulled him to the very edge of the moat.

"Come out, Caterina Sforza, and see your eldest son die!"

Young Ottaviano began to sob as Cecco held the dagger to his throat.

I looked to Caterina. She had heard the shout, and calmly nodded at her castellan, Feo; in response, he held a flaming cord to the cannon's touchhole.

She peered around the battlement and shouted: "Here is my answer!"

At once, she stuck her fingers in her ears; I did the same, and grimaced at the teeth-chattering boom.

The ball sailed over the heads of those assembled on the other side of the moat, followed by a puff of white smoke. Many in the crowd screamed, and, as the smoke began to clear, I saw Ludovico Orsi and Savelli begin to ride off.

Cecco was so unnerved, he dropped both his dagger and his hold on Ottaviano, who ran wailing back to the wagon as it lurched and began to slowly follow Savelli.

Caterina howled gleefully at the chaos. "Run!" she shouted scornfully at Cecco. "Go ahead, run home, and see for yourself how accurate Feo is with his cannon. I will destroy your palazzo and the homes of all those who would attack the Riario!"

As Cecco ran in pursuit of Ottaviano, who had managed to catch up to the wagon and was pulled inside, some of the Forlivese snickered.

Caterina turned at the sound. "Laugh at Cecco while you may," she shouted at the crowd, "but the homes of those who attacked my husband will suffer. People of Forlì, hear me! Destroy my enemies, and I shall treat you as my brothers from this time forth. Fail to act, and three days hence-forth, you will rue it."

The Forlivese grew silent. By then, Savelli and Ludovico were out of sight, and the wagon fast disappearing. Cecco had swung onto his horse and was cantering after them. When Caterina came down from the battlement, the crowd began to disperse.

By the time Feo fired the second and third shots—aimed at the palace of the Pansecco, who had supported the Orsi, and at the humbler home of Ronchi, the military captain who had finished Girolamo off—the crowd had disappeared.

The castellan, Feo, was an odd-looking man, short of torso and long of skinny limb, with red hair shorn so close I could see the scalp beneath it. His face was triangular, with a long, sharp chin and overlarge nose and mouth; his great ears stuck out from his head like two open doors. His uniform looked and smelled as though he had worn it for months without washing it, or himself; his cheeks and hands were grimy from soot and black powder.

One might expect crude speech from such a hideous, dirty little man, but when Feo swung down from his perch beside the cannon, he faced Caterina and cried, with diction that would have made any royal courtier proud:

"All hail our Lady of Forlì! All hail the Riario! Bow, my fellows, and let us cheer the courageous and brilliant Caterina Sforza!" With that, he bowed deeply, with a sharp glance about him to make sure his men did likewise, then he went down on one knee and removed his helmet.

"All hail the Lady of Forlì!" he crowed, and his men echoed the cheer. "All hail the Lady of Forlì!"

Caterina beamed, exultant; she grasped Feo's filthy hands and lifted him to his feet. "All hail to my clever castellan," she said happily, and beneath the grime, Feo's gaunt cheeks blushed. "Without your loyalty and wit, Ravaldino would not be mine! You shall be well rewarded!"

And with that, she pulled the velvet purse Savelli had given her from her bosom, and presented it to him.

Feo cleared his throat and dropped his adoring but reverent gaze, though he was not so overwhelmed by his mistress's generosity that he forgot to weigh the coins in his hand. "You are too kind, Your Illustriousness. I shall put this aside, lest we need it to further our cause." He shoved the bag into his pocket and gestured toward the staircase. "Our watchman will remain on duty and will call if anyone else comes to the moat. In the meantime, I took the liberty of having the cook prepare a feast from our finest provisions. Will you honor us by dining with us?"

Caterina grinned at him. There was not a whiff of flirtatiousness in Feo's tone, or in hers; they were comrades-at-arms who much admired each other's courage and cunning. "The honor shall be mine, Captain," she said.

The food—roasted game, bread baked in Ravaldino's ovens, and apples from the previous autumn—seemed heavenly after our imprisonment. To the music of the pipe and tambourine, Caterina danced with Feo and all of his men, and insisted I join them for a round.

Yet even in the midst of victory, I was apprehensive. Although I had never before been inside the fortress, the interior walls of Ravaldino were eerily familiar to me, as if I had always known them, as if I knew that I would see them again all too soon.

The very next day, a group of one hundred townspeople—the carpenter who had repaired the staircases in the Palazzo Riario and his family, the widowed seamstress who tailored Caterina's gowns, the hunter who sold us fresh game, and all the others who had made a decent living providing services and products to the Riario family—appeared at the moat and politely asked to join Caterina. They did not care for the Orsi, they said; Cecco Orsi was "wild with fury" and had defied Savelli, calling him an outsider who had no business meddling in Forlì's affairs. The townsfolk feared that violence would break out, and they wanted no part of it. None of them were rude enough to mention that they feared Caterina's cannon just as much.

Would the Lady of Forlì let them in?

"First," she shouted, "you must tell me what has become of my children."

The children were all safe in Savelli's hands, leaving the Orsi brothers without the ability to negotiate. Power had shifted, and the Forlivese were not fools.

We recognized each worker, who had brought with him his entire family. As the drawbridge was lowered, Tommaso Feo and his men stood on the battlements watching lest Savelli or Cecco Orsi take advantage of the situation. Caterina's instincts were correct, and the refugees grateful; Feo was relieved that he had recently restocked the larder. Ravaldino was large enough to house the entire population of the town, with the result that we were not overcrowded, but quite comfortable.

On the next day, the sixteenth of April, Feo's watchman spied four riders galloping across the plain toward Ravaldino; they came not from town, but from the north. Caterina and I ran to the northern battlements to watch them come.

As the riders raced toward us, they grew larger and larger, until my eye was just able to make out the banner one of them held: scarlet and white, the colors of the Sforza.

"Milan!" Caterina bellowed next to my ear, almost deafening me. "Messengers from Milan!" Her tone contained both relief and apprehension: relief that Ludovico had heard and responded to her request; apprehension that these four men might not be heralds announcing an approaching army, but messengers come to break the bad news that the army would never arrive.

She climbed down from the battlement and hurried down the stairs to meet them, but instinct held me fast to the spot. The riders grew closer, closer, until I could clearly see the scarlet and white tunics three of them wore, and the matching caparisons on their horses.

The fourth wore a plain gray tunic and rode an unadorned black horse, yet he caught my eye more than the others. I had seen him before, riding across the icy Lombard plain.

The next instant, I scrambled down from the battlement and ran after Caterina down the stairs, calling Luca's name.

Luca and I were still embracing as the herald from Milan and his two guards spoke briefly to Caterina before continuing on into the town of Forlì.

Luca's face was sun-browned and parched from the wind, his clothes dusty, his toothy grin dazzling. His lips did not pull away from mine until we heard the drawbridge start to retract; even then, he kept an arm about my waist, forcing me to bend with him as he bowed to Caterina.

"Your Illustriousness!" he said, with excessive good cheer. "I am delighted, but not surprised, that you have turned the tables on your enemies. I have a letter from your uncle." He reached into his pocket and retrieved a folded square of paper, sealed with red wax and worn at the corners. "May I tell you what it says?"

"Troops from Milan!" Caterina crowed, snatching the letter from him.

As she broke the seal and unfolded it, Luca was unable to contain himself. "More than just troops, Madonna. *Five thousand* troops from Milan and Bologna!"

I let go a whoop of joy, which prompted Feo, who was finishing raising the drawbridge, to do the same; one of his men dashed up the stairs to spread the good news. Five thousand troops would not only strike terror into the hearts of the uncommitted citizens and send the Orsi running, but would also discourage Savelli from attempting to take the city for himself; even Pope Innocent would it challenging, if not impossible, to raise such a massive force in such a short time.

Caterina waved us quiet and scanned the letter, her lips working silently, and frowned. "He does not say *when* they will arrive."

"It is not easy to move so many men so quickly," Luca offered, "but they are on the march and should be on Forlì's outskirts within four days. The herald has gone to the town square to read Duke Ludovico's warning to the conspirators and the Forlivese; he will tell them as much."

"Four days," Caterina murmured to herself, then spoke suddenly, giddily to Feo, as the realization of her triumph dawned. "These troops will attack on *my* command," she told him, gesturing at the creased letter in her hand.

As we stood together near the closed drawbridge, I heard another shout of joy from above us, followed quickly by another, and another, until word spread to the families housed inside the fortress with us. At that point, we could not hear each other talk for all the cheering.

The people who listened to the herald in the town square chose to believe that his announcement was just another of Caterina's tricks; they knew that Ludovico took no real interest in his niece's affairs, but they had not counted on his determination to keep Sforza allies in the Romagna. The Orsi brothers scoffed and begged an unimpressed Lorenzo de' Medici for military aid; Monsignor Savelli, revealing himself to be far from the disinterested observer who wished only to keep peace, sent a messenger to Pope Innocent asking for troops—not on behalf of the Orsi, but for "the papacy," knowing that he, Savelli, would be appointed ruler.

Even after the combined Milanese and Bolognese armies reached nearby Cosina and Villanova—both of which reported, in despair, that the soldiers and the vermin who followed them were plundering and terrorizing the villages—some Forlivese preferred to wait with Savelli for the massive army Pope Innocent was surely sending.

The Milanese and Bolognese, however, were eager to descend on Forlì; messengers went almost hourly between Caterina and the commanders. Wisely, she held them off, lest Forlì be razed; instinct told her that the townspeople would soon be reconciled to her.

"I have no wish to rule a razed city," she insisted.

Days later, troops *did* come from Rome—fifty of them, bearing the blue and gold standard of the Riario. Pope Innocent had decided against the foolishness of sending thousands of his own men to die in the Romagna over such a trifling bit of land as Forlì. But Cardinal Raffaele Riario, after learning from his aunt Caterina that she and his cousins were in grave danger, spared men at arms from his own private battalion.

As the anxious citizens (and no doubt, the horrified Savelli) watched, Ravaldino's drawbridge descended, and, in orderly formation, the Riario cavalry trotted into the fortress to join their new commander, Caterina.

We learned much later that, upon hearing the news, the Orsi brothers and Captain Ronchi rode to the gate of Saint Peter, whose little tower housed Caterina's children and servants. The conspirators meant to kill them all, but the guards knew where the true power lay, and pelted the Orsi and their supporters with rocks and threats.

That night, Girolamo's assassins gave up all hope, and they and their supporters headed east, into exile.

When dawn came again, Luca and I woke to a beautiful sound: the ringing of the town bell, summoning all citizens to the main square. We dressed quickly and ran up the stairs to the roof, where Caterina, her back to us, was standing silently beside the battlement facing the city, her palm pressed to the stone; the rising sun's rays pierced her gossamer nightgown, showing the outline of her firm twenty-five-year-old body.

Luca and I hurried to stand beside her. She half turned as we approached; her expression was solemn, her eyes shining with unwept tears. Unable to utter a sound, she turned her gaze back toward Forlì, rosy in the early-morning glow.

The bell still sang, but its loud cry was soon matched by the throaty shouts from the filling streets.

"Ottaviano! Ottaviano! All hail the Riario! All hail the Lady of Forlì!"

Twenty-nine

Over the next few days, most of the items stolen from the Palazzo Riario were quietly returned. Caterina sent the humbled Monsignor Savelli back to Cesena, minus the artillery he had brought with him in hopes of claiming Forlì. The city councillors expressed their loyalty to Caterina directly, although during our time in Ravaldino, they had sat on their hands waiting for the struggle between Savelli and the Orsi brothers to resolve itself. Caterina politely accepted their allegiance before informing them that they had all been removed from their positions. The townspeople had lost their right to any degree of self-government; from now on, the word of the Lady of Forlì was law until her ten-year-old son, Ottaviano, reached his majority at twenty-one.

In the meantime, she reminded her subjects of her power. Never again, she vowed, would she set foot in the Duomo, whose priests had refused to accept Girolamo's mangled remains on the night of his death; instead, she proclaimed the Basilica of San Mercuriale to be the Riarios' sanctioned church. Several masses of thanksgiving were held there, followed by Ottaviano's celebratory procession around the town square. On the same patch of ground, the people watched as the Orsi brothers' father, the respected patriarch Andrea, who had known of the murder conspiracy but had failed to warn Count Girolamo, was chopped into pieces while still alive. Caterina claimed the estates of all the escaped conspirators, and offered a thousand ducats apiece for their return. At the same time, she heaped rewards on Feo, the tower guards, and all others who had helped her in her time of greatest need. And she showed the people, who marveled at her coldhearted expression as old Andrea was butchered, that she was not just relentless, but benevolent, by lowering taxes.

Luffo Numai, whose loyalty had wavered in the first days after Girolamo's murder but grew stronger the instant it became clear the Orsi had no military backing, presented Caterina and her family with a lavish feast. In fact, Numai was so desperate to ensure that he stood in the contessa's good graces that he fed us for the rest of the week, and remained physically close to Caterina, offering his services at every opportunity he could be of use. Caterina tolerated him—Numai had the hearts and ears of the people—while I remained busy just avoiding Ser Luffo's lecherous clutches.

As for the Palazzo Riario, Caterina refused to set foot in it again; the slaughter of her husband reminded her all too much of her father's bloody end. Instead, the bounty from the conspirators' estates allowed her to create a lavish apartment in Ravaldino's highest tower, where she lived and slept and stored all her valuables. She was determined not to lose what possessions she had again, and most certainly determined never to put herself and her children in mortal danger. Wherever possible, the windows opened onto a panoramic view of the tranquil Apennine Mountains. My lady took great joy in furnishing the apartment with items that did not remind her of Girolamo or the lost glory of Rome. "For once," she told me, "I have a sanctuary truly my own."

"A paradise," I murmured.

A curious light came into her eyes; she smiled at me. "Paradise it is." And from that time on, we never referred to the apartment by any other name.

Years of relative peace followed, during which time Caterina's daughter, Bianca, grew into a beautiful young woman, and Ottaviano and his younger brother Cesare grew into youths. When she pleased, Caterina took lovers, none of whom truly had her heart. This provoked rumors that spread swiftly across the Romagna. Ludovico of Milan wrote stern letters, saying that such scandalous conduct was exposing Caterina not only to public shame, but also to the loss of her properties, since she answered to her overlord, the pope.

Caterina spat on the letter after reading it, and ground it under her heel. "I am discreet," she stormed, "while my uncle carries on with mistresses in public, under his wife's nose! Does he think I am less of a Sforza than he? That because I am a woman, I dare not love whom I wish, even though I, too, was born to rule?"

She answered him politely, of course, telling him not to believe such vile rumors, and proceeded to take whomever she wished to her bed.

The year 1492 brought much bad news. In April, Lorenzo de' Medici of Florence died too soon, at the age of forty-three; he had suffered from crippling gout, which left him disfigured and in agony until it finally weakened his kidneys and heart. Less sad, but more important, Pope Innocent VIII died in late July, from a more mysterious cause.

The latter tidings left Caterina troubled; she could confide only in me, for no one else knew of her real relationship with Cardinal Borgia, who would certainly fight hard for the papacy.

"If he becomes pope . . ." she said on one difficult night, when she had called me to her bed to sleep beside her; I did not need to ask of whom she spoke. "If he becomes pope, he can do whatever he wishes with me."

"It was a long time ago, Madonna," I answered, with feigned unconcern. "He has forgotten everything by now; he must be sixty years old, at the least."

She sighed. "I wish I were in Rome." At my gasp of astonishment, she continued, "Oh, I realize it's a madhouse there until someone is elected. But I've had no letter from Giuliano della Rovere for too long now."

"He is the most powerful cardinal in Rome," I countered truthfully. "Surely he will get the tiara this time."

Caterina stared up at the ceiling. "He should. He's as crafty as Borgia, and far richer."

"Whatever happens, you have Cardinal della Rovere on your side in Rome, and your uncle Ascanio, who has as much chance as anyone of becoming pope," I said. The youngest of Galeazzo's brothers, Ascanio was made a cardinal and sent to Rome, so that he could spy for Milan as well as represent her interests. "Or perhaps," I added lightly, "none of them will be elected, and we'll be surprised again."

At that, she gave a short laugh. "You're probably right."

On the eleventh of August 1492, Rodrigo Borgia ascended to the throne of Peter and took for himself the name Alexander VI. Although Giuliano della Rovere had received two hundred thousand ducats from the King of France and half that from Genoa, it was not enough to defeat the Spanish cardinal. Della Rovere was furious, and publicly charged that Borgia had bribed Ascanio Sforza with four mule-loads of silver; other cardinals spoke out similarly, and Lorenzo's son, the young Cardinal Giovanni de' Medici, called Borgia a "rapacious wolf."

Caterina was devastated; all my reassurances that her uncle Ascanio would have Borgia's ear and would protect her went ignored. Yet even as she fretted, she set about taking advantage of Cardinal Ascanio Sforza's new-found prestige by having him make arrangements for her second son, Cesare, to enter the priesthood, with the thought of someday sending him to Rome.

The contessa was not the only one to be deeply troubled by Borgia's election. Luca, who had been oddly restless ever since his master's death, seemed despondent as well.

When I approached him on the subject one evening after supper in Paradise, he folded his arms and stepped away from me to gaze out the window at the distant Apennines. Half his face was painted by shadows, which fell in such a way as to sculpt his remaining features handsomely. After a time, he said quietly, "You are the one who sees the future, not I. Don't you sense the coming scourge? There is talk of the French invading Italy; it would be the perfect excuse for Borgia to send papal troops marching through the Romagna. He is an evil man, Dea, more wicked than either you or the contessa know. I am not easily scandalized; I do not care that he has brought his natural children to live with him in the Vatican, or that his new mistress is almost fifty years his junior. But . . ."

I moved to him and, thinking to dispel the darkness in his expression, teased one of his hands from him and kissed it. "There's nothing we can do but wait for evil to come. When it does, we can deal with it bravely. Until then . . ."

He did not take my hand, as he always did, but instead let it lie limply in my grasp. "There are things *I* can do."

I laughed gently. "What things?"

He did not smile. "I have not spoken much of them, but when I went to Rome, my purpose was to help Girolamo."

"Of course," I said. "You were his scribe. And Lorenzo needed the information only you could provide."

Luca shook his head. "I'm not speaking of my *ostensible* mission, although that, too, was important. I tried, through my actions and words, to lead Girolamo gently toward his true self. Dea, you know what I'm speaking of. You do the same for Caterina."

"I . . ." I lowered my face so that he could not see my shame. "If you're speaking of the angel, I told you before . . ." My voice dropped to a whisper. "I don't know him. I'm still a fraud."

Luca tilted his head sadly. "After all these years, you still haven't given up your hatred for Matteo's murderer? Oh, Dea, how you suffer unnecessarily." His hand finally found mine, and drew me to him; he lowered his forehead until it touched mine. His breath was warm upon my cheeks. "But you have not abused your talent to find the killer?"

I shook my head.

"You do not know how close you are to your angel, Dea . . . but one step away. And your behavior toward Caterina, the effect you have had on her over the years . . . whether you know it or not, you are doing the work you're supposed to be doing."

I tensed in his embrace. "And what was Matteo's work, then? To suffer before dying young? His death, his sacrifice . . . those must have been for nothing then, because his master, the Duke of Milan, remained a monster up until the moment of his death."

"Then perhaps he was not in Milan to help Duke Galeazzo," Luca countered gently. "Perhaps he was there to help you."

I drew back from our embrace to stare at him. "Of course Matteo helped me," I agreed. "He looked after me, protected me from being married off to a horrible man. But his death did not *help* me."

Luca said nothing, but steadily held my gaze.

"It was meaningless and terrible and cruel," I said. Yet I began to consider what had happened to me in those awful days just after Matteo died. He had directed me to his private papers and the rituals to invoke the angel; he had sent me to Florence to meet the Medici, where I learned about our past and more about the angel, and received my mother's triumph cards. I had come close to knowing the angel then, but my all-consuming desire to avenge my brother's death held me back. And it had been all too easy, once I was saddled with looking after Caterina, to lose myself for years just trying to make sure she survived.

"It was terrible and cruel," Luca said, "but it will only become meaningless if you allow it to."

I pressed a hand to my brow, overwhelmed. "What am I then to do?" I whispered.

Luca dropped his hold upon my waist and took a small step backward. "It is not my place to tell you what you already know, Dea." He stiffened, and it was as though a chill breeze replaced all the warmth he had just lavished on me.

"I only know," he said, "that I am needed elsewhere. Just where, I do not yet know. But my heart leads me."

"I cannot leave Caterina!" I protested.

His expression grew wistfully sad. "On that," he said, "we are unfortunately both agreed."

"Oh, Luca!" I moved forward to seize his hands again. "You cannot leave me! I could not bear it!"

"Nor I," he whispered as a spasm of grief passed over his features; he recovered himself quickly and pressed my palms, one at a time, to his lips. "Not yet, not yet," he promised. "There is still time, Dea. If you think on it, I know you will come to understand."

Tearfully, I said, "But you will come back to me?"

"Yes," he vowed. "Yes, I will come back, as soon as my work is done."

I broke down and sobbed into his shoulder. He led me away from the public rooms and curious eyes, to our little bedroom in Paradise, joined to Caterina's chamber by a spiral staircase. There I spent the night clinging to him until dawn.

Two months passed. Luca and I never spoke of the matter again, nor did either of us mention it to Caterina, who would certainly refuse to let Luca desert me without adequate explanation.

During a night I spent with Caterina—who had been frightened again by nightmares of her father and Girolamo dying bloodily—I chanced, in the early hours of the morning, to hear stealthy footsteps on the stairs; a few moments later, there came the sound of hoofbeats galloping away from the stables. Caterina was dozing, so I rose and stole down to the room I had shared with Luca, making sure to leave the staircase door open so that my lady could call for me without getting up to ring the bell.

Down below, the bed I shared with Luca was made, the room clean, the lamp on the night table lit. I was just about to open the wardrobe to see what was missing when I spotted the letter upon my pillow.

> *My beloved,*
>
> *It grieves my heart to leave you, and I know, all too keenly, it does yours as well. But I go knowing it is for the best. There is work I must accomplish, in a city I must not name, and it is likely that I will not be able to contact you for some time—many months at least, and perhaps longer. Only know that I am always your faithful, loving husband, and that I will return to you as quickly as I am able.*
>
> *How I love you.*
>
> *Forever your faithful servant,*
>
> *Luca*

I came undone. There, upon our little mattress beneath Caterina's grand bedchamber, I clutched the letter to my chest and sobbed so loudly that the contessa was roused and, receiving no reply to her shouted questions, climbed down the stairs and found me.

I did not have the presence of mind to hide the letter or to make up lies about Luca's reasons for leaving; I was so lost in sorrow that I only vaguely noticed that Caterina tore the paper from my hand and read it herself, that she tried to pull my hands from my face to speak to me, that she gave up and sat beside me, her arms about my shoulders.

When I had calmed enough to catch my breath, Caterina withdrew her embrace and smoothed the letter out upon her knee.

"The bastard!" she said softly. "How dare he hurt you so! He seemed such a kindly, sensible sort. I'm of a mind to hunt him down and—"

Wisely, she left the rest unsaid, and her tone became more practical. She pointed to a phrase in the letter. "'Work I must accomplish, in a city I must not name' . . . Dea, he is a spy!"

"I don't know. I don't understand it," I said tremulously, but my lady was not fooled.

"You've never lied to me before," Caterina stated flatly, "and I must say that you're very bad at it." She faced me with a sympathetic yet unyielding stare. "For whom does he spy? Where are his loyalties?"

"To the Riario, of course," I said feebly, but was too exhausted, too angry, too heartbroken to prevail, and I knew it.

So did Caterina. "I have always put more trust in you than anyone else in this world. Do not betray me."

I drew a breath and closed my eyes, so that everything I saw in the little room would not remind me of Luca; even blind, I could still smell iron-gall ink.

"He has always been loyal to the Riario, and to you, Madonna," I said without opening my eyes, "but he was loyal first to his benefactor, Lorenzo de' Medici, who rescued him from the orphanage and educated him."

"Lorenzo," Caterina breathed respectfully. Despite her husband's vicious hatred of the Medici, the Lady of Forlì had always admired Lorenzo. But her tone hardened. "So he was a spy for the Medici," she said.

I nodded. "He warned Lorenzo that Girolamo was plotting to kill him."

She lifted the paper between her thumb and forefinger and held it up, a warning. "Had he not brought back such a great army from Milan, I would not trust him. I would send men after him, to hunt him down."

I finally looked at her. "He is good-hearted, Madonna. He means well. Please don't ever think—"

"I won't," she said, "if you will tell me for whom he works now. The hapless Piero de' Medici, Lorenzo's son? Or someone else? My uncle Ludovico?" A look of pure hatred flickered in her eyes. "God forbid, Borgia?"

"He would never work for the likes of Borgia!" I answered hotly. "Luca was as distraught as you when Borgia claimed the tiara. If anything, he has gone to work against him!"

"Wherever he has gone," she said, "his work must be dangerous, or he would have taken you."

Tears threatened again; I swallowed hard. "He told me he would leave, but he would not say when."

Caterina stiffened. "You knew and you did not *tell* me?"

I shook my head guiltily. "I did not. Forgive me."

At that, she scowled and rose indignantly beside me. "How long have you known that he was leaving?"

"Two months." I peered cautiously up at her; her eyes were bright with anger. "I wanted to go with him, of course, but we both knew . . . I told him, so he knew . . ." I paused, overwhelmed by emotion.

"Say it!" she snapped.

"That I could never leave you. My place is here, with you, always." I turned to face her directly. "I have read my own cards, Madonna. Like you, my future is the Tower. I will never desert you. I hope that you have always known that."

The anger drained from her so swiftly that she sat down heavily beside me. "Oh, Dea!" she murmured, blinking rapidly, and put a hand to her throat. I expected her to embrace me again; instead, she spat upon Luca's letter, then crumpled it into a ball and threw it across the room.

"Stinking weasel!" she shouted at it, as though it were Luca himself standing before us. "Miserable son of a whore! I will not forget your transgression against me, against your beautiful wife! When you return, I will throw you into the soldiers' latrine! I will make Marta use your head to scrub the chamber pots! No one dares break the heart of the Lady of Forli's sister!"

Sister, she called me.

With that, she threw her arms about me and kissed my cheek; uncomfortable with her own display of emotion, she lifted her skirts and hurried up the stairs.

When she had gone, I picked up Luca's letter and carefully wiped the spittle away before smoothing it out and placing it beneath my pillow.

Thirty

Months passed, and Luca did not return, nor did I receive a letter from him, though twice a folded, sealed piece of paper was delivered to Ravaldino by a street urchin, who could not describe the mysterious courier who gave it him.

Twice, I broke the seal in an agony of expectation, and twice read the single line, written in Luca's carefully even script: *Know that I love you and think of you always.*

I was desperately glad to read such words, even though they reopened the wound his departure had inflicted on me. Caterina tolerated my mournful visage and sighs without a word.

The political turbulence in those days served as a distraction. The year 1494 began with the death of King Ferrante of Naples in January, which encouraged the French king, Charles, to gather a huge army and march south through northern and central Italy. This terrifying event led to instability in Florence, where Lorenzo's feckless heir, Piero, was banished along with the rest of the Medici. Florence became a republic after the same fashion as Venice, and she sided with the French.

Caterina remained scrupulously neutral during the war, until the Neapolitan troops were upon Forlì, at which point she promptly announced her support for Naples. Fortunately, the French never visited our town, and the new king of Naples, Alfonso, had the good grace to rout them; King Charles also had the good grace to retreat after coming down with the pox.

The calm that followed was fleeting. Venice had her eye on the Romagna, specifically on the town of Faenza, which lay directly between Imola and Forlì. The Venetians saw Faenza as an excellent maneuvering ground from which they could launch an attack on Florence. Dismayed, Caterina sent several letters to her uncle, Duke Ludovico of Milan. Ludovico did what he could to influence the Serene Republic, but the matter was never fully resolved to Caterina's satisfaction.

In the meantime, King Charles of France had died and was succeeded by Louis XII, who also felt entitled to the Italian peninsula. France was unusually powerful, with a vast military force, owing to the fact that she was united under one ruler; and Florence allied itself with her, believing that this time the superior might of France would prevail. Well before King Louis announced his intentions, the Borgia pope, Alexander, had created a Holy League: an alliance of Rome, Venice, and Milan as well as other smaller city-states. Caterina announced her intention to remain neutral, which at once caused both sides to try to persuade her to join their cause. Ludovico sent several letters to Caterina, begging her to join the league; her uncle Cardinal Ascanio Sforza, now Borgia's right-hand man, informed her that Pope Alexander "recommended" that the Lady of Forlì join the league, as he was now her overlord.

And then, one fateful day in the first days of September 1496, there came the ambassador from Florence.

Giovanni di Pierfrancesco de' Medici was a beautiful man; at the sight of him entering Caterina's well-appointed sitting room in Paradise, flanked by ten attendants, I fought to contain a gasp of appreciation. I believe he was twenty-eight then, fully in his prime.

Save for his hair—full, dark ringlets that fell slightly past his shoulder and, where brushed out, dissolved into a soft, voluminous cloud—he had the even, classical features favored by ancient Romans: a thin, straight nose with flaring nostrils and a perfectly proportioned chin with a pronounced cleft in its center. He was clean-shaven, the better to show it off. His eyes were slightly rounded and brown-black, matching his hair, which was parted in the middle to show off a high, unlined forehead; his eyebrows were thin, lending a delicacy to his aspect. His neck was as long and white and graceful as Caterina's, though the muscles and tendons were more prominent. His hands were long, uncalloused, and slender—a gentleman's, not a soldier's.

He was slightly taller than the Lady of Forlì, with a powerful chest and wide shoulders accentuated by a narrow waist and hips. He wore simple black leggings and a tunic of sedate dark brown silk.

His voice, though not deep, was well modulated and pleasant to the ear. I first heard it as he passed over the threshold, joking and laughing with his attendants as if they were his friends and equals. He had been smiling, and that smile widened at his first glimpse of Caterina and seemed to illuminate him from within.

I stood beside Caterina, who was seated in a high-backed chair, the closest thing that she had to a throne. As distracted as I was by Giovanni's physical presence, I noticed that Caterina's hands gripped the arms of her chair tightly.

The Lady of Forlì had become acquainted with Ser Giovanni through business correspondence with him and with his older brother, Lorenzo di Pierfrancesco de' Medici. They were nephews of Lorenzo the Magnificent and had received an exquisite education from their uncle after their father died; however, they broke with il Magnifico after coming to suspect that he had spent most of their inheritance on himself and his more immediate family. Their disagreement with Lorenzo had saved them from exile, and to appease the new Republic of Florence, they eschewed the Medici name while in the city, instead using the surname "Popolano," "of the people."

The Romagna, with Forlì and Imola at its heart, was famed for its abundant wheat crop, which, in previous years, had led Giovanni il Popolano to Caterina in search of grain to buy. The business was conducted solely through correspondence; Caterina was so impressed by the brothers' quick payment and honest accounting that she did not turn Ser Giovanni down when he asked for a small loan in order to make a large purchase of grain. That, too, was swiftly repaid.

When Giovanni asked for permission to visit Caterina in August of 1496, she readily agreed, even though she realized that their talks would surely stray from business to politics. She had made too much money from her grain sales to the Medici brothers to offend them, and they had shown such courtesy in their dealings with her that she trusted Ser Giovanni's efforts to persuade her to side with Florence against the Holy League would be gentle and brief. She prepared a lavish suite in Ravaldino, bought a cellarful of the region's finest wine, and had several new, more elaborate gowns made so that she might properly entertain a Medici from Florence.

Now Ser Giovanni walked through the doors of Paradise, and with a gesture, bade his entourage remain several steps behind him as he walked up to Caterina and bowed from the waist with a courtier's practiced ease.

"Your Illustriousness!" he greeted her cheerfully. "How honored I am to set eyes on you at last!"

"Welcome to Forlì, and Ravaldino," Caterina replied, and extended her hand. "My home and everything in it are yours."

Ser Giovanni took the proffered hand and kissed it respectfully. Entranced, Caterina stared down into the soft dark nest of curls as he leaned over her, and scarcely breathed until Giovanni's lips touched her skin—at which instant she squirmed ever so slightly in her chair, and her free hand went to rest just beneath the hollow of her throat.

Giovanni rose, his pale skin flushed; he did not release Caterina's hand quickly, and when he did, she did not immediately withdraw it, but lingered a bit in his grasp.

"Your hospitality honors me," he said, his eyes still on her face. He motioned to his attendants; three of them stepped forward, and I noticed for the first time the objects they bore. "I have brought a few paltry gifts in recognition of your kindness. First, a painting from the hands of Sandro Botticelli, my dear friend." He waved a hand toward his gentlemen. "Enrico, please."

One of his entourage stepped forward, bearing a large rectangular item draped in black velvet. At Giovanni's nod, the man removed the velvet to reveal an astoundingly lovely portrait of a Madonna and Child in a large gold frame. To Caterina's delight, the Madonna resembled her.

"Forgive me," Giovanni said. "I did not have a likeness of you—only a coin, and the knowledge that you were beautiful and golden-haired. The rest came from Sandro's imagination. I must say, Your Illustriousness, that you are quite famous in Florence for your bravery. Sandro is so impressed with your beauty and boldness that he has included your likeness in many of his paintings."

"It's beautiful," Caterina breathed. "Simply beautiful. I shall have it hung in a place where I can see it often."

The man with the Madonna and Child stepped back into the group, and a second man came forward with a stack of folded fabrics in his hand. Florence was, after all, famed for its fine silks and woolen cloth.

"These are only samples," Giovanni said, "of a much greater quantity stashed in our wagons below. If there are any you do not like, we shall carry them back to Florence. If anything pleases you especially and you desire more than we have brought, let us know and we shall send it to you the minute we return home."

The man proffered the fabrics to Caterina; she lifted and unwrapped the first of them—a sheer, iridescent silk that began as deep purple, then slowly faded to lilac, at which point the hue shifted to rose and eventually a dark crimson.

"This is our cangiante silk," Giovanni said, "but there are many others."

Caterina ran her fingers over the next piece of fabric on the stack, burned-out black velvet, the sheer pattern shot through with glistening thread of gold. "They are all lovely. . . . I shall go through them later, after you have had a chance to rest and refresh yourselves. Dea, would you go and tell the kitchen to fetch us some of the wine I put aside for Ser Giovanni?"

"Ah," Giovanni interjected, "Madonna Dea, I have been so rude to ignore you! Forgive me, I was distracted by our lady's beauty. I am Ser Giovanni, and pleased to make your acquaintance."

He bowed from the shoulders, and I made a half-curtsy, then moved to obey Caterina's instructions.

Before Caterina could interrupt us, Giovanni said, "But first, Your Illustriousness, let us bring out one more gift; I think you will find it useful almost immediately."

With that, the fabric-bearer retreated, and a third gentleman stepped forward. In his hands rested an intricately carved wooden box, inlaid with gold and nacre in the shape of a fleur-de-lis, symbol of Florence and her ally, France. It was of sufficient size to hold a fortune's worth of jewelry or silverware. Caterina opened her mouth to utter thanks, but before she could speak, Giovanni held a finger to his smiling lips.

His gentleman held the underside of the box and, tilting it forward so that the contessa could easily view its interior, lifted the lid. It was connected to the bottom by a hinge, and as it opened, neither Caterina nor I could hold back frank gasps of awe.

Nestled against a lining of scarlet velvet was a pair of pure gold goblets fit for an emperor. The shapes of the cups matched exactly, but their adornment differed: one was encrusted with diamonds, emeralds, and rubies, the other with sapphires, diamonds, pearls, and malachite.

Two chalices.

Unnerved, I went to fetch wine and goblets for Ser Giovanni's attendants. When I filled Giovanni's gold chalice, then my mistress's, Caterina linked her arm through Giovanni's for a toast.

At long last, the King of Chalices had arrived, bearing with him the Two of Cups—love—and the smitten look in my lady's eyes confirmed it.

Giovanni's attendants departed to prepare his chambers while their master sat beside his hostess, enjoying wine from the glittering chalice. Caterina, who drank little and then only in the evening, took more than her usual share, perhaps because she was too distracted by her guest to notice that the cupbearer kept refilling her dazzling goblet. The grape allowed her to recover her confidence, and in the conversation that followed, she told Giovanni:

"I have no doubt that your Republic has sent you with orders to sway me to the side of the French alliance. But I *must* remain neutral; if I accept Florence's protection, Pope Alexander would have every right to seize my properties. I tell this to you now to spare you the trouble of arguing on your government's behalf later."

Giovanni gave a half smile, revealing a dimple in his left cheek. "Of course the Republic wants me to persuade you to join us. Why would they not? But I was born with the Medici brain for business, not diplomacy. I'm here to buy grain. No doubt you've heard of the poor harvest in Tuscany."

"I have," Caterina allowed.

"It's worse than you imagine. It affects not just the poor, but the merchants and nobles, too. People are starving in the streets." His gaze grew sorrowful at the thought. "I will sell the wheat to the city at a slight profit. The Republic did not send me; I saw a need, and made arrangements to come." The half smile returned. "Although the government begged me, of course, to speak to you about the advantages of allying yourself with Florence."

"So you are loyal to the Republic? You did not leave with the other Medici. And what shall I call you? Giovanni de' Medici, or Giovanni il Popolano?"

His grin turned wry. "Outside of Florence, I find the family name to be very useful. In my mind, I am a Medici, but it was necessary to avoid offending the Republic, so I took the name Popolano. But frankly, Your Illustriousness—and I trust you completely with such damning information—I believe as you do, that power is best kept in the hands of noble families who are educated and trained from birth to rule. It is frightening to see the uneducated and superstitious sitting in the halls of government."

Although Giovanni and his men were clearly tired and dusty from travel, Caterina would have continued speaking to him the entire day had he not graciously hinted that his men were in need of baths and beds. Instead, she let him be led to his recently refurbished apartment, where he rested until dinner.

He arrived in the dining chamber a few minutes before Caterina—as had I, with the precious goblets, to clean them and set them out for his and Caterina's use that night. I forced myself not to gape at his beauty and murmured a greeting. He nodded to me politely, and with the same dimpled half smile, said, "Good evening, Madonna Dea. Forgive me for disturbing you, but I could not help noticing that you and our lady are very close. I was wondering whether you would be willing to tell me something in confidence."

I tensed, suspicious.

"Is there anything the contessa has need of? I should like to buy her a gift she can truly appreciate."

Relieved, I held up the chalices in my hands. "Sir, you can hardly do better than these."

"Yes, but while such things are beautiful, they are used rarely, and will be hidden away when I am gone. I want to get her something more."

I could have pointed out that Caterina would see the portrait of herself as the Madonna every day, but Giovanni was determined. I hesitated, and suddenly remembered Caterina bitterly complaining about the need to pawn almost all of her jewels and silverware. They were still in Milan, at the pawnbrokers, and the interest alone was more than she could afford to pay.

"Jewels," I said, and told him the sad story.

He nodded happily. "And what do you have need of, Madonna Dea?"

"Oh, sir, you are too generous. I have need of nothing." But he continued asking general questions, which somehow led to our speaking of Florence. I told him how I had met Lorenzo, and Giuliano before his death, and Lucrezia, and Marsilio Ficino. "I even possess a short manuscript by him, and a letter to my late husband from him." And then I broke off, wondering whether I had said too much.

That night, Caterina and Giovanni feasted and danced late into the night; my lady was a fine dancer, but Giovanni's grace exceeded even hers. During a break in the music, Caterina took me aside.

"Go to bed now," she whispered into my ear. "To your own room, and be sure to shut the door to the staircase. Don't come out until morning."

When morning came—and I had waited for hours, dressed and fully awake—I finally ventured going up the stairs and opening the door to my lady's chamber, to see if she had need of anything.

Caterina was still sound asleep, fully naked, with the covers and linens kicked carelessly to the floor. She lay curled on her side, nestled in the crook of Giovanni's arm, her head upon his shoulder, her arm flung across his bare chest. The tightly coiled braid at the nape of her neck had mysteriously come undone, and golden waves of hair covered her own shoulder; the pins lay scattered on the night table beside her brush.

Giovanni lay naked on his back, his arm enfolding Caterina, his face inclined tenderly toward hers, and hers toward his, a breath away, as black and golden locks intertwined.

On either night table stood one of the jewel-encrusted chalices.

I smiled faintly at the sight of their bliss, though the sight stirred my pain. I stole out the main door to the rest of Caterina's apartments, thinking of my Luca, wondering where he found himself at this particular instant, and whether his thoughts were of me.

Caterina did not call for me until an hour past midday, at which point Ser Giovanni had retired to his own chamber to be dressed and groomed. The lovers met alone in Caterina's private dining hall, without Giovanni's attendants, while I hovered over the two and made sure plates and cups were refilled. Out of the public eye, Giovanni reached across the table for Caterina's hand, and she offered it to him shyly; they began their discussion by clasping hands above the table.

But they did not cling to each other for long. They were both stubborn businessfolk, and when it came to the amount and price of the grain to be purchased, Caterina balked and argued strenuously for her point of view. Ser Giovanni remained perfectly calm and reasonable, but held just as doggedly to his own numbers. In the end, the deal was reached after some swift, fierce haggling, with both sides making concessions, and when it was done, Ser Giovanni and Caterina both were satisfied.

As a good host, Caterina had readied horses and hounds for a hunt, but at her invitation, Giovanni smiled wistfully.

"I have so little time here," he said, "and I would rather spend it coming to know you and your family instead of bounding across the Romagna in pursuit of a hare. Where are the brave children who survived imprisonment after the death of their father? I should like to meet them."

I had the distinct pleasure of watching Caterina melt before my eyes.

"Of course you can, Giovanni," she said softly, "but they are with their tutors right now."

Giovanni favored her with a coy grin. "Does today not seem like a holiday, Caterina?"

"It does, doesn't it?" she answered, smiling back at him, and reaching for his hand.

With that, the hunt was canceled and turned instead into an outdoor picnic in the grassy meadow across the moat. Giovanni's men produced the most succulent food I had dined on since leaving Rome. Caterina's eldest, Bianca, had since been wisely married off to Astorre Manfredi, Lord of Faenza, but fifteen-year-old Ottaviano and fourteen-year-old Cesare brought blunted swords to show off their blade-wielding skills, and twelve-year-old Giovanni Livio challenged Ser Giovanni and his attendants to a number of footraces. Ser Giovanni wisely let his little namesake win most of the races; Giovanni Livio, the brightest and most exuberant of his brothers, celebrated by jumping into the murky waters of the moat and swimming its entire length. After a severe chastening by his annoyed mother, the soaked boy was pulled out and offered a cloak.

A few of Ser Giovanni's attendants disappeared for some time, and returned bearing gifts for the boys: a gold belt buckle in the shape of a fleur-de-lis for Ottaviano ("as I hear your mother has arranged your first military commission for you in Florence"), and one in the shape of the stylized Riario oak for Cesare. Giovanni Livio received a handsome inlaid wood recorder, which he proceeded to play badly for the rest of the afternoon.

Fortunately, Ser Giovanni had also hired musicians. When we all quickly tired of listening to the shrill blast of the recorder, Ser Giovanni signaled for them to begin playing, and the recorder was soon muffled by the sound of the lute, tambourine, and drum. This, of course, made Caterina take Giovanni's arm and pull him into a dance. Their joy was so evident that the rest of us were caught up in it, and the nurse, Lucia, and I danced with each of the attendants while Ottaviano and Cesare performed a mocking little dance, cooing at each other in falsetto tones.

We did not return to the fortress until the sun slipped low in the sky, and a cold breeze replaced its warmth. I was assisting Lucia in herding the boys back over the drawbridge when little Giovanni Livio, shivering a bit in his still-damp clothes, leaned forward to say, much too loudly: "Mama and Ser Giovanni are in love, aren't they?"

Behind us, the two principals in question giggled faintly, though the rest of us dared not.

I patted Livio's head and nodded, smiling.

"Well, that's good," Livio said. "He seems like a very nice man."

Caterina let go a faint strangled sound as she tried to hold back her laughter.

Supper was a more poignant, hushed affair, as Ser Giovanni was to start his journey homeward the next morning. This time, the boys were invited to dine with their mother and her guest; to my surprise—and that of the boys—Giovanni and Caterina once again held hands openly across the table. The conversation focused on the changes in Florence, and Ottaviano's first commission there. There were times when my lady's happy smile faded, and I saw the melancholy in her eyes. Ser Giovanni saw it, too, and each time pressed her hand to his lips and reminded her that he would return as soon as possible.

I sat between Cesare and his younger brother. By the time the meat course arrived, I noticed that little Giovanni Livio had eaten almost nothing and was slumped and shivering in his chair; I put a hand to his forehead, which was alarmingly warm.

"Madonna," I whispered down the table to Caterina, "he is unwell. I'd best take him to his bed and call Lucia."

Frowning, Caterina pushed herself from the dining table and, still sitting, opened her arms to her youngest son. "Come, darling, let me see you."

Livio was so ill that he swayed on his feet, squinting at the light. I bent down and put an arm beneath his shoulders, and helped him stagger to his mother's arms.

Caterina put a hand upon his forehead and blanched. "He's very sick," she said. "Take him to Lucia, and have one of the couriers fetch the doctor. I'll join you in an hour."

"Please," Ser Giovanni told her, as I took hold of Livio again. "I'll return soon enough, and all of us have been shown enough hospitality to last a lifetime. Take care of your child, Caterina. I've brought my own physician and I vouch for his competency. I'll send him to Livio immediately."

She gazed at him, her face taut with worry, and nodded. "I will help him to bed, then," she promised, "and return once your physician has come. I hope not to be gone long. I had hoped to speak with you privately once more before you leave."

Livio could not make it to the boys' apartments; after attempting a single assisted step down a half flight of stairs, he clutched his skull and retched weakly, though nothing came up. "I can't walk," he moaned. "My head hurts too badly."

He was almost his mother's height, but she scooped him easily up in her arms and carried him to his bed. Lucia, who slept in adjacent quarters, lit the lamp and brought out a bag of medicines, though Caterina asked her to wait for the doctor before dosing Livio with anything.

"I'm thirsty," little Giovanni whispered. His eyes were closed in response to the nearby lamplight, his face pale and slack with pain; he could not stop shivering. When Lucia held a cup to his lips, he began to cry in frustration, as he could not bear the pain of bending his head forward to drink. Near tears herself, Caterina sent the nurse off to the kitchen to find a ladle.

At that point, Ser Giovanni's physician arrived, dressed in rich brocades and a dark blue velvet cap atop his long gray hair. With an air of confidence born of many decades' experience, he examined the boy. To all his questions, Livio, his eyes squeezed shut, his head turned from the lamp, could only moan one reply: "My . . . head . . . hurts. . . ."

As a final test, the doctor put his hand beneath the back of Livio's head, and urged him to bow his head, touching his chin to his chest. The attempt to even begin to do so brought weak screams, and the doctor immediately told the child to stop trying.

As Livio fell back, huddled and trembling, the doctor rose from his bedside and beckoned for Caterina to join him in the doorway. I followed. The doctor was not unkind; his gaze was sad, with a distant weariness found in those who have witnessed too much suffering.

"I am so sorry, Your Illustriousness," he told Caterina in a soft, paternal tone. "The outlook is grave."

Caterina seemed not to understand him, as if he had just uttered something absurd. "Grave?"

The doctor drew in an unhappy breath. "I have seen this before, mostly in children—and of those, children who have recently swum in muddy or stagnant waters. The odds of your son recovering are very slight."

Caterina put a hand to her mouth and spoke through her fingers. "That can't be. . . . He was perfectly healthy this afternoon." She glanced back at the supine Livio in horror. "What will happen to him?"

"The fever will spike even higher. He might have a fit, but most certainly he will lose his sight and hearing, and fall into a stupor. Death will follow in a matter of a few hours."

Caterina emitted a short, gutteral sound, as if the air had just been knocked from her lungs. "What can be done?"

"I can bleed him with leeches, but that is not curative; it would only prolong his misery."

"What will ease it?" she demanded impatiently.

"Tea from the bark of white willow for the fever," the doctor said, his tone sympathetic. "Though it will be very difficult for him to drink. I have some powdered poppy that can be added to it, to make him comfortable."

By then, Lucia arrived with a small ladle and a kettle of hot water. The doctor dug in his satchel and produced the medicines, which Lucia promptly brewed into a tea. Livio screamed as his mother held him up, supporting his head while I stuffed another pillow beneath him, so that he half sat in the bed. Afterward Lucia got some of the tea into him by ladling it, sip by sip, into his mouth. After each swallow, he shuddered and grimaced.

At that point, Caterina dismissed the doctor and crawled into bed with her son. Very gently, she took him into her arms and held him, whispering sweetly into his ear. His lids fluttered open only once, to show eyes dulled by fever and pain.

Not long afterward Ser Giovanni silently entered the sickroom; his somber expression implied that he had spoken to the physician.

Caterina looked up at her lover and opened her mouth to explain the grim situation, but only tears, not words, would come. Ser Giovanni climbed silently into the bed with her and wrapped an arm around her shoulder as she held her son. By then, Livio was in the predicted stupor, and responded not at all to sight or sound or touch.

They remained so until the dark of night lightened to gray in the hour before dawn, when young Livio's breath grew labored and harsh. Ser Giovanni had the presence of mind to call for a priest; I hurried to rouse Caterina's chaplain and led him back as fast as I could. By then, the boy was scarcely breathing, and by the time the priest finished praying over him, he was gone.

Caterina was not ready to leave, but continued to hold Livio while Ser Giovanni carefully detached himself. Lucia and I were both sobbing when he came up to us.

"I will not leave her now," he said, "but will remain for as long as she desires. I shall go speak to Livio's brothers now, unless you think Caterina would prefer to do so herself."

I looked to my mistress, who was humming softly and rocking Livio in her arms; I directed Lucia to remain with her, and led Ser Giovanni to Ottaviano's room. At Giovanni's solemn knock, Ottaviano's valet opened the door. Ottaviano and Cesare were both dressed, and had been anxiously speculating about their younger brother's condition.

"I am so sorry," Giovanni told them, with heartfelt sadness. "Young Giovanni Livio has died of a fever. It came from swimming in unclean water."

He paused as Ottaviano burst into tears and Cesare tried to console him. After the youths had voiced their sorrow, Giovanni said gently, "I shall stay with your mother and do my best to help her in whatever way I can. She is alone now without your father, and needs a man who can help with the painful details that must now be arranged. Ottaviano, Cesare, I know you two bear your own grief, but can you be strong for your mother as she has always been for you? There are funeral arrangements to be made. I can help you with them, but you know best what would please your mother and departed brother, not I."

In the end, Ottaviano agreed to make the funeral arrangements, although Giovanni wound up doing all that was necessary, and paid for the priest and burial.

Ser Giovanni kept his promise and did not leave immediately for Florence; he postponed a good deal of business and remained with us a fortnight.

On the night before he finally left, he presented Caterina with another present: all the jewels and silverware she had sent, years before, to the pawnbroker in Milan.

Nor had he forgotten his conversations with me. On the morning of his departure, while his men were loading up their horses, he handed me a leather-bound tome. I opened it to find a collection of Marsilio Ficino's writings on the soul of man.

Thirty-one

Ser Giovanni was true to his word, and returned within six months for a much longer visit—a good thing, since Caterina was bereft and moody without him; whenever a letter arrived from Florence, she would snatch it from the messenger and run to her bedchamber to savor it. While I never approved of her affairs outside marriage—were Caterina to become pregnant again, the scandal could cost her her lands—I was glad that this time she had chosen the kindest of men.

When Ser Giovanni returned again after New Year's, all his belongings were taken to the lavish apartment directly next to Caterina's, and this time, neither he nor Caterina bothered to hide their relationship from anyone at Ravaldino, although the servants were all sworn to secrecy. The Forlivese would be scandalized, and there was always the chance a cleric might write a letter of complaint to Rome.

Pope Alexander would never allow a Medici to take control of any property outside of Florence, and if Caterina married outside the Riario–della Rovere lineage, it would cost her her regency.

Despite this, Giovanni and Caterina lived as man and wife, and there was no happier time in Paradise. Giovanni was naturally cheerful and slow to take offense, and his sweet temperament influenced Caterina greatly. She learned from him that it appeared magnanimous to make requests of an underling rather than to demand, and that a kind tone brought better results than a harsh one. He also taught her how to consider the opinions and feelings of others before reacting, and that it was no shame to show genuine affection, in private or in public.

He was good with her sons as well. Rather than scold Ottaviano for his gluttony and laziness, he praised the lad when he drilled harder, rode longer, and hiked more "as it is excellent preparation for military service." Cesare, who, like his mother, was lean and agile, received incentives to read more and study harder, and was generously rewarded for the slightest improvement. Both boys adored Ser Giovanni—as, frankly, did I, for he dealt with me as an equal. Never was a master more beloved in a household, and never the mistress and children and servants happier.

Months passed, however, and the inevitable happened. Early one morning, just as I had finished dressing, Giovanni opened the door at the top of the staircase leading up to Caterina's bedchamber. He was in his nightshirt, a look of panic on his face.

"Dea," he called down softly. "I am worried; Caterina is ill."

I shoved my feet into my slippers and hurried up the steps. Frightfully pale, Caterina was sitting on the floor beside the bed, the front of her lawn chemise streaked with yellow bile. She had pulled the chamber pot from beneath the mattress, and was doubled over it. Just as I stepped up beside her, she obligingly vomited up a bit of foam.

As she wiped the stringy remnants from her lips, she met my knowing gaze, and I met hers. We did not speak; we had been in this situation far too many times to need words. I brought a clean chemise and a towel from the closet, dipped the latter in the basin and wiped her face as she leaned back against the wall and closed her eyes. Only then did I speak to Ser Giovanni, who hovered anxiously over us.

"I am going downstairs to the kitchen," I said briskly, "to fetch salt and bread, and will be back soon." I rose, and handed the clean chemise to Giovanni. "If she feels better before I return, she might need some help changing into this. But no sudden movements. And..." I frowned at the chamber pot, which, though unused, smelled vaguely unsavory. "Perhaps she would be better off using towels than this." I replaced the porcelain lid, and pushed it back beneath the bed.

Giovanni's concern increased as I began to stride off. With an air of helplessness, he called after me, "Is it serious? Will you fetch the doctor?"

I had crossed the threshold, and did not turn, but I heard Caterina's low, muttered reply behind me: "I'm pregnant, fool."

Caterina Sforza and Giovanni de' Medici were wed in late September, in Ravaldino's chapel. The bride wore a wreath of white silk flowers and diamonds upon her hair; her dress was made from one of Giovanni's first gifts, an elegant gold damask trimmed with indigo satin. Giovanni wore black and silver and a look of profound panic. His older brother, Lorenzo—a thick-limbed, pudgy man with long golden curls, a round, handsome face, and startling green eyes—came from Florence bearing gifts. Such was the love between the two brothers that Lorenzo did not care that the marriage was politically dangerous and needed to remain a secret; he was happy simply because Giovanni was happy, and saw no reason not to celebrate.

To explain Lorenzo's visit, and the score of gift-laden carts that rolled into Forlì—not to mention Ravaldino's sudden, urgent demand upon the locals for flowers, decorations, and high-quality food and drink—the bride-to-be intentionally started a rumor that Lorenzo had come to speak to Ottaviano about a possible marriage to the former's daughter.

In fact, Ottaviano was not considering marriage at all, but his first *condotta*—a paying military post—in Florence, thanks to his new relatives.

The ceremony was short, to accommodate Caterina's passing spells of queasiness, but it was far from solemn. After the priest had declared the deed done and the new couple turned to face the group gathered in the pews, Ottaviano, who had been drinking the entire day, belched loudly. An air of uncertainty hovered over the assembly—should we acknowledge such rudeness?—until Ser Lorenzo let go an explosive, high-pitched giggle, which proved dangerously contagious. Even the priest left the chapel laughing.

. . .

On the fifth of April 1498, baby Giovanni was born after a short, easy labor. Like his father, he was dark-haired; time would slowly color his eyes a matching brown-black. Secret documents were signed, stating the name of the child's sire, so that the boy would be recognized as a Medici and heir to his father's fortune. A more public document, which Caterina would file with Forlì's Hall of Justice sometime later, listed no father, and gave the infant's name as "Ludovico Riario," supposedly after Caterina's uncle in Milan, who would be livid when he finally learned the truth.

Caterina and Ser Giovanni doted on the baby. Whereas all of Caterina's older children had remained confined to the company of their nurses or tutors unless on display, little Giovanni and his nurse always accompanied Caterina during the day, when she was in her apartments and not off drilling Ravaldino's small contingent of soldiers or hunting in the countryside. Ser Giovanni often joined her, and sometimes worked on his business correspondence while his son played at his feet.

Late that month, Caterina received a letter from the Bishop of Volterra announcing that he was already on his way from Tuscany to visit her at the request of Pope Alexander, "concerning a personal matter which shall certainly please Your Illustriousness."

The cheery tone of the bishop's letter left her unconvinced. Panicked, she sent Ser Giovanni back to Florence for a month, and everyone else in the household, including the soldiers, was instructed to say that the infant was Lucia's. The servants and I worked feverishly to move Ser Giovanni's belongings from Caterina's bedchamber and the adjacent apartment downstairs to storage. All this preparation did nothing to ease our anxiety. When the bishop's carriage finally pulled up alongside the moat, my knees were unsteady.

Waiting just inside Ravaldino's main entrance, Caterina hid her terror behind a smile as the bishop walked across the drawbridge to greet her. I knew that his name was Francesco Soderini, that he had been born a Florentine but detested the Medici, and that Rodrigo Borgia—Pope Alexander—was so impressed by his acumen that a cardinal's hat was in his future. But I had not expected him to be only twenty-five, or freckled, or so terribly thin. His black priest's frock hung limply on his bony frame.

"Welcome, Your Excellency!" Caterina greeted him as he set foot inside the fortress proper, but she did not step back or gesture for him to follow her; instead she moved to block his way. Soderini could not see the armed guards that waited around the first corner, nor did he realize that his next few answers would seal his fate.

Soderini bowed. "Your Illustriousness! I bring greetings from His Holiness Pope Alexander in Rome."

Caterina's smile never wavered, but a faint hardness crept into her gaze. "And pray tell, Bishop Soderini, what business brings you here? Your letter was rather vague."

Soderini suddenly grinned. "Business of the happiest sort, Your Illustriousness. I guarantee that you will be jubilant! But . . ." He looked uncertainly at the gatehouse's mildewed walls. "It would be wrong of me to dilute the impact of such a joyous announcement here. Is there a place where my attendants and I might retire and refresh ourselves after a long journey?"

I stood to one side just behind Caterina, and saw the hidden guards watching her keenly for a signal. She folded her hands carefully behind her back as she considered Soderini's question. A lift of one finger, and Soderini would be cut to pieces and sent back to Alexander in reply.

Caterina laughed quietly. "Forgive me, Your Excellency, but I am known for my impatience. I am eager to hear of this happy thing. Can you not give me one hint?"

Soderini gave a gaunt grin. "Very well, *one* hint. It has to do with a wedding!"

Kill him, I thought, and looked at Caterina's now-clenched fists. She studied the bishop and his attendants carefully, and curiosity crept over her features. The signal was never given.

"Thank you," she said earnestly, and turned to lead her guests up to her apartments.

Soderini and his group of priests and lay brothers were treated to a small but adequate banquet and plied with wine. Ottaviano's presence was requested and he, uncomfortable with unguided conversation and social niceties, spoke not a word unless pressed, in which case, he offered up monosyllables. Only those of us who passed in and out of the adjacent kitchen saw our lady's armed guards waiting, lest she call.

When the meat course was finished and the kitchen maid carried away the dirty plates, the tipsy bishop turned to his tense but faintly smiling hostess, and announced: "You and your family are privileged indeed, Madonna Caterina! His Holiness has entrusted me with a happy invitation. Ser Ottaviano, Pope Alexander is offering the hand of his beautiful daughter, Lucrezia, to you!"

Caterina drew in a sharp breath. It was not the judgment she feared, but certainly not what she expected. With the eyes of Soderini and his entourage upon her, she said, dazed, "I never expected this! We are so . . . honored."

What that, she glanced pointedly at Ottaviano, who could only repeat his mother's words. He looked to her, uncertain whether he should be fearful or rejoicing.

For Soderini's sake, Caterina forced a smile. "You must forgive us, Excellency. Such incredible news has left us stunned and overwhelmed. And as a mother, I am obliged to put at least a day's consideration into the matter. But here! Let us celebrate the honor itself! Let us drink to the health of His Holiness!"

She lifted her cup, and the others followed suit. At that point, she ordered several bottles of finer wine to be brought up from the cellar, and saw to it that the bishop and his companions drank their fill. By the time Caterina left, Soderini was incoherent and his head was starting to droop toward his plate.

Caterina, however, was fully sober and her mood was growing fouler by the moment as the implications began to occur to her. I half ran to keep up with her as she headed for the desk in her sitting room, and hurriedly supplied her with paper, quill, ink.

"To Florence," she dictated, "and Giovanni . . ."

My love,

The Bishop of Volterra, Soderini, has come from Pope Alexander, who has offered Ottaviano the hand of his daughter, Lucrezia.

Some would see this as an advantage; Ottaviano, after all, would have an indirect influence upon the papacy, and Forlì would at last have powerful military backing, no less than the might of Rome.

But I tell you that I know the mind of Rodrigo Borgia better than most. My time in Rome taught me that he can never be trusted. In fact, he tried to convince me to murder my own husband—which, of course, I would not consider—as part of his scheme to steal the papacy.

Because I refused him, he would not hesitate to strike back at me, even now.

My cousin Giovanni Sforza of Pesaro married Lucrezia, though, as you know, the marriage was annulled. He wrote to me about the Borgia household and the insults and threats he was forced to endure. I thought he was crazy at first because of the unbelievable, revolting charges he made—that Lucrezia was having affairs with both her father and eldest brother. I never doubted him, though, when he said he feared for his life. He was convinced that Borgia meant to poison him and seize Pesaro.

If I say yes to Borgia, my poor, unwitting Ottaviano will descend into that viper's pit in Rome. Borgia would claim his property, and Ottaviano would put up no defense. Imola and Forlì—and, I have no doubt, my poor son—would be lost.

If I say no, Borgia will find another cause to strip my lands from me.

Either way, this invitation strikes me as an omen that Borgia's lustful eye has finally taken notice of my possessions. It can only be a matter of time before he takes his revenge.

If you have other information, or are certain that my reasoning is faulty in some respect, send a messenger at once. Otherwise, I shall write a letter for His Holiness's eyes only and send it with the bishop.

So now you must come home. You know how terribly I love and miss you. Little Giovanni yearns for his papa's knee.

Your loving wife,
Caterina

Giovanni apparently concurred with his wife, for over the next week of entertaining Bishop Soderini and his entourage, Caterina received no urgent messages from Florence. On the last day of Soderini's stay, he again pressed the Lady of Forlì for an answer; she demurred, but gave him a sealed letter to deliver personally to Borgia. I wrote the text of the letter as Caterina dictated, and agreed with her logic: regardless of whether Ottaviano married

Lucrezia or not, Forlì and Imola were in danger. Why risk the life of her son unnecessarily?

To His Holiness the Pope, Alexander the Sixth
Most Holy Father,
   Greetings from Forlì. May this letter find you well.
   My son Ottaviano and I were deeply honored by the offer of your charming and beautiful daughter's hand. We do not take your favor and generosity lightly; indeed, we were surprised and overjoyed when Bishop Soderini relayed the happy news.
   It is precisely because I take your offer so seriously that I must, for now, decline, though I am sorely tempted. I have not forgotten our friendship of years earlier, and I remember too well the beautiful, well-mannered little Lucrezia, with her golden curls. I was always fond of her and would never wish to mar her happiness.
   For that reason, I must tell you that Ottaviano has been slow to mature and as yet lacks the discipline to be a good husband or papal emissary. I have recently secured for him a condotta, *whereby he can receive a year of military training. This is necessary for the development of his body and mind.*
   Your Holiness's affairs are too pressing for such a humble soul as I to demand that you wait in your search for a proper suitor. Rather than insult you with such a request, I instead humbly withdraw Ottaviano from your consideration. You and the lovely Lucrezia will surely be better served by a more worthy candidate.
   Your humble servant in Christ,
   Caterina Sforza
   Regent of Forlì

A few days after Bishop Soderini and his minions departed, sentinels spotted Ser Giovanni's traveling party on the outskirts of Forlì. Excited, Caterina changed quickly into one of her better dresses and I accompanied her, carrying little Giovanni downstairs so that he could be one of the first to greet his father.

Giovanni's unmarked carriage stopped in front of the lowered drawbridge. It was Giovanni's habit to throw open the door of his carriage, sprint across the bridge, and take Caterina in his arms. This time, the gleaming black carriage door stayed shut too long; Caterina frowned at the delay, and the baby grew restless. Eventually, Caterina stepped onto the bridge herself.

Two of Giovanni's strongest guards emerged from the far side of the carriage, their arms linked to form a chair between them. Giovanni sat in that chair of flesh, his arms wrapped about the guards' solid shoulders. He wore no boots; part of his left legging had been cut away to expose his foot and ankle. The same leg was extended straight in front of him, and supported gingerly beneath the knee and shin by a slender young page. With Giovanni's left foot leading, the awkward quartet made their way haltingly across the narrow wooden bridge.

"Is he injured? Did he fall?" Caterina shouted anxiously at the guards.

In reply, Giovanni shook his head and motioned for her to go back and wait. When the four made it across the bridge, Giovanni, who was clearly in a great deal of pain and could only manage a sickly smile for his wife, warned us all to stay clear of the foot and not even brush up against it.

Only then did he kiss Caterina and say sheepishly, "Gout."

A glance at his left lower leg confirmed it. His great toe was an alarming shade of deep red, and so swollen that the skin looked shiny and ready to burst from the pressure. The outer joint of the toe bulged outward.

Caterina looked stricken. Gout was not uncommon and often struck wealthy, corpulent men after an excess of meat and wine. But the form of gout that tormented the Medici family was especially virulent, attacking not just the joints but also the internal organs, and had brought Il Magnifico and his father early, agonizing ends.

Giovanni tried to kiss his squirming son, but the baby landed an innocent kick in his father's midsection that caused the latter to wince; I took the child back and followed as the largest man at arms scooped Giovanni up and carried him to the bedroom he shared with Caterina.

All linens were pulled aside, as Giovanni could not tolerate the touch of them against his inflamed skin. As the giant guard lowered his master carefully onto the mattress, Giovanni could not repress a cry of pain as his left heel touched down. His inner ankle and all the surrounding flesh were fiery red and puffy, and during the last part of the journey, his knee had begun to ache as well. Caterina cut away the leggings and pulled it back to reveal the angry, swollen joint, while Giovanni gritted his teeth and moaned.

Caterina called at once for the physician who had attended him on his trip.

"Poppy is the only thing that can ease this sort of pain," the doctor said. "Large amounts of cherries also help to lessen the severity of the attack, but he would not eat enough to prevent this one. Give him quantities of water, and no wine or spirits until the attack has passed."

With that, he mixed up a bitter potion that Giovanni drank eagerly. Within half an hour, Giovanni was groggy but in much less pain. Caterina brought a chair to his bedside and sat with him for hours, talking, though she said nothing about spurning Borgia's marriage offer to Ottaviano. Instead, she spoke cheerfully about little Giovanni and successful business matters as the elder Giovanni drifted drowsily in and out of the conversation.

When Giovanni finally fell asleep, Caterina took the doctor aside.

"There is no cure for the disease," the doctor said, "and no reliable treatment from preventing the attacks; each new one does fresh damage. But it's summer, and you should be able to buy fresh cherries; dried are good, too. I will show the kitchen how to cook them down to make a syrup, which he must take several times a day. His kidneys are paining him as well. This syrup will help dissolve any stones."

"We will administer it to him faithfully. But is there nothing we can do to ease *this* attack?" Caterina demanded. "Giovanni cannot spend his days sleeping, and I can't bear to see him in such agony."

The doctor hesitated a moment. "There is a natural spring only a few hours' ride from here," he said. "San Piero in Bagno. Have you heard of it?"

Caterina nodded.

"Other physicians and patients swear by it. There is some sort of mineral in the water that miraculously relieves the pain, cheers the spirit, and shortens the attacks. Overall, the effect of soaking the affected limb in the water for some hours, as well as drinking the water, is salutary." The doctor's tone grew candid. "You are braver than most women, so I shall tell you the truth: Ser Giovanni might well have died from this attack—not so much for what it has done to his legs as to his heart. He is very weak right now and needs a long convalescence. If he does not rest, but continues to have these attacks, I would not expect him to live many more years."

Caterina did not shrink from the truth, but asked bluntly, "If your wife were as ill as Giovanni—God forbid—would you send her to San Piero?"

"I would do so immediately, Madonna—the minute he is able to walk again. The journey is a short one, else I would not recommend it."

Caterina sighed. "Then it is done."

For three days, Giovanni languished, three pillows propped beneath his left foot and knee. He was restless and despite the poppy's sedating effect, managed to accomplish a good deal of business from his bed. When the swelling and redness finally retreated, he began to make his way around the apartment with a cane, cheerfully joking about his infirmity.

At that point, Caterina shared the doctor's grim assessment with her husband. She spared him nothing; she was frightened, and wanted Giovanni to be frightened, too—enough to take his cherry potion with him to San Piero in Bagno. At the same time, she was unhappy to contemplate his departure; she had missed him terribly during his absence, and could not bear the thought of being separated from him when he was ill.

Giovanni resisted. His doctor could care for him adequately at Ravaldino—wasn't the fact that he was better so soon proof of it? And he, too, hated the thought of leaving his wife and little son behind again for an indefinite period of time.

Yet Caterina persisted. Logic was on her side, and Giovanni eventually yielded. On the day he departed for San Piero, he stood with her on the opposite bank of the moat and embraced her as though he never intended to let go.

I waited just inside the fortress as Giovanni and Caterina reluctantly parted, and he balanced upon his cane and the coachman's shoulder in order to climb gingerly into the carriage. As it rolled off, Caterina stood in the meadow, waving and watching until it was out of sight.

Later that afternoon, a ragamuffin appeared at Ravaldino with a letter addressed to *The Lady Dea, Ravaldino Fortress, Forlì.* I excused myself in order to read it in the privacy of my downstairs bedchamber.

I recognized the handwriting on the address immediately, but was disturbed by the fact that the letter was somewhat thicker than usual; had something untoward happened to Luca? Was this some sort of good-bye letter explaining his reasons?

Anxiously, I slipped a letter knife beneath the unengraved seal and read:

Dearest beloved,

 With each passing day, I love you more.

 Today, I am moved to warn you: Forlì and Imola are not safe.

 Another day, and Pope Alexander's alliances change again. Young Cesare Borgia has been named captain general of the papal army. He and his father are negotiating a secret agreement with Louis XII. They have offered Milan and Naples to France in exchange for the French army's support in taking the entire Romagna. Cesare has dreams of ruling the region, and will be dubbed "Duke of Romagna" once the invasion has been successful. Right now only the might of Venice stands in their way.

 In May, Cesare married one of King Louis's cousins. He was made Duke of Valence, and has taken to calling himself Valentino.

 I fear for you. Go to Florence; it is your best hope for safety.

 These are exceedingly dangerous people; their word cannot be trusted. All the rumors you have heard are true. Cesare despises his father bitterly for taking liberties with his sister from the time she was a tiny child, yet Cesare now schemes with his father all the same, as Alexander is his one means to power. Still, Cesare loves Lucrezia desperately, and will stop at nothing to protect her; there are some who say he loves her too well.

 I pray that you remain in good health. How I miss you!

I did not share this immediately with Caterina, as she was still undone by worry over Ser Giovanni's illness.

Surely Luca knew that I could not leave Ravaldino without Caterina, and that Caterina had recently written to her uncle Ludovico saying, "If I must die, then I will die like a man, in battle." My existence was, as it had always been, in the Lady of Forlì's hands.

I waited a few days, but by then, Caterina was overcome by joy at receiving her first letter from her husband, stating that he had arrived safely and that the accommodations were adequate, if interesting. His note was intentionally cheerful and comforting, and for a day, Caterina forgot her cares.

The nearness of San Piero allowed for easy, quick correspondence;

Caterina was able to read about what Giovanni had done only the day before. For the first week, she received a letter from him every day, describing his fellow sufferers, the pools made by the rocks and the "brimstone-scented" waterfalls that filled them.

The second week, she received only two letters from her husband. Both were cheerful, but held fewer details. She wrote a private letter to Giovanni's physician; the doctor admitted that his patient had "suffered a small setback," but that he hoped for a full recovery. Only the doctor's reassuring tone kept her from hurrying to Giovanni's side.

For the first half of the third week, there was no news at all . . . until Thursday, when, before dawn, Caterina received an urgent summons from the doctor, who wrote that "Ser Giovanni's condition is dire, come at once."

Caterina dashed down the stairs and swung onto a horse. For once, I did not follow. Perhaps it was because I believed that Ser Giovanni could not have deteriorated so swiftly; he was too young and strong, and so recently in robust health. Even Lorenzo the Magnificent, who had been stricken hardest of all by gout, had survived to the age of forty-three.

Morning and midday passed with no word. In the late afternoon I climbed a parapet to look to the south, and the road leading to San Piero. I stood there until dark, and still there was no sign of a rider.

When morning came again I fell prey to a growing uneasiness and climbed up once more to Ravaldino's roof. It was mid-September, and the sun was strong, but the breeze cool. No doubt the sentinels thought I was simply taking the sun, but I remained, pacing slowly from battlement to battlement, staring south for almost an hour.

At last I spotted black forms moving steadily across the road, kicking up dust. As they neared, I made out two riders, a carriage, and two wagons, one laden with goods. The second wagon appeared empty from a distance.

I hurried down several flights of stairs to the main entrance, where the horses' hooves were still clattering. The riders were two of Giovanni's men-at-arms, and their gazes were fixed straight ahead as they reined their horses to a stop and dismounted. After they handed the reins off to a groom, one of them opened the door to the carriage. Caterina emerged, her features as set as stone; when she first caught my gaze, I saw a flicker of raw emotion behind the mask. She would not speak; her demeanor was a warning to those who might dare to trouble her with words.

Her steps echoed as she passed me. I turned finally to look at the last wagon, which was not empty after all, but bore a long, slender coffin made of freshly hewn wood.

Thirty-two

After Ser Giovanni left us, the world grew uglier with each passing day. Caterina immersed herself in silence; she would not discuss her grief, even with me, but went about her daily business with an unsmiling, strained expression. Her one desire was to entomb her beloved husband in Ravaldino so that she would someday be buried with him, but Giovanni's brother, Lorenzo, retrieved Giovanni's body so that it could be buried in the Medici-sponsored church of San Lorenzo in Florence, not far from where the old Palazzo Medici lay.

A grim Christmas passed, and not long after New Year's, unhappy news came: Venice had signed a treaty with France, which meant that the way was now clear for King Louis to march into Italy by way of Milan. The time came for me to show Caterina the letter from Luca stating that the Borgias had allied themselves with France and were eager to claim Forlì and Imola for themselves.

Duke Ludovico was extremely nervous about the invasion; try as he would, the French would not negotiate with him, nor would Pope Alexander. Distraught, he contented himself by buying as many mercenaries and artillery as he could afford. As he now had few friends, he promised Caterina his full support. Caterina had no illusions; the French army was one of the most powerful in Europe, and if Ludovico met them in battle, he had best have luck on his side. Yet after Ser Giovanni's death, Caterina had not been able to put her mind to anything, much less politics. I had hoped that Luca's letter of warning might stir her to action, but she did nothing.

That changed early in March, when a dozen horsemen bearing Borgia's papal coat of arms rode into the meadow across from Ravaldino and sounded a trumpet. The commander insisted on speaking to Caterina and Ottaviano at once.

The two appeared on the battlements. Caterina wisely would not go to meet them, nor would she let them enter the fortress. Instead, she forced them to read aloud the papal bull signed by Alexander and seventeen of the cardinals in the Sacred College.

"To that daughter of iniquity, Caterina Sforza, and her son, Ottaviano Riario . . ."

I was outraged that a man like Borgia could accuse my mistress of "iniquity." Interestingly, the bull never mentioned Caterina's marriage to Giovanni or her new son. Instead, it falsely claimed that for the past three years, Caterina had refused to pay the required annual tribute to the Apostolic Treasury "despite continual warning."

At that, Caterina let go a short, sarcastic laugh. "That's a lie!"

Girolamo's agreement when he left Rome specified that he would continue to receive his captain's salary. The Vatican never paid it, and for the past eleven years, Caterina had been allowed to deduct her tribute from it. If anything, the Vatican owed *her* money, but the commander ignored her and continued to read.

Such rebellious and arrogant behavior had forced Pope Alexander to invest the captain of the papal army, Cesare Borgia, with Imola and Forlì. Caterina and her family should pack their possessions and leave at once, lest Captain Borgia be forced to take military measures to claim his new property.

Caterina took Ottaviano's hand and cried out, in a clear voice: "These charges are false and easily disproven. Tell His Holiness Pope Alexander that I shall send an envoy to Rome who will prove that a mistake has been made."

I was surprised by her response, yet after a moment's reflection, came to understand it. She was responding to the bull in good faith, as though the charges were sincere, thus forcing Alexander either to find another excuse, or to give up all pretense and admit to his naked and illegal ambition.

More important, she was stalling the invasion, and winning herself more time.

Caterina immediately recruited one of Forlì's most prominent citizens, a Doctor dalle Selle, learned in medicine and law and the art of accounting. The very next day he was off to Rome, and was surprised and pleased to be offered access to the papal treasury's records. They revealed that the treasury owed the Riario sixty thousand ducats. Dalle Selle was ecstatic, and Caterina relieved.

Still, it made no difference. The pope refused to grant the doctor an audience, and not one cardinal in Rome, including Raffaele Riario and della Rovere, would receive dalle Selle to listen to his tale of injustice.

When the crestfallen dalle Selle returned, he brought back with him a new phrase that was on every Roman's lips: *the Borgia Terror.* Pope Alexander and his son needed money for their war, and had discovered that murdering their enemies in the Sacred College was an efficient way to raise it, since a cardinal's property and wealth reverted to the Church upon his death. And the wily Rodrigo Borgia had perfected a poison that killed slowly, within days instead of hours, without arsenic's telltale symptoms. Already the fearful citizens of Rome had given it a name: *cantarella.*

Even before Doctor dalle Selle had learned the truth in Rome, Caterina began making preparations for war, funneling whatever grief she felt over Ser Giovanni's death into decisive action. Despite the threat of a French invasion, Milan was still one of the mightiest forces in Italy, and Caterina made good use of her uncle Ludovico's sudden unequivocal support of Imola and Forlì. She took whatever arms he would spare, and recruited some of his most talented fighters, including her older brother, Alessandro Landriani, and Dionigi Naldi, a much-respected castellan. She even recruited the respected *condottiero* Scipio, a natural son born to Girolamo before he married Caterina, whom she treated as a favored relative. She hired the unruly mercenary commander, a French-born Italian named Gianotto, who brought with him an undisciplined group of Gascons; Caterina set them and the townsfolk to work on strengthening Ravaldino's fortifications and the city walls. Even Ottaviano set aside his slothfulness to work alongside the others, shoveling tunnels and pushing heavy carts filled with dirt.

But Caterina was too shrewd to rely upon a single ally, even though no one in those days believed that the powerful duchy of Milan could ever be overthrown. Besides strengthening the ties with her uncle, Caterina sent a message to Florence, asking to meet with a diplomat to discuss an alliance. Her marriage to Giovanni de' Medici and her close ties to his surviving older brother, Ludovico di Pierfrancesco, were proof enough of her predisposition toward the city—and there was also the fact that her preferential sales of vast quantities of wheat to famine-struck Florence had saved its people from starvation. At that time the Republic had been so grateful to the Lady of Forlì that they had made her an honorary citizen. Where was their gratitude now?

Florence was still a French ally, and would therefore be spared during the invasion. If Imola and Forlì could be inserted into the alliance, they, too, would be spared. If not, Florence still owed Caterina military support. And there was the matter, too, of Ottaviano's military *condotta*. An agreement concerning his price still had to be negotiated.

Months passed, but the Florentines gave no reply. Caterina pressed again, without success. Finally, in late July, their emissary appeared.

Niccolò Machiavelli was tall, with long limbs and wide shoulders, both of which emphasized the surprisingly small size of his egg-shaped head. His foreshortened jaw made his forehead appear abnormally high, especially given his receding hairline. His hair was odd, too, cut so short on the top that it seemed shaved, yet it was long in the back and on the sides, where he tucked it behind his ears. His eyes were small and darting, his brows narrow and thin; his long, straight nose was his most fortunate feature.

Caterina received him in Paradise, her thronelike chair set with its back to a great window that looked onto the Apennines. After introducing himself with an awkward bow, the unlikely diplomat stood back and waited for his hostess to speak.

Caterina did. Normally, such encounters took place over days, with much entertainment, food, and drink, yet Machiavelli looked to be impervious to distraction. He wore all black, like a priest, and clasped his hands at his waist like an attentive pupil. At my lady's urging, I poured her a cup of wine and offered one to Ser Niccolò; he refused it.

After numerous failed attempts to engage her visitor in small talk, Caterina proceeded to the matter at hand. "I have spoken numerous times to my uncle, the Duke of Milan," she said. "He is very eager to give Ottaviano a *condotta*, and has offered him twelve thousand ducats." Florence, at this time, was offering ten thousand. "And His Grace says that Ottaviano will receive a number of honors, as well." She paused. "I am very much tempted to accept it, even though Ottaviano wants badly to go to Florence."

"It is good," Machiavelli said pleasantly, "to have such loyal family."

Grasping the arms of her chair, Caterina leaned toward him. "I, too, would far prefer that Ottaviano go to Florence. But the *condotta* is meaningless to me unless it comes with military backing for Forlì and Imola."

Machiavelli regarded her impassively. "Are you asking whether Florence can provide you with men and arms?"

Caterina gazed at him with faint scorn; she was used to ambassadors who grasped delicacy and nuance and the importance of winning a friend, not just negotiating a contract. "Is that not why you are here, to discuss just such a thing?"

Machiavelli glanced down briefly at his carefully clasped hands. "I am here," he said, "to discuss your son's military position in Florence, and his recompense. The Republic has not granted me the authority to speak to you about an alliance."

Caterina clicked her tongue in disgust and recoiled. "Then you had best get permission as soon as possible," she countered.

The diplomat tried to stammer a reply, but Caterina waved him silent.

"Tell your Republic this," she said. "I have grain, and you have need for it; when the French finally come—whether Florence is their ally or not—your citizens will want for food unless you are well supplied. As for the *condotta*, twelve thousand is a paltry sum, considering that Ottaviano brings his own weaponry and armor."

With that, she dismissed him, and left him to wander about Paradise to find his own entertainment.

A week passed—sufficient time for Machiavelli to have received a reply from his government. Caterina summoned him a second time, again dressing like a queen and sitting on her "throne" in front of Ravaldino's best view of the Apennines.

"I have good news," Ser Niccolò said, his tight little smile a bit brighter than usual. "I have communicated with our city council. Owing to the fact that you are supplying Ser Ottaviano with weaponry and armor, we are pleased to offer him a *condotta* for a salary of twelve thousand ducats."

"Ottaviano will be happy to accept the offer," Caterina replied, "provided that Florence's protection of Imola and Forlì comes with it."

Machiavelli's cheeks and nose faintly reddened. "It does not, Your Illustriousness. The council refused me permission to discuss it."

Caterina rose. "If Florence can spare neither men nor arms," she said acidly, "then the least she can do is list me as her ally, so that neither the French nor Cesare Borgia have the right to invade my lands."

With that, she strode from the room, as Machiavelli called after her: "I will see, Your Illustriousness, what I can do."

Machiavelli was true to his word. Two weeks later, word came that Florence had listed Caterina Sforza as her ally. King Louis reacted by saying, "She is an enemy of His Holiness Pope Alexander; I cannot go against the pope's wishes."

Alexander scoffed, insisting that such a move by Florence was invalid.

Even as we were reeling at such news, worse came from Caterina's uncle. Louis XII's troops—more than ten thousand of them—had crossed the Alps and invaded Milan, forcing Duke Ludovico to flee for his life. Mighty Milan was now in French hands; the die was cast.

Those who did not know Caterina well expected her to take as many of her possessions as possible and flee; there was time, as the French army was well north of us, and Borgia had not yet reached the Romagna. Florence would welcome her, and she could remain there until Alexander, thirty years her senior, died. With luck, Cardinal della Rovere might finally be elected to the papacy and reinstate Caterina as Lady of Forlì.

But unlike her uncle, Caterina would not flee. She was too proud to bow to the likes of the Borgias; even so, she would not risk her children, especially her beloved little Giovanni. She sent him and his brother Cesare to Florence, where they would be tenderly cared for by the nuns at the convent of Le Murate. Ottaviano insisted on remaining with his mother. But many carts loaded with Caterina's valuables left Ravaldino for Florence, where her brother-in-law would keep them safe. There were a few fine things she kept: a slender mother-of-pearl perfume vial that had somehow survived unscathed, and the fine Toledo halberd Rodrigo Borgia had given her years ago.

I sent a few precious items to Florence, but many things I could not part with: the book by Ficino that Ser Giovanni had given me, my triumph cards, and all of my brother Matteo's writings, including the diary, magical diagrams, and the mysterious brown powder.

As if I could summon the angel after all these years, now that everything was lost. As if it would swoop down from Heaven and rescue us all.

Stripped of its brocade and velvet appointments, its carpets, paintings, tapestries, and fine furniture, Paradise was stark and ghostly; our voices echoed off the bare walls and floors. Gone were the sounds of children's laughter and servants' gossip; instead, we heard the commander's bark as the soldiers drilled down in the walled-in yard. Caterina dismissed all household servants who expressed fear of the coming invasion and had me move my things upstairs to her bedroom, where I slept beside her. By then it was almost winter, and the gray sky and ceaseless drizzle only added to our sense of gloom.

Late one night, in the hours before dawn, I woke to a crashing storm and realized that Caterina was no longer in the bed next to me. I called softly to her, but received no reply; concerned, I lit the lamp. She was not in the bedchamber, so I rose and walked barefoot on Paradise's cold stone floors searching for her.

On impulse, I went down the narrow, stifling corridor that led to the water closet. Caterina almost always preferred the chamber pot at night, especially in cold weather, and it was my habit to empty it every morning in the water closet, pitching the offal down to land in the latrine several floors below.

But this night, apparently, was different; I could see the glow of a lamp as I approached the open door. I covered my nose at the stench, and peered inside to find Caterina.

She was so engrossed in her work that she had not heard me come. On the stone bench, as far as possible from the opening where one sat to do one's business, sat the lamp, next to a shallow bowl with a sip's worth of water in it. Beside the bowl was a piece of parchment set upon a brass plate, and beside the parchment, a lovely mother-of-pearl vial lay on its side, its stopper in place. Save for her eyes and forehead, Caterina's face was covered by an old woolen scarf; thick leather riding gloves covered her hands. She dipped a piece of uncombed wool the size of a coin carefully into the water, then, working quickly so that it did not drip, brushed the wool over the parchment, and waited for the water to be absorbed.

"Poison," I blurted as the realization struck me. I had been puzzled by the fact that she had kept such a fine thing instead of sending it away.

Caterina deliberately set the wool back into the water, then turned, frowning. Her words were muffled, but her gestures were quite clear: I was to touch nothing, but leave immediately.

I returned to bed. When she at last returned, her scarf and gloves were gone—presumably tossed into the latrine—and the pretty vial, now stoppered, was in her hand. She disappeared into the closet to stuff it into the bottom of one of two remaining trunks. At her bidding, I poured water from the pitcher over her hands as she held them over the basin.

Once she had dried them, I voiced the question again. "That *was* poison, wasn't it, Madonna?" My tone held disapproval.

Caterina swung her legs onto the bed and pulled up the covers. "It was a gift," she said matter-of-factly, "from Rodrigo Borgia, many years ago. I'm simply returning it to him . . . without the vial." She paused. "The parchment is drying on the plate in the water closet. Don't touch them—either could kill you. When it's ready, I'll deal with it myself. Put out the lamp, will you?"

"You mean to murder the pope, then." It seemed a mad, unthinkable thing... and yet, knowing that the pope was Rodrigo Borgia, it did not seem so shocking.

My lady shrugged. "Call it preemptive warfare."

"But if you're caught, they'll kill you!"

"Please," she said, disgusted. "They intend to kill me anyway. Besides, what's the difference between my hacking Cesare Borgia's head off with a longsword and this? Now put out the lamp!"

I lifted the glass globe and snuffed the flame with my thumb and finger, then crawled beneath the linens. As I lay awake, listening to the storm, the horror of what my mistress planned faded. I thought of all the cardinals who had died at the Borgia's hands, and the thousands of innocents who would die in the Romagna, all to feed the Borgias' greed.

Suddenly, murder seemed a good thing—a *necessary* thing—and Caterina a hero.

When the parchment was dry, Caterina put on two pairs of long leather gloves and wrote a letter to His Holiness in her own hand, begging for his mercy and asking for compromise. After that, she impressed her seal upon the wax, and wrapped the letter in velvet—scarlet, the color of a proud Sforza. The whole was placed inside a container of fine cedar, and sent with couriers to Rome.

The assassination did not go well; seeing the container and knowing it was from Caterina, Pope Alexander would not open it, and immediately threw the men who brought it into the dungeon of the Castel Sant'Angelo. The head of the expedition from Forlì immediately confessed all.

In late November, a mass and public celebration were held in Rome, thanking God for saving His Holiness from the wicked murderess in Forlì. In the church square, Alexander addressed the public—and especially the Republic of Florence, which he warned would face "disastrous consequences" should it provide the "daughter of perdition" with any further support. Cesare and his father now had good reason to pursue her relentlessly, and punish her as cruelly as they wished.

Caterina never denied responsibility.

Thirty-three

December came, and with it Cesare Borgia and his army of fifteen thousand men. He rode with five hundred Swiss into nearby Imola, whose governor willingly opened its gates to him; within minutes of Borgia's arrival, the city was his . . . and within minutes, the citizens came to regret it. The fearsome Swiss immediately started pillaging while Cesare had the most beautiful of Imola's women rounded up and brought to him. Rumor said that he raped them all, a new one every night, and kept them as slaves until he tired of them.

The fortress at Imola, however, did not bow. Its castellan, Dionigi Naldi, was unreservedly loyal to Caterina and held off Cesare's army for days, despite the fact that he, Naldi, was wounded in the head. He sent word to the contessa, asking whether he might surrender in the face of overwhelming odds; Borgia was so impressed by Naldi's loyalty that his troops escorted the wounded castellan home.

At the news that the city had fallen, Caterina sent her eldest son, Ottaviano, off to Florence with his brothers; the youth put up little protest, but departed with alacrity before Borgia's troops arrived in Forlì.

He was not the only one to fear the approaching army. The next day, two Forlivese city elders requested an audience with Caterina in Ravaldino.

She granted it, expecting to receive a promise from her townspeople to defend her; instead she was informed that Forlì intended to open their gates to Cesare as well. When the contessa pressed them as to the citizens' change of heart, the elders confessed that Luffo Numai had been instrumental in swaying the Forlivese to surrender. Clearly, Numai's loyalties lay with the one who possessed the largest army.

Furious, Caterina turned the cannon on Numai's palazzo, but it was dusk and we could not see whether the palace had been struck. As we stood beside the gunners, watching the sulfurous cloud dissipate in the air, Caterina turned to me with an urgent air.

"Come," she said.

I followed her back to Paradise, where, at her urging, I put on my heaviest woolen cloak and changed into my sturdiest boots. Lamp in hand, she went into her trunk in the closet, where the mother-of-pearl flask was hidden, and retrieved a large black key, then signaled for me to follow her down the hallway leading back to the water closet. Halfway down the corridor, she knelt and ran her hand over the dark wainscoting on the western wall. I heard a faint click and stared, amazed, as a panel popped open. Like Caterina, I leaned toward the gap and drew in the stench of the latrine and mildew. She held up the lamp to the opening, revealing a narrow, apparently fathomless shaft leading downward; on one side of the mildewed stone wall were metal rungs.

Caterina set the lamp on the floor, then cautiously lowered herself into the shaft by catching the top rung with her hands and finding the lower rungs with her feet.

"Here it grows difficult," she said. "Tuck up your skirts, and mind the cloak doesn't get in your way. It's cold, but it's easier without gloves. Just keep climbing down, and follow the sound of my voice."

Her head soon disappeared. I drew a breath and entered the shaft. The metal rungs were slippery and freezing cold; I had to grip them with all my strength to keep from losing my balance. The farther downward we crawled, the darker it became, and the more I noticed the bitter cold and the stink.

After torturous minutes, Caterina's voice said beneath me, "I'm at the bottom. Get ready to step down. I'll be right behind you, to catch you. Don't worry, you can't fall."

I felt for the next rung with my foot, but encountered only stone. I felt

Caterina's hands upon my waist and, drawing a breath for courage, let myself drop. The soles of my boots immediately touched against solid ground, and I expelled the breath as a laugh.

"Hush," Caterina warned. "The soldiers might hear us."

I turned to her. My eyes had grown used to the darkness, enough to make out her form but not her features. We appeared to be in a gap between the fortress walls, and standing on bare earth; my nose told me that the latrine was very close by.

"Now turn to the left, and take two paces forward."

I did so, and nearly stumbled over what seemed to be a wooden hatch. Caterina put her hand over mine and guided it to the handle, made of rope. The hatch opened onto pure blackness.

"It's a tunnel," she hissed into my ear. "I went through it myself last night, while you were sleeping, just to be sure it was still open. It leads all the way past the city walls to an olive grove. You must leave, Dea. In another day or two, there will be armies marching through the streets of Forlì. But I can arrange to have a horse waiting for you in the grove by morning. I want you to go to Florence and raise little Giovanni for me."

I thought of Florence and wondered suddenly whether Luca might be there. But something rose in me, something as foolhardy and stubborn as Caterina's refusal to surrender Ravaldino to the Borgia.

"No," I said.

"You *must*! My son must be raised by someone I trust."

"You're meant to raise him, not I," I said firmly.

Silence followed. I could not see Caterina's expression, but I could well imagine the rage in it.

"How many times must I say that I will not surrender!" she hissed. "I am a Sforza, like my father, and I will die honorably—by my own hand if need be—but I will not give myself over to Borgia!"

"And if there is a third way?" I whispered.

She ignored the question. "Dea, I am ordering you to go."

"Caterina," I said forcefully, "I am telling you that I will not. You may punish me for my insolence, but I, too, must obey the instincts of my heart."

With that, I turned around and, after taking two steps, swung myself up onto the rungs and began to climb.

. . .

Caterina did not speak another word to me that night, nor did she acknowledge my presence for the next two days; instead, she took her secretary, Giovanni di Casale, to her bed, forcing me to sleep downstairs in my room or else in her closet. Of course, she had a legitimate reason to be sullen: our spies had revealed that the city fathers of Forlì had signed a document surrendering the town to Cesare Borgia.

On the nineteenth of December 1499, the Forlivese opened the city walls and Cesare Borgia, captain general of the papal army and the Duke of Valentino, rode through the streets behind a battalion of five hundred Swiss.

Caterina, her commanders, and I watched grimly from the ramparts, trying to catch a glimpse of the one called Valentino. The distance and the bitter, icy rain made it impossible to see his features, but we recognized him from the gold caparison on his black palfrey and the honor guard that flanked him. Few Forlivese came to watch, given the weather, and the streets were mostly empty. Rather than parade through town in such foul weather, Borgia rode directly to the palace of Luffo Numai—a fact that made Caterina swear like her soldiers. His army continued on, to encamp in the fields east of Ravaldino.

By sunset, the rain had tapered off, leaving the city coated in ice. It was not enough to discourage Cesare's soldiers, who could not wait to attack the helpless public; screams and shouts filled the air throughout the night.

Unlike his men, Cesare chose to bide his time and play the civilized Christian conqueror, holding his fire until after the holidays had passed. No doubt he would spend them in the luxury of Luffo Numai's palace.

By Christmas Eve, Borgia's troops had installed artillery on the other bank of the moat; more happily, Caterina had forgiven me for my refusal to leave. She seemed to be at peace, finally, with whatever fate awaited her, and the holiday found her in a strangely festive mood.

I could not say the same for myself. The fact that I was now truly trapped inside the fortress filled me with an urgent restlessness, the feeling that there was something that I needed to do before I died.

By dusk, Caterina and all her advisers sat in Paradise's great dining hall. The hearth had been lit and was blazing so fiercely I began to perspire immediately after entering; since Caterina could not go cut a Yule log per the Milanese custom, she had stacked the fireplace high with wood, so that the flames would last through the night. It was the only visible symbol of the holiday. I thought of my last Christmas Eve in Milan, just before the duke had been murdered, and felt a sudden sadness.

This Christmas Eve could not be the same. Inside, Paradise's heavy dining table, capable of seating a hundred people, was occupied by only a dozen, all sitting on hard wooden chairs at the edge nearest the fireplace. All of them, save Caterina, were near-strangers to me: her lover, the red-headed Giovanni di Casale; Alessandro and Francesco Landriani, her half brothers; an adviser, Ser Antonio; Caterina's favorite *condottiero*, Bernardino da Cremona; Girolamo's natural son, the huge and muscular Scipio; and the dreamy-eyed warrior-poet known simply as Marullo. I sat between Ser Antonio and Scipio and smiled with the others, though my thoughts were of Duke Galeazzo's marvelous singers and how we had listened to them in Bona's chamber the day the brick tumbled from the hearth and sent roasting pignoli scattering.

Caterina offered up the first toast of the evening. Duke Ludovico, she optimistically proclaimed to her guests, was already amassing an army to retake Milan. Once he was safely back, he would send several battalions to Forlì. This provoked shouts of approval.

Three roast geese, a platter of the obligatory chestnuts, and candied almonds were set before us. When these were devoured, the musicians— soldiers all—were summoned. Two pipers and three drummers played with such abandon that the floor beneath my feet vibrated.

Caterina, of course, grabbed di Casale's arm and pulled him from the table onto a bare stretch of marble floor. Immediately, she launched into the vigorous skip, step, hop of a driving saltarello; given the heat of the fireplace, her face soon flushed pink.

Before Scipio could turn and invite me to dance, I rose and called to Caterina. "Your Illustriousness, I am in need of fresh air."

I did not wait to hear her reply before rushing through the antechamber to the door that opened to outside, where the air was sweet and cold.

Without thinking, I ran up the stairs to the roof, and leaned against the freezing stone battlement to look down at Forlì below.

On the other side of Ravaldino's moat, slivers of moonlight gleamed dully off the long barrels of Borgia's artillery. Beyond them, lamps painted the windows of the larger dwellings in town. I could hear faint, off-key carols and the drunken shouts—in French, German, and Italian—of the conquering army. But these were nearly drowned out by the laughter and singing coming from the hundreds of inebriated mercenaries on the floor beneath me, and the driving music coming from Paradise.

I stayed until I began to shiver, at which point I headed reluctantly back toward my lady's apartment. As I descended the last flight of stairs, I met Caterina coming up; like me, she had come without her cloak. She was smiling faintly, but her eyes held something poignant and resigned.

"Come," she said gently. "I want to give you a present, in private."

"But I have none for you, Madonna," I said.

"You have already given me everything," she replied.

We walked into her stark bedchamber. She went to the wardrobe and brought out a plain wooden box half the size of her hand, then sat on the edge of the mattress and gestured for me to do likewise. She did not wait for me to open the little box, but pulled out what lay inside: a thin, un-remarkable golden chain with a plain, heart-shaped golden pendant hanging from it.

I was perplexed by the gift, but thanked her politely all the same. She held it beyond my reach and responded, "Just watch."

There was a tiny latch on the side of the heart; she pressed it with her thumb, and the pendant sprang open. Tucked inside was a neatly folded bit of thin paper.

"Don't ever open this unless you intend to use it," she warned. "I put the powder inside the paper so that it won't spill out when the latch springs open. One could take it with wine, if the opportunity arose. In an emer-gency, the paper could be swallowed easily enough." Her tone grew confi-dential. "It's a large dose. It should kill rather quickly."

I folded my hands in my lap and stared at the innocuous-looking piece of paper. "The *cantarella*," I said.

She nodded. "Cesare Borgia will never take me," she said. "Either I am killed in battle or I use this, a gift from his father." She snapped the pendant closed, unlatched the chain, and put it around my neck, then sat back to admire it with a faint, unhappy smile. "I have one, too. Would you help me put it on?"

I was too stunned to disagree, but waited while she fetched the second from the wardrobe. As I unfastened the chain and draped it around the tender skin of her neck, my hands began to quake.

"You must not do this, Madonna."

"If I am captured, I will. Would you prefer to see me raped and tortured by Cesare Borgia? Dragged back to Rome and sentenced to an even worse fate?"

I turned my face away at the thought.

"Now," she said softly, "it's Christmas Eve. Shall we read the cards one last time, to see what the new year holds?"

Despite the tightness in my throat, I nodded and retrieved them from my trunk. When I sat on the mattress and untied the black silk scarf that held the deck, I ran my hand over the worn plaster on the cards and thought of my mother. I wondered who would take the cards after I was dead.

I prayed silently to the angel, who had never seemed more distant. *Bless the cards, and let my words be true.* Then I opened my eyes and waited until conviction gripped me; these were not just Caterina's cards, but mine, too.

I shuffled the cards myself, slowly, thoughtfully, and set the deck down between us. "Cut them, Madonna."

She cut them into three piles, drew three cards from the top of the third stack, and set them down in front of me.

The first was, as we both knew it would be, the Tower, and God's gilded lightning bolt. I saw not the Tower of Babel, but Ravaldino itself, shattering into a hail of jagged stones.

Neither Caterina nor I uttered a word; we knew well what it meant.

I turned over the second card, wishing for a glimmer of hope, and there it was: the Nine of Batons. It was a simple-looking card, nine golden scepters arranged against a background of white, edged by green foliage.

"Strength," I said. "Whatever befalls you, Madonna, you have the strength to endure. There is success here, against all odds." I did not utter all that my instinct told me—that this was strength pushed to the limits of exhaustion, and victory earned at the bitterest cost. I looked on it with dread, but kept my expression carefully neutral.

Caterina nodded solemnly, and pressed a finger to her lips.

In silence, I turned over the third card.

On its face was the painting of a man suspended upside down from a gallows by a rope tied to his ankle. His free leg was bent at the knee and crossed over the other leg, so that his lower body took on the shape of an inverted Arabic numeral 4.

"The Hanged Man," I whispered. This card, too, needed no explanation. Sudden tears welled in my eyes.

Caterina saw them and put a comforting hand upon my forearm; surely she thought I was looking at her death. I drew a steadying breath.

"There are two possible fates here," I said at last. "The choice is yours, Madonna. Whichever you choose, you have the strength to endure."

Only then did I begin to sob. Caterina put her arms around me, and we wept together like sisters.

Caterina went back to her dancing that night, and did not return until the first black hours of Christmas morning. I slipped quietly from the bed at dawn, and as I dressed myself in the dark closet, I decided to find the leather-bound collection of Ficino's writings that Ser Giovanni had so kindly given to me.

I took it to Paradise's dining hall in hopes of finding breakfast, but the room was deserted, and the entire fortress as silent as the dead. I went to the deserted dining hall, where the Christmas Eve fire was reduced to a heap of white ash. Quiet hours passed as I read the words of Marsilio Ficino concerning the soul, God, the order of the heavens, and the proper use of magic, which was to bring enlightenment to humankind.

I remained distracted until the muted blare of a herald's trumpet brought me back to the present. I closed the book and hurried up to the parapet overlooking the moat.

I stared down. On the shore, in front of his own cannon and flanked by a uniformed trumpeter, the captain of the papal army sat astride his warhorse. Cesare Borgia wore a black velvet tunic with a thick insert of pleated white satin at the breast and collar, and a black velvet cape trimmed with thick gold braid and lined with white ermine. His beret was likewise black, with a great white plume that moved with the wind. The effect was one of severe elegance.

At last I could see his face: his lips were even but small, his profile rather flat, his jaw too long. But these irregularities were easily overlooked because of his beautiful dark eyes, which slanted slightly upward at the outer corners; his lids were lined with lashes as black and thick as kohl. His brows were nicely arched, the better to emphasize his eyes; his cheeks were lean and artfully sculpted, and his nose straight, of perfect width and length. His hair was the color of jet and fell without wave or curl to his shoulders. He wore a neatly trimmed goatee and thin mustache in the Parisian style.

If the Lady of Forlì was beautiful, then Cesare Borgia was surely handsome.

"Go fetch your mistress," he shouted.

I flew to Caterina's apartment and shook her awake; the instant she heard the word *Borgia,* she sprang to her feet. I dressed her quickly in the gown she had worn the night before, and covered her tousled hair with a veil.

Within ten minutes, the Lady of Forlì walked out onto the parapet, looking calm and supremely confident. Despite the cold, she would not wear a cloak; she wanted Cesare to see that she was still lithe and fit, still attractive. When she stepped forward to greet Borgia, I hung back.

Caterina looked down, and her eyebrows lifted slightly as she registered the young Borgia's attractiveness. A smile bloomed on her lips.

"Good Christmas morning, Your Grace," she called down, and Borgia called back:

"A blessed Christmastide to you, Madonna Caterina." His voice was deep and resonant, easily heard over the wind.

Caterina's brow lifted again, very slightly, at the insult. She had addressed Borgia as befitted a duke, but he addressed her not by her title, but as a civilian.

"Madonna," Borgia called, "I bring you good tidings on this holiday. Being a generous man of goodwill, Pope Alexander wishes to offer his hand in friendship. He has instructed me to call off the siege and grant you safe conduct to Rome."

Caterina moved to the dizzying edge of the stone precipice. "How very gracious of His Holiness! I trust you to explain to him that I am very happy here in Forlì, and so must decline."

Borgia's smile thinned, but he soon recovered himself.

"Madonna," he called, "Forlì is no longer legally yours; such is the price of attempting to murder a pope. But I have no desire to harm a woman of your courage and beauty. Nor does His Holiness, who in his piety is willing to forgive. Instead, we exhort you to submit to the law."

Caterina's smile vanished as she shouted, "I do not recognize laws when they become weapons wielded by wicked men!"

"You are beside yourself, Madonna," Borgia answered smoothly, "and understandably so, given your dire circumstance. It must be difficult to know that you have but nine hundred men in Ravaldino, whereas I have access to fifteen thousand. Surrender, and His Holiness and I guarantee that you will not be harmed. In fact, we shall make you a most generous offer in the spirit of friendship: come with your children to Rome, and we will give you property and a large pension."

Caterina was unmoved. "If I surrender to you, Your Grace, you will do with me as you please. Your words have no value."

"Untrue!" Borgia countered. "History is full of rulers who wisely chose to surrender and went on to lead prosperous lives. Do you not want to see your sons grow up to rule? Or will you doom them to die as their mother watches?"

Caterina flushed. "You would like to know whether my sons are here with me, wouldn't you? Actually, sir, history shows that the brave's legacy endures, while cowards' deaths are soon forgotten. I am my father's daughter; I am not stupid, nor am I afraid to die."

In her vehemence, she had leaned so far over the bulwark's edge that I stepped forward to get a secure hold on her arm.

"And I am my father's son," Cesare answered, a hint of impatience in his tone. "I swear on my family name that if you will come peacefully with me, none in Ravaldino shall be harmed. Not even your pretty lady-in-waiting, who seems to have a good deal of sense." He grinned up at me; there was something unsettlingly familiar about his wolfish smile. "You would not want her to die—or worse, would you?" He spoke to me. "What are you called, lovely one?"

"Dea," I answered stupidly, before Caterina pushed me aside.

"Dea," he repeated to himself, grinning. "I hope to make your acquaintance soon, Dea."

"Swear on the name Borgia all you like!" Caterina shouted. "But only an idiot or madman would take the word of anyone who wears it!"

With that the audience was over. Caterina turned and dragged me back to her apartments.

Christmas Day passed; the next day was the Feast of Saint Stephen, and the truce continued.

Even though the rest of the troops were enjoying a second day of freedom from the contessa's obsessive drilling, Caterina left me to discuss a "military arrangement" with one of her advisers. She returned after an hour with a slight, smug smile on her lips.

Shortly before noon, trumpet blasts sounded again outside Ravaldino's walls; as tradition demanded, the captain of the papal army had come again to make an offer of peace. This time, Caterina dawdled; when she finally went up to the battlement to look down at her visitor, she remained silent.

"Greetings, Madonna," Borgia called up cheerfully, removing his plumed cap with a sweeping gesture and bowing low in the saddle. "I trust you enjoyed a blessed Christmas."

"Greetings, Your Grace," Caterina replied sweetly. "Have you come to your senses yet and ordered your men to retreat?"

The duke laughed with good humor at the notion. "Not yet." His manner grew a bit more serious, though his tone remained light. "I felt that the offer I made to you yesterday requires clarification. As you know, most of my forces are composed of the French army, whose ultimate allegiance is to King Louis. I have discussed your situation at length with the *bailli* of Dijon, who rides with me; it is his duty to see that the king's troops and any prisoners of war are treated in accordance with French law.

"You are aware, Madonna, that under French law a woman cannot be taken prisoner of war? If you put yourself under the *bailli's* protection, it is his duty to protect you until you reach a place of safety.

"Do so, and I will see that you arrive safely in Rome—or elsewhere, if you prefer."

The Lady of Forlì tilted her head thoughtfully, and after a moment's pause, answered, "If you would have me trust you with my life, then do the same for me. Come to the gate; I will have the drawbridge lowered so that you can enter the fortress and speak to me in detail about your proposal. And have your trumpeter go and summon the *bailli* of Dijon; I would like to speak to him personally about the matter. If the two of you would be willing to sign a contract..."

She trailed off as Borgia's unrestrained laughter drowned out her words; his head was thrown back and he slapped his thigh, causing his horse to snort nervously. When he recovered, he called: "To paraphrase what you said yesterday, Madonna: I am my father's son, and am not stupid. I have no doubt that you would be pleased indeed to coax me alone into your fortress!"

Caterina's cheeks colored. "And you, sir, would be pleased indeed to coax me out of it. My offer is made in good faith. If I say that no harm will come to you, then you will be safe indeed. Your reluctance to trust me shows that *you* cannot be trusted."

Cesare banished his grin. "Madonna Caterina, I mean no offense. But it would be foolish of me to give such an advantage to you. You are surrounded, with no hope of rescue; I have come to offer you life instead of death."

Caterina's ill humor was replaced by a sudden coquettishness. "Will you not come at least to the drawbridge? I will come out to you. It is impossible to conduct such a delicate political discussion by shouting back and forth."

Cesare laughed. "Madonna, were I in your hopeless situation, I would try to lure my enemy inside my fortress. But I assure you, my men would continue the siege, whether you took me prisoner or not."

"Don't be so confident, Your Grace!" Caterina pressed a gloved palm against the side of the battlement and leaned perilously forward. "I've offered a considerable amount of money to anyone who brings you to me, alive or dead!"

"I know of your offer," Valentino said darkly. "I have offered ten times as much for you dead—and twenty more should you be brought to me alive."

With that, he signaled his trumpeter to depart and spurred his mount; the stallion kicked up tufts of mud and grass as it wheeled about and headed with its master back to Forlì.

With a faint sigh, my lady turned and I turned with her, to head back into the fortress and await the inevitable siege.

Thirty-four

Another day passed, and Borgia's artillery remained silent; apparently it took two days for Valentino's soldiers to recover from the holiday. But early in the morning of the twenty-eighth of December, I woke to the ear-splitting roar of the cannon as the mighty walls of Paradise shuddered. I leapt from the bed, only to feel the marble floor quake in earnest beneath my feet.

Caterina rolled from the bed immediately and grabbed my arm. "They've struck Paradise," she shouted in my ear as I scooped up our winter cloaks and handed one to her. "Come!"

We ran down to the lower floors of the main tower where the castellan and top commanders conferred and slept. These grim, Spartan quarters were the safest in the fortress, as they were on a low floor and completely sheltered by Ravaldino's walls. Caterina entered, calling for da Cremona, but he and the others were all manning the artillery. She deposited me in a meeting room beside the fire.

"I should have realized," she said, angry at herself, "that Borgia would not have the decency to wait until the new year. He has figured out that I live in Paradise; we will have to move down here for the remainder of the siege.

"Stay here," she commanded. Clad in only her nightgown and cloak, without even slippers, she went to join her men. I held my freezing feet to the fire and massaged them, trying to ignore the artillery's constant pounding.

It continued for the entire day. Despite the fiercely cold weather, Caterina remained with her artillerymen, giving orders in her bare feet. After a time, I found my courage and went back up to Paradise to collect our trunks and take them down to the main tower. Then I delivered a pair of shoes to Caterina, who was on the rampart shouting orders. She was grateful; by then, her feet had turned an alarming shade of blue.

When night fell, the explosions continued. Captain da Cremona gave us his apartment, which consisted of a small bedchamber and even smaller sitting room. Caterina slept upon a narrow, lumpy mattress while I took the narrower straw cot. The blasts were muffled in our new location, but loud enough to work on my nerves. Restless, I left the cot, lit the lamp out in the sitting room, and took out the book Ser Giovanni had given me.

I did my best to concentrate on Ficino's Latin text, but the more I read about God and the angels and the celestial order in the Heavens, the less I believed it. There was no order, no grace. Ficino himself had recently died, as had Lorenzo the Magnificent, his mother, my beloved Matteo, and kind Ser Giovanni—and the world had not changed. Now Caterina would die, too, and my great fear was that I should have to witness her violent end—or worse, force her to watch mine.

How pretty Ficino's lofty philosophy must have seemed when he wrote it down during Florence's halcyon days, in the lavish palace loaned to him by the Medici. He wanted for nothing, but wore the best clothing, ate the best food, drank the best wine; he did not listen to the thunder of artillery and wonder, each passing moment, how much time he was allotted to live, or how bloodily he would die.

"For nothing," I hissed aloud. "My brother died for nothing."

I began to weep—not gentle tears of sorrow or resignation, but of outrage, bitterness, and despair. I stood up, and, forgetting Caterina in the room next to me, hurled the fine leather volume across the room.

It sailed through the air, opening in mid-flight. The fluttering pages struck the wall first, badly creasing many of them before the book fell, spine side up, to the floor.

Stunned, I stared at my crime for an instant before tiptoeing to the half-open door of the bedchamber; the exhausted Caterina was still snoring loudly. I went over to the splayed-open book and lifted the binding carefully. The spine, alas, was broken and the pages permanently damaged. To my dismay, one of them had come altogether loose and slipped to the floor.

I lifted it gingerly. It was deeply creased, as if it had been folded and unfolded often. The edge was not torn; I realized then that it had never been part of the bound manuscript. The paper was worn and discolored by age.

The text, written in a different hand, was not a continuation of Ficino's text; in fact, it was not in Latin at all. It was a vertical list of the Italian alphabet, and directly across from each letter was a different letter, number, or symbol, written in an even, elegant script.

A script I recognized well, despite the passage of two decades. The writing was Matteo's, and this was one of his cipher keys.

I felt the sort of physical chill one experiences when mortally frightened. Yet I was not afraid, only gripped by anticipation and fragile hope. Carefully, I closed Ficino's book, thinking that the weight of the unharmed pages would press the creases out of the damaged ones. Then I stole into the bedroom and quietly fished Matteo's little diary out of the bottom of my trunk. I went back out to the writing desk, lifted the top, and found paper inside. With the key beside me, I opened the diary—careful lest the already cracked spine fall apart—and turned to a random page in the middle of the little book.

"Matteo," I whispered foolishly. "Dear brother, help me."

Letter by letter, I translated the first line:

. . . warfnsmtethastcbounvtginrolcamoscangnotpbetcrusitedoonethezmatgterdofiamolsa

It was gibberish. I set down the quill and put my face in my hands, angry at myself for trusting in something other than a cruel God. But I could not cry; the restlessness still had hold of me, and I stared down again at Matteo's key.

At the very bottom of the page was a tiny note, so small that I had to hold it to the lamp:

ev 4th

I looked from Matteo's key to the diary, again and again; in the end, I struck out every fourth letter. This gave the result:

... warnsmethatcountgirolamocannotbetrustedonthematterofimola

When properly spaced and capitalized, it rendered this:

... warns me that Count Girolamo cannot be trusted on the matter of Imola ...

I had known that Marsilio Ficino had also been Giovanni de' Medici's teacher, yet it had never occurred to me that Giovanni, like Matteo, might have been exposed to the same teaching about the Egyptian mysteries and the angel. Or perhaps it had simply been chance that Matteo had read the same book in the Medici library and accidentally left his key there.

It didn't matter; I was still grateful.

"Thank you," I whispered. "Matteo, Ser Giovanni, thank you."

I never went to bed; instead I sat translating Matteo's diary throughout the night. At times, I had to stop because emotion overwhelmed me, especially when I read lines such as:

My poor sweet sister, I have confused her so. When I return home, I will take her to Florence and let her learn the truth of her past. Like our mother, she has a great talent for understanding symbols and portents, too great a talent to be ignored or misused. I pray the time is soon ripe for her to discover the angel. ...

A later entry was more melancholy, as if Matteo had finally glimpsed his approaching doom:

If only I could live long enough to teach Dea all that I know. ... But I understand too well the symbol of the Hanged Man. My one prayer is that my sacrifice—whatever it may be—will be of great help to her. I want only happiness for her. I want her to experience the joy that knowledge of the angel confers.

The next morning, Caterina found me asleep at the desk, my cheek upon Matteo's diary, the quill still in my hand.

Even though I was not even halfway finished with deciphering Matteo's journal, I went to bed and slept through the artillery's constant thunder until midday. When I woke, I took advantage of my solitude by retrieving the rest of Matteo's papers from the bottom of my trunk. There was the little pouch with the gray-brown powder and the diagrams of the stars and circles in Matteo's hand, as well as the ancient Egyptian invocation written in another.

Caterina was in her element, commanding her artillerymen. I spent the entire day reacquainting myself with the rituals and rehearsing the motions I had seen my brother make in the air so very long ago. It wasn't rational, but it gave me something to do besides listen to the battle.

It also distracted me so that my mind was free to think clearly. I knew that the last cards I had dealt Caterina were also intended for me: the Tower, the Nine of Batons, the Hanged Man. I, too, had the strength to make the choice between total destruction and sacrifice. But what sacrifice could I make that would save Ravaldino and the Lady of Forlì?

By the time Caterina returned, well past nightfall, I was back to translating the diary, where I learned that Luca had always been honest with me. He had not only befriended Matteo during the long journey back from Rome, but had privately warned him of Girolamo's determination to take Imola at any cost, and Matteo had informed Luca of Galeazzo's equal determination, at his dear friend Lorenzo de' Medici's request, to keep Imola under Milan's rule.

Borgia's artillery fired upon us continuously until the sun set on the eve of the New Year of 1500—a year that many preachers declared would bring God's judgment and the end of the world. At Caterina's urging, I joined her and her commanders in Paradise's stripped dining chamber that evening and drank a few cups of wine before retiring early. The Lady of Forlì danced until well after midnight to the pipes and drum.

As a result, I woke earlier than all the others on the first day of the year to deep, blessed silence. Caterina was fast asleep and looking haggard after long days of battle; I closed the door to the bedchamber and slipped outside, where my brother's diary awaited me on Captain da Cremona's desk. I was grateful for the quiet and eager to start, as only a few pages remained undeciphered.

Matteo's melancholy tone persisted, as if he had been aware of his fate. He spoke of his deep gratitude to Lucrezia de' Medici, the benefactor who had rescued him and who had tried to rescue me, and his affection for Lorenzo, Giuliano, and "my teacher," Marsilio Ficino. Such reverie was interrupted by details of the journey and the mistrust he felt toward the legates whom he escorted from Rome. He feared that they had been so thoroughly corrupted that Duke Galeazzo's person might be in danger.

One of them in particular concerned him.

Luca has shared with me even more disturbing news. The Spanish legate has created a powerful new poison, which he might well have brought with him from Rome in order to assassinate the duke, should His Grace refuse to cooperate on the matter of Imola. Rodrigo Borgia is a shrewd and wary man, with a keen mind that captures every detail, so I must be careful—but before we arrive in Milan, I hope to find where he has hidden the poison, and to dispose of it without his being the wiser.

The quill dropped from my hand onto the desk, where it left a black blot; I stood up so quickly that the chair skittered backward, screeching against the uncarpeted stone.

Borgia. Was he the priest who performed last rites for Matteo? Had I been so stricken by grief that I had not remembered? For the first time, I intentionally recalled that horrible moment. The priest had not worn black at all, but a finely tailored scarlet robe.

In the end, my swirling thoughts coalesced: Rodrigo Borgia had killed Matteo, and now he intended to kill Caterina. For fear of him, Luca may have returned to Rome. Perhaps Luca, too, had already been killed for his efforts to stop a most dangerous man.

Borgia had cost me everything.

From my very core, a vile, bitter brew of emotions—impotent rage, vengefulness, hatred, grief—swept over me. I understood the depthless hatred Girolamo and his father had felt toward Lorenzo de' Medici, believing as they did that he had stolen from them a brother, a precious son. I craved vengeance more than air.

It was no accident, I decided, that Matteo's cipher key had appeared after all these years. It was no accident that I had still had the diary and the wits to decipher it. And I now understood the two fates the cards had presented to me.

I could sit upon my hands and die with Caterina when the steady pounding from Borgia's artillery breached Ravaldino's walls.

Or I could sacrifice myself by going directly to Cesare and feeding him his father's poison in an act of perfect justice. It did not matter that I would likely be caught and killed; Caterina would be saved, and Matteo avenged at last.

My plan was simple and relied on chance, but I convinced myself that the angel would protect me as I made my way to Cesare. I would go into Forlì on the sixth of January, Epiphany, a holiday that the French and Florentines held dear and celebrated with copious amounts of wine. By late Epiphany night, Cesare and his troops would be drunk and sated and, I hoped, asleep, as they would have to rise early the next morning to return to war.

Caterina often watched as Cesare came to and from his artillerymen. He was definitely sleeping in Luffo Numai's palace. Numai was playing the courteous host, as he had for Caterina and Girolamo when they had first arrived in Forlì.

I shared nothing of my intentions with Caterina. When the fighting began again on the morning of the second of January, she went to oversee her artillerymen while I spent the day preparing to escape.

After Ser Giovanni died, I had taken his clothes down to the guest quarters in Paradise, where he had stayed after his first visit. I stored them in a trunk at the very back of the closet, so that Caterina would never have to look on them again. Indeed, she never visited those quarters, as they reminded her of the early days of her relationship with Giovanni. There I found a woolen tunic and winter cloak, leggings, a belt, and a man's broadbrimmed hat, all black save the belt, and set them aside.

I knew that Caterina kept a sheathed stiletto beneath her pillow; I took it and a pair of my winter riding boots to Ser Giovanni's old apartment and left both next to the pile of clothing.

That night, Caterina returned and went straight to bed after supper, where she slept so soundly nothing would wake her.

This pattern repeated for three more days; each day, I remembered some other item critical to my mission—a scarf to cover my face; a pair of lined gloves and the key to the shaft, both of which I put in the pockets of the cloak; the small black bag that held the dried, gray-brown powder—and practiced the rituals.

The fourth day was Epiphany and we rested. From the battlements, Caterina watched the pageant and procession staged by the French army chaplains. The weather was brutally cold; the streets of Forlì soon cleared, and so did the parapets of Ravaldino. After attending a mass in the military chapel, Caterina retired early to da Cremona's quarters to sleep. I worried that she might waken again after sunset, but dusk came and went and she never once stirred.

I watched her sleep for a time, wishing that I could say a proper farewell to her; instead, I silently put my mother's triumph cards into my pocket and slipped out to the small sitting room to retrieve the written rituals from inside the desk. As I lifted the desktop, I paused, and took not only the rituals but also a single piece of paper. On it, I wrote:

Do not look for me. Just know that I am happy.

I left the note upon the desk and, with the sheaf of papers tucked beneath one arm, took the lamp and headed for Paradise.

Ser Giovanni's former apartment was dark, forlorn, and cold—the shutters were all closed, and no one had lit a fire in the hearth since the siege had begun. The light from my lamp swept ghoulishly over the bare floors and walls as I made my way to the closet.

I set the lamp down, filling the closet with light; nearby rested the stack of masculine clothing. I would do my work here rather than risk one of the soldiers noticing the light coming through the cracks in the shutters of the long-dark chamber. Hurriedly, I undressed and pulled on Ser Giovanni's too-long leggings and tunic, then held both in place by strapping on the belt with the stiletto and pulling on my boots. I hung the wool scarf around my neck and threw on the cloak and hat.

I placed the deck of cards in the center of the closet, brought out the worn piece of vellum containing the invocation ritual, and faced east, toward Forlì. Recalling the solemn reverence of Matteo and Luca's gestures in the dark of night, I sanctified the space with the ritual of the five-pointed star first, and then that of the hexagram. Afterward I realized I had forgotten to take some of the dried brownish powder in the pouch. Without it, the angel would not appear—and I was not ready to risk my adventure without divine aid.

Half a small teaspoon, Ficino had said, would suffice. Remembering my previous encounter with the magical powder, I opened the little black pouch beside my abandoned gown and carefully measured out the proper amount. But if I were to succeed, I needed to overcome the languor and disorientation the drug produced.

I looked at the powder in my palm, thought of the long climb down the shaft, and flicked a third of the drug onto the floor. The rest I licked off my palm, and spent a miserable moment gagging it down.

Only then did I recite the ritual of the barbarous names. The nonsensical syllables took on poignant, urgent meaning: this was my last opportunity to contact the angel before I died, and I was determined to understand my life and my brother's death.

The recitation lasted several minutes. At the end, I bowed my head and whispered, "Please guide me. I want to understand, and I won't be able to ask again."

I stood waiting for the walls to disappear and the angel to appear as it had so long ago. Instead, there was only the silent flickering of the lamp, and my gown, discarded like the past, and my mother's cards, resting at my feet.

A phrase surfaced in my mind: *The key to your past is also the key to your future.* These had been the words of the angel to me two decades ago.

Take up the cards. Were these the words of the angel, or my own?

I picked up the triumph deck. With my eyes closed, I shuffled the cards, kissing each one with a fingertip until I sensed the one that waited for me. I pulled it out and, opening my eyes, set the others back down on the floor.

The card that remained was the Nine of Swords. As I stared at it, I remembered how the card had looked to me when I was under the powder's sway: each sword's golden tip had wept copious scarlet tears.

I stared at the swords now and could almost see the dripping blood as the angel's past warning replayed silently in my head.

This is the key to your past and future: cruelty and self-cruelty; pain to the point of madness. It gnaws at you; if you do not expel it, it will devour you.

"I will expel it, then," I said aloud. "I will kill Cesare Borgia. You must go with me and help."

There came a pause so long that I despaired. In a voice raw with grief, I asked, "Will you not come with me? Will you not show yourself? I am frightened and need comfort."

At last there came a faint, faint answer, as if the angel had distanced itself from me. *I am always with you. I will never desert you.*

I sighed as my belief faltered; my previous vision had no doubt been prompted by the powder, not any magical operation, and my thoughts had just told me what I most wanted to hear. But the reality of saving Caterina's life and avenging Matteo's death still remained.

I closed the circle for superstition's sake, and instead invoked the bravery of Caterina Sforza. She would not have shirked from my dangerous venture; with shrewd daring, she would have found her way to Cesare Borgia and killed him. As I put the Nine of Swords in my cloak pocket, where the gloves and key waited, I thought of my lady as my talisman and smiled.

Ser Giovanni's apartment was adjacent to Caterina's former rooms in Paradise, where Captain da Cremona now dwelled. Fortunately, he was in the dining chamber with his fellow *condottieri*, drinking wine and discussing the next day's plan; I slipped through the door connecting Caterina's old bedchamber to Giovanni's without a sound.

The lamp on the night table was lit. I darted through the bedchamber into the narrow corridor leading back to the water closet; halfway, I crouched down and held the lamp to the dark wainscoting until I found the tiny keyhole.

I unlocked it and began to reach for the top rung inside the shaft when I realized I did not want to leave the lamp behind, as it would announce both my escape and the presence of the tunnel. I threaded my belt through the lamp's handle and, praying I did not set myself ablaze, grasped the top rung and climbed into the shaft.

Closing the wall panel behind me was unnerving; I was forced to hold on with one hand while I pulled the panel shut. It didn't help matters that the globe of the lamp was painfully hot and scalded my hip and thigh as it bounced off them each time I moved down a rung. I had made it only a quarter of the way down before the lamp swung so hard that it went out, and the globe nearly slipped off.

Somehow I kept my balance and prevented the heated glass from falling and shattering down below me in the darkness. The shaft and the rungs were both freezing, and my scalded leg and aching hands kept me alert. I kept thinking of Caterina, who would scoff at such minor inconveniences.

The moment came when I reached down with my boot and could not find the next rung. I lowered myself as far as I could. I had a sense, even in the profound darkness, that there was ground not far beneath me, but sensing was far less reassuring than seeing.

Let go, I imagined Caterina saying. *I'm right behind you.*

I let go and immediately landed on solid earth. I remembered to turn sharply left and take two paces; the sole of my boot scraped against rough wood. I opened the door to the tunnel and, fumbling, managed to remove the useless lantern from my belt before continuing.

Without light, I had no way of knowing what awaited me. I pawed the frigid earth beneath my feet, finally found a stone half the size of my fist, and dropped it into the tunnel opening, perhaps twice as wide as my shoulders. It struck the soft bottom with a muted sound that indicated I would fall too far should I jump in; I sat on the edge of the opening and dangled my legs over, searching with the tips of my boot for purchase. They revealed a clumsy staircase of wood and piled earth leading downward. Drawing a deep breath, I stumbled down the makeshift steps and, proceeding by touch alone, came to an opening the height of my shoulders.

This was the tunnel proper—freezing airless gloom that stank of the nearby latrine and the piss of rodents. I crouched down as I entered; even then, my hat and the shoulders of my cloak scraped the dirt ceiling.

As I forged ahead, my hands stretched out in front of me, I felt my fingers tear through the webs of spiders and heard the nearby squeak of rats. My hat fell off, and I was obliged to reach down and feel about for it; just as my one hand found the brim, my other found tiny crawling legs in the dirt. I straightened quickly, hitting my head against the ceiling.

In the impenetrable gloom, I brushed off my hat and set it back on my head. *A true Sforza would never fear a rat or a spider,* I imagined Caterina saying.

I lumbered on; soon I began to wonder whether there were holes in the tunnel, for in the distance I saw what looked like infinitesimal colored glass balls in the air, or translucent glittering atoms alight with shifting colors, one blending into the next like cangiante silk. I blinked, and when I looked again, I saw that they were suffused with thin, silvery rays of moonlight—though there was no moon that night.

I felt a sudden exhilaration and laughed softly. "Angel, angel," I whispered giddily. "I grow drunk; now you must come to me."

My eyes were dazzled by a flash, like lightning; I shielded my face with an arm, and when my eyes cleared again, I saw a shape in the distance beyond. It might have been the outline of the angel, glittering darkly, but when I focused directly on it, it shifted to the periphery of my vision.

"Angel, lead me out of here," I said. There was no response, in my own mind or outside of it, but I followed the glittering, shifting blackness ahead of me, and the swimming colored atoms. As I did, my legs grew heavier and my balance uncertain; I stumbled upon a split log half-buried in the dirt, and fell against the third step of a steep staircase leading upward.

I half crawled up the uneven dirt stairs, and hit a wooden hatch with the covered crown of my head. No light came from above, and the hatch was so reluctant to open that I had to push my entire weight against it before it finally gave way.

It did so with a groan and the snap of twigs; sand spilled through the opening and would have blinded me had it not been for the brim of my hat. I emerged from the earth spitting out sand to discover that I had displaced a withered bush. Above me were the limbs of olive trees, and beyond those, a hundred thousand twinkling stars in an indigo sky, a sight so dazzling that I opened my arms as if to embrace it. This caused me to notice my bare, freezing hands, and I put on my gloves—not only for the cold, but to avoid poisoning myself with the *cantarella*. I remembered, too, the black scarf around my neck, and wrapped it around my face, covering all but my eyes.

Although my mission was a gruesome one, I felt a pervasive euphoria that left me grinning like a madwoman. The lights of Ravaldino were behind me, and the city gates to my right. I completed the walk through the gates with only minor difficulty, but it was enough for the pair of shivering guards inside the gatehouse to interrupt their game of dice to call out: "You there! Are you drunk?"

I dared not answer in a woman's voice, and had to bite my lip to keep from laughing. I kept my gaze on the glittering blackness that kept slipping in and out of the corner of my eye, and shook my head. The act caused me to have to shift my feet to keep from falling over.

"He *is* drunk," the other guard sneered, and leaned out the open window. "I've a mind to arrest you! You know very well that Captain Borgia would hang you for wandering outside the city gates—not to mention the fact that no one is to be on the street after Vespers."

I bowed in apology and, when I tried to straighten, staggered a few paces to my right.

"Go home, drunkard!" the first soldier shouted. "Go on, before I come out!"

I steepled my hands together in an expression of gratitude, and made my unsteady way down the road that Cesare Borgia had traveled as Forlì's conqueror. I stumbled down the near-deserted streets, grateful that there was no moon, grateful that I had dressed in black, grateful that the few lights still burning in the houses of Forlì sparkled like pretty yellow diamonds. I did not follow the road to its end, where hundreds of French, Swiss, and Italian soldiers had encamped, and where a few horsemen were patrolling; instead, I turned onto the main road leading to the town square.

There, torches burned on sconces hung on the front walls of the distant Duomo. I walked past a row of empty shops with broken shutters and doors torn from their hinges; these gave way to public gardens, now denuded by winter and trampled by soldiers and their horses. I crossed to the other side of the street before passing the Duomo, lest the torches reveal me, but I paused a moment to lose myself in the flames, which appeared as long, jagged bolts of shifting colors: red, green, blue, yellow.

Past the shops and Duomo, the trees grew more numerous, providing privacy in summer for the homes of the wealthy. The leaves were all gone now, and the bare, skeletal branches served as reminders of winter's bleakness.

Luffo Numai's house was the second grand palace in the neighborhood, buffered from the street by a large island of trees—some evergreens—and a now-dead flower garden. Between the house and trees was a broad, curving driveway covered with cobblestones, and a tiny plaza.

I stole up to an evergreen in the island and stood in its shadow to assess what lay before me. A campfire had been lit in the driveway, not far from the main entry, and four soldiers huddled around it as they passed around a jug of wine. Like me, they wore drab wool cloaks and scarves over their mouths and noses, but their brows were colored sunset by the blaze, which seemed far more alive and beautiful.

Just beneath my euphoria lay panic. I had thought of some clever tactic to distract the guards, so that I could speak to Ser Luffo alone—and now, I had abruptly forgotten it. I had to make a decision, and quickly, but I was beginning to lose my bearings to the drug.

I stared at the men huddled off to one side of the fire, and as I stared at their dark cloaks, I imagined I saw another form in between them, dark and glistening.

Obey me, the angel said, *and I will show myself.*

Get me inside Numai's house, to Cesare Borgia, I answered silently, *and I will obey you for the rest of my life.* No matter that I didn't expect it to last very long.

There seemed no way around the four soldiers, and the sides and back of the palace were sealed off by a tall stone fence. The only hope I had of getting past the men was to reveal myself. Intuition and the angel both failed me. Shivering violently, I thought of Caterina. She would not have feared these men; she would have approached them boldly.

I let go a breath of pure desperation and forced myself into motion. I crashed out of the trees and onto the cobblestone, waving to the soldiers to get their attention, and calling in the deepest voice I could muster:

"Numai! Numai! I must speak to Ser Luffo at once!"

Obviously, my appearance was less than daunting; the soldiers turned toward me with a look of vague amusement mixed with puzzlement, as if they suspected someone was playing a joke on them.

"Who is this?" one asked in a thick French accent.

Another—an Italian, with a distinctly Roman intonation—rose from his haunches to study me. "Lad, you're *very* drunk."

A third said, with disinterest, "He doesn't sound like a Forlivese, does he?"

"I have a message for Luffo Numai, for his ears only," I said in a deep alto. I wanted badly to lie down and stare up at the night sky, or watch the beautiful fire; at the same time, I was afraid for my life.

The Italian studied me curiously. "And why should we let you speak to Ser Luffo? What proof do you have?"

"I am his cousin," I answered gruffly. "Tell him I bring a message from the Lady Dea. He will want to see me."

The Frenchman glanced up at the Italian. "There is no harm in telling Ser Luffo, is there?"

The Italian considered this thoughtfully. "No," he answered at last, and beneath my scarf, I beamed with triumph. "Of course," he said to me, "even if you are Ser Luffo's cousin, we will still have to search you for weapons."

"Here," I said and, like an idiot, held the stiletto out to him. "You needn't search me. This is the only weapon I have."

The other three soldiers burst into laughter; beneath his woolen muffler, the Italian's lips moved, and the corners of his eyes crinkled deeply.

"Oh," he said cheerfully, "now you most definitely *will* be searched!"

He reached for me and I pulled back from him, almost falling into the fire. As I regained my footing, the Frenchman came up behind me and pinned my arms. I howled Numai's name repeatedly as the Italian parted my cloak to feel for hidden weapons.

When he reached my breasts, he drew back, grinning, and pulled down the scarf, revealing my face. "Oho, boys, we have here a lady! Would this be the Dea who has a message for Ser Luffo?"

He pushed me over to one of his fellows, who gave my breasts a quick squeeze before pulling off my hat to reveal the long braid coiled at my crown. In an instant, the others were upon me, groping me, pulling the pins from my hair. I struck out with my fists, my boots, screaming for Numai.

The torment lasted until a window on the second floor opened and a man stuck out his head to bark, "Enough noise! What the hell are you doing down there with a woman? You're on duty!"

The soldiers immediately unhanded me and came to attention. "Ser Luffo," the Italian called, "a woman came to see you, dressed as a lad. We were searching her for weapons."

"Ser Luffo," I called up, too inebriated to consider the fact that Cesare Borgia might hear. "It's I, Dea. I've come to see you."

He leaned down to peer more closely at me, his bald crown looming, his coarse black hair falling forward about his face in long, limp strands. "Dea," he said, in recognition and disbelief. "Have you a message?"

"Yes," I called. "My own."

He lifted a brow at that, and addressed the guard. "Go ahead and search her thoroughly for weapons," he said. "I will come down and escort her in."

Thirty-five

Ser Luffo appeared at the front entrance in a burgundy brocade dressing gown trimmed in black velvet. I winced at the glaring lamplight in the foyer and the pair of guards sitting just inside the door.

"Dea!" Ser Luffo whispered as he studied me, his brow furrowed in dismay and disbelief. "My God, what has happened to you?"

"Please," I whispered back, glancing at the curious guards. "Ser Luffo, may I speak to you? In private?"

"Of course," he said, and snapped at the soldiers, "She is, in fact, my cousin."

We trod softly on the stairs, I clutching the railing to keep from stumbling. By then, it was almost midnight, and it was clear that Numai had guests he did not want to wake. He led me into a small bedchamber on the second floor, with a pair of chairs by the hearth to serve as an antechamber. Cesare, no doubt, was sleeping in Numai's magnificent apartments.

I stumbled inside and sagged into a chair to soak up the fire's glorious warmth. Numai did not light the lamp; the hearth's glow was sufficient. Indeed, I shielded my eyes from it while Numai sat across from me and stared. The golden glow pulsed upon his features, which at times swirled and shifted so that he seemed a stranger.

"Look at you, darling," he breathed. "You're as dirty as the artillerymen. Why are you here, Madonna Dea? Do you bring a message from Madonna Caterina?"

As lost as I was, I registered the intentional omission of my lady's title. I shook my head. "I've come of my own accord," I said.

"If it is to seek sanctuary," he answered with a faint leer, "you have come to the right place. I will tell no one who you are." He glanced at his empty bed, then back at me. "I will, of course, keep your secret . . . provided you cooperate sincerely. Perhaps I might mention that I sent my wife and children away before His Grace, the Duke of Valentino, arrived in Imola."

"I . . . Ser Luffo, I must see Cesare Borgia." *Angel, only let me get to Cesare Borgia, and I will obey you in all things. . . .*

He shrugged his shoulders. "Why?"

"I need only a moment with him. Only a moment . . . As you can see, I have no weapons."

"That would be impossible, of course. There are two guards at his door. Even if you got past them, His Grace is extremely athletic and an excellent swordsman. Of course, he is partial to beautiful women and might wait to hear you out before he kills you."

"Please." I dropped from the chair onto my knees, but found myself unable to clasp my hands in a pleading gesture; instead, I sank onto all fours. "If you could get me past the guards . . ."

Numai was unimpressed. "So that you can assassinate him? They would quarter me and hang the pieces in the public square!" His tone grew wheedling. "My darling Dea, you are clearly drunk—and perhaps even a bit mad—after so much time under siege. Stay with me, and I'll protect you. I can promise you a life much finer than your mistress has ever given you."

Fury welled up in me. I crawled to Ser Luffo's chair and pulled myself up to stand over him while he waited, delightedly, for what he presumed would be an embrace. Instead, I seized him by his velvet collar and pulled it so tightly that he coughed and began to struggle for air.

Angry lies poured out of me. "There are troops on their way to Forlì even now," I snarled. "An army so mighty that Borgia's will flee before it. You will be quartered and hung, indeed, if you do not cooperate with the Lady of Forlì. Do you remember the night when Lord Girolamo was assassinated? When Her Illustriousness was trapped in her own bed-chamber, awaiting slaughter? No doubt, the assassins swayed you to their side—enough for you to wait and see whether she could battle her way out of impossible circumstances.

"She did. And she graciously forgave your hesitancy. But I swear to you now, Ser Luffo, that she *will* recapture Forlì—and should you not aid her now, she will make a public spectacle of your execution."

I pushed Numai backward as I let go of his collar. Red-faced, gasping, he coughed hoarsely and put a hand to his throat as he stared—frightened and entranced—at me.

"Is it true?" he rasped. He was trembling badly, not so much from my attack as from physical arousal. "Troops are coming? Where from? Ludovico Sforza has not retaken Milan. . . ."

"Not as of this evening," I hissed, still leaning over him threateningly. The lethargy had passed, and I felt suddenly energized and invincible. "But by tomorrow morning all in this house will know. By tomorrow morning it will be too late for you . . . unless you help me."

Numai shrank in his chair and looked up at me with timid hope. "I cannot! I cannot help, Madonna Dea . . . unless you slap me."

I slapped his cheek with such stinging force that it hurt my hand.

He put a hand to his face and closed his eyes in a moment of sheer ecstasy. Panting, he looked at me again and gathered himself. "If I help you get into Borgia's room, and you kill him, how will I be protected if you fail? Or even if you succeed?"

"If I fail," I countered, "you can tell them that I overcame you and escaped."

He frowned at that. "Overcame me?"

"You have weapons in this room, don't you, Ser Luffo? Perhaps I could do something as simple as strike you on the head with the fireplace poker . . ."

He looked at the poker and lifted a thoughtful brow as he weighed the consequences of shifting loyalties once again.

I saw my advantage and pressed. "But Borgia will not die quickly. If I can get into his room, where he sleeps . . . It will take me a moment, no more. He will not become sick until morning, and then it will seem that he has a fever. If I return without detection to spend the rest of the night with you, who will be the wiser?"

I did not mean the invitation sincerely; I had never stopped to consider what would become of me should I actually succeed. I took a step back from Numai's chair. His face was half in darkness, half gilded, as if a painter had captured firelight upon his brush. In the gold, I began to see tiny, intricate patterns, as beautiful and possibly as meaningful as Matteo's handsome ciphers.

Something moved in the gloom behind him; I glanced up to see the more profound shadows gather and coalesce into human form, glittering darkly. The angel was fully with me now.

Forgetting myself, forgetting Numai, I spoke to it aloud.

"Only let me get to Cesare Borgia," I whispered, "and I vow to obey you forever."

Once convinced that he would not be held responsible for my failure or success, Numai offered up a plan. Borgia was sleeping in his apartment, the door to which stood roughly in the center of the third-floor corridor. This corridor could be accessed from the servants' back staircase, which approached from the west, or the main staircase, which approached from the east.

"I will take you to the servants' staircase," Ser Luffo offered, "so that when I call for the guards, they will run down to me as you run up the other way. Don't worry; I'll think of a distraction to give you enough time. Oh, my darling, I shall make you so happy."

Before he would let me leave, however, he went into the small closet and brought out one of his wife's gowns. It was a ridiculous confection of lace and pearls and golden beads, but it would prompt less suspicion than my dirty men's clothing.

"There are always ladies coming and going in this house," Numai said wryly. "Cesare prefers to have a new conquest every night; the soldiers will notice you less this way, and certainly won't look on you as a threat."

I threw Ser Luffo in the closet—a game he seemed to enjoy—and quickly changed into the gown and threw one of his wife's scarves over my ravaged hair. Fortunately, the neckline was high and covered my heart-shaped pendant. I emptied the pockets of my cloak, making sure to move my talisman, the Nine of Swords, to the side pocket sewn into the gown.

As Ser Luffo begged softly to be let out and I responded with harsh threats, I ran a hand beneath his pillows quickly and discovered a sheathed stiletto. I hid it in my pocket before finally setting my prisoner free. Numai emerged grinning, with a large brass key in his hand.

"The key to Lord Cesare's apartment," he said smugly. "*My* apartment, that is. No one knows I kept an extra one."

At Numai's suggestion, he put his arm around me as we went out into the corridor, and I pretended to weep upon his shoulder. He was correct; this brought no notice whatsoever from the guard patrolling the second floor. Numai led me to the other side of the palazzo and an alcove next to the servants' steep, rickety staircase that originated down in the kitchen. I could see why the soldiers never used it.

"When you hear me shout, run up one flight and turn right. You'll know Lord Cesare's apartment by the chairs in the corridor, where the guards sit."

With that, he kissed my ear—timidly, apologetically—and I caught his nose between my thumb and forefinger and twisted it cruelly. He left smiling.

In the minute that I spent waiting, my surroundings came alive; the walls began to swell and recede like waves in the sea, and the staircase looked as though it were breathing. In the corner of the ceiling, a spider patiently wove its web, and I watched, enthralled by such beauty. At the same time, I giggled silently at the realization that I could see in the dark with such clarity.

I also knew that the angel was with me. The drug's effects seemed to be growing stronger, affecting not just my vision, but also my emotions. It was as though I had split into two beings: the lower Dea, who was quaking with terror at the prospect of a violent death, and the higher Dea, who was soaring past all petty mortal fears and ready to ride the currents of fate with exhilaration.

"Guards! Guards!"

Ser Luffo's muffled shout—just loud enough to summon Cesare's men but not wake their master—emanated from the second-floor landing on the other side of the palazzo. As it did, the rickety staircase tilted forty-five degrees in front of me; startled, I drew a deep breath and ascended them anyway, clutching the railing and finally breaking into a run.

As I made it to the third-floor landing, gasping, I paused in the alcove to peer around the corner down the hall. As Numai had promised, the guards were gone. Midway down the corridor, two empty chairs were pushed against the wall on either side of a heavy wooden door. I could hear Ser Luffo down below, speaking urgently to someone on the other stairs.

I hurried silently to the door, unlocked it, stepped inside the ante-chamber, and closed the door behind me.

Cesare Borgia's quarters smelled of sweat, horselather, and gunpowder. Although the room was unlit, I could see everything easily. A large table surrounded by several chairs held a stack of unscrolled, annotated maps, the edges furling upward; nearby, a poultry carcass, dirty dishes, and several near-empty goblets sat beside an uncorked flagon of wine. Dusty saddle-bags sat heaped upon the fine carpet, accompanied by crumpled pieces of paper, careful diagrams, an overturned chair, and a woman's dropped shawl. The stucco wall near the table was stained with irregular purple splotches, as though someone had flung a goblet of wine at it.

The open door to the bedchamber glowed with dancing hearthlight. I had never seen a room so lavishly appointed, save at the Vatican, but my focus remained on only one item: the large, magnificent bed in the center of the room, heaped with velvet pillows and fur throws of sable marten, leopard, and rabbit. The thread-of-gold tapestry bedcurtains had been drawn back to admit the fire's warmth.

Huddled near the pillows was a woman—more a girl, really, of perhaps sixteen years. She sat with her back pressed against the mahogany headboard, her arms tightly hugging her bent legs; a fine wool chemise the color of candlelight draped over her spare form, suggesting wide but delicate shoulders and long, slender legs and arms. She was beautiful, with thick brown hair streaming to her waist, and dark eyes that made me think of the mourning Magdalene. One of them was bruised and badly swollen; her creamy throat bore red marks made by fingertips.

She saw me and did not stir or speak, but watched mutely as I moved toward the man who lay snoring lightly beside her.

In sleep, Cesare's face was slack and innocent, free of the ambition and arrogance that propelled him. He lay on his side, his legs stretched out beneath the covers, his left hand beneath his pillow, his right dangling over the mattress's edge. On the night table beside him was a half full goblet of wine, a stoppered flagon and—prominently, perhaps so that he would see it first upon awakening—a miniature portrait in a solid gold frame.

The woman in the painting looked vaguely familiar. She was younger, but not as handsome as her brother, having inherited her father's weak chin. Nor did she share either's black hair; hers was golden and crimped in long, narrow ringlets, which she wore loose, like an unmarried woman.

I drew my uncertain attention from it and quietly removed the golden heart Caterina had given me from my neck. I set it on the night table beside the flagon, and removed the crystal stopper.

I glanced up at the mute girl. She did not move, but her breathing had quickened; in her troubled eyes, I thought I saw approval. Beside her stood the coal-colored form of the angel, from whom I sensed nothing at all.

Between us, Cesare slept, oblivious, with the portrait of his sister, Lucrezia, beside him. I looked at his handsome face and remembered, with uncommon keenness, how he had appeared as the clever little boy who proclaimed he would be king. I remembered him lost outside Rodrigo's pleasure garden, sobbing in my arms in the dark. I remembered, too, nine-year-old Cesare who could not bear to see his little sister hurt, Cesare whose father grabbed his wrist and slammed him to the floor. Sobbing, Lucrezia had thrown herself upon him and begged her father not to hurt him anymore.

And young Cesare had sworn, *I will kill whoever dares harm her again.*

My resolve began to falter. I looked away from Borgia's face, away from his sister's, and pushed the latch on my pendant. The golden heart sprang open, revealing the neatly wrapped paper that held the *cantarella*.

I had removed my gloves; I dared not unwrap the paper, lest the powder scatter and I become its first victim. I looked about for something to cover my hands with, until I remembered Ser Luffo's stiletto.

It was a deadly little dagger, narrow as my finger and sharp on both sides, with a tip that could halve a hair. It was not long enough to reach the bottom of the flagon, but close enough, and I could use it to retrieve the paper after the poison dissolved.

I lifted the golden heart carefully and tilted it over the decanter's opening; the paper dropped into the garnet liquid. I swirled the decanter once, twice, then gingerly lowered the narrow blade into it and stirred, careful not to strike the glass.

Perhaps it would be quicker, though not as satisfying, simply to stab Borgia with the poisoned blade and disappear. I looked over at him, his features relaxed and innocent in sleep, and thought again of him as a child, and of his love for his sister, Lucrezia. No matter what it had grown into, it had been pure then, as Matteo's love had been for me.

Abruptly, I no longer saw Cesare or the portrait, but only the blade in my hands, held above the flagon, its wicked tip dripping dark red wine.

The key to your past, the angel had said. *The key to your future.*

The Nine of Swords, with each blade dripping blood from a pierced heart.

At once I recalled the bitterness on Count Girolamo's face when he visited his brother's tomb—his brother, whom he mistakenly thought had been murdered by Lorenzo de' Medici. He had struck out, killing Giuliano instead, and wounding Lorenzo's heart. Who knew what revenge il Magnifico had taken as a result?

I saw the rage in Cesare's eyes as he tried to protect his beloved sister, in myself as I swore to avenge my brother's death. All the bitterness, all the hatred, all the blood, because we could not let go of our angry grief.

I looked at the blade in my hand, and saw my own fury over Matteo's death. I was no less a poisoner than Rodrigo and Cesare Borgia, no less a prisoner of hatred than the violated girl sitting in Cesare's bed. The stiletto gleamed dully in my hand as I turned it in the light.

An unbidden thought came to me: What would my brother think, to see me at this very moment?

I looked to the angel. It had changed; its glittering blackness was swirling now, and tiny gaps as small as stars in the night sky began to break through the darkness, radiating blinding light.

Vow to obey me even unto death, the angel said, *and I will reveal myself to you.*

"I vow," I whispered.

I did not need to ask what to do; I had always known. I looked at the dagger in my hand, at the poisoned wine with a soggy bit of paper floating in it, and began to weep quietly.

At the sound of my soft tears, Cesare's body stirred beneath the covers. Apparently thinking it was his young companion, he began to turn onto his other side. But in mid-roll, his eyelids fluttered, and he sat up, swift as an asp, with a short sword in his hand.

The mute girl beside him covered her head with her arms and emitted a wail. All the while, the angel watched, growing so bright with each passing second that I soon could not look upon it. Instead, I studied Cesare's threatening expression, and finally understood why I had come.

"Dea," Cesare said, marveling. "You're Dea, Caterina's lady-in-waiting, aren't you?"

In response, I obeyed the angel: I plunged the stiletto into the poisoned wine, and left it there. At once, all my grief lifted, replaced by weightless peace. I could be angry no more.

Truthfully, I said, "I will not hurt you. I bear a message for you."

I moved to reach into the pocket of my gown. He tensed and waved his blade at me, but I made a reassuring gesture, and slowly pulled the card from my pocket and set it down beside the dagger and the cup.

"This is yours now," I said, pointing to the Nine of Swords.

They did not kill me at once, as I had hoped. Perhaps the triumph card had given Cesare pause; before he called for his guards, he looked from me to the Nine of Swords with the awe one reserves for madmen and saints.

By then, the sheer relief of revelation—assisted, no doubt, by the drug— had transported me to another realm, one where reality and consequence had little meaning. When the guards responded to Cesare's shout, I smiled at them, and went so willingly that they laid not a hand on me.

I walked cheerfully into the makeshift dungeon created in Ser Luffo's wine cellar, where groaning, shivering men were manacled to the walls near the devices used to torture them: the rack, the boot, the strappado.

I had experienced Heaven in Cesare Borgia's bedchamber; now I experienced Hell.

The French forbade the torture of women for political purposes, but Borgia's men shared no such compunction. Despite the cold, they stripped me of my boots and gown, leaving me with only a filthy, torn chemise to cover myself. I was manacled to the wall, unable even to sit upon the freezing ground, and waited—still content and jubilant in my emotional freedom, and rendered passive by the drug.

Then my turn came. It began with endless questions about Ravaldino—about the layout of the fortress, the artillery, the soldiers, the food and ammunition—and Caterina. What secret plans had she? Were the Milanese indeed coming? What had the last message from Duke Ludovico said?

My general ignorance of the subjects cost me several beatings. I endured them well enough, for I as yet felt no fear. The pain was only physical; it would not last forever, and death would come soon enough. My only regret was that Borgia would use my imprisonment against Caterina.

Then came the fateful question: *How did you leave the fortress?* The drawbridge had never been lowered. I must have left by another way, one that should be exploited.

I vowed to obey you, I told the angel silently. *Help me now to hold my tongue.*

I would not utter a word. The beatings grew more brutal; I lost a tooth and gained a cut, a swollen eye, and a broken jaw. I began to move in and out of consciousness, yet remained silent.

This earned me the strappado. I was freed from my manacles and placed beneath a thick chain suspended from a pulley on the ceiling; the other end of the chain was fastened to something resembling a ship's wheel. My arms were pulled behind me, bound together tightly at the wrists, and attached to the dangling chain. This seemed ominous enough, but my tormenter—a pleasant-faced youth wearing a rumpled papal army uniform and a benign expression—had not yet added the final touch: a heavy iron weight connected to shackles, which went around my ankles.

With something approaching boredom, my lad repeated the question: *How did you escape Ravaldino?*

With that, he gave the wheel a turn, to the clank and squeal of metal and the groan of wood. My wrists rose first, followed by my shoulders and elbows, both of which were forced into such an unnatural position behind me that the pain was immediately unbearable; the bones strained so hard against my flesh, I thought they would tear through the skin. I let go an involuntary cry as I was pulled higher.

By the time the iron weight attached to my ankles cleared the floor, I was screaming. The searing anguish in my upper torso was now matched by the lower, as my hips, knees, and ankles were slowly being pulled out of joint.

This made me consider loosing my tongue, but my sweet-faced lad was far from done. He gave another mighty turn of the wheel, and my wrists grazed the ceiling. I thought I could bear no more . . .

Until the lad let go of the wheel. The chain went whizzing downward, and I with it, until the torturer abruptly clutched the wheel again, jerking me sharply in midair.

I could answer nothing; pain consumed the entire world, leaving no place for the lad or the dungeon or even me.

I must have fainted, for when I came to myself again it was night and the soldiers were gone. The tiny hearth, which had provided some slight warmth while the torturers did their work, was cold and dark; there was nothing but the groans of the suffering.

I discovered that I was lying on my side on the floor, my ankles shackled to the wall. Although I had been freed from the strappado, it was still doing its work; every bone, every muscle in my body throbbed, and shrieked at the slightest movement. Yet the pain urged me to shift my position. Gritting my teeth, I pushed myself up to a sitting position, my back against the dank wall, my chained legs sprawled in front of me. It was then that I realized I was unsure not just of the hour, but of the day; my memory was blurred, distorted. I could not have said whether I had been in the dungeon for a day or a week.

The drug had worn off completely, but my emotional relief and sense of revelation had not. Perhaps I had been mad not to use my opportunity to kill Cesare, but I did not care. Like me, like Girolamo, like Caterina, he had been wounded, and I could only pray that he lived long enough to understand his angry grief and transcend it.

I heard squeaking, and shuddered as a pair of rats scurried over my legs;

I would have lifted an arm to shoo them away had I been able. Instead, I closed my eyes and whispered to the angel.

"If you *are* real," I breathed, "you must appear to me now, because I have finally obeyed you unto death. Grant me that, at least, before I face the executioner."

In response, there came the patter of the rodents over the stone, and the faint sobs of a fellow prisoner begging God to let him die. I leaned my head back against the cold wall and hoped for sleep. The rat's squeaks grew gradually louder, but none came close to me.

Perhaps I dozed, for by the time I opened my eyes again, their squeals had transformed into a woman's screams.

I was no longer in Luffo Numai's cellar, but in a place I had been only once, after the Duke of Milan's assassination: Galeazzo Maria Sforza's lavish bedchamber in the Castle Pavia. The beautiful strains of the duke's choir singing Christmas carols emanated from the private chapel, two rooms away.

But in the duke's bedroom, the festive sound was muted by shrill screams. From my perspective on the floor beside the massive bed, I watched as a leering Galeazzo, his leggings bunched about his ankles, struck the young woman pinned beneath him; I sat too low to see her face. Galeazzo had insinuated himself between her legs and pulled her skirts above her waist, revealing the long sweep of her white flesh from hip to slipper.

"I will not suffer this a second time!" she roared in French beneath him. "I will kill you, I swear! You have cost me my life, my sanity!"

Galeazzo struck her again, then pushed his erect member inside her with savage force. Pushing his victim down with the weight of his body and covering her mouth with one hand, he began to rut.

For the first time, I realized that another voice—high-pitched and childish—had been shouting all along. "*Maman, Maman!* Stop it, *Monsieur,* you're hurting her!"

I watched as a slender young boy ran up beside me and crawled onto the bed to try to pull the duke off his mother. "Leave her!" he shouted. "Leave her, please!"

The duke reached back with his free hand to knock the boy squarely in the jaw; the boy fell backward and, unable to keep his purchase, slid onto the floor.

I began weeping. "Stop!" I shouted. "Someone, help her!" I scarcely noticed that my words came out in French, like the boy's; I struggled to lift a leg, an arm, but the violent pain kept me still.

The boy was on his feet again. I feared for him; he was a lovely child of perhaps ten, tall for his age and slender, with hazel eyes and dark auburn hair. *How like Matteo he looks,* I thought, until I saw the blood on his upper lip, split right at the bow.

Helpless, I watched as Matteo swiftly scanned the room and grabbed a heavy golden candlestick from the table near the hearth. Again he crawled onto the bed behind the prone Galeazzo; this time, he struck the back of the duke's skull. The duke roared and turned the upper half of his body in an effort to seize the weapon from the boy.

Matteo struck Galeazzo's crown a second time, so fiercely that the candlestick shuddered and let go a faint, metallic ring. The duke fell still, and the woman pulled herself out from under his limp body.

"*Guillaume,*" she said, holding out her arms to the boy. "My savior, my darling!" They embraced tearfully.

She was a beautiful woman, with ebony hair and eyebrows, and striking features. I thought at first I looked upon myself, but there were differences; her dress and hair were long out of fashion, her cheekbones and chin more becoming than mine.

She released her son to spit upon the duke's still form. "She is yours, you bastard, and you know it," she hissed in his ear, "and you have cost me my marriage, my life, everything. Will you not even take responsibility for your own child?"

And then she turned and held out her arms to me. "*Desiree,*" she said. "Sweet girl, we must hurry! We will find no help here!"

"*Maman!*" I gasped. I tried to open my arms and reach for her, but could not. I squeezed my eyes shut, sobbing, and when I opened them, she was gone.

I was back in the unlit dungeon, trapped by the agony in my limbs as much as by my shackles. Yet my mind was working to piece together what I had just witnessed. I understood why the pious Duchess Bona had treated me so kindly all those years; she was trying to make amends for another of her husband's sins. Once Duke Galeazzo was dead, her obligation to me ended. What more perfect solution than to send me off to Rome with my half sister?

As I considered these things, the anonymous form of the angel appeared before me. Once again, its glittering blackness was slowly fading, replaced by larger and larger gaps of blinding white light until I was forced to shut my eyes and look away. Even then, the brilliance increased steadily, until it pierced my eyelids like the naked sun.

"Dea," a man's voice whispered, and laughed softly. "Dea, look at me."

I opened my eyes. The dungeon was illuminated by a gentle golden glow.

Beside me crouched Matteo, dressed in the same tunic he had worn the day he set off for Rome. He was radiant, as if from an internal light, and he grinned broadly at me. The scar upon the bow of his lip had disappeared.

"Matteo?" I whispered. "*You* are the angel?"

"I have always been with you," he said. "I never left." He put his hand upon mine, and my pain vanished. I reached out to him, and pressed my cheek to his, and sobbed.

"Don't cry," he said, embracing me, and I let myself melt with him into the bliss of overwhelming love. "Dea, my existence is pure joy. And none could be happier than this moment. Don't you see?

"Duke Galeazzo, your father, could not be redeemed. But you have reclaimed our mother's work, and allowed me to know the joy of spiritual union. And you have led your sister, Caterina, away from her father's dark legacy. You, who thought you had no family, have saved us all. And I will be with you forever."

I held my brother and felt my heart soar, free from the fetters of fear and sadness. "I can die now," I whispered to him. "I am happy."

Matteo drew back and gazed down at me tenderly. "Your service has only begun," he answered. "You have obeyed me unto death; now you are a true magus."

I bowed my head and whispered, "I surrender to my fate."

At once, the door to the dungeon swung open.

Thirty-six

When the door opened, I looked up toward it to discover that I had returned to the dungeon completely; back were the pain, the shackles, the aching cold. A guard and Luffo Numai, holding a torch, were walking toward me. No doubt they were coming to take me to my execution.

Numai's lips parted in shock when he set eyes on me, but he soon recovered enough to address me as the guard knelt down to unlock my shackles.

"Madonna Dea," he said solemnly, "we have come to release you."

I tried to speak and found I could manage no more than a hoarse whisper. "Why?"

He looked on me with genuine pity. "It's over. Ravaldino has fallen."

I sobbed at the news; the sounds emerged from my throat as grating rasps. Caterina, then, was dead.

Even with my shackles gone, I was too weak to rise. The guard bent down and slipped his arms beneath my armpits, then lifted me straight up as I let go a yelp. I could not bear any weight upon my hobbled ankles, so he scooped me into his arms and carried me away from the stinking dungeon, up the stairs to Ser Luffo's house.

I was taken to an empty nursery and laid upon a bed. Two female attendants came and washed my face and hands, then dressed me in a clean gown, gloves, and slippers, and wrapped me in a fine woolen cloak; a third brought a bitter potion, which I drank eagerly. Numai and the guard returned again, and held me upright between them; I could not bear the pain of holding on to them, as both my shoulders were dislocated, but they supported me well enough so that, as we approached a well-lit sitting room on the ground floor, I was able to stagger a few agonizing paces through the open door.

Inside the chamber, Cesare Borgia stood dressed in black velvet, his arms folded in disapproval as he glared across the room at an older, meticulously groomed and uniformed Frenchman, who glared back. It was clear that neither man acknowledged the superiority of the other; the hostility between them was palapable. Borgia was accompanied by a trio of bodyguards, the Frenchman by one of his officers and a woman.

It was Caterina, in her best gown, now torn and covered in dust—the dust, I realized, of Ravaldino's shattered walls. The golden heart around her neck was gone. Yet she was very much alive and unharmed, and keenly interested in the argument Borgia and the Frenchman were having. Even defeated, she was not bowed, but listened with an imperious, confident air; despite my pain, I smiled with joy to see her.

"Forgive me, Your Grace, and Captain Bissey," Numai interrupted as we entered. "This is the prisoner in question."

Captain Bissey lifted a graying brow and turned his gaze on me. He was much taller than Borgia, with a long, hawkish nose and tiny lips. "My *God!*" he exclaimed in horror. "This is grotesque barbarism! It is horrible enough to imprison a woman, but this one you have tortured! A disgrace! Were His Majesty King Louis to learn of this, he would charge you with a crime!"

Caterina saw me at last, and put a hand to her mouth; I watched as her eyes filled with tears.

"No, no," I rasped. I wanted to wave my hand to stop her from crying, but pain stopped me from lifting it. "I am all right, Madonna. Everything is all right. . . ."

Cesare continued his argument, his tone smooth yet cutting. "I am Italian," he said, "and as difficult as it may be for you to believe, Captain, our laws are not yours. I am the king's ally, but not his subject; I have committed no crime."

"And I am the *bailli* of Dijon," Bissey thundered, "and therefore King Louis's representative when it comes to legal matters. I am also responsible for seeing that women and children are not taken prisoners of war, but protected and well cared for until they can be returned to a place of safety. The lady Caterina will not be harmed or imprisoned. And *this* poor lady . . ." He gestured at me.

"Arrangements have been made for the Lady Dea," Caterina interjected, her eyes still taking in my injuries, her expression one of grief and outrage for my sake. "She is guaranteed safe passage as a condition of my surrender."

"She is indeed," Bissey said pointedly to Cesare. "One of your couriers, Your Grace, waits outside now to escort her. Although, seeing what you have done to her, I doubt she can mount a horse."

"Let her go," Borgia said in a bored tone, and waved Numai and the guard—and me—off. "She's quite mad. I have no use for her."

I struggled not to fall as Ser Luffo and the guard turned toward the door. I turned my head to say farewell to Caterina, and she strode up to me and gently cupped my face in her hands, then touched her forehead to mine.

"I chose the Hanged Man," she whispered. Her eyes were bright with tears, but radiant, her voice tremulous.

"As did I," I breathed.

"They breached Ravaldino's walls," Caterina said softly, so that Cesare could not overhear. "Still, we could have repaired them and I could have kept fighting. But when I learned that you were gone, and later that Borgia had captured you, I could no longer remember why Ravaldino and Forlì were so important. I remembered the Tower, which leads to total destruction; at least the Hanged Man brings us the promise of a happier future." She drew back to study me tenderly again, and let go a deep, shuddering sigh. "I am so sorry that monster hurt you."

"And if he hurts you?" I asked, with sudden anguish.

"I thought I had courage," she murmured, "because I never feared dying in battle. But now I understand what bravery is: being frightened, yet persevering. Your act was far more courageous than anything I have done. The time has come at last for me to be truly brave and face what I dread most of all."

I lost my composure and began to weep in earnest; Caterina had chosen defeat and humiliation by surrendering herself to Borgia, knowing that she would be raped, then dragged to Rome and publicly humiliated. If unlucky, she might die in some filthy dungeon in the Castel Sant'Angelo. All this she had chosen for love of me.

"I don't want to leave you," I sobbed. "Caterina, I am your sister."

She gave a short, tearful little laugh. "It took you all these years to figure that out? Why *else* would Bona have made such a fuss over you?" She grew solemn again. "And here our paths diverge."

"*No*," I whispered. "I won't go." I could not bear the thought of leaving her with Cesare Borgia.

She let go another sad, short laugh. "So our positions have reversed; you don't want to leave me, and I am telling you to go. Go now, Dea, before I change my mind. Go and be happy, so that my surrender is not in vain."

I turned my face away briefly, as if by doing so, I could hide my anguish from her. "Our paths will join again," I told her truthfully. "By then, something beautiful will have been born of our sacrifices."

She nodded; a spasm of sorrow passed over her features and was gone. "Take care of my little Giovanni," she said into my ear.

"Only for a little while," I whispered, "until his mother joins him."

We kissed, and the guard and Ser Luffo led me away.

The courier was waiting out in the cobblestoned driveway upon his horse, the hood of his cloak pulled up against the cold. Beside him stood a placid white mare, my intended mount, but when it became clear that I could not stand, a wagon was brought, and I lay down and let the poppy do its work as I stared up at the moon and stars. A pair of Cesare's soldiers rode beside us until we passed safely through Imola.

In time I drifted off to sleep, and when I woke again it was day, and we were in the Tuscan countryside with not a soul in sight. When the driver reined in the horses, I struggled to sit, but surrendered and instead waited until he crawled into the wagon and took me in his arms.

I thought at first that the poppy had deceived me, but I found the strength to reach up and touch his face. It was Luca, my Luca, who had served again

453

as scribe and courier to the captain of the papal army; he and Caterina had plotted together to rescue me. He was older, his face more weathered, his brow lined, but he was Luca all the same, as if the years had never separated us.

"Now I am a deserter from the Duke of Valentino's service, for your sake," he told me. We rode on to Florence, where Caterina's children and the future waited.

In my old age, I grow uncertain as to whether Matteo actually appeared to me in the cell or was the product of a dream, or the drug, or the pain. It matters not even if the angel exists, or is simply the product of my own mind; I know only that, when I hear his silent voice, it guides me true. Do I regret not killing Cesare Borgia? Never, though he went on to leave thousands of victims in his wake. Those, too, are souls who must continue the struggle and fight their way out of darkness into light.

May we all find our way.

AFTERWORD

Caterina Sforza invoked the protection of the French king when Ravaldino's walls were breached; even that, however, did not spare her from being raped by Cesare Borgia. But at the *bailli* of Dijon's insistence, she was treated not as a prisoner but as a guest, and thus escaped torture. In this manner, she was forced to travel through the Romagna with Cesare's army until his triumphant return to Rome.

There, she was publicly humiliated and thrown in the dungeon of the Castel Sant'Angelo, where she languished for more than a year due to her refusal to legally surrender her lands to the Borgia. In May 1501 her spirit was finally broken, and she signed the contract granting Imola and Forlì to Cesare.

She returned the same year to Florence, where she devoted the rest of her life to training her son, Giovanni de' Medici, in the military arts.

Giovanni, who in later life was known as Giovanni delle Bande Nere, became one of the greatest *condottieri* (military mercenaries) in Italy; his courage was legendary. He married into the Salviati family and sired Cosimo de' Medici, who became the first Grand Duke of Tuscany. Caterina's other descendants include the kings of France and Spain.

Dea and Luca are fictional characters; outside of them almost all of the characters are based on real historical figures.